SEDUCED *by the* STORM...

"I can always make room in my schedule for a beautiful woman," he said in a rich, whiskey-smooth southern drawl that made her want to drink him in. And those eyes...even in the hazy, dim light from the beer signs, they glowed clear green. She'd never seen anything like it.

And as a telekinetic who had grown up alongside people with gifts even more incredible than hers, she'd seen a lot.

"I'm not usually so forward," she said, tearing her gaze away from his when the pub door opened. "But see that man walking in?"

The stranger inclined his head almost imperceptibly, as though he hadn't looked, and she gave him points for his astute assessment of the situation.

"He's my ex-lover," she lied. "He's a loon. Completely mad, and he's stalking me. I told him I have a new lover—"

"And I was the first guy you saw?"

"Yes." No, but when she'd detected a tail as she strolled along the moonlit boardwalk, she'd slipped into the nearest public place that would be full of men, and as luck would have it, these weren't just men. They were bikers, oil drillers and roughnecks, and the man who now held her had stood out as the toughest of the tough.

Marco watched from near the entrance, not bothering to hide his annoyance.

"Well," the stranger said, threading one ha̶n̶d̶ ̶t̶h̶r̶o̶u̶g̶h̶ ̶h̶e̶r̶ ̶ to pull her face close to his, "I ca̶n̶ ̶e̶i̶t̶h̶e̶r̶ ̶k̶i̶s̶s̶ ̶y̶o̶u̶ ̶o̶r̶ ̶ take care of him."

Also by Sydney Croft

UNLEASHING THE STORM

RIDING THE STORM

SEDUCED
by the
STORM

Sydney Croft

DELTA TRADE PAPERBACKS

SEDUCED BY THE STORM
A Delta Trade Paperback / August 2008

Published by Bantam Dell
A Division of Random House, Inc.
New York, New York

Delta is a registered trademark of Random House, Inc., and the colophon
is a trademark of Random House, Inc.

Library of Congress Cataloging-in-Publication Data
Croft, Sydney.
Seduced by the storm / Sydney Croft.
p.   cm.
ISBN 978-0-385-34082-3 (trade pbk.)
1. Psychic ability—Fiction.   2. Storms—Fiction.
3. Weather control—Fiction.   I. Title.
PS3603.R6356S43 2008
813'.6—dc22   2008006630

Printed in the United States of America
Published simultaneously in Canada

www.bantamdell.com

BVG 10 9 8 7 6 5 4 3 2

Acknowledgments

As always, there are so many people to thank for helping us take this book from idea to finished product.

To our agent, Roberta Brown, for all her support in ways too numerous to count.

Thanks to everyone at Bantam who has helped make this book the best it can be, from cover to cover, especially our editor, Shauna Summers, for her continued guidance and belief, and Jessica Sebor, who goes above and beyond on a daily basis.

Special thanks to Saskia Walker for being available to help out with some of the special British details, and to Michelle Willingham, for sharing her knowledge of the beautiful Irish coast.

And we certainly can't forget our families, who have supported us through deadlines and marathon writing spells. To Zoo, Lily, Bryan and Brennan, we love you.

SEDUCED
by the
STORM

CHAPTER
One

Faith Black had been beaten, drugged and imprisoned, but none of that scared her. No, what frightened her to the core was the man confined with her. Chained to an improvised medieval rack and bare from the waist up, he lay on his back, arms over his head, his incredible chest marred by bruises and a deep laceration that extended from his left pec to his right hip.

He might have been rendered immobile, but he was in no way helpless.

His weapon, far more dangerous than the telekinesis—to her, at least—was his overpowering sexuality, a force that tugged her toward him, made her burn with need despite their grave situation.

Head pounding from a brutal blow to her cheek, she pushed to her feet and padded close, her nudity barely registering. She'd been stripped naked while unconscious, her clothes tossed into one corner of the windowless, steel-walled room. The weak yellow light from the single bulb emphasized the deep amber of Wyatt's eyes, no longer green, as he settled into the transitional period many telekinetics experienced when their powers flared up. The air in the room stilled, and the chain around his right ankle began to rattle.

"Don't," she said quietly.

He shifted his head to look at her as though he hadn't realized she'd regained consciousness. "Faith." His voice was rough, as haunted as his gaze. "I didn't tell him. I swear."

"Tell who what?"

"Your boyfriend. I didn't tell him about us. He knew."

"Sean's not my boyfriend," she said, and Wyatt cocked a dark eyebrow like he didn't believe her. "And I know you didn't say anything."

She knew, because she'd been the one to spill the beans that she and Wyatt had been sleeping together.

Wyatt's head lolled back so he was staring up at the steel beams crisscrossing the ceiling. The corded tendons in his neck strained and tightened as he swallowed. "I'm sorry I got you into this."

"You didn't."

A growl rumbled in his throat. "I seduced you. I shouldn't have. Not here. Not on the platform, where he could find out."

She inhaled him into her, the masculine scent that threw her off balance whenever he came near. No, she couldn't blame him for anything, least of all her out-of-control desire for him. He was here to do a job, just like she was, which meant getting the assignment done by any means necessary.

"I'm not here because Sean is jealous." Though Sean was, furiously so, but Wyatt didn't need to know that.

"Then why?"

Dragging her gaze from the strong, ruggedly handsome features of his face, she let her mind focus on a realm of existence most people never saw. Instantly, Wyatt's aura became visible, a shifting, undulating layer of light around his body. And God, something was wrong, so wrong she nearly gasped.

Wyatt radiated power, so his aura should reflect the same. Instead, it stretched thin around his body like an ill-fitting, secondhand coat, ridden with weak spots and holes, as though he'd suffered repeated supernatural attacks. She could repair the damage, but her efforts would amount to little more than a patch job on his psychic garment. Replenishing his aura, renewing it... that only he could do, subconsciously, through healthy living and mental wholeness.

For now, she concentrated on the cut on his chest, worked her power into a psi needle and thread that knit the wound together. The muscles in his abs rippled, carved so deeply that they cast shadows on one another. She knew how they felt beneath her touch, how they flexed when they rubbed against her belly, and she had to clench her hands to keep from reaching for him.

The wound closed in a whisper of sound, and Wyatt sucked in a harsh breath. "Jesus. You're a fucking agent."

His eyes glowed amber again, and the chains binding him rattled.

"Please don't," she said, letting her psychic fingers slide south on his body. "Let me. Follow my lead."

He moaned and then grit his teeth against the sensations she sent streaming into his groin.

"I'm going to need you to scream, Wyatt. Scream like I'm killing you."

His shaft began to swell with each of her virtual caresses deep inside his body, and his eyes flashed green fire. "You are, Faith." His voice rumbled, dark, dangerous. "I've been through the gates of hell and survived, but somehow I think you're going to be the devil who takes me down."

CHAPTER *Two*

Two Days Earlier

Wyatt Kennedy was a dead man, and other than a few problems, like being unable to use his credit cards, it hadn't been so bad.

Of course, he'd already been declared dead once before, a long time ago, so he knew the drill. Lay low, use cash, watch your back.

When he'd dropped off the face of the earth years earlier, he'd had ACRO—the Agency for Covert Rare Operatives, of which he was one—on his side. ACRO had recruited him, changed his name and killed him off so he wouldn't face a murder rap for the death of his half brother.

Which, for the record, he still wasn't sure he was responsible for, thanks to a memory lapse that had lasted for the past five years, despite ACRO's best efforts.

This time he got to keep the same first name, at least. The most important part of being dead this go-around was letting everyone at ACRO think he'd been killed—for reasons he didn't quite understand but when orders were given, orders were followed. The rest of the world, and Itor Corp—ACRO's major nemesis, had never known Wyatt existed anyway, and he knew the mission he was dealing with—finding the weather machine that Itor Corp had built and hidden on an offshore oil platform—was some serious we-plan-on-destroying-the-world shit.

He'd handle it easily enough. It's not like he looked as if he had special powers. But he was tall enough that most men gave him a wide berth, which was cool with him. He tended to live mostly inside his own head anyway and preferred his own space, big-time. Even when he was in a room full of people, like now.

The bar crowd tonight was rough, made up mostly of roustabouts who wanted to be roughnecks and roughnecks who wanted to be drillers, all either preparing to rejoin their offshore crew or just coming off their fourteen-day workweek. Wyatt was just coming off his own two-week break, prepared to go back in and finish up the job he'd started for ACRO. He'd been on the rig, doing recon on the weather machine—ACRO wanted to make sure there weren't any more out there like it. So he'd spent the first days getting the code and transmitting it back to Haley at ACRO. Now he'd been ordered by Oz to actually destroy the machine.

Wyatt had grown up in this life, under the name of James Jasper. His father owned his own drilling company by the time Wyatt had been born, and he'd already had two sons from his first wife.

Wyatt had been thirteen at the time all the other crazy shit had started happening around him.

For as long as he could remember, he'd always had what he'd thought of as secret powers. He remembered moving an object with his mind when he was just two years old, and it had gotten worse when he hit puberty. Out of control, until every time he lost his temper even slightly, shit would fly.

At first, the doctors at the mental facility he'd been forced into were concerned, and then they became downright fed up with him. Especially because he became really good at ripping up their offices, all while sitting in a chair, looking innocent.

One minute, he'd been drilling, the next, learning how to avoid medication he didn't want to take by hiding it in his mouth. He never did tell anyone at that mental institution about the sex thing, a power that ACRO scientists now believed had roots in his telekinesis—it hadn't begun full force until he was fifteen. Even then, everyone just assumed he was getting laid on a regular basis because he was good-looking.

Yeah, totally *One Flew Over the Cuckoo's Nest,* only not as fun, and he'd escaped before the electroshock therapy, by seducing all the female nurses and pretending to be normal.

Pretending. Wyatt did that a lot. Pretending to not be telekinetic. Pretending to be dead...

So far, pretending to be dead this time around was pretty cool. He'd always wanted to come back as a ghost, thought that would be the coolest part of actually being dead. Creed, another operative at ACRO—a ghost hunter—had assured him that most ghosts were on the up-and-up, but Oz, a medium who spoke to ghosts who were the worst of the worst, disagreed.

Oz had temporarily taken over for Devlin O'Malley, the head of ACRO. Oz was the one responsible for Wyatt's death and his current assignment, which placed him back on the job as a roughneck.

Like fucking being reincarnated.

Just concentrate on getting your shit together, man.

When his concentration went elsewhere, his gift began to scatter like loose marbles on a slick, hardwood floor. But then, he always felt scattered, not fully whole, not integrated. Motherfucking crazy. Like maybe he really did belong in a padded room somewhere. He'd tried to explain it to the psychics at ACRO, told them it felt as if his powers were Legos missing the connecting pieces.

When he'd been released from the mental ward at sixteen, he'd worked on the oil rig with his father and brothers until he was nineteen and then he went the military route. Learning to drill had been cool, and in his blood—learning to destroy had been equally

so. Fuck the middle-of-the-road bullshit. As bent on extremes as
he was, he went straight for the roughest route possible.

Special Forces—SEALs, specifically. The drill sergeant at
boot camp had taken one look at Wyatt's lanky six-foot, three-
inch frame and laughed. Wyatt had knocked him out cold with
one punch, spent the night in the brig and found himself in
BUD/s two days later. As punishment.

He loved it—every single brutal minute.

He'd passed his psych evals for the Navy with no problem.
He'd faked it, the way he'd faked a lot of things, and the Special
Forces community wanted its men to be a little bit on the crazy
side anyway, even if they didn't outright admit it.

Fuckin' A right.

But the sex thing, *oh*, *yeah*, he'd let his handle on that slip, especially this past week. Mainly because it was fun as hell letting it
go out of control and he'd known he wasn't going to get laid at all
during the next phase of his mission.

He'd been tamping it down hard when he'd been rigging for
two weeks straight—so hard that it made his head hurt.

When you could have any woman—or man, if he'd swung
that way—sex got old fast. If his libido wasn't in constant over-
drive, he'd have given up sex altogether long ago, shaved his
head and become a monk.

He'd tried the monk thing once, when he was seventeen. His
apprenticeship lasted exactly three weeks, until he couldn't stand
the other men trying to break into his room to have him. The
head of the abbey agreed with Wyatt's decision. Didn't stop him
from trying to screw Wyatt, though.

Wyatt was still learning to control his pheromones—most of
the time they only worked on people he wanted them to work on,
unless he let himself go too long without, or if he and the object
of his desire were around other people when he got turned on. In
that case, everyone and their mothers—literally—needed to
watch out.

And there was an even bigger price to pay for the sex mojo—
the women he'd been with never remembered the sex once he left

the room. So yeah, that would be great when trying to have any kind of long-term relationship—waking up in the morning with a woman who would soon forget sleeping with him in the first place.

He'd put the mojo to rest completely yesterday after a round with two women in a ménage à trois that lasted all night and into the afternoon. Sex wasn't a severe drain on his powers, but it did mess with his head.

When a man's fucking, his walls crumble, Dev always said. And yeah, that was the truth in plain English.

English. Like the accent purring against his ear: "Got any plans for tonight, love?"

FAITH BLACK'S PLANS for the night hadn't included a tall, dark and handsome man, but with someone trying to kill her, she'd had to make some adjustments.

The stranger she'd propositioned wrapped his arm around her waist. Before she could so much as blink, he tucked her between his long legs. The bar stool bit into the front of her thighs and his fingers bit into her hip, and for some reason, all she could think about was biting into *him.*

"I can always make room in my schedule for a beautiful woman," he said, in a rich, whiskey-smooth southern drawl that made her want to drink him in. And those eyes...even in the hazy, dim light from the beer signs, they glowed clear green. She'd never seen anything like it.

And as a biokinetic—a specialized telekinetic with the ability to manipulate living tissue—who had grown up alongside people with gifts even more incredible than hers, she'd seen a lot. She'd seen even more since the day she and her partner, with funding from the British government, had started up The Aquarius Group, a small, secret agency employing people with special abilities, like herself.

"I'm not usually so forward," she said, tearing her gaze away from his when the pub door opened. "But see that man walking in?"

The stranger inclined his head almost imperceptibly, as though he hadn't looked, and she gave him points for his astute assessment of the situation. She gave him extra points for having the most gorgeous, stout-colored hair, which just brushed the collar of his tee.

"He's my ex-lover," she lied. "He's a loon. Completely mad, and he's stalking me. I told him I have a new lover—"

"And I was the first guy you saw?"

"Yes." No, but when she'd detected a tail as she strolled along the moonlit boardwalk, she'd slipped into the nearest public place that would be full of men, and as luck would have it, these weren't just men. They were bikers, oil drillers and roughnecks, and the man who now held her had stood out as the toughest of the tough.

Not to mention the best-looking.

Marco watched from near the entrance, not bothering to hide his annoyance.

"Well," the stranger said, threading one hand through her hair to pull her face close to his, "I can either take care of you, or I can take care of him."

A sweet offer, but no matter how capable this guy looked—and he did look capable, all steel-strapped muscle and broad shoulders beneath his black AC/DC T-shirt—Marco was a trained killer, an excedosapien with reflexes ten times faster than the average person's. She knew because she'd gone head to head with him a year ago, and though her combat skills couldn't be better, his speed and fondness of the wire garrote had nearly spelled her doom.

She fingered the black velvet choker that hid the thin scar circling her neck, before catching herself and dropping her hand to his shoulder. "I'd love it if you'd play along, for just a bit."

One corner of his made-to-please-a-woman mouth turned up like she'd picked the right answer, and suddenly she was experiencing just how much that mouth was made to please.

The contact was gentle, more a brush of lips than anything, but her body's response was immediate and alarming. A blast of heat that had nothing to do with the Florida autumn temperature licked at her breasts, her belly, her inner thighs. When the expert sweep of his tongue opened her mouth, her legs opened too.

At least, as much as they could open with her caged between his jean-clad thighs.

This was not good.

Mustering all her self-control, she concentrated on Marco, using her unique form of telekinesis to probe his aura with her mind, searching for a weakness, a chink in his armor. On average, it took her thirty seconds to penetrate the protective weave of energy around a human, but in the heat of battle, thirty seconds was about twenty-nine and a half seconds too long—which was why she'd honed her hand-to-hand combat skills to a machete edge. Fortunately, she had time now, but this wasn't going to be a thirty-second jobber. It figured that Marco's aura would be the psychic equivalent of Kevlar.

"What's your name?" the stranger murmured against her lips, and for a moment, she forgot about Marco.

"Faith Black. Yours?"

"Wyatt." He dragged his mouth across her cheek to her ear. "What did he do to you?"

Marco sauntered toward them, his khaki business-casual out of place in a rough crowd like this. Men jeered . . . until Marco shot them a dark look that shut them up in an instant. Even predators recognized when they were in the presence of something higher on the food chain.

His flat, black eyes remained trained on her as he took a seat at a nearby table.

"Nothing I want to talk about," she said finally.

Wyatt pulled back as though he wanted to say something, but the bartender, a pit bull of a man with gray hair pulled into a low ponytail, interrupted.

"Can I get you anything, lady?"

Taking the opportunity to peel herself off Wyatt, she sank down onto a bar stool. "I'll have what he's having."

The bartender palmed a highball glass. "Jack neat with a beer back, coming right up."

"So, Faith," Wyatt said after the bartender slid her drinks to her, "where in England are you from?"

She sent out another probing pulse toward Marco, and—thank God—found the chink in his aura. "All over, really."

Standard answer. She'd spent a lifetime cultivating an accent that wouldn't reveal a background from any particular region, especially Devonshire, where she was born, or Yorkshire, where she grew up after her parents were killed. In order to blur the lines even more, she threw German inflections and American phrasing into her speech.

Blending in helped keep a secret agent alive.

One of Wyatt's hands came down on her knee, but she felt it to her core. Moisture drenched her panties. Her head felt light, her breasts heavy. The sensations breaking over her body were strangely intoxicating, and she had to give a little shake of her head to clear it. No man had ever affected her like this. Not even Sean, the one and only man she'd ever loved.

It had been a year since she'd last seen Sean, since they'd played cat and mouse, pain and pleasure. He couldn't resist her even when his job was to kill her.

She was counting on his predictability once more, because this mission could get her very dead if Sean's love for her had finally taken second place to his job with Itor.

"It's a little hot to be wearing leather." Wyatt's gaze took in her goth attire, which went against the whole blend-in thing—her black leather pants, the crimson silk-and-lace corset top and her leather jacket—his appreciation obvious in the way his lids grew heavy.

"The heat doesn't bother me." Neither did the cold. She'd always been able to regulate her own body temperature, though that was the extent of her powers over her own bodily functions. She could, however, do anything she wanted to anyone else.

Sliding a glance at Marco, Wyatt downed the whiskey in his glass. The fine muscles in his throat worked beneath the golden, whisker-roughened skin there, holding her gaze for a moment.

When he finished, he spun the glass across the polished bar top and nodded to the bartender for another.

"Think the heat will bother khaki-boy?" he asked.

She grinned. "It might," she said, knowing full well that nothing would deter Marco from his goal, but needing time to finish breaking through his aura.

"Let's find out, because the way he's looking at you is bugging the shit out of me." He palmed the back of her neck and slanted his mouth over hers once more.

Even though she'd anticipated the kiss, her breath caught. The way he maneuvered his lips, teeth and tongue with gentle, dominant skill...Christ, the man could probably make her orgasm from kissing alone.

"We've got to be convincing, right?" he whispered, and then licked the swell of her bottom lip, and a ragged moan escaped her. "Open for me."

She didn't hesitate, welcomed the slide of his wet tongue against hers. He tasted like whiskey, smelled like earth and man, a potent combination that made her loosen up more effectively than if she'd poured the entire fifth of Jack Daniel's down her throat—her throat that throbbed in a grim reminder that Marco wanted to slit it.

Again.

Doing her best to ignore what Wyatt's hand was doing to her thigh, she used her mind to pluck at the weak strings in the weave of Marco's aura. Finally, with Wyatt trailing kisses along her jaw, visions of the internal workings of Marco's body filled her brain.

Marco still watched, but had leaned forward, elbows propped on knees, enjoying the show. The dozen or so patrons in the pub could care less, too fascinated by the two scantily clad women near the pool table who were doing a lot more than kissing the four guys they were with.

Marco's heartbeat gave nothing away. Slow, steady, strong. She could stop it in an instant, give him an aneurysm, or boil his blood.

But all of those things would attract attention. Besides, killing one of Itor's men when she would be meeting with a top Itor operative tomorrow was not conducive to a good working relationship. Even if—or especially because—she was going to be faking the relationship.

In the back of her mind, she knew Wyatt was nuzzling her ear, knew he'd pulled her nearly into his lap and that he had a monster erection nudging her hip. She knew her fingers were gliding over his hard, bunched biceps, and that her sex had flooded with silken cream.

If Marco weren't a threat, she'd drag Wyatt No Last Name to her hotel room and rock his world.

But she wouldn't put it past Marco to try to take them both out before they made it to her bed.

A psychic flare-up drew her to Marco's stomach, full after a meal. In her mind, she reached for his pylorus, the ring of muscle that separated the stomach from the small intestine. With a mental nudge, she opened it, allowing unprocessed food to spill through.

Marco winced, rubbed his belly. He'd cramp up soon, but she needed something more immediate to distract him until the cramps started.

"Wyatt," she gasped, when she felt the slide of his palm beneath her corsetlike top.

His tongue swirled against her neck. "Do you think he's convinced?"

"I don't know, love, but I certainly am."

His smile tickled her skin, and before she became distracted again, she dropped south inside Marco's body, located his bladder, and gave a mental squeeze.

The expression of horror on Marco's face as his pants darkened with urine brought immense satisfaction. He looked around wildly for the toilet, and then, clutching his gut, he ran for the Men sign near the back of the pub.

"Brilliant," Faith said, pulling away from Wyatt and ignoring her body's protests. She slid the bartender a sultry smile. "Wyatt's picking up my tab. Cheers."

She darted out the door, Wyatt's curse following her. She'd nearly made it the three blocks to her hotel when she realized someone was following.

Spinning, she threw out her fist. Recognition bloomed, but she pulled her punch too late. Wyatt blocked the strike, lightning fast, and then she found herself against a building, Wyatt's body pressed against hers.

Sloppy work on her part, letting it happen, but a small part of her had wanted this from the moment she recognized his face beneath the streetlight.

Relaxing, because doing so rolled her hips into closer contact with his, she dragged her gaze up from his broad chest, past the dazzling white teeth that flashed in a smile, as though he knew she was taking his measure now that they were alone.

The look in his eyes confirmed it. Amusement swirled there in the green depths, amusement and wariness and a touch of wild, as if he'd seen one too many horror movies.

Or had lived them.

"Tell me to back off and I will."

"Back off."

Grinning, he tugged her hard against him so she had to crane her neck to look up at him. *Oh, my.* She'd known he was tall, but at five-ten, she wasn't short herself, and he topped her by at least five inches. For all that height, he moved like a cat. Powerful muscles sang with reserved energy while in motion, went loose-limbed at rest.

A flicker of unease made her tense. This man was even more dangerous than he'd appeared to be in the pub. Prior military, maybe a merc.

It worked for her, the whole danger thing, since that was her life, but on the eve of what might be the riskiest mission she'd ever accepted, she didn't need any extra stress.

"You didn't back off," she said.

"Because you didn't mean it."

No, she supposed she hadn't. Sex oozed from every pore in his smooth, tanned skin, the promise of eroticism so tangible she could feel it rumble through her like a purr.

"Did you want to go at it here, then?" She skimmed her thumb over the massive ridge in the fly of his jeans, and he arched into her palm. "Where anyone driving by can see?"

His hand dropped to grasp her ass and hold her as his hips undulated against hers, driving his cock into her belly. "I'm not into exhibitionism. No one sees my woman but me."

"I'm not your woman."

Dropping his head, he nipped at her earlobe, held it between his teeth as he growled, "Tonight you are."

Somewhere deep inside, she wanted to protest, but when her mouth opened, only one word came out.

"Yes."

Her voice sounded husky, needy. It had been so long since she'd allowed herself an indulgent night of pleasure. Normally, sex was a tool, whether she offered her body or merely the promise of her body. Seduction played a big part of her job as a special operative for TAG, and tomorrow it was back to the job.

Tonight... tonight was for her, because if her mission aboard Itor's oil platform met with success and she nabbed the weather machine, someone she loved might die. If her mission failed, someone else she loved *would* die.

Either way, she'd lose Sean or Liberty, and either way, she didn't have a lot of time left for pleasure.

Reaching up, she took Wyatt's face in her palms and captured his gaze with hers. "Your room or mine?"

CHAPTER
three

It was definitely going to be Faith's room. Wyatt's own was a piece of shit off the side of the highway. Most nights, he slept outside, on the beach, until the cops rousted him and called him a vagrant. Besides, they determined that Faith's room was the closest, and he let his body send out enough pulsating mojo to make her realize they needed privacy—and fast.

He'd slung his arm around her as they walked past the snooty desk clerk, to the elevator. They rode up to her floor with an elderly couple, who smiled at them—as if they knew what was going to happen once he and Faith reached her room. Or what would be happening right here in the elevator if they were alone, based on the way Faith was rubbing against him.

When Wyatt's hormones called out, they *called out*, brother. Even the old lady was edging closer to him, on what seemed like the slowest ride ever to the top of a building.

"This is us," Faith said, tugging him along by the front of his belt. Wyatt felt the older woman caress his lower back as he left the elevator, towed along by Faith, and he tossed her a wink over his shoulder as the elevator doors shut.

That old man was getting lucky tonight, on him.

"Come on in," Faith said, holding the door to her room open for him. She was staying in a suite, very posh, and fitting of her accent.

"Fancy," he said, noting the ratty stuffed animal sitting in the middle of the plush bedding, out of place and somehow strangely comforting.

She wound her arms around his neck, looked up at him as she pressed her belly against his erection. "Yes, well, work is paying for it all, so I figured I deserved the splurge."

"What kind of work do you do?"

"Nothing special." She sucked lightly on the skin above his collarbone.

"So you dress in leather and run from ex-boyfriends on your time off to spice things up," he said.

"Anything to keep it exciting. What about you?"

"You didn't invite me here to talk work," he said.

"Actually, I wasn't going to invite you at all."

"Then why did you?"

"I don't know," she murmured against his neck, her lips hot against his already overheated skin—and, *oh yeah*, they were going to have fun tonight.

He turned the lock on the door to Do Not Disturb mode with his mind and kept on kissing her.

She was so enthralled, she didn't notice that he was unbuttoning her leather jacket with his fingers and unzipping her leather pants with his thoughts, pulling them down and ripping off her corset top.

She'd made short work of his T-shirt, yanked it off impatiently and nibbled along his shoulder as she unbuttoned his jeans. He wasn't wearing underwear, found that in most cases it wasn't necessary, and this was definitely one of those cases.

"God, this is crazy," she murmured. Her nipples were dark pink and already stiff, begging for his touch, and he knew, just knew that if he reached between her legs right now she'd already be wet and ready for him. One long stroke and he'd be fucking her.

He wondered what it would be like to actually make love, when things weren't at such a frenzied, fever pitch, thanks to his mojo. The times he did slow it down, the women he was with would have a complete fit, practically force themselves on him.

No, slowing down wasn't worth it, and from the looks of things, this night with Faith wouldn't be any different. Her pupils were already slightly dilated, her lips fuller, her scent calling out for him.

His head was getting fuzzy, a side effect of turning another person on this much. But he wanted her to want him badly, even though she hadn't been drawn to him originally because of his sexual pull.

He hadn't realized that back in the bar, but he'd been concentrating too hard on his past to put anything else out there. And he was nearly beyond concentration now and she was completely naked, save for the black goth choker she wore. He was going to make sure she kept that on, since it was sexy as anything.

He walked around her body, surveying, taking it all in. She turned her head to watch him circle. He stopped at her back, rubbed himself against her, his jeans brushing the bare backs of her thighs, his cock brushing her high, tight ass.

She'd let him fuck her this way, he thought, caressing a butt cheek in each hand as she continued to watch him over her shoulder.

He noted a scar on her right shoulder, his sex-addled brain not registering it as anything important as he ran his tongue over it, back and forth. She shivered at that intimacy, as if the scar was something she'd tried to keep hidden. Nothing could stay hidden from him for long, not when his hormones were calling out to hers, begging her to unveil everything to him. She was powerless.

And when she turned toward him and took his cock in her hand, so was he.

"You're a big man," she murmured.

"Compliments will get you everywhere. And I mean that literally," he said, letting her drag him down to the most comfortable bed he'd been on in months. Years, maybe.

She made short work of his jeans and he could see her assessing his body, looking at the various scars that graced his chest and thigh—remnants more of his SEAL days, less from ACRO work—but not really taking them in because she was completely focused on sex.

She crouched, on all fours like a stalking panther, above his jutting cock and nuzzled it with her cheek. He put his hands behind his head, content to wait and watch for the moment.

She ran her tongue up the length of his shaft, stopping to swirl the broad head and then gently suckle the bead of pre-cum before sliding her tongue along his slit and, Jesus Christ, his hips bucked up with a force of their own.

"You like that, Wyatt?"

"Yeah, baby. I like."

Another beautiful smile before she slid him into her mouth. His back arched, his eyes closed, and for a few merciful minutes his mind went completely blank of anything but the incredible pleasure she was giving him.

He wanted to do the same for her, curved his long body sideways in order to grab for her thigh. She understood what he wanted immediately, let him pull her hips toward him, even as her mouth formed an O around the outer ridge of the head of his cock. The dark hair of her sex was manicured into a neat triangle, and he angled his neck so he could get his mouth on her. He blew softly on her center and then gave a long lick down her wet, hot folds, imbibing her sweet scent like a mark that would follow him for life.

Her thighs clenched involuntarily and he used that opportunity to bury his face in her, to inhale that sweet, tangy scent she'd been giving off, and goddamn, he was going to move in and set up shop.

Her tongue flattened against the smooth spot behind his balls and he was going to come, good enough and hard enough to push away any coherent thoughts that might break through.

Faith had one of the most talented mouths he'd ever run across, and yes, he could definitely do this for a long, long time.

At least until morning.

His balls tightened as he flirted with the edge of his orgasm, tried to hold off as long as he could, until Faith came against his mouth and moaned around his shaft, and then it was over for him. His cock pulsed, the edges of his sight blurring, the way it did right before he went telekinetic. But this was not the time for any more special gifts to barge in on his party. No, he wanted to savor the way shivers tightened every muscle in his body to an almost painful level as he came.

She gripped his hips as she milked him—he did the same for her, his face still buried in her pussy. Keeping his tongue on her pulsing clit with just the right amount of pressure, he worked her over the edge again.

Slowly, he let his cock slide from her mouth, licked his way up her body, stopping to tease each nipple again while she moaned. Her fingers stroked through his hair, her nails raking lightly along his scalp.

He put his knee between her thighs to spread them, but she protested, pushing back against him.

She was trying to flip him because she wanted to be on top— even though she was overtaken by him, her dominant streak was still fighting.

He didn't let that happen, not so much because he needed to be on top, but because he was in the mood for it. And Wyatt always went with his moods.

His mood also had him not wanting to use a condom. Yeah, he used them if the woman asked or if he wanted to contain the mess, but he didn't *need* to use them. ACRO had recently acquired immunizations developed to prevent all sexually transmitted diseases—immunizations that would never be available to the public, for the same reason the drug trade would never be stopped: There was too much money to be made off human misery.

"You on the pill?" he asked, because ACRO had yet to steal a patent on an anti-pregnancy drug for men.

"Mmm . . . yes . . . hurry."

Pressing her down, he held her wrists against the sheet. He wanted to bury himself inside her, watch her face, see her with that cool choker. And that's exactly what he did, took her hard and fast while one of her legs wrapped around his lower back, and proceeded to fuck her into the mattress. Not roughly, but he wasn't gentle either.

Faith had no problem with it. She kept one foot firmly on the mattress, used it to give herself leverage so she could rock her hips up to meet him, stroke for stroke, and she was moaning. Uncontrollably.

"Keep fucking me, Wyatt."

And he did, through a multiple orgasm that shook her, body and mind, until she was incoherent and his own body demanded release.

The beauty of the sex thing, when he was deep in the throes of it, was his own ability to have multiple orgasms, something that most men couldn't experience. It was like falling, closing his eyes and trusting his body's responses. White light blasted from under his lids; his legs straightened as she contracted around his cock.

His body shook and he let himself fall onto his elbows, his forehead pressed to hers. Her arms went around him as a contented groan escaped her throat while he nuzzled against the velvet fabric of the choker.

"Your weight feels good," she murmured. "Don't move."

"I wasn't planning on it, but my body has other ideas. Plenty of them." He was hard again, and he was still inside her.

THE LOVELY MAN was still hard.

Faith wrapped her legs around Wyatt's waist and smiled up at him as he watched her with those fabulous eyes. His mouth was open slightly, lips glistening from kissing her. He thrust slowly, each slide of his cock scraping over flesh already sensitive after several orgasms. It wouldn't take much for her to climb the peak again—a peak that would punch with sharp clarity through the fog of bliss in which she seemed to be stuck. For a split second she'd wonder what had gotten into her, and then Wyatt would kiss her, or lick her neck, or thrust deep, and she'd fall under his spell once more.

Like she was right now. "Want to mix things up a bit?" she asked, and he cocked an eyebrow.

"What did you have in mind?"

She jerked her chin toward the four-person Jacuzzi near the panoramic windows that overlooked the dark Atlantic. "Do you like to get wet?"

"Oh, yeah."

They padded to the hot tub, and she entered first, hissing at the intense heat as she immersed herself. When she was waist deep, she kneeled on one of the benches and told Wyatt to stay where he was, standing at the edge of the tub. He watched her with open curiosity as she ran her hands up his muscular legs, over wicked scars she'd have asked about if she ever planned to see him again.

His thighs quivered at her touch. His cock, thick and wrapped in dusky, smooth skin, jumped when she leaned in to kiss his hip. She trailed kisses inward, each one making Wyatt's breath come faster.

"What do you want me to do, Wyatt?" She licked the base of his shaft up and down like a candy cane and looked at him. His eyes glowed with a feral light, a trick of the full moon shining through the window. The raw hunger in his expression was no trick, though, and when he spoke, the hunger dripped from his deep, growling voice.

"Put your mouth on me. Suck my cock."

Smiling, she trailed her tongue down, planning to suck him, but not like he wanted. The soft musk of his arousal heightened her own, and her mouth watered as she pressed her lips to the velvety sac below his erection.

A low groan escaped him, encouraging her. Slowly, she sucked one heavy testicle into her mouth and worked it gently with her tongue. He threaded the fingers of one hand through her hair and palmed his erection with the other, stroking himself as she suckled his balls, giving each special attention.

"You're so good at that," he said, and she almost laughed, because if he only knew what she could do with her gift, how she could stroke him from the inside as well as the out, it would blow his mind.

She could make him come without laying a finger on him.

Which would ruin her fun, because she wanted all her fingers on him.

Gently, he pushed her away and joined her in the water, his big body filling the tub and blocking her view of anything but his broad chest. He circled around behind her and cupped her breasts, used his thumbs to flick their wet tips until they peaked, flushed and ripe. His erection slipped between her legs, and she reached down into the water to run her fingers over the head as he rocked his hips.

"You're so beautiful," he murmured into her hair. "Tall. You're a good fit."

Wrapping his arms around her, he sat, pulling her down onto his lap so her back rested against his chest. He slid both hands over her breasts, across her belly, and between her legs.

She let him spread her thighs wide, exposing her sex to the hot water. His tongue traced the shell of her ear as he dipped one finger between her folds and began to stroke, slowly, back and forth through her slit. The water jets massaged her legs, her waist, her feet. Wyatt might as well have had ten hands.

Curls of pleasure swirled up from between her legs where the tip of his finger pushed inside her. She couldn't remember the last time she'd treated sex as a luxury, a relaxing indulgence, and after the fast and furious pace of what they'd done earlier, this was a double treat.

In no way had her drive slowed down, though, and she wanted his touch as badly as ever. Somewhere in the back of her mind she knew they should have used condoms even though she took contraceptive pills and even though physicians at TAG purged the body of all diseases after each job. She also knew she shouldn't have brought him to her room. Not when she was on a mission.

Then again, this man didn't strike her as an enemy agent, didn't come across as anything but a roughneck with some military experience.

He definitely had some sexual experience, and he wielded it like a weapon, using it to devastate her willpower.

Every push of his finger inside her, every circle of his thumb around her clit, had her panting and squirming against his hand.

"Please," she gasped. "Please make me come."

Wyatt scraped his teeth over the back of her neck and shifted, spreading her legs wider, and surprise sucked the air from her lungs. He'd turned her so one of the Jacuzzi jets streamed water against her sex.

"Oh, God." Groaning, she threw her head back onto Wyatt's hard shoulder.

"You like that. You like the water licking your pussy, fucking you hard."

She couldn't answer, could barely breathe as he spread her swollen flesh with his fingers, exposing her even more to the frothy jet. She pulled her feet up against her butt, braced them on his knees so every inch of her sensitive flesh could benefit from the gurgling spurts.

Hot bubbles danced over her clit, stroking and pulsing. She whimpered, and Wyatt closed his mouth over hers, swallowing the sounds of her climax as it took her with such force her hips came up out of the water.

The walls of her pussy were still convulsing when Wyatt lifted her and settled her on her knees on a bench so she was bent over the edge of the Jacuzzi. He entered her hard, stuffed her deliciously full. She pushed back against him, taking everything he could give.

"Oh, yeah," he said, his voice guttural, breathless. "Talk to me, baby."

His cock knocked against her womb, making her cry out with pleasure. "Talk naughty to you?"

"Naughty, not naughty"—his fingers dug into her hips as he pumped—"anything. I want to hear your voice."

"Naughty, then," she managed between panting breaths. "Because I love the way your cock feels inside me. It's almost as good as when you licked me there."

His moan vibrated through her, sweetening the already hon-eyed pleasure building at her core.

"You liked going down on me," she continued. "Liked push-ing your tongue deep, liked sucking my clit. God, it was good. Your face buried in my pussy, my mouth milking your cock and caressing your balls, so tight, so filled with come. Do you know what you taste like, love?"

"No," he rasped. "No one has ever, ah, damn..." He stopped thrusting, gripped her tenaciously and panted, his control nearly breaking. After a moment, he rocked into her again, slow and easy. "No one has ever told me."

"You taste salty and heady, like the ocean and ale. I could suck you off all night long."

"Fuck." His thrusts came faster, and she felt him swell inside her, knew he was close. So was she.

"Yes, fuck. Fuck me, Wyatt. Harder."

The sound of water sloshing against the edges of the tub min-gled with the wet slap of his balls against her sex, and then his roar of release joined in. His seed pulsed inside her, hot, silky, and bursts of pleasure shot through her as her own orgasm shook her apart.

For a full minute, they remained where they were. When their breathing and pulses slowed, Wyatt wrapped his arms around her and dragged her back into the water, where he caressed her arms and back with lazy, long strokes.

They kissed, leisurely smooches that led to another round of sex, in the shower and again in bed, and after what must have been her tenth orgasm, he pressed her into the mattress and rested his forehead against hers, smiling sadly.

"I have to go."

"I know."

There was nothing left to say. They were strangers, even if what had happened between them felt like more than meaningless stranger sex. At least, it felt like more to her. He might do this all the time.

She did what she had to when she was on a mission, but in her personal life, she preferred to actually get to know a man before she had sex with him. Doing something like this wasn't like her.

What really annoyed her was that she couldn't even blame her behavior on alcohol. Maybe her nerves about seeing Sean tomorrow had affected her. She'd been wound tight lately, knowing that a nightmare was about to begin. One last fling before throwing herself into the lion's den was probably just the thing to take the edge off.

And Wyatt had done that, brilliantly. She'd never been so relaxed.

She threw on a hotel robe and held Mr. Wiggums while Wyatt dressed. The tatty stuffed rabbit went everywhere with her, had been all that remained of the twin sister she'd last seen when she was five and whose status had been unknown—until one week ago. Now Liberty might very well die before they could be reunited, if Faith failed this latest mission.

She could not—would not—fail. The images of a very young Liberty, in tears and handing over her favorite toy to Faith as she was being carried away by "people who could help her," was burned into her brain. If only Liberty had hidden her biokinetic gift better—a gift identical to Faith's, but that had developed much earlier—maybe they would still be together. Then again, maybe Liberty would have died in the storm that had killed their parents and that Faith had barely escaped.

Putting aside both her thoughts and Mr. Wiggums, she watched Wyatt approach, his eyes glowing.

"I'd ask for your phone number," he said, cupping her cheek, "but I doubt you'll even remember this if I called."

She swatted his hand away. "You think I'm such a slut that I won't remember which guy is calling me?" And why the hell was she getting mad, when she knew damned good and well that they couldn't see each other again? They were from different countries, different worlds.

"It's not that. I'm just not memorable." He lowered his mouth to hers and kissed her so thoroughly that by the time he was done, she was clinging to his shirt as though desperate to keep him from leaving. "See ya, Faith Black."

He swept out of the room, leaving her standing on wobbly legs. Not memorable? Was he daft? Because she knew, without a doubt, that Wyatt No Last Name would be the lover to which she'd forever compare all others.

CHAPTER Four

Devlin O'Malley opened his eyes and blinked and then blinked again and again and then he smiled because, *hoo-fucking-rah,* let there be light. Real light, not filtered through his second sight, and his body relaxed on the bed in the guest quarters on the ACRO compound, where he'd been staying for the past four months because his blindness was officially gone.

Ten years in the dark gone in an instant last spring, the same way the light was taken from him all those years ago when he'd been piloting that C-130. Yes, the heavy weight—and the bad karma that had come along with it—was finally gone.

Today, he was going home, to his own house, and returning to his role as leader of ACRO. Taking back the helm, a job his lover and best friend had been handling for him—a job Oz hated doing, which made Dev appreciate him all the more.

It was time to take back his life, to find a way to deal with the man named Alek—who was not only his biological father, but the mastermind behind Itor Corp, ACRO's rival agency—once and for all. The one who'd almost taken the agency Dev's parents had built from the ground up—and nearly taken Dev's soul with it.

But first, it was time to stop a man-made hurricane from wiping out a major U.S. city, and after that possibly the entire free world.

"Devlin, it's nearly time." Sam, ACRO's most respected psychic, one who'd been with the agency since its inception, stood in the doorway, and automatically, for a split second, he thought about using his controlled remote viewing to see her—a habit that was hard to break, since his psychic gifts were as strong as they were before he'd gotten his sight back.

Sam had known his parents, had worked hard with them to ensure the agency's success. She did so again when she'd taken care of him over the past months, helping to shield his mind from Alek, so the head of the enemy agency couldn't learn any more of ACRO's secrets.

Like the fact that one of ACRO's operatives, Ryan Malmstrom, had infiltrated Itor. And hadn't been heard from since Alek announced last May that he knew about the spy, something that ate at Dev like acid. He'd tried to use his CRV to get an image of Ryan, but after one clear, disturbing impression of the operative strapped down to a medical table, he'd only been able to conjure fuzzy, distorted images that grew darker and more distant with every try.

"I'm getting up," he told her, rising to look out the large window overlooking the acres of land where the Animal Division horses roamed freely, and wondered if he could take up one of the small Cessnas this afternoon, a spin through the wild blue yonder...

"You have too much work to do to think about flying today," Sam teased.

"There's never too much work to stop flying," he said, and the thought of being able to get into the cockpit as more than just a passenger heated his body with excitement.

"You still need to keep your mind shielded as much as possible," Sam told him. "You know I believe in the power of the mind over the power of drugs."

Still, she handed him the bottle of pills specially developed by a team of ACRO scientists to totally and completely block Dev's mind from being read or broken into. A way to control the dreaded mind rapes that I-Agents had no compunction about utilizing at whim, leaving their victims nearly paralyzed with pain and violated memories.

"You're ready, Devlin."

"I know, Sam, I know. But you're going to miss winning our nightly poker game," he teased. Ever since he'd been here, he hadn't been allowed near op reports or other agents, save for a handful of psychics. In fact, he hadn't done this much of nothing since forever—but the return of his sight smoothed out many of the rough edges.

"Oz saved your life by getting rid of the spirit who haunted you," Sam continued. "We owe him."

"But I'm sure the rest of the agency is giving him a hard time." Dev knew Oz, his longtime, on again/off again lover and the love of Dev's life, was strong enough to take it, to handle the role of leader in Dev's stead. But Oz had been gone for so long from any sort of teamwork environment, Dev knew he had to be squirming.

"Is he staying?"

"Oz is staying, Sam." For four long months, his memories were the only way he had of communicating with Oz. Memories full of restless, inherently forceful sexual urges that comforted him—because that meant Oz was thinking of him, dreaming of him. Sharing the memory. "I don't know if he'll continue to work at ACRO, but he's staying." Dev wasn't going to make that mistake again, wasn't going to let Oz take off into the night.

When the ghost, the tortured spirit of a murdered ex–Itor agent named Darius, began haunting Dev years ago and then returned for more this past spring, he hadn't been sure he had the strength left to deal with it. Both times, Oz was the one to help him—and now that issue was literally dead and buried.

And Dev needed to get back and deal with the most pressing issue, the one that had been weighing on his mind heavily—the weather machine that was still in Itor's hands. Although, if his calculations were correct, Wyatt would be ready to take it down.

Still, he never expected things to happen that easily, and he had a strong sense of dread that this time he was right.

"HALEY, WE HAVE all the forecast models you asked for." Jeremy Bondy, ACRO's hydrometeorologist, stood in Haley Begnaud's office doorway. Nervous energy had him bouncing on his toes, his shaggy red hair sweeping into his eyes.

"Thank you," Haley said. "Great work." Better than great, considering that just an hour ago she'd burst into the weather lab's workstation and shouted out a list of demands that had ended with *"I need it yesterday. Move it!"*

"Your husband and Mr. O'Malley are here."

"That was fast." She grabbed her laptop and various charts and hurried through the weather station, where several meteorologists worked on the state-of-the-art equipment she'd brought in since taking over as station chief a year ago.

"Are you going to let us in on what's going on?" Melissa Abel, her climatologist, asked as Haley breezed by.

"As soon as I can."

Which probably meant that she'd be telling everyone about the weather machine the moment the meeting ended. She'd been studying weather patterns for months, trying to determine how many of the machines might exist, all the while hoping the transmissions from Wyatt would help. She knew he'd been sent on a recon mission only—until last week, when she'd finally concluded that the machine sitting on the Atlantic oil facility was probably the only one in operation. Now his assignment was to destroy.

But he might have been sent too late.

She entered the briefing room, where Remy and Dev waited at the twelve-person oval table. She barely glanced at Dev; she hadn't seen him in months and rumor had it that he'd regained his sight, and she didn't want to stare. Remy, though...him she stared at plenty. After nearly a year of marriage, she still drooled over her dark-haired, blue-eyed husband when he wore his black BDUs.

Well, she drooled no matter what he wore—or didn't wear. But the BDUs gave him an even more commanding presence, which set her libido on fire—it was crazy, considering that when she'd met him she'd hated military men. Now she sometimes asked him to wear his uniform at home. Maybe tonight...

"I guess this means you broke the code." Dev leaned back in his chair and folded his hands over his abs.

Snapping out of her lust, she pulled an Atlantic map down from its roller on the wall. "It wasn't that difficult. Your cryptographers were thinking like secret agents, not meteorologists. It was modified synoptic code. How did Wyatt get it anyway?"

Haley was one of the few people who knew that Wyatt was alive and well, and while she had no idea why the deception was so critical, she did know that he had somehow transmitted a code he'd come across a couple of weeks ago while on the oil platform.

"I don't know how he got it. What does it mean?"

Haley spread out the charts she brought with her—hurricane predictions, forecast models and climate data. "Remy, remember when you asked me why we've had such a quiet hurricane season?"

He nodded. "Itor could have pounded us. Why haven't they?"

"I couldn't answer that until today. See, I've been watching every tiny disturbance that popped up in the Pacific, the Atlantic and the Gulf of Mexico. Some of the storm development contained weather machine signatures, easy to spot now that I know what I'm looking for. Those storms were bizarre in their behavior, almost like Itor was playing around. The conclusion I came to is that their machine has limitations. For instance, it can steer a storm or it can strengthen one, but doing both strains the machine's capabilities. Hurricane Katrina is an example of that."

Dev frowned. "Katrina was an Itor storm?"

"Absolutely. And I'm sure New Orleans was the target. Thing is, she should have weakened more than she did. I think Itor tried to keep up the intensity, and doing so caused a problem with steerage. The storm slid east instead of striking New Orleans head-on. The irony is that Itor's mistake actually caused more damage overall than a direct strike would have done. The way it turned out, the city still took massive damage because of the levy failures, and everything to the east was devastated in a way that might not have happened if Itor had gotten its way."

"Bastards," Remy growled. Louisiana was his home state, and the bayous, food and people held a special place in his heart. After the time she'd spent with him there, the state was in her heart as well.

"So what's the bottom line?" Dev leaned forward, and finally Haley allowed herself to meet his sharp gaze.

She could barely contain an astonished gasp. The man had always been striking, but there was a new spark about him, a glint in his seeing brown eyes. She wanted to tell him how great he looked after his sabbatical, but her relationship with him had always been extremely professional, much more so than he required.

She cleared her throat. "Basically, I believe that in order for the Itor machine to achieve maximum effectiveness, its operators have to wait for the perfect atmospheric and oceanic environments. That's what the synoptic code was about. Normally, synoptic code communicates existing weather conditions, but this code was more of a plan of optimum conditions. And unfortunately for us, the optimum conditions for a strike are taking shape." She moved to the map she'd unrolled. "Right now there's a minimal hurricane in the Atlantic, moving toward Florida."

"So you think they're going to strike, what, Miami?"

"No. I believe the plan is to make us *think* they're going to hit Florida." Dev tapped his fingers on the table as though annoyed, so she hurried on. "Late-season hurricanes are often East Coast strikes. The storms can move fast. Terrifyingly fast. If all the conditions fall into the perfect alignment suggested by Itor's code, Itor is going to aim a hurricane at Florida, and while everyone is watching the south and resources are diverted, at the last minute Itor will slide the storm up the East Coast. They'll strengthen it here"—she pointed to a spot on the map—"and here, and here."

She took a deep breath. "This sucker will move so quickly that no one will have time to get out of the way. We're talking a matter of hours."

"Jesus," Dev muttered.

"Where are they going to bring it in?" Remy asked, but his tight expression told her he already knew the answer.

"New York City."

Dev pegged her with a hard look. "Is that possible? That a hurricane could hit New York?"

"Powerful storms are rare, but they happen. And New York is due. The last bad one struck in 1938, a category three that killed six hundred and changed the landscape around Long Island. The geological impact is still being felt today. In 1893, a minimal hurricane wiped an entire island off the map." She pointed to Manhattan. "The area is far more built up and populated now. Imagine what will happen if Itor brings in a category five, or even what could amount to a category six hurricane. It'll flood the city, the subways. Wind will funnel and strengthen between the high-rise buildings. Tens of thousands will die. Maybe more. It'll take years to recover. This will be the most devastating occurrence in the modern history of North America. Wyatt needs to destroy that machine. Fast. If he doesn't do it before the hurricane crosses this point"—she pinned a tack to a spot on the map—"it won't matter if the machine is destroyed or not. We need to put a backup plan into motion."

Dev, face pale and appearing a little shaken, turned to Remy. "I don't know how easy it's going to be to contact Wyatt. Looks like you're our backup plan."

"I can't affect man-made weather. As long as the machine is controlling the hurricane, I'm useless. We found that out the hard way."

Haley's gut clenched at the memory of how Itor had used their tiny prototype weather machine against Remy—an act that had nearly cost both of them their lives.

"True," Haley said, "but Itor will use existing natural conditions to maximize the effects of the hurricane, and the thing is,
those same conditions can be Itor's enemies. I know you haven't
done anything this big, but our only hope is for you to drive
faster a front coming from the west. Itor won't be able to main-
tain the storm's strength if it has to push against the front, which
means that if they manage a direct strike, the storm will be weakened. The problem is that even if Wyatt destroys the machine
after the point I showed you, the storm will have become self-
sustaining and will still be a threat to the eastern seaboard. In that
case, you'll have to nudge the hurricane itself out to sea."

"That's some big shit, Haley." Remy sat forward in his chair
and braced his forearms on his knees, his gaze intense, masculine,
having shifted into the mission-mode sharpness that always made
her heart trip with appreciation. Yeah, he was definitely wearing
the BDUs home tonight. "I'll need you with me."

"I know."

"Not an option," Dev said. "I need Haley here at the weather
station."

"I can't do this without her," Remy said. "You know that."

Dev dragged his hands through his hair, leaving wild tufts behind. "I do know that, but just this once—"

"No woman but Haley." The fierce tone in Remy's voice put
an end to any further argument—an argument Haley hadn't been
surprised to hear put on the table. Dev would do anything to
make sure a mission as critical as this one reached a successful
conclusion, and if that meant Remy getting blown by one of their
Seducers while Haley manned the weather station, then it was a
sacrifice Dev was willing to make.

It was not, however, a sacrifice either Remy or Haley would
ever make.

Dev turned his gaze on her, and she didn't flinch. Everyone in
ACRO's top tier knew about Remy's sexual ties with the weather,
and a handful were aware of her role in the weather-sex thing, but
she'd gotten over the embarrassment.

"Then you'll stay in touch with your weather lab?"

"I'll take all my portable equipment, and I'll stay in constant contact with you and them."

"How much time do we have?"

"Remy and I will need to be in place in two days. If Wyatt and Remy can't take care of this thing, then on day three cartographers can start rewriting the U.S. map."

CHAPTER
Five

"Wyatt, great save on drill four—we would've lost it for sure if you hadn't been quick on your feet." Don, the rig manager, slapped him on the back and Wyatt couldn't even bring himself to smile at the guy. Instead, he nodded and worked his way down to the lower platform, where he drew in shaky breaths and tried to shrug off the praise.

He could almost hear his father's voice berating him, mocking him. Wyatt's fists clenched at the memory and he shook it off the way he did all his shitty ones, because he was not back on his family's rig feeling like a pariah. This was a job and he couldn't afford the brain drain.

You're not the same.

Not the same scared kid he was at twelve and thirteen and fourteen, not the same young man who pushed his gifts down so hard it hurt him physically, sometimes so badly that he had to curl up in a tight ball until the pain receded. In order to ease it, he'd allowed himself to use his telekinesis in the privacy of his room.

Yeah, being back on a rig was full of memories, none of them particularly good, some of them indifferent and a few that were downright scary. The distrust in his father and brother's eyes tended to weigh heavily on his mind, haunted him with every drill he did for this particular job, even though he was a million miles away from his family.

A platform wasn't the place for distrust. Neither was the military... and he'd deserted his men and his country after he'd been accused of murder.

More than twenty years had separated Wyatt and his two half brothers. One brother, Tim, had been killed the week Wyatt was born—bringing Wyatt onto the earth during major family chaos.

The other brother, Mason, lost an arm and a leg in a rigging accident a week later—but continued to live on the platforms and help his father run operations both in Texas and on the Indian Ocean. And thus Wyatt's birth was always tied to the two tragic events, at least in his father's eyes.

And so, from an early age, Wyatt felt guilt for something he didn't do... and for those things he did nothing about, except run.

Wyatt's mother had died right after Wyatt had enlisted. Four years later, Mason was found murdered, his neck broken in a mysterious accident the police blamed Wyatt for, since he'd been in the military at the time and more than capable of snapping a man's neck... and there was also surveillance video of Wyatt sneaking aboard the rig. Then, mysteriously, the video had been cut off. Another thing Wyatt would've been able to accomplish.

He hadn't stuck around to figure out any of it—fight-or-flight response kicked in and ACRO helped him to save his ass. But he still didn't know for sure whether or not he was guilty.

His hand wrapped around the deck railing and he shifted from foot to foot, hating *that* particular uncertainty with a passion.

These days, he was still working for his country, the only way he could. The best—and only—way he knew how. He was loyal, faithful, and a fucking better-than-great operative.

But no, he wasn't the same.

THE HELICOPTER PILOT said the oil platform was ahead and to the left, but from her seat directly behind the copilot, Faith couldn't see a damned thing other than endless ocean and massive storm clouds.

Screw it. She sat back in the seat of the Chelbi passenger helicopter used to transport rig crews to and from work. She'd never been on an offshore installation, and would have looked forward to the experience if it weren't for the reason she was going to be there.

Liberty.

The call had come last week, had left Faith stunned, trembling and unable to think clearly for half an hour.

We have your sister. She will die if you don't cooperate.

At the time, Faith hadn't known whether or not Liberty was even alive. Their parents had sent Liberty to a psychiatric hospital, and three years later, the Great October Storm of 1987 had struck southern England, killing their mother and father. Traumatized, fledgling powers running wild, Faith had been whisked away by agents of the British government, eventually ending up in the school for special kids where she'd met Sean. By the time she was old enough to search for her sister, the trail had grown cold, and the mental facility her sister had gone to had no information beyond sketchy medical records. There had been rumors, but nothing substantial.

Faith hadn't given up, but she'd reached a dead end years ago.

Until the call, and the accompanying video feed.

The woman tied to a chair, one eye blackened and blood streaming from her nose, had been the spitting image of Faith. Liberty's black hair was shorter, jaw-length, and straight rather than long and wavy like Faith's, but there was no doubt as to the identity of the woman who swayed in her seat, a Kalashnikov rifle pointed at her head.

"Help me, Faith," Liberty had said in a lilting Irish accent. "I'm scared. This old boardinghouse is—"

The man had struck Liberty with the butt of the gun before she could slip in more clues. Liberty fell over with the chair, and Faith had screamed obscenities and threats until the man who'd hit Liberty approached the camera.

"If you want her to live, you'll listen."

The man's accent, also Irish, had been muffled by the knit mask he wore, but Faith understood. "What do you want?" she ground out.

"Itor has developed a powerful weapon. A weather machine. We want it."

"I don't know who Itor is."

The man turned, and though Faith couldn't see it, his action and the resulting grunt told her that he'd kicked Liberty.

"You bastard!"

"Don't jerk me off, Ms. Black. You will contact Sean Stowe, the man in charge of the weather device. We know you have a relationship with him. Tell him you love him. Tell him you want to join Itor. We don't care. Just get the machine's motherboard."

That day, Liberty's captors had sent a disposable phone and custom-made, waterproof carrying case for the motherboard, along with more instructions. Once the motherboard was in her possession, she was to contact them. She had two weeks. After that, Liberty would start losing body parts.

Bastards. Faith had her agency on the case, had given them the video, but she didn't expect much. Anyone who could track her, who could have found Liberty and used her against Faith, wasn't going to make mistakes.

And how had they known about Faith and Sean in the first place? Where had they found Liberty? Where had Liberty been living all these years? She needed answers, and she needed them now. Unfortunately, Liberty's captors hadn't been very forthcoming.

"We're landing," the pilot said, and grateful to tear her mind away from the images in her head, Faith peered out the window.

For a moment the air and water seemed to shift, shimmer. Suddenly, a monster offshore platform appeared out of thin air, and how the hell did Itor do that? What kind of men did Sean have working with him?

Her stomach churned, because she'd find out in a minute.

Once they landed, a man in black-spattered orange coveralls helped Faith out of the helicopter. She could feel eyes watching her. Lots of eyes. But then, any woman wearing a sleeveless black leather dress on an oil platform staffed with men had to expect stares and wolf whistles.

"Ms. Black, I'm Don Goss. I'll take you to Mr. Stowe, if you'll come this way."

She nodded briskly at the man who stood before her on the helipad, shielding her from the humid gusts that pushed ahead of the approaching, roiling storm cloud. A sense of unease shivered through her, but she couldn't be sure if the new case of nerves came from the storm or from the impending meeting with Sean. She wondered if he was watching. He wouldn't be out in the open—he was too dramatic for that—but he could have security monitors, and he was, no doubt, getting off on the sight of his men drooling over what he'd had. And would have again.

Ignoring the conflicting emotions that thought stirred, she followed Don through the maze of metal.

They climbed several flights of stairs, and she mentally thanked TAG's research specialist for advising her to wear boots instead of high heels, or she'd have killed herself on the grated metal plating.

She took note of the cameras, the placement of the men and of the fact that many wore sidearms. What the legitimate oil workers thought of that, she had no idea.

At the door to an inside hallway, two men required ID, which she gave to them in the form of her passport and British driver's license, and they motioned her inside. Alone.

She entered the hallway, and immediately a man dressed in jeans and a casual jacket joined her.

"I'm Giulio," he said, his Italian accent bringing back memories of the last time she'd been in Italy, six months ago, on assignment. "This way, please."

Flanked by her new escort, she memorized the path that led to a door guarded by two men holding AK-47 rifles. One moved forward.

"Ms. Black, I need you to raise your arms and stand with your feet apart."

"Of course." She did as she was told, and the man ran his hands down her body, ending at her crotch. There was nothing sexual or personal about it; the man just as easily could have been searching a corpse.

He finished, reached for the door lever, but paused, putting his hand to his earpiece. After a moment, he turned to her. "Mr. Stowe is taking an urgent call. He suggests that you take a look around the platform, and he'll join you shortly."

Faith smiled. "Perfect. I'd love to explore."

Explore, and map out the platform in a way the schematics she'd studied couldn't. The reprieve from having to see Sean for a few minutes wouldn't hurt either.

WYATT DID NOT like Sean Stowe. Didn't like, didn't trust—and sure, Wyatt could say that about most people, but this Sean guy made Wyatt take his nontrust issues to a new level. ACRO had determined that Sean Stowe was a high-ranking Itor agent, but his exact talents remained a mystery.

Didn't matter. The weather machine was getting taken out *today*. No exceptions. Wyatt's escape route was all mapped out, dive equipment ready, and although he hadn't heard back from ACRO about the code he'd transmitted—a code that might indicate Itor's immediate plans for the weather machine—his gut told him that waiting any longer wasn't a good idea.

He rounded the corner of the dive platform and stopped dead.

Faith Black was standing on the platform—not the safest place to be, given that the approaching storm had stirred up the ocean swells just feet below, but he already knew the woman was anything from safe.

He hadn't stopped thinking about her since he'd kissed her good night. Had thought about her all the way back to the crap motel room, dreamed about her, jacked off thinking about her in the shower and found himself hard again almost immediately.

Then he'd thought about stopping by her hotel room this morning, but instead took the early flight to the rig to check things out. Thought about Faith some more. Wished there was some way he could make her remember the sex they'd had.

"Hey," he called. "You're too close to the edge."

She turned on one high-booted heel to face him. Hot mama in all leather, and *shit,* the breath squeezed right out of his lungs.

At least Faith had her mouth partially hanging open too, but she got it together quickly. More so than he did. He was happy in the knowledge that she'd remember nothing beyond their time in the bar, and a little sad as well. None of them ever did. All part of the gift and the curse of the sexual portion of his talent.

"Still running from your ex?" he asked, and she smiled, that killer smile she'd used on him last night.

"Not exactly. This is part of my job."

"You don't look like a roughneck."

"You don't either, but you are," she countered as she moved away from the edge and closer to him. "As for me, I'm an auditor for the company that owns the platform. Here to check the books."

"I don't know too many accountants who wear leather."

"Glad I could be your first."

"I hope I'm around next time you need to get away from your ex. Although I sure wish you hadn't left in such a hurry."

"You were the one who left my bed—and I don't remember anything rushed about last night."

"You *remember?*"

She bit her bottom lip and he had a hard time not taking her, right here and now, against the pipes. "Of course I remember."

Something was wrong. *Really motherfucking wrong.*

"Are you trying to play it cool or were you drunk last night? You didn't seem to be. Do you want me to talk about it—remind you how often we enjoyed each other?"

He blinked, and she continued. "In the hot tub, in the shower, again on the bed . . ."

The thunder, which had been merely a distant rumbling minutes earlier, grew louder. More forceful.

As the wind picked up, the platform began to shake and shudder, and Faith held the metal railing behind her for support. Wyatt grabbed the same railing, one hand on either side of her, his body protecting her from the rain that began to fall nearly sideways.

"I don't want you with other men," he said suddenly, because whenever he was feeling strongly enough about something those thoughts tended to fly the fuck out of his mouth.

Faith stared at him, again as if he were crazy. Didn't matter—when his feelings pulled him, he went with it. But before she could answer him, the platform's alarms began to ring.

"What's wrong?" Faith asked.

"Could be a blowout," he said.

"Len's not coming up!" Don shouted from the upper portion of the platform. "He went down to fix one of the leg floats. He should've been up by now—he'll be out of air soon."

Len was one of the divers—a job Wyatt would've much preferred, and had the training for, thanks to his SEAL days. But being under the water most of the time on this hunk of junk would not be conducive to destroying the weather machine from hell.

"Why the hell was he down there alone?" Wyatt demanded.

"Clarence didn't feel well. It was calm as shit ten minutes ago—the weather wasn't supposed to turn like this."

The way this storm was behaving, it had to be man-made.

Yeah, that weather machine had to go, and soon. But right now, there was a man down and Wyatt had too much training to ever leave a man behind. He knew that no one else on the dive team was going to volunteer to go either, even though they wanted to. They weren't rule breakers and refused to go against the foreman most of the time. Pussies.

"I'll go," Wyatt said. "Get me a drysuit, fins and a weight belt."

"You can't go until we unload the tanks and rebreathers off the supply boat. Give it ten minutes," Don said.

"He might not have ten minutes."

"There's no other choice. He's too deep."

"I'll free dive."

"Are you fucking insane?"

"Yes," he said calmly.

He yanked on the equipment Don brought him without further argument and prepped to head into the swirling ocean.

He looked at Faith. "Stay under the deck. Hang on tight—it's going to be wild."

"Are you sure you should be doing this on your own?" Faith's voice held an urgency, let him know she heard what he'd told her about not being with anyone else. And she liked it. "Wyatt, it's dangerous."

"So am I, Faith," he drawled. "So am I."

FAITH WATCHED WYATT jump into the water at the crest of a swell, her heart pounding harder than it did even during situations more hazardous to her own life. The man was insane, diving with no air tank. Though she had to admit that watching him strip in order to put on the drysuit had been half the reason her pulse rate had doubled.

Wyatt sank into the dark depths after shooting her a cocky wink that set fire to her blood. Even up to his neck in water, he was a menace to women everywhere. Mermaids would probably flock to him in the deep.

"Ma'am!" the foreman shouted from the deck above, "get off the dive deck! It's too dangerous."

A medic crew had arrived, the men waiting in yellow slickers at the top too, because as the storm churned up the ocean, the swells were crashing into the platform, splashing her with water. Soon, the low-hanging dive deck would be overtaken by the waves. But no matter how freaked by the tempest she might be, she couldn't leave until she knew Wyatt and the other diver were safe.

"Faith!" She looked up to see Sean hurrying down the caged metal stairs, toward her. His black overcoat billowed out behind him in the wind, and rain had plastered his sandy blond hair to his head.

Sweat dampened her palms, a silly nervous reaction that irked her even as her heart seized up for just a moment. He was striking, as handsome as she remembered, and she drank him in like a recovering alcoholic facing an open bottle of expensive Scotch.

He was shorter than Wyatt, but broader in the shoulders; light in coloring, where Wyatt was dark; and why in the hell was she comparing the two? She had a job to do, and her hormones would have to wait.

Sean halted at the base of the steps, apparently oblivious to the rain pelting him. His lips quirked in the barest of smiles, his sharp gray eyes leveled on her face, and she knew they wouldn't scan her body until she looked away. The moment she averted her gaze, she'd feel his stare like a lover's touch, would know exactly where he looked at any given time.

It was one way his gift—the ability to temporarily zap energy from living things—affected her, and to her knowledge, she was the only one who felt it.

She also had no plans to look away. Sean was not a man to be met with anything but eye-to-eye confidence. More than one person had failed to make a strong impression, mistakes which had proven fatal.

"Babes," he said, in the deep voice that seemed to grow more husky with every passing year, "did you enjoy your flight?" He stepped forward, as though he wanted to embrace her, but she backed deeper under the overhanging deck.

"As much as I've ever enjoyed a heli ride."

"You arrived just in time." Another step, and she slipped to the right, keeping space between them. "This test storm decided to follow its own timetable."

They moved in opposite directions, circling like two rival tigers—a game they'd played ever since they'd become professional adversaries. "I'm not surprised," she said. "Nothing is calm around you."

His smile socked her in the weak spot of her heart, the one that remembered him as a frail, mousy child who used to try to protect her from bullies at the academy.

"True. But I'm more fascinating because of it." He moved forward, his long legs carrying him smoothly, a predator with his prey exactly where he wanted it.

She stepped closer as well, not willing to give an inch, though she kept alert to what was going on around them. She wanted to know the moment Wyatt emerged from the ocean. "Your ego remains intact, I see."

"Did you expect anything to change in the year since we last met?" His cleft chin came up, and his gaze darkened. "You remember the night in Paris."

It wasn't a question, and yes, she remembered. She remembered having such violent sex in Sean's hotel room that afterward he'd had to pay for the room service dishes, the telly and a mirror. She'd paid too, in blood.

He'd been there with a team from his agency; and she'd been alone, an operative from her much smaller one—though, like now, he believed she was a free agent who did jobs for the highest bidder. His team had tried to kill her, and then they'd gotten away with the prize—a religious artifact associated with deadly curses.

"I remember that I didn't much like your friends," she said, resisting the urge to grab the railing when the deck shuddered from the force of the driving wind. "And speaking of which, I'm quite sure Marco intended to kill me yesterday." No doubt he wanted to finish the job he'd started in Paris.

A muscle in Sean's jaw ticked. "I'm sure he was only playing with you."

"Is that what we're doing now?"

He lunged at her, and though she could have fought him, she didn't, letting him spin her behind a huge beam and away from the prying eyes of the medics and riggers above.

"We are definitely not playing," he growled. He traced the edge of her bloodred chain choker, and it took everything she had not to flinch. "When you called, I wasn't sure what to expect."

He dropped his finger lower, wiped drops of water off the exposed swell of one breast. She'd come to him knowing they'd shag like rabbits, but the idea no longer appealed to her, thanks to Wyatt's skill in bed last night. The amazing sexual chemistry she'd had with Sean had never been topped. Until Wyatt.

"I didn't know who else to turn to."

He drew back, and abruptly the rival agent was gone, and in his place was the man she'd fallen in love with so long ago. "You said you were tired of being alone. Of working alone. You didn't tell me why."

She'd worked hundreds of jobs, lied to five times as many people to get those jobs done. But lying to Sean... it was such a betrayal, even though he'd gone over to the dark side a long time ago. At times like this, she truly believed he could turn himself around.

"There's something to be said about being your own boss," she said as she pulled away from him, too distracted by what was going on around them and in the water to fully concentrate on Sean. Which, she knew, could be a fatal mistake. "But it's also nice to have backup."

"We've always backed each other up." He grinned. "Remember the time our calculus professor accused me of cheating?"

She smiled at the memory, of how she'd come to his rescue by making the man's lips swell so he couldn't talk. "He was such a tosser."

Sean's gaze darkened into something she couldn't read. Startled, she tried to shake off the feeling of dread that rippled down her spine. She'd always been able to read him, but before she could ponder the new development too much, he murmured, "Remember how I paid you back? How I came to your room that night and used my tongue to make you beg? Now that we're together again, I'll do that every night. I'll make you beg."

"I don't beg anymore," she said, even though she'd begged Wyatt last night. God, she hoped he was okay. Biting her lip, she looked out at the boiling ocean and wondered how much worse it was going to get. She'd thought she'd gotten past her fear of storms—or had at least gotten a grip on her fear—but with Wyatt in danger, bad memories had started to surface. Surface...

something Wyatt hadn't done yet. How long had he been down there anyway? Too long, dammit.

"So stubborn. And beautiful. You've always been so beautiful, Faith...Faith?"

She blinked, shook her head, unable to believe the mistake she'd just made. If she wanted to survive this mission, she had to make Sean believe he was her sole focus. She couldn't make an error like that again, for her own sake, and Liberty's.

"Yes, sorry. I was thinking about how nice it is to be on the same side again."

"As it was always meant to be. We should never have gone our separate ways."

She hadn't wanted to, but he'd grown increasingly jaded with Britain's Secret Intelligence Service, the patrons of the school they'd attended and the agency he'd joined after graduation. She had struck out on her own and watched helplessly as he degenerated into something cold and hateful. Three years ago, he turned his back on the British government and defected to Itor. Still, even as enemies they couldn't deny their fierce physical attraction or the sentimentality of their past, and their encounters always ended in sex, when they should have ended in the death of one of them.

This time, one of them would probably die, and even if they both escaped unscathed, Sean would never forgive her for the betrayal she was about to commit.

"If all this is going to happen," she said, "we'd better discuss what Itor expects of me."

"We will. But first, I want to show you what my weather machine can do. Come on."

She didn't budge. "This storm over us...it's yours?"

"Absolutely. We'll turn it up a few notches. Spawn a waterspout in honor of your arrival."

As though the storm agreed, lightning flashed overhead, followed by a deafening clap of thunder, and she couldn't hide her flinch.

She shouted over the noise, alarm sharpening her voice. "Sean, you've got to shut it down! There are divers in the water."

"So? They're deep. No worries."

"They're coming up. They'll have to decompress shallow. The waves could crush them against the supports."

Sean gave her an indulgent smile. "It's just a couple of divers. Let's go."

She stared in disbelief, water splashing her bare legs and filling her boots. "You'd let them die? What is wrong with you?"

"You need to toughen up if you're going to work for Itor, babes."

"Yes, fine, I'll work on that." She gripped his arm hard enough to make him wince. "Just, please, turn it off. If those men die, there'll be an investigation, and that will only cause trouble. Please. You know how much storms terrify me."

She hated to play that card, hated to show weakness of any kind around him, but it paid off when his gaze softened.

"Oh, babes, I'm sorry. I'm such a bastard. I completely forgot." He sighed and shook the rain from his hair. "I assume you're going to stay here until the divers are safe? You always were one to rescue strays." When she nodded, he started up the stairs, but halted on the third. "I had your bags delivered to your room. I'd rather that you stayed with me."

"Me too," she lied. They'd both agreed, to her relief, that it wouldn't look good to the men if the auditor bunked with one of the company bigwigs. Technically, Sean was one of the owners, since Itor held a major share in the company stock, but for the purpose of his mission, he was posing as a bigger owner than he was.

"It won't matter soon," he said with a cryptic smile, and once again, she wondered about his mission here. He'd assured her that all would be revealed in a few days, but she didn't plan to be here that long. "Lunch will be served in my quarters in an hour. I have the galley deliver all my meals, and you'll be eating with me. I'll see you then."

He climbed the stairs, and she turned her attention back to the water where Wyatt had gone in. God, she was in trouble. His presence on the installation turned a highly dangerous mission into an impossibly dangerous one.

I don't want you with other men.

Wyatt's words blew through her head louder than the wind funneling through the steel beams.

Shit.

She'd been shocked to see Wyatt here, had meant to tell him they couldn't see each other, but when he'd caged her in his arms, all she'd wanted to do was wrap her legs around him and let him give her just one more orgasm. She fell apart around Wyatt, got fuzzy with lust, and somehow she had to keep a straight head. Because Sean would kill the guy.

Or worse.

Shit.

Her only hope was to do this thing, and do it fast. She'd spend today and tomorrow learning the lay of the land and figuring out when to strike and how to escape. Sean already trusted her, so getting to the machine wouldn't be a problem.

The problem would be in coordinating and executing the actual theft. She'd have to take out the team monitoring the security cameras. Then the machine's guards. She'd have to make sure the helicopter was on deck and that the pilot was easily accessible. Then she'd have to hope that no one discovered anything out of the ordinary before the pilot, probably at gunpoint, could lift off the rig. Even once in the air, it might not be safe, as she had no idea if Sean employed an Itor agent who could take out the helo.

No, she definitely did not need the complications another man would bring into the situation. When Wyatt made it back up, she'd tell him that what they'd done at the hotel stayed at the hotel. She had to, even though the very thought of that night made her clothing feel too tight, too restrictive, like she needed to shed it and join Wyatt that very second.

Yeah, she had to tell him to forget last night, because dammit, her sister's life depended on her focus. And now so did Wyatt's.

CHAPTER
Six

Wyatt had been free diving since BUD/s, had perfected it during SQT training and practiced the depth, time and distance on a single breath technique every chance he got. You just never knew when you were going to have to do some breath-hold diving to save someone's life.

Like now.

He'd limited his predive breathing to two breaths per minute before he'd lowered himself into Mother Ocean, who was royally pissed in her own right, and with his headlamp on, he readied to begin his descent into the darkening water.

He jackknifed, used minimum effort to move toward the bottom—stiff-legged kicks, sleeping his way down at twice the speed he would've been able to gain if he'd had full scuba gear on.

The free dive, when done right and for pleasure or practice, was one of the ultimate rushes—a Zen thing, an ancient skill. And he was comfortable here, with the water crushing down on him, floating in that suspended place that could literally become life or death. The ocean molded around his frame, sucking him down into her depths and holding him tight, like a woman's legs and arms wrapping around him when she was right about to come. The way Faith had last night...

Faith. A fitting concept right about now.

Mammalian diving reflex kicked in almost immediately, his body understanding what he expected of it, allowing him to endure the depth he was headed toward with the lack of oxygen.

Heart rate slowed—80...70...60—ultimately, the bradycardia would lower his rate to less than 55. Vasoconstriction followed, then splenic contraction, and finally blood shift, which saved his lungs as he got down past thirty meters.

The weight belt kept him in a moderately straight line—he had to steer clear of using the rig legs as guides because he didn't want to get caught against them. The water grew colder and churned hard and it took everything he had to not let himself get pulled off course.

Fucking man-made storm. He'd kill Sean Stowe the second he got the chance. All part of the mission.

Lungs squeezed, the pressure in his ears nearly unbearable, letting him know he was rapidly approaching his max.

The water was so churned up he could barely see even with the dive light, and he slammed against something that was either human or shark—and shit, he hoped it was human.

Whatever it was had bounced away, and he only had one shot of getting it back now, and no time to waste.

Hooking his foot on one of the hundreds of steel cables that spiderwebbed between the rig legs, he closed his eyes and let the tingle start at his toes. He reached out with his mind and drew the object toward him, until he was able to grab an arm—Len's arm.

The diver was clinging to a line tethered to the inoperative dive bell, both legs hanging motionless. Not good. Wyatt grabbed Len around the waist and snapped the line free. Len, weak and barely conscious, went loose-limbed as Wyatt held the other man's back to his chest.

He released the weight belt and kicked the fins hard enough to gain the momentum for his upward travel, hanging on to Len, who was heavy as shit in his dive gear. The full helmet kept slamming backward into Wyatt's face, and the way he had to crane his neck to the side to keep from getting whacked wasn't making things any easier. The ocean turned ferocious on him halfway back from the depths—spun him and his charge around and nearly fucking upside-down.

His lungs ached, the natural instinct to exhale excruciating to hold off, and he fought like hell to get them upright.

Once he did, he prayed he was going in the right direction. He added another prayer that Len survived the ascent. They didn't have time to decompress, not with Len's air running out. Hopefully, the boys on deck had the hyperbaric chamber ready.

He broke the surface, exhaling hard through the snorkel, his body heavy as it began to pay back its O_2 debt. As gently as he could, which was damned near impossible in the fifteen-foot seas, he pulled the deadweight that was Len toward the dive platform.

The first person he saw was Faith, waiting for him on the mid-level deck, safe from the violent swells. That was the best part of all.

A wave slammed into him. He twisted, took the brunt of the impact against the side of the platform. Pain jammed the breath in his throat, but he fought through it, hooked his free arm around a ladder rung. Exhaustion screamed through him. Gritting his teeth, he used the last of his strength to haul Len up.

Driving rain stung his face and crashing waves nearly dislodged him twice, but finally, panting with effort, he got Len within reach of the men gathered at the railing edge.

"Get him into the chamber!" he said, or at least tried to say, but he didn't have enough breath to make a sound.

They grabbed Len and eased him to the mid-level platform, his pained groans audible even over the howling wind. A small hand appeared in front of Wyatt's face.

Faith.

"Grab hold." Her grip was surprisingly strong as she helped haul him up out of the water.

Shivering, he gulped air into his lungs, content to kneel on the cold steel as Faith's warm hands patted him down in a rapid but thorough search for injury. The deck beneath them shook, the massive structure groaning from the force of the storm's growing intensity.

"We've got to take shelter," he said.

"Agreed. Wholeheartedly." She pushed her wet hair out of her eyes and helped him to his feet. In the gale-force gusts, they used each other for balance as they walked away from the edge and up the steps to the upper deck.

"Is Len all right?" Wyatt called out to the men at the top.

"He's in the chamber," one of the medics said. "We'll medevac him as soon as the storm lets up."

Relieved, Wyatt leaned on Faith, his muscles trembling, his head still heavy.

Combining the telekinesis with the free dive had zapped him. He'd need rest before he attempted to take down Sean and the weather machine. And judging from the way the scientist-types were racing toward where the weather machine was housed in the lab, Wyatt knew it was going to be a while before he would have any hope of getting to the thing.

So yeah, let them spend precious time fixing it while he recouped and recovered—because then he was going to take it out six ways from Sunday.

"Come on, let's get you out of the rain and into something dry." Faith moved forward, even though he was leaning on her pretty heavily. Wind gusts knocked them around, but Faith held tight, and yeah, he could work with that.

Once they arrived at the covered threshold to the Accommodations Module, she began to help him out of the drysuit.

"Do you know Len well?" she asked.

"I met him this morning," Wyatt told her, and she stopped mid-zip, leaving the suit hanging open, exposing his chest.

"You risked your life for someone you barely know?"

"Does that turn you on?"

"You can barely stand. I don't think you're in any shape to—"

She stopped mid-sentence as his cock pressed against the suit and into her hip. "Well, parts of you are in shape."

Yeah, and that part of him didn't get that it wasn't going to get what it demanded. At least not now. "It's still touch and go," he told her earnestly. "You might have to nurse me back to health for a few hours."

FAITH HAD NO INTENTION of nursing Wyatt in any way, shape or form. Being with him in any capacity was a risk; being with him in private could get him dead if Sean ever found out. The only reason she risked it now was that clearly something had gone wrong with the weather machine, so Sean could be tied up for hours. And God, she hoped whatever was going on didn't make the weather worse. Give her a dozen armed enemies, a hungry shark, a pissed-off ghost. She could handle it. But a clap of thunder? Not so much.

"Come on," she said, hoping Wyatt didn't notice how her teeth chattered. "Let's get you to your room and out of this storm. Which direction?"

"I knew you'd see it my way."

She huffed. "I'm taking you to your room and leaving you there. Alone. Understood?"

"Mmm-hmm. Sure."

"You're insufferable."

They started moving down the hall, him leaning on her even though she suspected he'd recovered well enough to walk on his own. "I love it when you talk like that."

"Like what?"

"A stuffy Brit in need of a good loosening up."

"And I suppose you think you're the one to do the loosening."

One big shoulder rolled in a lazy shrug. "I'm handy with lube."

"I've no doubt about that," she muttered as they halted in front of one of the nondescript steel doors lining the hallway.

He grinned and reached for the door handle. "Shit. My clothes."

"You left them outside. Was your room key in them?"

"Yeah." He stared at the door for a second. "But I left it unlocked." Sure enough, the door swung open.

"That's not very safe," she commented, as they stepped inside the room that was smaller than most water closets. It contained bunk beds she doubted Wyatt could sleep in without bending his legs, lockers and a desk sized to accommodate a laptop computer and nothing more. A narrow walkway down the center was just large enough to fit the two of them.

As long as they were touching.

Wyatt turned into her and settled his hands on her hips—which she promptly removed. "You may think you're irresistible," she said smartly, "but you're not. And now that I've done my duty and escorted you to your room, I'm going to set about my business."

"But I still need help out of this suit," he said, his green eyes going all big and innocent and, bugger all, irresistible.

Unbidden, her gaze dropped to the exposed skin of his chest, the sculpted muscles beneath the damp hair plastered there. The suit stretched like a second skin over the rest of his body, doing nothing to hide his lean, powerful frame. He was built for both battle and sex; in ancient times he'd have been a warrior who won the day and then won a female over in bed.

The thought made her ridiculously hot. The idea of him coming to her after war and then coming inside her . . . She had to get away from him.

"You can get your own self out of the suit." She fumbled for the door handle behind her, only to find it locked. When had he done that? And why couldn't she unlock it? "The lock seems to be jammed."

His dark eyebrows climbed up his forehead. "Really? Weird." He reached around her, the close quarters forcing their bodies together, his weight trapping her against the door. "You're right," he said in her ear. "It's stuck. Happens sometimes. I keep meaning to shoot it with WD-40."

"Bloody hell."

"Yeah." He inhaled deeply, and on the exhale, his warm breath fanned across her neck like an invisible caress. "Sucks, huh?"

"Wyatt," she began, and then couldn't speak because his tongue was a wet lash of heat on her neck. Oh, God, this had to stop.

When he was done licking her.

Groaning, she tilted her head to give him better access, and he took advantage in an instant, like the predator he was. He sank into her, covering her entire body with his, attaching his lips to her throat below her choker and sucking as if he had a direct link to her sex.

His brutal erection prodded her belly as he pushed one thick thigh between her legs, making her rain-soaked dress bunch up indecently. Hard muscle created intense, melting pressure at her core, and she went utterly wet, her body preparing itself for him, even if her mind hadn't yet arrived at that same place.

"We can't," she said, sounding more breathless than she thought she should. "What about your roommate?"

"Don't have one."

"Well, still, it's too..." Dangerous. Not that she didn't make a life out of danger, but she wouldn't put an innocent at risk because she couldn't control her hormones. Which was strange, because she'd always been perfectly capable of controlling her carnal desires.

"Too...intense? Explosive?" He nuzzled her throat, dropped his hands to her thighs and pushed the hem of her dress up to her waist. Then, in one quick move, he ripped her panties in two. She felt them flutter against her skin as they fell to the floor. "What we did last night was those things. But as good as it was, it can be better. I can feel it. You can too, can't you?"

Yes, God help her, *yes.* Her feminine instincts were screaming with the knowledge that this man could take her places she'd never been.

His hand slipped between her legs. Long fingers brushed over her folds, lightly, teasingly. "Tell me you can feel it." He pushed a finger inside her. "Oh, yeah...so wet...spread your legs...

yeah, like that..." His voice was ragged and rough, blessed evidence that he was as affected by the white-hot chemistry between them as she was. "Tell me. Say it."

"Yes," she whispered, gripping his shoulders, though she wasn't sure if she wanted to pull him closer or push him away. "I feel it, damn you."

"That's good, baby. That's good." A second finger joined the first, his hand creating a slow, easy rhythm that she undulated her hips to, wanting deeper, faster.

"Now unzip me."

He stepped back, withdrawing his fingers from her body. As she reached for the zipper tab, he brought them to his mouth. His gaze held hers, forcing her to watch as he sucked the evidence of her desire from his fingers.

"Oh, sweet Jesus..."

Blood pounded in her ears and her sex throbbed to the same beat. Unable to move, she remained rooted to the spot until he'd licked himself clean. When he finished, he grabbed her hand in his and forced her to drag down the zipper on his drysuit.

Not that he truly had to force her, but she'd frozen in some sort of lust-shock, something that had never happened to her before. She'd had lots of sex, had been in lust several times. But what Wyatt did to her went way beyond anything she'd experienced; the way he made her feel so feminine, dominated—and yet, worshipped.

He wasn't *making* her do anything. He was making her *want to do* anything.

He peeled himself out of his suit, and she salivated at the sight of him naked, his magnificent length jutting upward so hard, the tip curved into his six-pack abs. She reached for him, but he caught her around the waist with both hands and lifted her.

"I have to taste more of you. Grab the pipe."

Above her, a network of pipes and wire runs coiled deep into the overhead. Unsure of his intention, but on fire and crazed with need, she seized a metal tube with both hands. At the same time, he heaved her up so that her thighs came down on his broad

shoulders and his mouth met her pussy. She didn't even have time
to gasp before he speared her with his tongue.

"Yes," she moaned. "Oh, God, yes." She gripped the pipe so
tightly she was afraid it might crack, and when she started to rock
her hips, he tightened his hold on her ass, where he held her
firmly against him.

He lapped at her with an almost out-of-control hunger, his
tongue first sweeping her inner walls and then swiping up the
length of her. Broad, fast licks met deep, stabbing penetrations.
Pure, erotic sensation assaulted her—her body, her mind—and
she heard herself begging for release. He didn't tease; he caught
her clit between his lips and suckled hard and it was all she could
do to hang on to the pipe and not scream as she came apart.

The moment she stopped bucking, Wyatt slid her down his
body. In one smooth, raw move, he entered her and forced her
back against the lockers. One arm went behind her to bear the
brunt of her weight against the metal, and the other held her
thigh so she could wrap her legs around his waist. She locked her
booted feet at the base of his spine and held on for the ride.

His eyes were wild, emerald lasers of possession as he pumped
into her with the same focus and near-desperate need he'd dis-
played when he'd feasted on her sex.

"*Faith.*" A low moan vibrated his chest. His lips drew back,
baring his teeth. "You feel so good. So fucking perfect. Can't...
wait."

He threw back his head and surged into her, his thick shaft
stretching her, heating her, making her burn. The tendons in his
neck strained, the veins in his arms bulged on top of rolling muscles, and oh, he was a thing of masculine beauty. A force of nature
no less powerful than the monster machine two decks above
them.

The sounds in the room, from their panting breaths to the slap
of skin on skin, even the metallic clanking of something distant,
heightened her desire, made her pulse catch, her blood sizzle, and
then she was coming, moaning through the pleasure. He was
right there with her, his breath hissing between clenched teeth,

his hot jets of semen filling her, his hips pounding into her without mercy.

The way he held her, the intensity of his thrusts ... something told her this was more than a quickie shag. This was a claiming, of sorts—a wonderful yet terrifying message to her and other men.

Which was ridiculous. But she couldn't shake the thought that she'd just made a terrible, perhaps fatal, mistake.

When it was over, she dropped her legs to the floor and he collapsed against her. They were both trembling, struggling to breathe and stay upright. Eyes closed, Wyatt fumbled with the locker to his left, grabbed something, and then she felt the soft rasp of a cloth between her legs.

"Sorry," he muttered, pulling back. "I meant to grab a condom. I just ... shit. What you do to me ..."

Shocked that he cared enough to tidy her up, she stared at him, wishing they'd met under any other circumstances. Maybe someday, if she survived the next couple of days, she could ring him—

Fool. Nothing could ever work between them. She lived in England, he lived in America. He was a simple roughneck, she ran an agency full of superhuman spies. Their worlds couldn't be farther apart.

Then again, maybe that was part of the appeal. Most of the men she met were part of her world, the good side or the bad, and to them, she was a soldier in a global war for power. She didn't have many opportunities to get to know men outside of her business, and when she did, she didn't allow herself to get close. She wasn't exactly a prize—she brought to the table a side dish of danger, something a man living in the "normal" world had no defense against. The last thing she wanted to do was risk the life of an innocent simply because she wanted a relationship with someone who saw her as a woman, not a warrior.

Wyatt tossed the cloth to the bottom of a locker and reached for another, and she used the opportunity to slip from beneath him. Tugging her skirt down, she moved toward the door, intent upon breaking it down if she had to.

"You're not leaving," he said, as he wiped his cock clean.

"I have to." She couldn't look at him, so she looked at the floor—and groaned at the sight of the panties Sean had sent to her upon finding out she would be arriving on the platform, shredded and in a pile. "Oh, shit."

"Ah, hey, I'm sorry about that." Wyatt swept them up and tossed them into the locker that seemed to be the repository for everything. "I'll buy you new ones."

"That won't be necessary." She reached for the door handle. "This can't happen again, Wyatt. We're done. It's over."

A palm slapped against the door, right next to her head, so hard she jumped. "I don't think so." He leaned in close, once more trapping her with his body, using his size and height in a primitive me-man-you-woman message that would have chafed if it hadn't made some small, shameful part of her feel so desired. "If you think I can spend the next thirteen days seeing you, hearing you, smelling you"—he inhaled deeply and growled a little—"without touching you, you're very, *very* mistaken."

Shivers skittered over her skin at his words, at the possessive tone, at the heat his body was sending out again. When she felt the hot head of his cock slip beneath the hem of her dress to brand her ass cheek, she nearly sobbed. The erotic menace, the danger he threw like a scent, scared the piss out of her.

Oh, she could take him out if she wanted to, could kill him where he stood. But this wasn't about a physical fear of him. It was about what he could do to her soul, and ultimately her mission to save her sister.

"Please, Wyatt. Let me go." She didn't mean from the room. He knew it. But he opened the door as though it had never been stuck.

"It's not over, Faith. It's just begun."

"You're crazy," she breathed, staring out into the deserted hall because she dared not turn to him.

"You don't know the half of it."

She fled. Faith Black *never* fled. She'd held her own against Syrian assassins, Itor's lab-created beasts, ACRO's top agents...

but with Wyatt, an apparently normal guy who might or might not have some military experience, she was losing her footing for the first time in her life. Maybe too much had happened at once: her sister reappearing after more than twenty years, feeling guilt over having to betray Sean and now protecting Wyatt from Sean's wrath if he learned what had happened.

Normally, she thrived on stress. Right now she wanted nothing more than to run from it.

It figured she'd be stuck on an oil platform with no way off and no way to hide.

All she could do was hurry to her quarters, shower and then hope to God Sean hadn't been looking for her. No matter what, she was stepping up her timetable for grabbing the weather machine.

For the sake of all concerned—Liberty, Wyatt and herself—she had to get off this platform.

CHAPTER *Seven*

ACRO agent Annika Svenson loved Athens in the fall. Really, Greece was one of her favorite places in the world, so it was only fitting that the man she hated most was going to die here.

"Don't do it, Annika."

Creed McCabe, a ghost hunter who communicated with earthbound entities through the spirit that had been attached to him almost since birth, watched her from the doorway of her hotel room as she strapped a throwing knife to her thigh beneath her skirt. She didn't need the thing for self-defense; her own electric shock security system was a weapon in its own right. No, the knife was for fun.

"Would you mind shutting the door? I don't need the entire world watching me dress." She pulled a slinky tank top over her head. "I can't believe you followed me here."

He tossed his duffel bag to the floor and stepped inside, closing the door behind him. "Dev sent me to bring you home."

Annika started. *"Dev?"*

"He's back."

Thank God. She'd bucked Oz's authority at every turn, had,

in fact, disobeyed him to come to Greece. But now that she was here, not even Dev could stop her.

"I'm not leaving until I've completed the mission."

"You aren't on a mission. You don't have orders to kill a CIA agent."

She snorted. "I don't need orders."

Her earbud crackled with static, and then Troy Modine's voice rang out as he ordered wine at the café where he'd met with his Hamas contact. She'd bugged his pants while he'd lounged at a nearby spa, and now she could track his movements with ease.

Enjoy the wine, asshole, because it'll be the last thing you ever drink.

"Annika, you can't do this. Dev needs you back at ACRO. There's some major shit going down with Itor's weather machine, and he wants everyone not on assignment on base."

"If you think you're going to talk me out of killing the man who murdered my mother, think again." She slid him a look, saw that he already knew the details about the murder. How? "I didn't tell you how she died."

He shoved his hand through his shoulder-length, dark hair. "Yeah, shock," he said, and great, it looked like they were back to how she never talked. "Oz told me."

"That fucker." She slid her feet into sandals as she pulled her long blond hair into a ponytail. "Not that it changes anything. Troy is going down. But hey, on the bright side, you can turn me in and get me kicked off assignments again."

"When are you going to get over that? It happened almost four years ago."

She shrugged, because yeah, she was still bitter.

She'd led a team to Madrid, where they'd been ordered to locate some mystical artifact Dev had his heart set on acquiring for ACRO. Its purpose was a mystery to her, but it didn't matter. Her job was to secure it, not study it. Unfortunately, the thing was protected by a nasty ghost that no ACRO psychic had been able to subdue. Oz had been tasked to come in at the last minute, but when he suddenly quit ACRO—leaving Dev an emotional mess—Creed had been sent. Unfortunately, just as Creed arrived at the old cathedral, an Itor agent had somehow stolen the artifact from under her team.

Annika had pursued, had discovered the I-Agent engaged in discussions with two CIA agents.

It had been an interesting development. Itor was always a concern, especially on missions as sensitive as that one had been. But she'd done her research before the assignment, had learned that the CIA—including one of the very agents who had murdered her mother—also had an interest in the artifact. Her plan had been to root out the agents, but Itor had done it for her. Clearly, the CIA had paid Itor for their help.

Perfect. Disturbing, but perfect.

ACRO's rules were strict in regards to revenge: not allowed during a mission. Annika didn't give a shit. Not when the son of a bitch who was responsible for her mother's death was right in front of her, laughing with a powerful enemy operative the CIA should know better than to make deals with.

Rage had short-circuited her smart switch, and she'd let the Itor man escape and instead followed Norris Welsh to his swanky hotel near the center of the Spanish city. When she'd sauntered into his room, he'd nearly had a heart attack.

They went at it, good old hand-to-hand combat because electrocuting him would be too quick. He was stronger, but she was younger and more experienced despite her age of eighteen. Five minutes later, they were both bloody, but she had him on the floor, was straddling his chest and holding him paralyzed with a low-voltage buzz through his body.

"So," she said softly, "did you kill my mother?" She traced a fingertip lightly along the edge of his jaw. "Or were you the one who raped her?"

His eyes shot wide and she released the buzz so he could answer. "I don't know what you're talking about."

Yeah, and she believed in Santa Claus.

"Don't fuck with me, Norris. I know. Mike Duffy told me everything before I took him out."

The blood drained from the man's face.

"He told me how you tranq'd me and then he tore me out of her arms. He said he waited outside the bedroom while he listened to her struggles with you and Troy. He said one of you raped her, and the other slit her throat."

The sound of footsteps thumped behind her, and a pulse of energy shivered through her—an energy signature unique to Creed and that he couldn't control. "Annika."

"Not now, Creed," she ground out.

"Annika, don't do this."

"Shut the fuck up and go away."

Creed stepped closer, and she grabbed the clock off the nightstand. She threw it, but he swatted it aside.

She'd zapped Norris with about a million volts, ending any further discussion. Then she'd pushed past Creed and headed out to find the I-Agent. She'd lost him, and it took two days to locate him and recover the artifact. The mission had been accomplished, but that didn't stop Creed from ratting her out to Dev.

Who had been pissed. Angrier than she'd ever seen him.

She'd broken the rules. She'd nearly lost the artifact. Norris had been working on a mission vital to national security, and his death had set back that mission. The CIA wanted her head. Of course, they'd wanted her head for years, but ACRO had protected her. Her actions had shattered that fragile peace.

Dev had had to spend weeks digging out of that mess, and he'd thrown the book at her. Six months of no missions. Nothing but never-ending training. And on her way out the door to find Creed, he'd tacked on a curt "If you so much as touch Creed, I'll double your sentence."

She hadn't touched Creed, at least, not until that night a year ago when they'd been locked in a haunted mansion together. It had been there that she'd learned he was immune to her electric shocks. The discovery had led to his taking her virginity, something she'd held on to because she couldn't control her electric pulses at orgasm.

Since that night, they'd maintained an on-and-off sexual relationship that burned hotter than the sun. But now he wanted more. Way more. Because four months ago, he'd learned that the ghost Kat—who followed him everywhere and made his love life difficult—could be banished, but he'd only agree to get rid of her if Annika committed to a permanent relationship.

Annika hadn't known how to react to his announcement, and he'd walked away—she'd taught him well. They hadn't spoken for weeks, until ACRO's annual Fourth of July picnic. He'd been cold and distant, she'd been a bitch who'd had one too many beers, and somehow she'd let it slip that she missed him. He'd pounced, and suddenly they were tearing off clothes and breaking into the nearest building—Paranormal Division's headquarters—to do it. Creed had laughed later about the vibe they'd left behind on a department head's desk, one that would shock the old biddy psychrometrist.

Creed hadn't brought up the idea of a real relationship again. The window of opportunity to get rid of Kat was closing fast, though Creed wouldn't explain why, and Annika had yet to make a decision.

Which was why slamming the door on her CIA past was so important. She needed to get her head on straight.

Creed remained near the door, like he was going to prevent her from leaving. He had to know he couldn't stop her, but there he stood, all six feet, five inches of masculine goodness, in jeans and a white Corona T-shirt that set off his body piercings and deeply tanned skin. Tanned skin that was marked on his entire right side with tattoos he'd apparently been born with.

Grabbing her purse, she made sure she had her fake passport and assorted weaponry. "Get out of the way, Creed."

"I'm not letting you go."

"Is this because of Wyatt?" He'd been weird ever since Wyatt had been killed, had been anxious about her missions, wanting her to constantly check in with him. The loss of a friend and operative who did the same jobs as she did had made him see danger around every one of her corners.

"It's not about what happened to Wyatt. It's about keeping you from making the same mistake you made last time."

"Killing Norris was no mistake." She shoved past him.

Creed grabbed her arm and wheeled her around.

"No."

She stood on her toes, but it did her five-foot-six self little good. "Fuck. You."

Breaking out of his hold, she spun for the door, but once again, he grabbed her. Cursing, she twisted behind him, pulling his arm back with her. He snarled, and then she found herself pressed between the wall and his back.

"I said *no*."

She hooked his leg and dropped him hard to the floor. Quickly, she grabbed for the door handle, but he snared her ankle and pulled her down on top of him. For the hundredth time, at least, she wished she could shock him.

Instead, she whipped out her knife and, straddling his torso, pressed it to his throat. "You can't stop me."

"You're prepared to kill me, Annika?"

Not long ago, she could have done it without hesitation. Now she hesitated. Another reason she had to kill Troy. She'd grown weak. Sentimental. Emotional. It had to stop.

"I'll do what I have to do," she began, but broke off with a gasp. Creed was aroused. The man had a blade to his jugular, and he had a raging erection nudging her butt.

"So will I." He arched his hips, pushing the full bulge between her legs.

"You fight dirty."

Creed had once said that sex was the only language she understood, that it was the only time he could ever truly communicate with her. It was ridiculous, especially since they'd been talking more and spending more time together since Dev disappeared. She'd even been cooking for him, something she used to do only for Dev.

And Creed still bitched that she didn't share enough.

In her ear, Troy droned on and on to the waitress about dolmades and moussaka. Annika had a little time for play. Creed's eyes darkened as she trailed her fingers along the hard ridge behind the seam of his jeans. Desire funneled a rush of moisture through her slit, and she couldn't wait any longer.

She drew down his zipper and released his gorgeous length, pierced, the right side decorated with the same Native American symbols that marked the rest of that half of his body. Tugging her underwear aside, she sat down, whimpering as she sheathed his entire cock inside her.

"So. Good." She closed her eyes and rocked on top of him.

"It'd be better if I wasn't worried about accidentally bleeding out."

She still had her knife pressed to his jugular. Grinning, she flipped it into the air, and in one smooth motion caught the tip of the blade and sent the weapon sailing across the room to impale the wall.

"Show-off," Creed said, running his hands under her skirt.

"You love it," she teased.

"Damn straight."

Her heart did a painful somersault at the intensity in his voice, his eyes. He'd never told her he loved her, thank God for that, but she knew, and at times like this she didn't know if the way he felt about her was a good thing or a bad one.

His fingers found her pussy, and she cried out when his thumb pressed against her clit. "Fuck me, baby. Ride me."

Noncompliance wasn't an option. Creed always had the control in bed. She gave it freely, would let him do anything he wanted, and she didn't analyze the whys of it. Especially not right now, when his thick shaft was thrusting in and out and the slow, sensual massage of his thumb was making her crazy.

The friction built swiftly, his right side burning hotter than the left, even inside her. She ran her palms over his abs, so taut, the hard ridges not giving an inch.

Jolts of pleasure and electricity shot through her, and he drew a harsh breath. He didn't feel the shocks themselves, but he'd said the pleasure she felt transferred to him if she was touching one of his piercings...which she was, and not only the one inside her. She'd grabbed the ring on his right nipple and was rubbing it between her fingers.

"Not yet," he panted, and rolled her, pinned her beneath him on the carpet.

She loved that about him, the way he always kept her guessing about what would come next. But when he withdrew and flipped her onto her stomach, she knew what was going to happen. Lifting her to all fours with one arm circling her waist, he entered her from behind, her favorite position.

He took her to the very edge, the place that walked the line between pleasure and agony.

The first tremors of orgasm started, but he eased back to stop it, pulled her upright onto her knees, so her back was flat against his muscular chest. "No," she moaned, "not this."

From this position, his thrusts were shallow, and he'd discovered he could hold her on the precipice for as long as he could hold out. He'd timed it once. Five minutes of hell for her.

"No," she repeated, but he held her immobile. Slowly, easily, he pushed the head of his cock inside her, massaging the ring of nerves at her entrance with just enough stimulation to keep her on the brink.

"What do you want, Annika?" He dipped his head so his lips brushed her ear.

"Make me come." She flexed her back, tried to drive him deeper, but he tightened his grip, caging her against him. "God, Creed. Make me come."

"Don't say it like it's an order. Ask for it."

His pierced tongue rimmed her ear, and she let loose a whimper. "No."

"That's my Ani," he murmured. "Too proud to beg."

The wet slide of his cock easing in and out of her was torture, his breath against her ear plain cruelty. She slid her hand down between her legs, needing release, but he grabbed her wrist and pinned it to her belly.

"You get what you want when I get what I want." His voice was low and guttural, but too breathless for her to think he wasn't affected by the rhythm he'd set.

"Please. Please make me come."

"Too late for begging," he said against her ear. "I want more now."

She groaned, because she'd started to tremble with the need for release, the ache so deep Creed had to feel it in his cock.

The cool air-conditioned breeze swirled around her, doing nothing to ease the heat that was making her sweat. "What do you want?"

He ground against her, pushing her forward just enough that he could drive deeply, once, twice. Oh, yes, he was going to let her climax. But her excitement faded when he pulled back again. He'd teased her, and fuck, ACRO wasn't using him the way they should. He was a sadist, and surely the agency had uses for those.

"I want the truth," he said. "I want to hear you say you want me."

"Creed..."

He brought one hand up to wind in her hair to restrain her. His teeth scraped her lobe as he bared them. "Say it."

Panic speared her chest as his cock speared her pussy, and suddenly she was torn between two worlds, the one where she might have to admit her feelings and the one where all she wanted was to banish them.

"Can't." She tried to shake her head, but he wrenched her head around so they were cheek to cheek.

"Say it." His thrusts quickened, the slap of flesh on flesh ringing in her ears.

Heart pounding so hard it hurt, she struggled, but for escape or for deeper thrusts, hell, she didn't know. She only knew she couldn't take the confinement of Creed's embrace anymore. He didn't let up, as if he knew better than she did what she wanted, and when he bit into her shoulder as yet another way to hold her, to force her to yield to his dominant, primitive bonds, she relented, sinking bonelessly against him.

"I want you," she blurted, unable to stop herself or the giant sob that followed.

Relief flooded her when he pushed her forward to her hands and knees and drove into her fiercely, his thrusts powerful, hard, his fingers gouging the flesh of her hips. Her internal muscles clamped around him, intensifying every ridge, bump, and vein on his cock. He filled her, stretched her, slammed into her faster and faster, her cries of ecstasy urging him on.

She came in a tide of emotion and pleasure that threatened to kill her with its intensity, to drown them both. His roar, of victory and release, vibrated through her, setting off another orgasm that had her writhing on quivering limbs until they both collapsed onto the floor in a heap.

Shit-oh-shit. This had gone way too far. Shaking, her eyes stinging with the threat of tears, she wriggled out from beneath him. She didn't look at him as she used a tissue to wipe away the remains of their lovemaking and then removed her knife from the wall and jammed it into the sheath. Behind her, the sound of rustling and a zipper told her that Creed was still ready to try to keep her from doing what she needed to do.

Troy had to die, now more than ever.

"Don't think that forcing me to say something I didn't mean can change my mind about this."

"You meant it." His footsteps drew close, but he didn't touch her or make her feel trapped. "Why is this so important to you?"

She stared at the hole her blade had made in the wall. "He killed my mom. If you don't get that—"

"I get it," he said softly. "And he deserves everything you plan to do to him. But this isn't about your mother."

"Fuck you." The words were harsh, but her voice gave away her defeat, and she braced her forehead against the cool plaster of the wall.

"Annika? You've killed a lot of people. Why is this one so important?"

Saliva flooded her mouth. She swallowed hard, her stomach churning. "I didn't care about the others. They were jobs. Bad guys." Reaching between her legs, she fingered the hard rubber hilt of her knife. "Troy . . . I fucking hate him. Hate is an emotion. It has to go."

Creed sucked in a breath, and she heard him take a step back. "Jesus."

"Yeah, you get it now. If I purge him, I purge it all. I get myself back." She turned. "You opened some sort of door, Creed. You made me feel things I don't want to feel. I want it to go away. All of it. Not just the hate."

He shook his head, pain and disbelief swirling in the black depths of his eyes. "You really want me gone, don't you?"

Creed stood there, his face so pale that his tattoo stood out like a throbbing, angry wound. When she didn't answer him, because the word *gone* had affected her in some crazy way, he snatched his duffel and strode to the door.

Did she really want him gone? She wanted what she felt for him to be banished, but Creed himself? With the exception of Dev, Creed had been the only person she'd ever enjoyed being with and felt comfortable around. He was definitely the only man she could have sex with. Why couldn't he be happy with no-strings sex?

She should let him go. Instead, she felt her mouth open. Heard herself say, "Creed, wait."

"Why? So you can tell me again how you only want me for sex? How you have Dev to fill your emotional needs?" He stopped at the door, scrubbed his face with a shaking hand. "Jesus. All this time I thought I could get through to you eventually, that you would come around. But you don't even want to try. I'm nothing to you, and you don't care."

"That's not true," she said, because she did care. Too much.

"Bullshit. If you could fuck anyone else, you'd be with them just so you wouldn't have to be with me."

Something inside her broke, releasing a wave of nausea. She hadn't considered what would happen if she could have other men—mainly because she'd known for years it wasn't possible. But her mind worked quickly, taking in the idea of sleeping with any of the countless men who'd propositioned her since she started sleeping with Creed, and no, none of them appealed to her in the least. None of them made her hot, made her laugh, made her feel wanted.

Oh, they wanted her. For *sex*. The idea turned her stomach. Turned her stomach and blew through her like a bullet, because she'd wanted Creed for the same reason. Sex. On *her* terms. She'd been treating Creed like a piece of meat, had been using him with no regard for his feelings.

She glanced at him, saw the way he was staring at her with a mix of sorrow and pain—and worse, resolve. He was cutting his losses and taking himself out of the game.

Oh, God. She'd blown it. Big-time.

If she could kill Troy, she wouldn't care. She knew it. But right now she did care, and the hurt that she'd caused Creed was unforgivable.

"I'm so sorry. I didn't...I never realized..." Dev had been right all those months ago when he'd said she wasn't ready for a relationship. That her upbringing in the CIA had caused her to be emotionally stunted. And now Creed was paying for her arrogance in thinking Dev was wrong.

"It's too late, Annika. Go kill your guy, purge your feelings for anything except Dev and fuck who you can. But leave me the hell alone."

The low buzz in her ear told her that Troy was on the move, heading for his hotel room. This was her chance. Now or never.

Creed opened the door. She clamped down on his arm with one hand and grabbed the earbud with her other.

"Please, Creed." Fear made her awkward as she dropped the tiny device on the floor and crunched it under her foot. "Give me a chance. I've been so stupid."

His body was so taut his bones must feel ready to come apart from the strain. "Too late," he rasped.

"No." Taking his hand in both of hers, she stepped in front of him. This time it was she who blocked the exit. "I'll let Troy go." God help her, she'd let that murderous fuck escape, but he wasn't off the hook. "I'll go back to ACRO with you."

"Do you think that's enough? Do you think going back to us fucking like porn stars and then me watching you take off so you won't have to have any kind of intimate conversation is enough? I can't do that anymore." He jerked out of her grip, grabbed her shoulders and moved her aside.

His long legs carried him down the hall, each footstep ringing louder in her ears, even though they should be growing quieter. Panic made her heart ping around the inside of her rib cage. She couldn't let him go. Something told her that if he got away this time, there would be no more second chances.

"I don't know my dad's name," she yelled, and Creed stopped in his tracks.

"What?"

She could barely see him through the tears welling in her eyes. "My dad. I don't know who he is. The CIA forged a birth certificate and destroyed all original records."

He moved toward her, slowly, as though he suspected she'd planted land mines between them. "Why are you telling me this?"

"A long time ago, you said I didn't let you in." She took a few shaky steps. "I want to let you in. I'll tell you the answers to everything you've asked and I've avoided answering. You want to know why I had to eat fish pudding when I was a kid? You want to know when I learned that the people who were raising me weren't my parents? You want to know why I never celebrated Christmas or my birthday? I'll tell you." Another step brought her within ten feet of him. "Let me tell you."

She dashed away the tears and saw that his expression had softened, but not enough. "Annika——"

"I don't want this to be the end," she croaked.

"Why?"

She trembled. Swallowed. Worked saliva into her mouth because she couldn't speak for the dryness.

"Why?" he repeated, his voice as hoarse as hers.

"Because I'm afraid of losing you." She stared into his eyes, made sure he understood how much this meant to her. "And I've never been afraid of anything, so this must mean something."

Suddenly, Creed's arms were around her, and he was holding her up, which was good, because emotion had made her legs rubbery. He was murmuring into her ear, sweet, comforting words, and she sighed with relief.

Things would be different from here on out, no question. Creed would no longer settle for just sex, would require a real effort from her. The idea brought her both joy and dread, because she had a feeling that Creed's ability to share her with the other man in her life had just come to a screeching halt.

CHAPTER
tight

Shortly after Faith left his quarters, Wyatt walked outside and stood on the edge of the platform, looked out into the swelling ocean that seemed unable to calm itself since the earlier storm. The entire atmosphere seemed strange, discontented, and the unease settled deep in his gut.

This mission—the failure of this mission—could bring on the end of the motherfucking world, and there wasn't a thing he could do to help beyond destroying the motherboard to prevent future disasters like the hurricane currently threatening to strike the United States.

At that point, it was all on Remy's shoulders.

He moved back and gripped the deck rails hard, hung his head and tried to get rid of the dizzy feeling that had been rearing its head more and more often. The off-the-rails feeling was related to his gifts, had hit him hard since he'd gotten onto the platform. Had hit him even harder since he'd been with . . .

"Wyatt, are you okay?" Faith's voice floated over him, half-lost in the wind.

"I'm great. Fine. Perfect," he said. He lifted his head but didn't look at her. Couldn't. He knew every emotion would show on his face and he took a minute to compose. To get back into Wyatt-the-roughneck mode, to a place where it was all good and nothing could shake his game.

"Okay, then, if you're sure."

"I'm not sure of anything," he admitted. "But I didn't mean to freak you out before. I just can't seem to keep my hands off you. I don't want to keep my hands off you."

"I'm not freaked out," she said, but he had the feeling she was lying.

"That makes one of us, then."

She turned to him and he shifted his weight and moved to hold them both steady as the wind churned up and rocked the platform. He locked his arms around her, holding on to either side of the pipe railing. "It's all right—I've got you."

"Why are you freaked out, Wyatt?" she asked, concern in her eyes.

"Lots of complicated reasons, Faith Black. Too complicated to go into here."

"Funny thing, I understand complicated pretty well."

"I thought you didn't want to get close to me."

"I didn't say that, not exactly."

"You didn't have to, Faith. You ran out of the room before. Literally."

"You're the last person I expected to find out here. And you didn't seem too thrilled to see me either—you didn't want me to remember you."

Yeah, he wasn't about to get into that one now. *Hey, Faith, you've been sleeping with a crazy man who has special gifts.* "I grew up on a rig," he said finally. "My family—everything—was all fucked up. Still is, I guess. So I don't have great memories of rigging."

"So why do you keep working on one, then?"

He shrugged. "Catharsis, maybe," he said, hoped she'd keep her hand on his chest because, God, it felt good. He felt upright, like two halves closing in to create a whole, and he wondered what it was about this woman that made him feel so connected.

He knew that he wasn't going to let that feeling—or Faith—
go easily. At first, he'd figured it was something to do with the incredible sexual energy that flowed between them, but he'd
figured out in this instant that it went far beyond sex. "I want to
see you, Faith. I want to keep seeing you once we get off this platform."

She shook her head. "I don't know if I can do that. I certainly
can't think about it now."

"You're all I can think about."

"Wyatt!" Don's voice rang out over their heads.

Wyatt turned toward the rig manager and Faith broke off contact with his chest. The empty, scattered feeling returned instantly. "What's up?"

"Boss wants to see you."

"I thought you were the boss."

"Cute, Wyatt. Real fucking cute. Stowe requests that cuteness
in his office. ASAP."

That was not a good sign—Wyatt had given the man a wide
berth, not wanting to trigger any suspicions that an ACRO agent
had infiltrated the rig operations. But he now had a sneaking suspicion of his own, that everything was about to change rapidly—
it was time to move it forward.

"Are you in trouble?" Faith was asking. "Is this about the free
dive before?"

"Who knows. The guy's a total control freak. It'll be fine." He
gave her shoulder a light squeeze, her energy zipping through
him, and for a moment—just a moment—he wondered if there
was something special about Faith Black. Something really special. "We'll talk later."

He reluctantly left her behind on the deck and ran the options
in his mind to get back into agent mode as he strolled casually to
Sean's office. He'd dressed earlier with a few concealed weapons
under his clothing. His powers were back at full force—he'd talk
to Sean, take a licking for the free dive and then it was weather-
machine time.

The door was open and Sean, the man responsible for the

weather machine that could take out entire countries with the touch of a button, was waiting for him, standing behind the desk, staring at his computer and not looking happy.

"In—and leave the door open," Sean told him.

Wyatt nodded, tried to keep the scowl off his face. "You wanted to see me, sir?" he asked, arms behind his back in perfect SEAL posture. Because he could pretend to kiss superiors' asses with the best of them.

"That stunt you pulled today, with the free dive, endangered too many other men. It pulled attention away from shoring up the rig during the storm."

"That stunt saved a man's life. And that's something I won't apologize for," Wyatt shot back—so much for the ass kissing. It had never really worked for him beyond the initial *sir* anyway.

"That stunt is why you're being fired," Sean said, hand on the button, probably ready to call in his thugs and have Wyatt immediately escorted off the platform, which would not work for Wyatt. He could handle them, sure, but then he'd be giving away his hand even more, plus any shot at the weather machine. He couldn't blow it now, not when he was this close. And so, he would do what he needed to do.

And he wasn't going to like it.

Damn, he did *not* want to have to pull out this card, to have to seduce any man—this man in particular—but when his back was up, and firmly against the wall, he'd do what he needed to do to survive.

Wyatt drew in a deep breath and took a step toward Sean. "Can I be honest with you?" he started, letting the familiar tickling begin at his feet and travel up between his legs and outward at a much faster pace than he'd normally allow. He'd need a cloud of the mojo to release fast and furious, a pheromone promise that Sean wouldn't be able to resist.

"I can't guarantee that I'll reward honesty," Sean said, but his hand dropped from the button. Wyatt watched him shift his feet and throw his shoulders back, posturing, and yeah, this was working.

"I pulled that stunt for you." Wyatt hadn't made a move, feeling the vibrations in the air between him and Sean, and shit, he needed a plan for after this plan.

"For me?" Sean cocked his head and smiled, his eyelids heavier than they'd been.

"Yeah." Wyatt shrugged, sucked his bottom lip in and saw the hunger in Sean's eyes, could nearly read the man's mind. Men were so fucking easy, much easier than women. "I can't ever seem to get you...alone. Can't seem to get your attention. I figured, maybe, if I impressed you, I could."

"What would you need to get me alone for?" Sean asked, his tone lighter, teasing, and Wyatt noted that the man had taken several long strides to close the distance between them. He was seriously buying Wyatt's cheesy bullshit.

Wyatt had let out extra pheromones on Sean and maybe, just maybe, this was going to backfire badly. But if he could get the guy so turned on he couldn't think straight, Wyatt could escape and leave Sean a panting but memoryless mess on the floor.

Or maybe he'd have to go all the way.

"How about I tell you—no, I'll show you. Once you switch off the security cameras and close the door," Wyatt suggested.

They were inches apart, Sean's breathing quicker than it had been seconds before, the change no longer subtle as his body leaned in toward Wyatt's as he spoke.

"Why don't *you* shut the door? Perhaps there's something we can work out that would be mutually acceptable for both of us." Sean's voice was low, husky, with more than a hint of suggestion bleeding through the proper British façade as he flipped open the security panel on the desk and paused the cameras.

Office space—space in general—was at a premium, enabling Wyatt to shut the door quickly and move back into position in front of Sean within seconds.

"What did you have in mind, Mr. Stowe?"

"Many things, Wyatt. I wish you'd come to me sooner about this. Why did you wait?"

"Because last I looked, I was just a lowly roughneck."

"Last I looked, you were much more than that." Sean's hand hooked the back of Wyatt's neck, caressed it with a lover's touch before attempting to pull Wyatt's mouth toward his.

It would be so easy, too easy, to kill Sean now, to snap his neck like a dried twig. But killing him now was the surest way to death—although the other option sucked dick as well. Literally.

Well, hell, this was going to be more interesting than he'd anticipated.

Wyatt, one of these days your pheromones are going to get you into big trouble—use them wisely, Sam, one of ACRO's top psychics, had told him just a few months ago. Of course, that's when she'd been in his lap.

She'd been trying to figure out if there was a way someone could actually put up a barrier against it. She'd had no luck at all in that department.

Sean hadn't let go of Wyatt's neck and now his gaze—and his hand—traveled down between Wyatt's legs.

When Sean began to kiss Wyatt's neck, Wyatt wondered just how far he was going to let this go.

This will save your ass.

This would eventually get him killed. All of it. Killing with his bare hands was a skill he had, and one he used often enough, but it wasn't going to be enough against this enemy. And sex—the ultimate power—would get him far, but he suspected it wouldn't be far enough.

FAITH HAD a very bad feeling about the meeting Sean had called with Wyatt. She hoped it was about the free dive, but she wasn't going to bet Wyatt's life on that. If Sean knew that she and Wyatt had been sleeping together...

Shit.

She'd paced for a few minutes after Wyatt had gone, but her concern had gotten the better of her. Earlier, right after she and Wyatt had screwed in his room, she'd showered, changed, and had taken a brief sojourn into Sean's office, where she'd planted a micro–video camera that fed into her cell phone. TAG's tech team was top-notch, and the device, as long as it wasn't in operation, couldn't be detected by security sweeps. When activated, it did put out a signature, but the chances that someone would be sweeping Sean's office right at this moment were slim to none.

She slipped into her tiny cell of a room, sank onto her bed and switched on her phone's feed. There was no sound, but the picture was clear, and ... *holy shit.*

Wyatt and Sean were ... She swallowed. Surely it wasn't what it looked like, because what it looked like was the beginning of a male-on-male sexfest.

The two men stood chest to chest, Sean's hands on Wyatt's hips, his fingers delving beneath Wyatt's waistband and his mouth on Wyatt's neck. Wyatt's head was thrown back, his eyes closed, his lips parted in that sensual way that made her shiver.

A surge of jealousy spiked in her veins. Wyatt was hers, not Sean's, dammit.

Oh, bloody hell. This line of thinking was insane. Wyatt was *not* hers, and if he was gay, then there was nothing to be jealous about.

Except he wasn't gay. She knew that as surely as she knew how his skin tasted on her tongue.

Wyatt's eyes peeled open, and that was when she saw it. The reluctance. He didn't enjoy Sean's hands on his body any more than Faith enjoyed watching it. When Sean bit into the straining tendon between Wyatt's shoulder and neck, Wyatt's teeth bared like he wanted to kick Sean's ass.

No, Wyatt was definitely not into it—she knew because she'd bitten him there too, back at the hotel, and his reaction had been swift and sure. He'd gasped in pleasure, put her against the wall and had pumped into her until she screamed.

So what kind of game was Sean playing? She knew him, knew he'd do *anything* to complete a mission—which made him no different from any other secret agent on the planet. But as a rule, he'd never been into guys.

He was up to something. Maybe he was toying with Wyatt, trying to humiliate him. Sean did have a cruel streak, something that had developed over years of being bullied. It didn't take much imagination for her to picture him telling Wyatt he could keep his job if he'd give Sean a blow job.

But that didn't explain why it was Sean whose hands were all over Wyatt. No, something wasn't right here.

Including her jealousy over the way Sean was touching Wyatt, because as insane as it was, she thought of Wyatt as hers.

I want to see you, Faith. I want to keep seeing you once we get off this platform.

At his softly spoken words on the deck, excitement had curled in her stomach. Her heart had raced at the tenderness in his gaze. The men in her past and present saw her as a challenge, a powerful operative who could hold her own in a fight and in bed. For the first time ever, a man was looking at her as if he could offer her a safe haven, arms to hold her when she could no longer be strong. Arms to protect her so she could rest, could truly relax instead of always keeping a trained eye on everything and everyone around her.

Now those arms were around Sean.

Snapping shut the phone, she darted out of her room and made a beeline for Sean's office. The guards, who had been ordered to allow her in at any time, stood aside as she opened the door.

The situation had gone further in the time it had taken her to get from her room to the office, and now Wyatt was sitting on the desk, legs spread and his jeans undone. Sean's hand was down the front, working the other man with hard, firm strokes.

The moment she closed the door behind her, a blast of lust hit her, so powerful and sudden that she could barely gasp out, "Someone want to tell me what the fuck is going on?"

Not that it mattered, because now she felt the fierce urge to join them. To sink to her knees in front of Wyatt and take him into her mouth while Sean ... well, Sean didn't even need to be there, because she wanted Wyatt, and she wanted him *now*.

The next moment was a blur of motion as Sean leaped away from Wyatt, drew a weapon from his desk, and smashed his hand down on the security button.

"Get in here!" Sean shouted.

Wyatt rolled off the desk, hit the floor in a fighting stance.

Faith stood there, too stunned to move. Her heart pounded and her breath came too rapidly and her aching body still hadn't gotten the message that it wasn't going to have sex.

She rubbed her face with a trembling hand, needing a moment to think. To clear her head, because God help her, she had no idea where the uncontrollable desire to have sex had come from. Sean seemed to be wondering the same thing. His eyes were still glazed and he looked as confused as he was pissed, and all the while holding a Tokorav 9mm at Wyatt's temple.

Wyatt just looked pissed. But he had the presence of mind to zip up his pants, and for some reason, Sean let him.

Had they all been drugged with some sort of airborne aphrodisiac? She wouldn't put it past Itor to try something like that, but why would they?

The door to the office burst open, and four of Sean's goons swarmed inside. Three leveled their weapons at Wyatt, and one aimed his at her. Idiots.

"Sean—"

"Not now." Sean nodded to one of his men. "Take Wyatt to the holding area. String him up."

She hoped Sean wouldn't notice that the blood had drained from her face. "Sean, be reasonable. Let him go. He didn't do anything."

"It's okay, Faith." Wyatt's voice was low and soothing, with the protective edge she'd seen earlier in his eyes. "Don't get involved in this."

The hell she wouldn't. Whatever was going on, it wasn't his fault. Sean was obviously in shoot-first-ask-questions-later mode, which didn't bode well for Wyatt's future. Especially if Sean suspected that they'd slept together, which would explain his fury—in part, at least. Sean wasn't usually the jealous type, but he believed she was joining Itor and that they would finally be together again. He didn't like to lose, and if he saw Wyatt as any kind of competition at all . . . he'd destroy the man.

She stepped forward, earning a blow to the cheek from the goon closest to her. Her head snapped back and the coppery taste of blood filled her mouth.

Pure murderous rage burned in Wyatt's eyes. "Bastard," he snarled. "She's a fucking accountant!"

He struck like a snake, knocked two of the goons to the ground with his fists and spun to the third, kicking his weapon out of his hands. The fourth got in a punch to Wyatt's kidneys. Wyatt grunted but didn't miss a beat. He traded blows with the other man, who clearly knew his shit and was throwing Hapkido kicks and hits like a master.

In the small space, Wyatt managed to hold his own, his lean body moving with a grace she wouldn't have expected from someone so tall.

Sean's nasty curse rang out. She felt the familiar tingle that signaled the use of his energy-draining power, and Wyatt stumbled.

"Wyatt!" Her warning came too late. He went down on one knee, and Sean cracked him on the back of the head with his pistol.

"Dammit, Sean! Don't hurt him!"

Sean ignored her, still focusing on Wyatt, who crumpled to the floor. The goons, limping and wincing, had him bound in moments. And they'd taken no special care to be gentle.

"You," Sean said, pointing to the guy who had hit her, "are fired." From the deadly expression on Sean's face, she knew the guy was lucky to have gotten away with nothing more than losing his job.

Head swimming from the blow, the residual sexual haze and the confusion of whatever was going on here, Faith watched helplessly as Wyatt was dragged out of Sean's office, semi-conscious and bleeding.

As soon as the door closed, she turned on Sean, intent on getting Wyatt out of this. "None of that was necessary. And overkill, don't you think? He's a civilian, and you used your powers on him!"

Strangely, she got the feeling that if not for Sean's unsporting use of his gift, Wyatt might have been able to fight his way out of the situation despite the fact that he had been outnumbered and outgunned.

Sean seized her wrist. "You fucked him, didn't you?" He squeezed until she had to grit her teeth to keep from crying out. "You're both a little too concerned about each other."

His words sank like a rock in her gut. This was precisely why she'd tried to keep her distance from Wyatt. Well, one of the reasons anyway. And now he was in danger because she'd allowed herself to care.

"Well," Sean snarled, "are you going to deny it?"

"No." There was no use. It was far more dangerous to lie and be discovered than to tell the truth.

She rubbed her bruised cheek with her free hand, using the time to collect herself and bring back the cool-agent persona she needed. "It was just sex." Smiling seductively, she trailed a finger down the center of his chest. "I like my playthings. It meant nothing."

So much for not lying.

"Wait." She frowned. "You didn't know we slept together until after you pulled the pistol on Wyatt. So what was the commotion about, then?"

"I have no idea!" Sean shoved her away and kicked his desk in a fit of temper. "I called him in to fire his ass, and then I got this e-mail...bloody one-liner from some 'informant,' telling me I had an enemy operative under my nose, here for the weather machine, and the next thing I know, I'm jerking him off and what the fuck was going on?"

All kinds of warning bells made her heart stop like it had been flash-frozen. Someone had told Sean he had a spy in his midst. Her heart started again, leaped right into her throat.

"What do you remember?"

Sean paced, ate up the small office in five long strides. "I was getting ready to call in an escort to take him off the platform," he muttered. "Then everything's fuzzy until—"

"Until I walked in, and you snapped out of it."

"Exactly."

She replayed the video feed in her head. No way had Wyatt enjoyed Sean's hands all over him. Sean, however, had been crazed with lust, something that had been very apparent even on the phone's small screen.

And when she'd stepped into the office, she'd seen Wyatt's expression, one of mild concentration, as though he'd been fantasizing about being somewhere else, maybe with someone else. He'd been detached, but she'd suddenly felt like she'd taken a dive into a pool of ecstasy. Like the very air in the room had been infused with a drug that took away all thoughts except those that originated below the waist. She hadn't cared about anything but getting Wyatt naked and getting the relief she needed.

The effect had been powerful, intense ... and unnatural.

Bloody hell.

"He's an agent." Her voice was a stunned whisper, but her shock only lasted for a second, veered quickly to hurt and fury.

A sickening sense of betrayal weakened her knees, and she had to brace her palm on the wall to keep from falling. Had he known about her all along? Had he planned to use her against Sean or to take the weather machine? Or maybe he worked with the bastards who had taken Liberty, and had been sent to keep an eye on Faith.

She pictured him just half an hour earlier, out on the platform, his arms caging her against the rail and telling her how freaked he was about what was going on between them. She'd felt fissures form in her chest wall as he talked about growing up on a rig, and yeah, he could have been playing her like James freaking Bond, but something about that theory didn't ring true. He'd been too outraged when the goon hit her a few moments ago.

He truly believed she was an accountant, something that shouldn't make her feel better, but did.

Sean spun on his heel in the middle of the room. "An agent? Do you really think so?" Sarcasm dripped from his voice like acid. "And you fucked him."

"Calm down." Easy for her to say, when inside her emotions

churned. "He doesn't know who or what I am. He thinks I'm a company auditor. And we don't know who he's with. We don't even know what special skills he possesses."

"Besides seduction powers any Seducer would kill for?" Sean scrubbed a hand over his face. "Christ. What was I about to do?"

"I should think that would be obvious." She caught herself playing with her choker and dropped her hand. "What do you plan to do with him?"

Sean barked out a laugh, snuffing any hope that he'd show mercy. "What do you think?"

She wasn't surprised, but she did feel ill. She knew what Sean, and Itor, were capable of.

She also knew she couldn't do a damned thing to help Wyatt. And when Sean poked her in the chest with a finger and said, "He's your lover, so you're going to do the honors," she knew she couldn't do a damned thing to help herself either.

CHAPTER
Nine

If Wyatt was lucky, he had five minutes left to live—unlucky would make it ten, because the fucking rack they'd strung him up on was starting to massively get on his nerves and pull his bones to the point of no return.

Not that the sensory dep had been a walk in the park, but at least he'd enjoyed the mental torture. This slow stretch of his limbs, however, his arms and legs spread-eagled by chains attached to slow-moving winches, would not be the way he'd go down.

His telekinetic powers were drained significantly, both from his own use of the mojo plus Sean Stowe's apparent ability to drain powers—something ACRO hadn't known about. Hurt like a motherfucker too when the guy did it, which was why Wyatt had been forced to remain here all night long and take this shit.

What doesn't kill you makes you stronger, his old CO would tell him, but right now he was walking along that dangerous kill line.

The beating hadn't worked; neither had the cat-o'-nine whip, made specially ordered with nails. The loud music and the blaring lights were easy enough to ignore—he'd had far worse in training and at one point he'd told his current torturers so. They hadn't appreciated that much, which was why he found himself in this predicament, ready to be torn literally limb from limb. The thing was, they'd do it whether or not he'd talked.

Faith lay unconscious on the cement floor—they'd dragged her in this morning, right before they'd jacked him up in chains. She'd been beaten, and when they'd started to take off her clothes, he'd gotten that sick feeling that came out of helplessness and rage combined.

But they'd left her alone in favor of continuing to have their fun with him, something he was grateful for. He'd taken the punishment with even more strength after that—his sense of protection was too strong to let himself die and leave her behind.

Breathe. Concentrate and breathe.

The feeling began the way it always did, a tremor that started at the back of his neck, vibrated through his skull like a freight train running straight through hell, and just when he was sure his skull was going to break apart, he saw the world through a hazy, lime green veil that let him know everything was under control, and that it was time to start shooting from the hip.

His eyes shot open. When the first object he laid his eyes on, the cat-o'-nine whip his torturers had left hanging on the far wall to taunt him, flew across the room and hit the opposite wall hard, he knew that despite the hours upon hours of torture, his powers were still there. Muted. Compromised. But there.

Faith's head jerked upward and she stared at him in disbelief. She came to her feet, an unspeakable pain in her eyes that he couldn't get a handle on.

Clearly, they'd drugged her, or she had some kind of head injury. But when he tried to focus on moving the heavy chain that bound his left leg he felt an unmistakable stir in his groin.

He shifted to look at her.

"Don't," she said.

From the uncontrollable sensations traveling through his body, he realized he wasn't going to have much of a choice. "Faith, I didn't tell him. I swear."

"Tell who what?"

"Your boyfriend. I didn't tell him about us. He knew." Sean had come in twice during the night to question him about Faith, had taunted him with his own lurid tales.

"Sean's not my boyfriend. And I know you didn't say anything."

He stared up at the steel beams above his head, thinking, planning, looking for any kind of escape hatch in all of this, and *fuck*, he was still weaker than he was comfortable with. "I'm sorry I got you into this."

"You didn't."

A growl rumbled in his throat. "I seduced you. I shouldn't have. Not here. Not on the platform, where he could find out."

She drew in a deep breath and he knew she was inhaling *him*, the scent he gave off whenever he was around her—because he wanted her whenever, wherever. Even now, in his weakened state.

But he was here for one thing only—to get his job done. Rescuing Faith would happen in tandem, but the weather machine couldn't be left to chance.

"I'm not here because Sean is jealous."

"Then why?"

Faith didn't answer, instead focused her gaze over his body and her face whitened visibly.

She concentrated on the cut on his chest and for a minute there was a hot stab followed by intense relief. He looked down and saw the wound's edges close and disappear and he sucked in a hard breath.

"Jesus. You're a fucking agent." He strained against his bonds as it all came together in his mind—Faith was working with Sean, and she was a hell of a lot more than an accountant.

He'd screwed himself, right to the fucking wall. Or the rack, as it were. All they needed to do was threaten him with electroshock therapy and he'd spiral down nicely.

He rattled the chains and felt the rack stretch him out again.

"Please don't," she said, and her fingers, with their psychic needle and thread, slid down his body until they hovered over his already hardened cock. He arched again, as if that would be sufficient enough to break the bonds, but her voice cut through his consciousness. "Let me. Follow my lead."

He moaned and then grit his teeth against the pleasant sensations she sent streaming into his groin and the pain her healing waves caused everywhere else.

"I'm going to need you to scream, Wyatt. Scream like I'm killing you."

"You are, Faith. I've been through the gates of hell and survived, but somehow I think you're going to be the devil who takes me down."

"Scream, Wyatt. Just scream."

He closed his eyes and let the primal sounds from inside his head out, the way he'd been resisting for the past twelve hours. The way he'd been resisting his entire goddamned life. Let it all out, held nothing back until he was sure he had nothing left inside. Until he wasn't sure he hadn't screamed away his very soul.

WYATT'S SCREAMS tore through the air, tore through Faith's heart and soul. She wasn't hurting him; far from it. But the raw roar that was ripping from his throat couldn't have held more agony.

She knew he felt betrayed by her, but there was more behind the screams, something dark and scary that went so deep she couldn't reach it even with her gift. At least it was convincing.

She'd warned Sean that she wouldn't perform for an audience. No one watching. No one listening.

Except she knew that guards would be outside the door, and while they wouldn't hear low-level chatter, screams would carry.

"That's good, Wyatt," she whispered, keeping up the psychic stroking of his pleasure centers at the same time she was healing his wounds. Her biokinetic healing waves could cause excruciating agony as the gouges and slashes knitted together, so giving pleasure at the same time kept the mind off the pain.

Even better, the conflicting sensations kept him busy and

unable to use his telekinesis. The drugs Sean had given him must have worn off—bad news for her.

"Why?" he rasped. "Why are you healing me?"

"Because I can't hurt you like Sean wants."

And Sean had definitely wanted. She'd gone to his private quarters after a fitful night, and a morning visit to the weather lab, where she'd covertly studied staff schedules, security and Itor's immediate plans, which were horrifying. She needed to make her move today, or a lot of lives besides Liberty's would be at stake.

Sean had been up nearly all night as well…torturing Wyatt. When she'd asked him if Wyatt had talked, he'd been curt.

"The only words he's spoken have been curses and taunts. We've tried everything. Physical and mental torture, sensory depriva-tion…but so far, nothing." A note of admiration crept into Sean's voice, and he seemed to realize it, and drew his upper lip into a sneer.

Fighting a wave of nausea, Faith sank onto a chair at his mirrored wet bar. "What about truth drugs?"

"The drugs we've had to use to keep his telekinesis under con-trol interfere with truth serums."

"Telekinesis? So you're sure he's an agent? ACRO?"

Sean moved close, his linen shirt untucked from his beige trousers, but the casual appearance was deceiving. She'd never met anyone as intense. "He could be a merc. Or a free agent, like you. We can't be sure." He poured a glass of wine and ges-tured to the empty glass next to it. She shook her head, wanting to keep her mind clear. "We need to find out why he's here and who sent him. We also need to know how he—or whoever he's working for—learned about this operation."

She should be grateful for the commotion. Wyatt's presence had focused all attention on him and taken it off her. His unin-tended sacrifice may have made her own mission much easier. In fact, if she timed her raid on the weather lab with the next time

Sean and his torture team were busy with Wyatt, she might increase her chances of success.

Except, dammit, she wanted to help him. Especially if he was playing for the good guys.

"What do you plan to do?"

For a moment, Sean swirled the wine in his glass, studying her with hooded, hawklike eyes. When his gaze dropped to her legs, she felt the instant tingle of his caress. The tingle moved upward, along her shins, over her knees. Her pulse raced with nervous energy as his visual caress stroked higher, to the skin just beneath the hem of her short black skirt.

He reached out, caught a lock of her hair in his fingers. "I love you. You know that, don't you?"

"Of course."

"Then you'll understand when I say that I wish I didn't need your help."

Shaking her head, she pulled back to look at him. "I'm not following."

He tugged gently on her hair. "I need you to get the information out of Wyatt." He tugged again, this time wrenching her head back so she was forced to look into his eyes. "Though I hate the thought of you being anywhere near him. Again."

"It meant nothing, Sean. And now I suspect that his powers of seduction played more than a small role."

She frowned, because she wasn't sure how much of a role. Did he have to activate them, or were they a part of him, always surrounding him like a web of lust that captured anyone who came close? Because she definitely felt an erotic magnetism when she was near him, but what she'd experienced yesterday in Sean's office had been very different.

"You'll have to resist this time, Faith," Sean said. "Think of it as a test. Pass, and Itor will accept you into our fold. And then I'll take care you. I've always taken care of you, haven't I, muffin?" He eased his hold on her hair, and she resisted the urge to rub out the kink he'd put in her neck.

"We've taken care of each other," she said tightly, and took a sip of Sean's wine so she wouldn't have to talk about things that were nothing but lies now, given how she was about to betray him by stealing his agency's weapon. Neither did she doubt he'd betray her for as big a prize.

He smiled, bent and pressed a tender kiss to her forehead. "I'm sorry, muffin."

"Why—"

His fist smashed into her face. Pain exploded in her head and behind her eyes. She flew backward from the chair, crashed to the floor.

Sean's foot crunched into her ribs, and then the toe of his boot caught her jaw. Through double vision, she saw blood spray into the air and splatter on his pants.

Groaning, she rolled away from him. She swung one leg around, catching him behind the knee. With an "Oof!" he fell, crashing into the coffee table. Before she could get to her feet, he was on top of her, his weight pinning her and his hands locked on her wrists, so all she could do was scream and wriggle uselessly.

"Shh, darling," he said, in a soothing voice that made no fucking sense. "I'm sorry. So sorry."

"Bastard," she rasped, spitting blood into his face. "W-what the hell?" Pain made her woozy, pissed her off even more, and she rocked her head up so her forehead connected with his in a sharp crack.

"Ow! Fuck!" He glared down at her, wincing when blood from his split scalp dripped into his eye. "Bloody calm down!"

"Calm down? You attacked me, you asshole."

Her voice sounded mushy from the swelling of her nose and lips, and a little bubbly from the blood filling her mouth for the second time in two days. She hoped he could understand what she'd said, because her ears were ringing and she couldn't tell if her words had been clear through the swelling and blood.

"We need you to be convincing," he said, and dipped his head to wipe the blood onto his arm. "You're going to be a prisoner with Wyatt. You'll gain his confidence by saying that you *are an enemy spy, and I caught you. You'll heal him...but don't use that pleasant side-effect thing you do."*

"So you had to beat the shit out of me?"

"Like I said. Convincing."

She swore, jerked her arms out of his grip, which he'd loosened. "You could have at least fucking warned me before you hauled off and decked me."

Grinning, he rolled off her with the lazy exhaustion of someone who'd just had sex.

"What?" She lurched to her feet and used every ounce of willpower to not jam the heel of her shoe through his jugular. "What's so goddamned funny?"

"You, darling. I actually feel sorry for Wyatt." He reached out, ran a finger up her calf, and her skin crawled. "He withstood my best interrogators, but he doesn't stand a bloody chance against you."

Wyatt most certainly did have a chance against her, because she'd healed him, but not for the reason Sean wanted him healed. No, she'd done it to give him a shot at escape. Sean wanted her to make it look like she was being nice, but he had a more sinister reason: healing Wyatt after each torture session would keep him alive indefinitely.

She didn't plan to be around for the next one.

Wyatt's throat worked on a hard swallow and she wished she had some water for him. "You work for Itor."

"I'm a free agent." His injuries healed, his skin smooth and perfect again, she pulled back her powers, let him relax. At least relax as much as he could with his limbs being pulled out of their sockets. She found the lever that operated the contraption and loosened the tension.

Wyatt exhaled slowly, riding what must have been a wave of relief. "Thanks."

"I'm going to release your arms and legs, but I don't trust you to behave, so I'll restrain you myself. You'll feel pressure, like I'm holding you down."

She couldn't risk him coming at her, because as good a fighter as she was, he was bigger and stronger, and right now his self-preservation instinct had to be in high gear.

Summoning her gift, she froze his muscles. Once he was fully immobilized, she reached to unlock the cuffs around his ankles.

Just as her fingers brushed the heavy iron, the manacles snapped open. Instinctively, she increased the amount of power she was using to keep Wyatt immobile and hoped to hell he didn't find something in the cell to throw at her. The drugs they'd given him had definitely worn off.

While she watched, his wrist cuffs sprang open, and suddenly he was free and the only thing that kept him from attacking her was the power of her mind.

He tested it; she felt him trying to push against her invisible force. In the corner, the cat-o'-nine whip rattled, and she wondered if she could knock him out before he did the same to her.

"Easy," she murmured, releasing her hold on his head, so he felt at least a little less restrained.

The rattling stopped. "Who do you work for?" she asked, now that he'd settled down.

His gaze sharpened. "Free agent. Like you." He licked his dry lips. "So if you're a free agent, why are you working for Sean?"

This was the question she'd been afraid of. So many answers, only one true, the rest only partly true, but any could get her killed.

She settled on telling him the truth about Sean's intentions. If Sean found out, she could talk her way out of his wrath easily enough by saying that she was trying to gain Wyatt's trust.

"He wants you to think I'm an enemy of Itor. That after he caught you, he learned I was undercover as well. I'm supposed to be getting information from you, pretending I'm getting it for myself. Not for him."

Rolling his head forward, he stared at the ceiling, and she had no idea if he believed her or not. "You're fucking him."

It wasn't a question. He knew.

"We do what we have to do." The memory of the near-sexfest

in Sean's office burned like a drop of acid in her brain, turning her words caustic. "You nearly fucked him yourself. I'd say you have no room to judge."

"I wasn't." The way he said it, flat and completely emotionless, set her off. Why, she had no idea. Well, that wasn't true. She'd wanted to hear ... what? Anger in his voice? Jealousy? She was an idiot. But that didn't stop her from asking the question that had plagued her since yesterday.

"You used some sort of enchantment on me, didn't you? Some power of seduction. To get me to sleep with you."

He smiled, still staring at the ceiling. "You wanted to sleep with me all on your own."

"Bastard." Abruptly, she became aware of her nudity, her vulnerability. Furious that she'd bothered to help him, she stalked to her pile of clothes. "I must have been one hell of a joke to you."

Keeping her power on full strength to hold him down until she was out of the cell, she dressed and called for the guards. She didn't so much as glance at Wyatt when the door opened.

"Faith." Wyatt's voice was soft as she stepped through the doorway. "You were never a joke."

Allen County Public Library
Friday September 26 2014 11:23AM

Barcode: 31833056345744
Title: Seduced by the storm
Type: BOOK
Due date: 10/17/2014,23:59

Barcode: 31833056036244
Title: Pursuit
Type: LARGEPRINT
Due date: 10/17/2014,23:59

Total items checked out: 2

Telephone Renewal: 421-1240
Website Renewal: www.acpl.info

CHAPTER
Ten

The evening Creed and Annika returned from Greece, Creed had a meeting with some ACRO agents, about prelim storm prep and possible locations for emergency shelters at HQ.

Annika was sent on a debriefing mission with Devlin, who was back at ACRO's helm, and for a second the thought made Creed clench his fists. He hated that, cursed himself for allowing himself to think badly of Devlin. This thing that kept cropping up between himself and Annika had nothing at all to do with Devlin's feelings, and rationally Creed knew that. But the way Annika ran to Dev anytime something went wrong, anytime she needed advice...well, it cut straight through his heart.

Still, he knew she was also worried, more so now about what would happen now that Dev was back in action. Her relationship with the head of ACRO hadn't been a problem for them for the past few months, because Dev had been busy battling his own demons. Literally.

But ever since yesterday when he'd stopped Annika from murdering the man who'd killed her mother, she'd been weird to him. Oh, sure, she hid it well, hid it behind the mind-blowing sex they always had, but Creed knew Annika's breakthrough—telling him that she cared—had taken more out of her than she was willing to admit.

The fact that he also had an opportunity to get rid of Kat—the spirit who'd been bonded to him since he was born—was also freaking both of them out. If Kat left him, she could take his powers of communicating with ghosts and spirits with her. Creed would be giving up everything he'd known, all his protection, his livelihood, for Annika. The way Kat protected him was by keeping women at bay, letting Creed only have the most superficial relationships with them. Until he'd finally broken through to Annika months earlier. Their road hadn't been easy—because of Annika's gift, the electricity that coursed through her body, Kat couldn't force Annika away as she had other women. And so Kat made life hell for him, wailed in his head for hours after he'd spent too much time with Annika.

He hadn't mentioned that to Annika, although he suspected she knew Kat was tough on him. And still, Kat was such an important part of him, important enough that the decision wasn't an easy one. Either way, he'd suffer.

His right side was chilled and he rubbed his bare arms, thought about how Kat had been unusually quiet lately. Helpful, even. And better yet, she'd actually started leaving him and Annika alone. As if she was trying to show him that the three of them could live in some sort of crazy ghost domestic peace.

He walked out his front door and hopped on his Harley, letting the crisp air clear his mind as he cut through the dirt roads that led to Annika's house.

There was too much confusion. Between Kat and the possible hurricane from hell, all he wanted to do was find Ani and wrap his arms around her for a little while, to have the mind-blowing sex they could always seem to lose themselves in. To forget about all the obstacles that kept cropping up in front of them.

And so he stopped the bike up the road from Annika's house on base and walked it the rest of the way in an attempt to surprise her. She was sitting on her couch, watching an old episode of

Buffy the Vampire Slayer when he snuck up on her. Or tried to anyway.

She had him on his back on the floor within seconds. Her sheer physical strength never ceased to amaze him. Or turn him on.

"Gotcha." Her smile was smug as she held her elbow against his windpipe, her thighs clenching around his shoulders.

"I planned this," he grunted.

"Yeah, sure—keep telling yourself that, ghost boy." She moved quickly, replacing a sharp elbow with a cool palm—a loving concession, coming from Ani—while her free hand roughly untucked his shirt from his pants and slipped beneath it to find one of his nipple rings. She tugged lightly and he grunted again.

"You like being my prisoner, don't you?"

"Take off your pants," he murmured, ignoring the truth of her question.

She cocked her head as she absently tugged on his nipple ring a few more times. "I'm supposed to be back at ACRO soon."

"Not before you come at least three times."

"Is that so?"

Or three times in the space of ten minutes, if he knew Annika and the way she responded to him. Not that he was any better— he hadn't known men could have multiple orgasms until he'd been with her.

She made his eyes roll to the back of his head so often, he'd memorized the inside of his eyelids. And he liked it.

"Pants, Annika," he repeated, and she made a show of taking off her top first, even though he knew she'd do exactly as he asked.

Outside of the bedroom, not so much, but hell, one thing at a time. Rushing Annika ahead of her internal timetable was a mistake he'd already made a few times, no matter how carefully he'd promised himself he'd tread around her. His protective male macho side came out full force in her presence.

Like right now.

Her breasts were perfect—high and firm, with dark pink nipples she kept threatening to pierce. But no, he wouldn't let her do

that, no marring her body any more than her job necessitated—
and he already hated seeing the scars, mostly bullet wounds, that
she'd borne during her years with ACRO and before.

She looked so hard on the outside, but really, Ani was soft and
so fucking sweet.

"Sit. On. My. Face."

"Now who's giving the orders," she murmured as she shifted
so she could get out of the rest of her clothing. Impatiently, he
helped with yanking off her jeans, and ripped the hot pink thong
right off her body.

"Hey, that was new," she protested.

"I'll buy you more. Anything you want. Just come here."

She straddled his face and he grabbed her hips hard, pulled
her down to him so he could taste the fiery essence that was
pure Annika—a combination of Red Hots and chocolate-covered
cherries—and he was lost with his tongue buried deep inside
of her.

She'd leaned forward, her palms flat on the floor above his
head, her back arched as she pressed her pussy against his face,
seeking relief. "God, Creed...your tongue." She groaned as his
piercing flicked her clit, her body shuddering with the force of
tiny electric shocks. He tightened his grip as she tried to crawl
forward to escape the torture he knew she loved, especially when
he suckled the tight bud, suctioning it in between his lips and tugging it until she was literally screaming with pleasure.

She came hard against his mouth, but he didn't let her relax.
No, he eased her away and urged her onto all fours so he could
plunge inside of her, let the piercing cause both of them an immense shock of sensation as he buried it deep inside her body.

Taking her from behind was the way she liked it, had always
told him she could feel him more. Now his hand stayed on the flat
of her belly as he drove into her. "Remember this, Ani...remem-
ber that this is always how it's going to be."

"Yes! Creed, don't you dare stop now."

He wanted to, wanted to draw this out, to tease her even
longer, but the shock waves her body naturally gave off when she

was under tremendous pressure like this were too much for him to handle. Every nerve ending tightened, his chest was tight and his balls pulled up high, because he was ready.

"Come now, Ani—come with me now," he murmured as they both reached the peak together, as she twisted her neck so she could touch her mouth to his briefly before the orgasms wracked their bodies.

DAMN, BUT THE SEX had been good. And it wasn't over. Annika and Creed had showered, dressed, and then she'd pounced on him in the hallway when he wasn't expecting it. They both had work to do—she had an afternoon full of martial arts classes to teach, and he had some research to do on post-hurricane hauntings—but she wasn't ready to go back to the real world yet. So she'd slammed him against the wall and fell to her knees in front of him.

Impatiently, she ripped open the fly of his leather pants, releasing his gorgeous cock, which had already gone rock hard. She'd always liked giving him head, but the piercing gave her a new toy to play with, new ways to make him shiver.

Gently, she pulled his heavy sac forward so it bulged over the V of his open fly. Creed's breath hitched. She loved that.

Saliva filled her mouth as she opened it over one of his balls. She sucked it between her lips, used her tongue to lift, to jiggle the testicle with tender little bounces. When she moved to the other one, she heard Creed's head hit the wall.

"Oh, yeah," he murmured. "That's it."

Digging her fingers into his thighs, she concentrated on his balls, sucking, licking, stabbing her tongue between them to separate them even as she used her teeth to create sensation on the rapidly tightening skin.

Creed's breathing grew more rapid and shallow, and he began to thrust, his patience wearing thin. "Enough teasing." His voice was a low, rough demand that made her shudder with feminine appreciation.

Using only the tip of her tongue, she licked her way up his

shaft, taking her sweet time, inhaling his soapy clean scent and tasting his musky arousal. A bead of cum seeped from his slit, and she sipped it greedily, sucked the broad head of his cock like a straw. He groaned, but the best was yet to come.

Smiling at her own pun, she nibbled her way down to the curved barbell decorating his dick. She wet her lips and slipped one round end of the jewelry between them. Creed stopped breathing, well aware of what she was going to do next.

She hummed and charged herself with electricity. He shouted, an erotic roar as his body jerked with pleasure. She closed one hand around the base of his cock and squeezed, pressing firmly with her thumb to prevent him from spewing, and she used the other hand to tug gently on his sac, keeping him from coming.

Nevertheless, he was as close as he could get, and she could keep him in this mildly orgasmic state for several moments. She'd discovered that going too long would eventually lead to a full release, but until then, he would be at her mercy, his body coming but his cock and balls not quite there.

After a slow count to ten, she released her electric charge and took him fully into her mouth.

"Annika..."

She smiled around his cock. This was her favorite part, right before climax, when he moaned her name, grasped her head and started pumping because he couldn't control himself anymore.

Deep-throating him, she grabbed his hips and let him go. His piercing tickled the back of her tongue on every stroke. She applied strong suction and used her tongue to lash at the underside of his shaft. The wet sound of him fucking her mouth had her squeezing her thighs together to ease her own arousal, and yeah, she'd have to either masturbate or make Creed do it for her after this.

With an explosion of breath, he went taut and released, and she swallowed everything he had. She loved the way he tasted, loved the sounds he made, loved him... even though she hadn't said it out loud. Neither had he, and it irked the shit out of her.

"Damn, Ani," he panted, as she licked him clean and then tucked him into his pants. "Where did you learn that?"

"Adam."

"*What?*" Creed had dropped his hands to her shoulders, and they tightened into claws.

"Adam Yates. You know him. The Seducer? Ow. Your fingers—"

She found herself hauled to her feet so fast she barely had time to plant them on the floor. Creed's nearly black eyes burned like coal, were practically smoking. Right... he hadn't really wanted an answer to where she'd learned how to blow a guy. Rhetorical question and all that. God, she was always making stupid missteps when it came to personal relationships. Probably because before Creed she'd never had one.

"When?" His voice matched his expression, filled with rage and raw possession. It was kinda hot, and a little scary.

"I had sessions with him a long time ago. I needed to learn to seduce guys for assignments. He taught me to kiss and touch a guy and give blow jobs and do that thing with my tongue and your—"

"Stop. Jesus Christ, *stop*."

"You asked," she muttered, and stepped back, out of his grip, which had been digging into the tendons between her neck and shoulder. "It was a job, Creed. He was teaching me and I was learning. Most of it happened in a damned classroom."

"Trust me, for him it was no job."

She rolled her eyes. "What's your deal? I have a past. You have a past. I don't flip out when we run into all the skanks you've screwed and they look at you like you're a steak and they're a lion. And there are a *lot* of them."

No, she always let him handle it when they smiled and drooled, or when they approached him the second Annika turned her back. Of course, she hunted them down later and made it clear that if they so much as looked at him again, she'd pull a Viking and rip their lungs out of their chests, flip them over their shoulders and turn them into wings. Usually, the skanks needed a change of underwear after that.

She didn't blame Creed for the ungodly number of women he'd slept with, though...Kat had never let him sleep with any woman more than once or twice. As a result, he'd gone through women like most people went through paper towels. It wasn't until he and Annika had hooked up that he'd been able to settle down a little—and the ghostly bitch had made it difficult for them as well.

"It's a guy thing," he said between clenched teeth. "Every fucking time I talk to Adam, he's secretly laughing his ass off at how he's seen the top of your head on a regular basis, and I'm a fucking clueless jackass." Wheeling around, he grabbed his jacket and keys.

"What are you doing?" She grabbed his forearm, but he jerked away.

"I'm going to have a chat with Adam."

This time when she grabbed him, he didn't get away. She planted her feet in front of him and refused to budge. "You're acting crazy. Besides, Dev already took care of it. Poor Adam won't even be in the same room with me anymore. The other day I snuck up on him and tapped his shoulder, and I thought he was going to pass out. I have no idea what Dev did—"

"Dev. Of course. Leave it to Dev to handle it so I can't."

"I still don't know what there is to handle!" Criminy, men were dumb.

"You, Dev and Adam all know Adam's had you, and I'm the idiot in the dark."

"Adam didn't *have* me."

"Right. He only had his cock in your mouth. That's better how? Because, baby, when it comes to sucking dick, you're a pro. Are there others at ACRO I should know about?"

Her mouth worked soundlessly for a few seconds, before she was finally able to whisper, "You bastard."

Wetness filled her eyes, and she spun around so Creed wouldn't see. She'd been such an emotional wreck lately, crying all the time, losing her temper...she'd taken a pregnancy test just to make sure she wasn't knocked up, and thank God that had turned out negative. Desperate, she'd finally paid a rare visit to one of ACRO's psychologists, who said that all of her emotional suppression during her CIA years had caused a backup, and by opening herself up to Creed she'd opened a floodgate.

No word on when it would all even out so she could feel normal again.

"Ah, shit. Ani, I didn't mean that. I'm sorry." His boots thumped on the floor and then his arms came around her. She turned into his embrace and settled her forehead on his broad chest.

"It's okay."

"No, it's not. I'm a jealous asshole." He pressed a kiss to the top of her head, his lips warm and comforting. "I guess I figured all the guys you've, um, been with, have been assignments and I'd never have to see them."

She ran her hands up his back, loving how his muscles rippled beneath her palms. "It was years ago. And it didn't mean anything."

Creed let out a low, rumbling sound, something between a growl and a purr. Whatever it was, it vibrated into her soul, leaving her feeling...marked, weird as that sounded. "I'm tired of sharing you, Ani."

She stiffened in his arms. "This isn't about Adam, is it? It's about Dev. Again." Creed couldn't let loose his anger on Dev, so he was lashing out at a Seducer who hadn't so much as looked at her in years. "You're both important to me. You know that. And you know I'm not sleeping with Dev."

His bark of laughter startled her out of his embrace. "Tell me, Annika, when you're upset, angry, hurt, where do you go?"

To Dev's. Shit. She'd gone to him the second she'd returned from Greece. Had gone straight from the plane to his office. She'd been thrilled to learn that his sight had returned, so thrilled she hadn't cared that he'd dressed her down like a green military recruit for the Greece thing. Of course, she'd done the same right back, asking why the hell he'd disappeared for so long, why he'd shut her out of his life and let Oz take over ACRO.

What he'd told her had left her stunned and shaken.

"Remember last fall when I sent you and Creed to my parents' mansion to check out the ghost living there?" At her nod, he said, *"Well, it got out. It was the spirit of a former Itor agent named Darius. He tried to possess me."*

"Why?"

"He wanted revenge. Itor's director, Alek, tortured him to death for helping Alek's pregnant girlfriend escape Itor."

Annika leveled a suspicious stare at him. "That's sad and all, but why would he want to use you for revenge?"

"Because Darius figured I'd want revenge too. Turns out Alek not only killed my parents, but he's also my father. My parents took me in after Alek's girlfriend gave birth."

Yeah, that had been a holy-shit revelation if ever there was one. Dev had gone on to explain that Oz had banished Darius but that Dev's mind—and ACRO's secrets—had been left wide open to Alek, thanks to a fun father-son mental link, so Dev's absence had been about keeping him isolated from everyone except the psychics who had maintained a mental shield on him twenty-four hours a day.

Annika realized Creed was staring at her, arms crossed as he waited patiently for her to answer his question about where she went when she was upset and emotional and crap like that.

"Creed, I'm trying. I answered all your questions on the plane ride back, and I even promised to go with you to that crazy monster-truck thing next weekend—barring a natural disaster. But I can't...I can't choose. Please don't ask me to."

Shaking his head, he sighed. "I'm not. I just want you to need me."

"I do need you," she said quietly. "Especially now. With everything going on, it's you I need."

In a heartbeat, she was in Creed's arms and she knew, for the first time in their relationship, that she'd finally said the right thing.

CHAPTER
Eleven

Wyatt's time with Faith had been the furthest thing from a joke he could think of—she was the first woman he'd ever admitted anything to about his family, the first woman he'd admitted any kind of weakness to. And now she'd seen him beaten, physically, seen his mental drain as well . . . and still she'd laid her hands on him and healed him.

With what barely seemed an effort, she'd held his entire two-twenty-pound body to the table, so hard he couldn't move a finger, let alone a muscle.

The only thing given free rein to move had been his cock— and it still ached from her touch. Longing for that touch was what propelled him off the table and onto the floor after he took out with the cat-o'-nine the security cameras located in all four corners of the room. He had two missions now—the weather machine and finding out if Faith Black could be trusted with his life . . . and possibly with his heart.

He figured he had maybe ten seconds before the goons came back in, felt his body flex with readiness as he grabbed a loosened line of chain that had held him to the rack and wrapped it around both fists.

The first man got a box to the ears, the second had his neck broken with a quick wrap of the chain. The third and fourth got equal punches to the nose, which took them out.

He killed the three unconscious men quickly, with the phrase *it's them or me* running through his head. Speaking of running, it was time to get his ass out of there.

He had keys, one of the dead men's talkabouts, clothing and his chains. The Chelbi helo was parked on the landing pad on the other side of the rig—that was his best and fastest option off this place. With the weather machine. And with Faith.

He knew that Sean wouldn't let Faith off this platform alive, not after what she'd done to help Wyatt...not after sleeping with him either.

Enough.

Find Faith.

Get out of Dodge.

He slipped out of the room that had been his prison and moved swiftly down the narrow hallway lined with sheet metal. At a corner, he slowed, eased his head around and smiled when he spotted his quarry ahead, near a door. Faith was standing there, her forehead braced against the wall.

With the pumalike quietness he'd perfected, he sprang on her, immobilizing her arms by her sides, and placed a hand over her mouth. "You make a sound and we're both dead. You try to throw me across the room and we're both dead—right now your best choice is to just come along for the ride," he growled in her ear.

He didn't wait for an answer, simply lifted her and pulled them both into the small room that housed the boiler, even as he slowly shifted the security camera slightly to the left with his mind so they had a clear hiding place in the corner. A good hiding place for now, until the chaos died down.

"What the fuck, Faith? Who do you work for?"

"Who do *you* work for? I think a little truth from your end for the woman who saved your life is in order." As she spoke, he could easily see that she was an agent—the calm, cool and collected vibe of a seasoned operative, at that. How the hell he had missed it the first night was above and beyond him, but he was done missing things.

"You're the one who nearly got me killed in the first place." He put a hand above her head, leaned against the wall and into her, and even here, with the danger surrounding them, he wanted her with a force he could barely contain.

"We're not out of danger yet."

He cocked an eyebrow at her, especially as her hands wrapped around his waist to pull at him, tug him closer to her body. "When did we become a *we?*"

"When you told me you didn't want another man touching me. Or was that just a joke too?"

He kissed her then, yanked her hard to him and crushed her mouth with his to let her know that none of this was a fucking joke. She yielded, her body softening against his, and he kissed her until he was certain she was certain that nothing he said or did around her was a joke.

"We're in big trouble here," she said, her breathing fast once he ripped his mouth from hers, and she wasn't only talking about Sean. "I can't concentrate on anything when you're around."

"Yeah, right back at you, Faith," he growled against her cheek. "We're getting off this platform, ASAP."

"I'm not cooperating unless you tell me who you work for," she said. "Even free agents answer to someone."

"ACRO. The good guys." No use lying now that they might have to work together. Better that she knew the wrath of the major agency could come down on her head.

And even though he knew she got it, she still played it cool as shit, a small smile curving those perfect lips. "You want the weather machine."

"I'm going to destroy the weather machine, and then we're out of here."

"I can't let you do that," she said.

"Ah, babe, don't tell me you really do work for Itor. I'm into you and I don't want to have to snap your neck because you're working for my arch enemy."

"I don't work for Itor, and I have my own reasons for wanting the weather machine."

"No good comes of that piece of man-made shit, Faith. Nothing good at all."

The sounds outside the room grew louder as alarms continued to sound. He put his forehead to hers and they remained pressed together, immobile and part of the shadows in the corner of the room, until the danger passed them by for the moment.

"We're going to have to wait them out." She jerked her head toward the closed door where the sounds of security guards were rising.

"It won't be long," he murmured against her ear. "They can't risk catching the riggers' attention and raising suspicion."

"They're still going to want you dead, no matter how long we wait," she said, and he smiled, because hell, he was already dead twice over.

"What about you? Do you want me dead?"

"If that's what I wanted, I could've done that back when you were on the rack."

She was still rubbing against him—his hips responding in like fashion with a life of their own, until the length of their bodies made a rhythmic connection that promised to set them both on fire. Dry humping against the wall of the boiler room might not be the best use of his time right now, but you couldn't beat it as an interrogation method.

The thing was, with Faith, he didn't even have to use the love jones before she responded to him.

And she remembers—remembers every time we've made love.

She shifted so she could wrap her hands around his ass and pull him into her even more tightly. "In the office—with Sean—you did something special," she said, and he nodded. "Is that why I felt different when I walked into the room? Drugged?"

"Yeah. It's part of my powers, tied to the telekinesis."

"Would you have slept with him if I hadn't come in?"

"I'll do whatever I need to do in order to save the world from the weather machine. That's why I don't judge anything you might've done, honey. But that doesn't mean I would've liked it."

"So those powers—you've used them on me, haven't you?"

"The first night, in the alley," he admitted.

"And all night long?"

"Once I let the pheromone out there, it's out there. It even affects me. But that didn't make that night any less special."

"I don't like being deceived," she told him. "If I have feelings, if I want someone, I need to know that it's all me, not because of some magic trick."

He pulled his upper body back slightly so his finger could trace her already hardened nipple through the fabric of her nearly see-through white blouse. "Just know that the way you want me now, it's all you, Faith. Nothing to do with my magical powers of persuasion. You'll know the difference. In fact, you do know the difference."

He pulled her in for a soft kiss—something that nearly killed him, since all he wanted to do was take her, right there, in the boiler room. But no, gentle was the answer for the moment—she had to believe him.

"You're the first woman who remembered me, Faith. This gift can also be a curse—the pheromones act like a memory erase. Convenient when sex is just a means to an end. Shitty when you want to be remembered," he said quietly. "I was really glad you remembered me. You have no idea how glad."

"Funny, because it might have been safer for us both if I'd forgotten," she said, and he knew she was thinking about Sean.

"I meant what I said earlier. I don't want you with other men."

"You're very proprietary."

"You're the sexiest woman I've ever met," he murmured, his free hand sliding down the length of her body to cup her ass as she arched against him again.

"We need a plan, Wyatt. Need to get the weather machine and get off this platform." She'd groaned the last part of the sentence, as his hand slid under her shirt and cupped her bare breast, a nipple pressed between finger and thumb.

"Any ideas?" he asked, glad multitasking had always been high on his list of talents.

"We're going to have to use some good old-fashioned brute force." She jerked under his touch and hissed as he pressed her nipple again and again. Her hand had made its way between his legs—she wasn't going to make any of this easy. "Overpower Sean and take the weather machine."

"Destroy the machine," he corrected, as she opened his pants and took his cock in hand, stroked him with a cool palm and a lick of her own bottom lip that made it almost impossible for him to think.

"I've got a buyer—he's willing to spend millions to get his hands on the machine—and I'll split the proceeds," she said as she traced a thumb over the slit and spread the pre-cum over his head. He retaliated by pushing her skirt up and moving her flimsy thong panties aside to stroke her already wet sex.

"Bullshit, Faith." He spoke as slowly and deliberately as his fingers moved over her clit. Her body threaded tightly, like a drawn bow, quivering and on the edge of being let loose. And he'd keep her on that edge as long as he needed her to be there, ruthlessly, breathlessly holding back his own orgasm. "I don't believe that you do anything for money. For the job, yes, but not for money."

She drew a deep breath and pushed herself toward his fingers, frantically seeking a relief he would not give her. Her own hand lost its momentum around his erection as her thoughts clouded from impending pleasure. "Just checking to make sure *your* motives are clean."

"My motives—and the motives of ACRO—are above reproach. But the actions of an independent agent might not be."

"I can help you take the machine, get it away from here." She was moaning in between her words, soft ones as the perfume of her arousal filled the room, as effective as any drug. If there was time, he'd lift her and take her with his mouth, lick her sweet juice until she was a quivering, whimpering mess.

He'd have to make do with his hand.

"I'm destroying it. And then we're out of here. Mission accomplished," he told her, moved his fingers to just the right spot and watched her explode, watched her eyes close and her mouth drop open to emit a soft cry of pleasure as she writhed on his hand.

"God, Wyatt . . . just bloody God." She bit into the soft flesh of his neck to keep from making any louder sounds.

"Did you hear me, Faith?" he asked, knowing full well that conversation wasn't her strong suit right now. But he'd gone beyond any sense of fair play a long time ago. "We're going to destroy the weather machine before we leave this platform."

She shuddered in his arms, her hands gripping his shoulders for balance as he eased her skirt back down, smoothed it with both hands and tried to catch his own breath.

He hadn't come, but damn, it had been close.

"Did you hear me, Faith?" he asked again.

"I heard you." She lifted her head finally, her eyes clear and bright, the smile of contentment still on her lips. "It's just that right now, right this second, I have a different mission."

First one arm and then the other went up over his head—wrists together, she held them there with her mind without a hint of strain.

What a fucking turn-on—more so, of course, if both their lives and the fate of the world weren't on the line, but Dev always reiterated that sex was about power and control, and never more so than when you were on the bottom, so to speak.

"Do you trust me, Wyatt?" she asked. He shifted slightly and realized that the only thing he could still move were his hips. She'd nudged his legs slightly apart, held them fast too, the way she had on the table.

"What do you want, baby?"

"Besides you?" she asked, stroking his still rock-hard cock

with an expert touch, cool fingers against hot flesh, and his body practically sizzled with need. "I want off this platform. That's one thing we agree on."

For the moment, it was enough. He was suspended basically by nothing but her mind, longed to stretch out with her on the floor and drive into her as hard and fast as he could, to drive her to the edge again, to hear her call his name in a way she'd never, ever called out any man's name before.

"Can you bring yourself over a chair?" she asked, and he didn't bother to question it. In seconds, he had the metal folding chair moving silently toward them. "Good boy. Now sit for me."

She released his body long enough for him to do so, and fuck, that was a cool power she had. Deadly, but cool. "Our powers complement one another well, don't you think?" she asked.

"I want to get beyond thinking, Faith. I want you to fuck me instead. Because when you do that, when I'm inside you, when you're touching me, I feel whole. And I like that feeling."

She immobilized him again, arms at his sides, legs spread and unmoving, her eyes never wavering from his as she slid her skirt up and her thong off.

"Yeah, oh, yeah, baby. Come on down," he murmured as she lowered herself, excruciatingly slowly until she accommodated every inch of him. Her nails bit into his bare shoulders, still sore from the beating he took, and he didn't care because, holy fuck, watching her ride him was worth that price.

"You make me want more, Wyatt," she murmured as she rocked against him, taking him in deeper and deeper, until he nearly screamed with the frustration of not being able to rock his own hips upward. "You make me crazy."

All the power, all the pleasure was located in his cock and balls, so intense he nearly lost consciousness.

"You like this, baby? Like when I hold you down and take you?" she asked, but he was beyond words, nearly incoherent as her body overwhelmed his, took him with a frantic pace he'd never known before.

They remained well hidden in the dark corner, her pussy

contracting around his cock, wet and hot and pulsing, and *fuck*, he was about to bite off his own tongue, and holding back was fast becoming a nonoption.

"Come with me, Wyatt. Come right now," she commanded him, and he did, shooting hard inside her as her own orgasm overtook her.

His arms and legs went immediately free when she came—he made a mental note about that as he held her against his chest and closed his eyes for a brief moment.

FAITH HAD BEEN in a lot of lose-lose situations. There'd been times when she'd been ninety-nine percent sure she wouldn't get out of a situation alive. But as bad as things had been during those missions, nothing could come close to the clusterfuck she was living through right now.

She'd always preferred to work alone, but when team action was required, she wanted to know she could trust her teammate. Which was one of the reasons she and her partner, Paula Archer, had, with the British government's support and financing, started The Aquarius Group—named for their birth sign. She and Paula, friends from their "special school" days, handpicked the operatives, trained them and tested them. Regularly.

Now she was on the most dangerous assignment of her life, easily the most critical one, and suddenly she had a partner she needed, didn't trust, and whose mission objective directly opposed hers.

Worse, every time she had sex with him, she sank deeper into an emotional place that threatened to derail her. The smart thing to do would have been to kill Wyatt while he was stretched out on the rack. Instead, she'd saved him, and now she'd have to battle him for possession of the weather machine.

"What do you think Sean is doing right now?" Wyatt slipped behind her, pressed the length of his body to hers as she peeked through the crack in the steel boiler-room door.

She knew Sean inside and out, knew exactly how he'd handle this situation. "He's got men looking for you, but because they didn't find you right away, he's scaling down the search, making it less obvious. He'll have figured out that I'm MIA, and he'll think you have me."

"Then that's how we'll play this."

"I'll be your hostage." Smart. The longer Sean believed she was on his side, the better.

"He did something to me in the office. What exactly is his deal?"

There was an unspoken rule amongst special-ability operatives, something that went along the lines of *Never reveal another agent's special gifts*. Sean was a childhood friend, a confidant, a lover...but he'd turned into something sinister, a stranger she barely recognized, and she didn't owe him anything anymore.

"Faith?" Wyatt's warm hand came down on her shoulder, to give her a gentle but firm squeeze—a not-so-subtle message telling her that they might have just had sex, but playtime was over, and he had a job to do. "I need to know what I'm up against. All of it."

"Yes, of course." The words were crisp, as devoid of emotion as she could make them. She had a job to do too. "He can tap your energy."

"Yeah, I got that. But how bad?"

"He can drain you so that in seconds you're nothing but a quivering blob on the floor. Or worse. You only got a very mild taste of it."

"That's just great," he muttered.

"There's something else you should know. It's difficult for me to use my gift on him, and vice versa."

"Why?"

"Sean and I go way back. We grew up together. Developed our powers together. And we learned to recognize each other's power signatures. We can't completely block each other, but we at least get a warning."

"Soon," he said so close to her ear she felt the scrape of teeth, "we're going to have to talk about how well you know good ole Sean."

Her breath hitched, but before she could catch it, Wyatt turned her and caged her between his arms and the door. "But first, we need to work out what we're going to do with the machine. Because I don't want to battle Sean and his goons and then have to fight you."

Her sense of self-preservation kicked in, and she reached deep for her power, prepared to do whatever was necessary if he even thought about doing his neck-snapping thing.

"I won't allow you to destroy the machine."

"And I won't let you take it."

The sound of footsteps on some grating above them created a tense silence, though she wouldn't be surprised if Wyatt heard her heart pounding crazily. When the men had passed, she lifted her chin and met his hard gaze with an equally hard one of her own.

"Do your orders specify that you have to destroy it while on the platform?"

He narrowed his eyes at her. "No. Why?"

"Then let's take it, and once we're safely away, we can decide what to do with it. There are probably a million ways you can destroy it once we're in the air." And there were a million ways she could either convince him to let her have it, or deal with him so he'd have no choice but to let her have it. The odds tipped in her favor if they could just get off the platform with the thing intact.

"I don't think so."

"Dammit, Wyatt. I'm not going to back down on this. I need that machine, and I will do what I have to do. Whatever it takes."

"What's this really about, Faith? I'm going to be real fucking disappointed if it's about money, after all."

"It's about family," she said gravely. "If I don't get that machine, my sister dies."

CHAPTER
Twelve

Family. Again with the family. The universe was trying to tell him something about synchronicity and karma—all things Sam was always talking about.

Look for the signs, Wyatt, look for all the signs.

Faith held his arm. "I know you might not understand . . . what you said before, about your own family, about not being close with them . . ."

"If you're fucking with me—"

"Why would I do that? I'm letting you take me as a hostage. I saved your ass and your life. I'm turning against my childhood friend."

"And former lover," he pointed out, mainly because that still chapped his ass.

"Exactly. I need this machine."

"I can't let it get into the wrong hands."

"It won't. I just need to get my sister *out* of the wrong hands." She fumbled in her skirt pocket and pulled out a cell phone. "Here—you want proof, this is the best I can do on short notice."

He watched the small screen, saw the woman Faith said was her sister, tied up, looking beaten and bruised and begging Faith for help. He heard the man's voice in the background as well, instructing Faith on the first steps toward assuring that Liberty went free and unharmed, and his stomach twisted. His own family was destroyed—ACRO was his family now, an amazing fucking family at that—but sometimes Wyatt longed for closure, for real answers about what happened.

He looked at Faith's face and saw a pain there that couldn't be faked. He felt his own pain every time he thought about his half brother.

He knew he was skating on cracked ice, that someone who would do anything for a family member would do *anything*, including hand over a machine that could kill half the world's population.

Her powers were strong, but he still had his most important talent—he'd hate to use that against her again, but if he had to, it would stop her from trying to crush his internal organs with her mind. Because *that* would be a real fucking drag.

"We'll deal with the fate of the machine after we secure the motherboard and get the hell off the platform."

"That works for me," she agreed.

"You owe me and ACRO for this, babe. Now, let's move. My fucking life is in your hands if that Stowe motherfucker gets through—you know that, right?"

"I know that, Wyatt. I've never been great at working as part of a team, but I'm a quick study," she said quietly. "Now, how are we going to move around this installation without getting you caught?"

He grinned. "Baby, I grew up on rigs and platforms. Took my first steps a hundred feet above the ground. Cut my teeth on steel cable. I can get us where we need to go."

She went up on her tiptoes and brushed her lips over his in a feather-light kiss. "Very sexy."

They moved swiftly but cautiously between piping and beneath out-of-the-way support beams, the sound of machinery drowning out the clank of their footsteps on metal plating. The familiar odors of oil and hot steel brought back memories of doing this same thing as a kid, when offshore platforms had been his playground.

This was his turf. Sean and his city-civilized minions didn't stand a chance.

The accommodations module loomed ahead, and his mind worked quickly. No way would they be able to waltz in—Sean's goons would be watching his quarters.

When Faith cocked a questioning eyebrow at him, he winked and scaled a pipe running along the backside of the module. She followed, didn't complain when he opened the cover on an air duct barely large enough for them and squeezed through.

The going was hot and dusty, but they made it to the ceiling above his room with a minimum of wrong turns. As quietly as possible, he pried the vent grating loose and dropped into his room, where he changed quickly, grabbed the important things, like his cell phone, weapons and ammo—one round definitely had Sean's name on it.

Faith whispered from the air duct above, where she'd remained. "Hurry. We still have to stop at my room so I can get a bag for the motherboard."

He looked up. "We don't need a bag."

"It's specially made. Waterproof and crushproof," she insisted, and something in her eyes told him he wasn't going to win this one, and that they were wasting precious time. He climbed back into the crawl space and led her to her quarters. Once they were there, they both climbed down. They'd go on foot from here.

He guarded the door to her room, watched as she took the bag from the closet. Watched as she placed the stuffed animal she'd had on her hotel bed the day they'd met inside, and he turned away and found himself both smiling and sighing.

This mission was too personal for both of them.

He snared two sets of coveralls and hard hats from a deck locker as they made their way to the weather lab, and once they were dressed, they used the hide-in-plain-sight ruse to work their way toward the weather lab.

It was game on for both of them.

Two guards stood at the entrance to the main offices, unarmed but no doubt deadly.

"Sean said that since the module housed the company offices used by legitimate workers, he couldn't have men toting semi-automatic weapons hanging around," she whispered.

"Probably I-Men," he said. Probably excedosapiens with minor abilities—which still made them more dangerous than the average, well-trained soldier. "I want the one on the left first."

"Got it," she said, and they both sprang into action, a fucking thing of beauty.

Their skills were complementary when they weren't being used against each other, and the guards went down like a choreographed dance Wyatt would've enjoyed if the situation weren't so mind-blowing dire, with Faith doing the immobilizing so Wyatt could kill them in a quick and quiet order, assembly-line fashion, snapping necks efficiently to preserve his telekinetic powers for when he'd really need them.

"Cameras," she said, and Wyatt quickly disabled them by blowing out the internal wiring, and did the same with the coded locks on the door.

"I'll take the alarms on the inside—hold them off for me while I do that," he instructed.

"The men inside aren't going to give you a problem," she assured him. "Trust me."

They opened the doors and burst into the lab that housed the massive wall of·computers that made up the weather machine, and were greeted by three men who had been hunkered over the weather equipment. Faith standing there with her arms crossed was enough to have them practically on their knees while Wyatt shorted the alarms.

That wasn't going to stop Sean for long, though.

"You guys meteorologists?" Wyatt asked, and one of them nodded. "Special abilities?"

All of them shook their heads vigorously. They were definitely

Itor, but like ACRO, Itor employed people who didn't possess special abilities but who were the best in their fields.

Wyatt glanced around, jerked his head at the closet at the rear of the lab. "In there. All of you."

"Wait," Faith said. She grabbed the nearest guy and pointed at the radar. "What's going on with that hurricane?"

"We just turned it to the north. It's going to move up the East Coast."

Wyatt moved close. "Turn it out into the mid-Atlantic."

The guy shook his head. "It'll take a little more than a push of a button. Once we turned it, the Bermuda High took over its steerage."

"Can you weaken it?"

"Yes," the guy said cautiously, as if he wasn't sure he was giving the answer that would keep him alive, "but it'll take hours."

"Shit. Okay, get in the closet."

Faith herded the three guys to the closet, closed the door, then Wyatt concentrated, bent the lock so the door wouldn't open.

"Motherboard," he said, and she pointed.

"There. Get it out first and then we'll have to destroy the entire wall."

"That will be my pleasure," he said, and with her help they gently extracted the motherboard, the key to the entire operation, up and away from the main components. Faith slid it into the lined protective pouch she wore on her person.

"Stand back, baby." He methodically began to blow out the computers, screens, the hard drives and even the keyboards for good measure. The TVs and phones went too, and one by one he lifted them and flung them against the far wall, until every single component was thoroughly destroyed.

The most important thing left to destroy had, however, just entered the room. And when Wyatt turned with deadly force to connect his fist to Sean Stowe's face, he knew he was taking his life into his hands in more ways than one.

* * *

ONE MINUTE Faith had been double-checking the motherboard in her satchel, and the next she'd been thrown into a pile of debris when Wyatt's punch knocked Sean into her.

Wyatt and Sean were going at it, fists flying, legs kicking. They pounded each other, slamming into equipment, desks, walls. Their faces were masks of rage, teeth bared, eyes promising no mercy. They could strike with their weapons or their powers, but this wasn't a fight over just the weather machine. This was personal, a fight to cause pain, a fight to the death.

She'd always thought Sean was beautiful in battle, but Wyatt blew her ex-lover out of the water. Every motion was clean and efficient, vicious and deadly.

And Wyatt was going to win. Sean knew it too. His chest heaved with panting breaths, sweat dripped down his temples and he was foaming at the mouth.

Faith shoved at the computer monitor pinning her ankle, moving it just enough to allow her to slide from beneath it.

A shadow filled the doorway, and a man burst inside, his movements so fast she could hardly track him. An I-Agent. Excedo-sapien with a gift for speed. He wrenched Wyatt's arm behind his back, forcing Wyatt to turn his attention away from Sean...a move that cost him. While Wyatt exchanged blows with the excedo, Sean found the focus he needed to use his gift.

Sean's eyes darkened as his power peaked. Ignoring the ache in her side, Faith clutched her leather satchel and lurched to her feet.

"Wyatt!"

Too late. Wyatt delivered a fatal, crushing blow to the other man's throat, but as he spun to Sean, he stumbled.

"Son of a—" Staggering, Wyatt reached out, his fingers only brushing Sean's shirt. He crumpled to the ground as though his bones had turned to rubber.

Sean retrieved his Tokorav from where it had fallen to the floor and disarmed Wyatt. Then he completely dismissed Wyatt as a threat, could afford to, since anyone falling victim to his energy-drain would be helpless for several minutes. Of course, the use of his power also left him physically weak for just as long.

Blood ran in a stream from his nose, and his bottom lip was split. He glanced at the empty slot in the machine where the motherboard had been housed. "How long have you been working with him, Faith? From the beginning? Don't tell me you're ACRO."

Keeping her eyes on Sean, she opened herself to her power. She couldn't use it on him, but she sure as hell could send a beam into Wyatt, get him up and running well before Sean expected.

"I didn't even know Wyatt until a couple of days ago."

"You betrayed me for a man you just met?" The hurt in his eyes shifted to raw fury. He swung around to Wyatt. "Did she tell you she loved you? Did you fall for her lies? She seems to throw the love thing around rather freely. She's turned into quite the whore since we last were together."

So like him to strike out when he was hurt. Now wasn't the time to mention his childish tendencies, however. Nor could she risk striking back like he'd expect. Not when he held the pistol pointed at Wyatt, who watched with cool, unreadable eyes.

"Sean, I never lied about loving you. I loved who you were. Who you can be. Please, come with us. Leave Itor behind."

For a moment, he appeared to consider her offer, and her heart soared. They could never be together like they once were, not after all that had happened. Not after how her heart was starting to beat for another man. But she did love Sean, as a friend. As family. If she could lead him away from the evil that was Itor—

He pivoted back to her. "Give me the motherboard, Faith. Give it to me, and I'll forget how you betrayed me."

"I can't." She doubled the size of the power ray she was sending into Wyatt, hoping Sean wouldn't sense it.

"This isn't like you. You've never cared about money. Or power."

No, she'd never cared about those things. But Sean always had, and those very desires had led to his corruption. "Do you hear yourself? Do you know what you were about to do with this machine?"

"I'm following orders."

"You were going to kill thousands of innocent people." She clenched her fists to keep them from shaking. "People like my parents."

There was a long silence. A softening in his expression. "I'm sorry, muffin. I didn't think. I shouldn't have allowed Itor to bring you in on this job."

"What about the people you planned to kill? Are you sorry about that?"

"My job is to execute the plan. Not to care about the people who die. Now give me the motherboard."

Behind Sean, Wyatt stirred, slowly, like an uncoiling serpent, his eyes conveying a message. *Keep him busy.*

She hugged the satchel closer to her body and glared at Sean. "I don't think so."

Sean raised the Tokorav, held it casually across his chest, reminding her he had it. "I'm losing my patience with you, muffin. I understand the trauma you went through, really I do. But it was a long time ago. Your parents are long dead. And your sister—"

"Liberty is why I'm doing this. Someone is holding her for ransom. They want the machine in exchange for her life."

His eyes widened. "Liberty? Why didn't you tell me? We could have used Itor's resources to handle the situation." He held out his hand. "We still can, if you'll just give over that satchel."

"How stupid do you think I am? The weather station is destroyed. The machine along with it. Itor is going to blame you for letting it happen. Do you really think you'll be in a position to help me after this? You'll be lucky if you're assigned to a remote office in Siberia."

They wouldn't kill him; someone with his experience and level of ability was too valuable to kill. They would, however, make his life unpleasant.

"Give me the fucking motherboard!" he shouted. "I don't want to have to kill you. Don't make me, Faith."

He was at the end of his rope, the gun shaking in his hand. She'd never seen him so rattled. So unstable. Shit. He had a hair trigger on a good day, but now, like this...

Wyatt came to his feet, smoothly, silently, the aura around him shooting off sparks. A stapler came out of nowhere, slammed into the side of Sean's head. Sean rocked backward and grabbed his temple with one hand, even as he aimed at Wyatt with the other.

The gun flew out of Sean's hand. It discharged, and the dull thud of a bullet lodging in the ceiling sounded like a bullet hitting a body. A body that could have been Wyatt's.

From the pile of debris near the door, a computer arced into the air, catching Sean full-force in the chest.

Faith dove for the pistol as Wyatt lunged, his shoulder connecting with Sean's gut.

Sean and Wyatt slammed to the floor, crushing a rubbish bin and sending a chair crashing into Faith's thigh. Biting down on a curse, she raised the pistol before Wyatt could kill Sean.

"Stop! Both of you!" She unloaded two shots into the smashed weather machine, and the men froze mid-punch. Though Wyatt slipped in one more to Sean's jaw a heartbeat later.

Wyatt bared his teeth at Sean, a clear warning, but he stood, wiped his bloodied mouth with the back of his hand.

Sean shoved to his feet, shot Wyatt a triumphant sneer. "I knew you'd come around, muffin."

"Shut up." She hefted the satchel firmly over her shoulder and leveled the pistol at Sean's chest. Wyatt's expression turned cocky. "Here's the deal. You're going to provide safe passage, walk us to the helo. Then you're going to order the pilot to take us wherever we want to go."

"I can fly," Wyatt offered. "So go ahead and off him."

"You bitch," Sean snarled, and she knew he was gathering his power. "I'll drain Wyatt dead. You've got three seconds, *muffin*. Hand me the gun and the motherboard, or he dies."

Draining a human completely would leave Sean weak and vulnerable for hours, the reason he rarely did it. But this time, she knew he would. Then again, all around them equipment rose into the air, giant machines, shards of metal ... all aimed at Sean. He and Wyatt would end up killing each other.

"Fuck. You." She raised the pistol an inch, aiming directly at his heart.

"You won't kill me. You don't have it in you."

"I'm sorry, Sean." Her voice cracked, but her resolve didn't.

His eyes shot wide with realization and terror. She squeezed the trigger. He crumpled to the floor, but she wouldn't allow herself the chance to feel anything. Wyatt gave her a look she couldn't read, but like the professional he was, he didn't waste time asking her questions. Quickly, he tucked the pistol Sean had taken from him into his waistband and stripped the dead excedo of his Glock. Once he checked the ammo, he and Faith slipped out of the lab.

Slipped out, and in the evening shadows ran right into Marco.

Wyatt raised his weapon.

"No!" she snarled. "He's mine." He was going to pay for what he'd done to her in Paris, and what he'd intended to do to her before she'd found Wyatt in the Florida bar. Her throat throbbed beneath her choker, as if it sensed revenge.

Marco was fast, a blur when he fought, so fast she didn't feel his blows until the next one landed. She barely blocked half of them, and she certainly didn't have time to concentrate on finding a weak spot in his aura with her power.

Good thing she'd found it two days ago.

She was taking a brutal beating, could hear Wyatt in the background cursing. Finally, he couldn't take it anymore, made a sweep with one of his legs that cut Marco's out from under him.

The break gave her just enough time to punch through Marco's aura and focus all her hatred on him. Marco made a nasty, hissing sound and drew a dagger from his boot.

"I'm going to skin you alive, you English cunt." He grinned. "Finish the job I started in Paris—" He cut off with a gasp, his eyes bulging.

Rage poured from her in a wave of heat, which found its way to his vital organs, his bloodstream. His skin turned red, blistered, and he fell over, a victim of the world's worst fever.

"That's a scary power you have," Wyatt muttered, grabbing her hand. They ran, ducking behind equipment when they could.

The path to the helo was clear...Sean obviously hadn't had time to tell his goons that he'd found her and Wyatt in the lab. But as they neared the stairs to the helipad, all hell broke loose.

Guards at the base of the stairs shouted, started firing.

"Shit!" Wyatt took aim at the nearest guard as they ducked behind a steel container.

Return fire exploded in the air around them, the bullets pinging off the metal grating and thunking into the container.

"More guys will be coming." She peered down at the main deck, where workers were scrambling for cover. "We have to get to that helicopter before we're surrounded."

Wyatt nodded grimly. "Just keep firing. Distract them."

She did, keeping the half-dozen armed guards busy, hissing when a bullet grazed her arm. A mild abrasion. She'd live.

Wyatt went still, his gaze fixed on the activity below. Men with AKs swarmed, but their guns were ripped from their hands by an unseen force, sent spinning over the railing. A row of pipes on the lower deck began to rattle. Faith couldn't watch for long, her attention focused on the goons in front of them who still had weapons, but she gasped when a giant pipe shot upward. She watched in awe as it swung like a baseball bat, taking out every guard blocking their way.

"Brilliant," she breathed. "Absolutely brilliant!"

The pipe tipped over the far railing, plunging toward the ocean below. Wyatt grabbed her hand, led her at a run up the stairs.

A man burst from the helicopter, his MP5 trained on Wyatt. Before she could blink, Wyatt slammed her to the ground, rolled with her as rounds sparked on the deck all around them. Abruptly, the gunfire stopped. Mainly because the butt of the rifle was lodged in the guy's chest in a creative use of Wyatt's power. And he'd said *her* power was scary.

"Asshole," Wyatt muttered.

He grabbed Faith's hand again and pulled her to her feet. They hauled ass to the helo.

"Good show," she said.

"Save the praise until after we make it off this platform. We'll need a small miracle."

"I thought you said you could fly a helo!"

A bullet pinged off the door as he held it open to shove her inside. "This bird is a little more advanced than what I'm used to."

"You could have warned me."

"No fun in that," he said as he climbed into the cockpit. "This is way more exciting. Hold on."

The man was crazy. They settled into their seats. He started up the helicopter, the low drone of the engine sounding as beautiful as anything.

"Faster would be good." She pointed to the men running toward them on the outer catwalk. "They're almost here."

"I can see that."

The helicopter rose, the fluid sensation of catching air giving her a moment of relief. Until a shudder shook it, sent it crashing back down to the pad. The jolt nearly knocked her out of her seat.

"Fuck." Wyatt pulled back on the stick, and the bird lifted, shuddered again. "Someone's holding her down!"

Bullets smashed into the windshield, which, thankfully, was bullet-resistant. Tiny spiderwebbed cracks formed, but the glass held. For now. Faith scanned the area. One man, dressed in black coveralls, stood to the side, no weapons, concentrating on the helo.

Wyatt saw him at the same time. "Bingo."

Faith's blood pumped faster in anticipation. "I got it. You fly."

She opened herself up, feeling the seductive buzz of power, the rush that normal hand-to-hand combat never provided. The I-Agent's aura became visible, his protective shield flaring and waning the way it did when a person was using their own psychic power.

Heart beating wildly, veins shot full of adrenaline, she probed for a weak spot. Found it, near his abdomen. Instantly, she pierced his body, used her energy to wrap around his heart and squeeze.

His mouth fell open. He clutched his chest. The helo launched upward with a sharp spin that threw her into the side window.

"Shit. Sorry," Wyatt said. "Oh, hey, we're free!"

Bullets punched holes in the helo's skin, and the acrid scent of fuel filled the cabin.

"Fuckers." Wyatt flipped the guys below a middle-finger salute, then sent a cargo container smashing down on top of them. The gunfire stopped.

He smiled, and they were out of there.

Exhaling a long sigh of relief, Faith closed her eyes and sank back in her seat. Her adrenaline crash turned her into a noodle, and her hands shook so badly she had to dig her fingers into her legs.

"You okay?" Wyatt's voice, deep and soothing, rumbled through her, and she knew he wasn't asking about her health. Not her physical health anyway. She'd killed a man she'd known for almost twenty years. A man she'd loved.

A man who had turned irreversibly evil.

She could no longer deny that fact, and today had been a long time coming. She mourned for the boy Sean had been, but amazingly, she found that she couldn't regret what she'd done to the man he'd become.

She opened her eyes and studied Wyatt's rugged profile, his intelligent eyes, his talented mouth. He was tall, lean and sinewy, his very presence so commanding that he seemed larger than what the cockpit could hold. He was one of the good guys, one of the rare humans people called heroes.

And for now, he was hers.

"I'm okay," she said. "I'm really okay."

HALEY WATCHED the satellite loop one more time, hoping the result would be different. But no matter how many times she witnessed the hurricane spin across the screen, nothing changed.

The atmosphere in ACRO's weather station was a strange

blend of tension and excitement. Only meteorologists would get hard-ons about the destructive power of a hurricane.

Well, Remy did too, but that was different. He was, at that very moment, inside the observation tower, trying to force the cold front to advance in order to push the hurricane away from the coast. So far, his efforts had been in vain. The Bermuda High was too strong, effectively holding off the front no matter what Remy did.

"Haley?" Jeremy waved his hand in front of her face. "We have the latest projections."

She rubbed her eyes, exhausted and not wanting to look. When she finally did, she wished she hadn't.

Stomach aching and hands shaking, she silently went to her office, closed the door and dialed Dev.

"Give me good news, Haley," he said in his usual clipped, businesslike tone.

"I wish I could."

There was a long silence. "What's the situation?"

"Hurricane Lily hit bingo. She's self-sustaining."

"Which means she's a threat even without the weather machine."

"Exactly." She spread the projections across her desk. "Every forecast model, including those from the National Hurricane Center, are bringing Lily in somewhere between New Jersey and Connecticut."

"They can't be more specific?"

"*They* can't, but Dev, a strike anywhere in that zone will be devastating. Lily is a category five storm, and she's strengthening." She cleared her throat. "Since we know what was going on with the machine, we were able to make a more specific storm-track projection. I think Itor knew what they were doing. I'd stake my reputation on the fact that even without the weather machine's help, Lily is going to make a direct strike on New York City. We need to step up preparations, and we need to do it now."

CHAPTER
thirteen

Dev hated showing weakness or fear, refused to in front of anyone beyond a select group of psychics at ACRO, and to Oz, who
understood. Now that he was back from what the majority of the
ACRO agents and workers assumed was a vacation, he needed to
be in complete control, to reassure the staff that even though Itor
had allowed the hurricane to gain the upper hand, ACRO was
still going to win the war.

They had no choice—if New York City was destroyed, tens of
thousands could die, and the entire U.S. economy would suffer
for years, leaving the country vulnerable to any low-life terrorist
with a few million dollars and a burr up his ass. And if another
natural disaster followed on the heels of the first . . . Jesus. He just
prayed that Wyatt had destroyed the machine, because it was too
late for Lily, but Itor could follow up with more hurricanes, bliz-
zards, droughts.

Sick bastards.

And what the fuck had they done with Ryan? That still bothered Dev, gave him nightmares, since he was solely responsible
for compromising the undercover agent. Because ACRO had
been dealing with a mole, Dev had taken precautions to make

sure he alone knew about Ryan's insertion into Itor. When it turned out that Dev had been the unwitting mole, that Alek had been sifting through his mind, Ryan had been found out, and his unknown fate was something that would haunt Dev for the rest of his life.

"You're ready, Devlin. I know you are."

Dev looked up to see Oz standing in the doorway of his office. Oz had been his rock through so much of Dev's life—starting when Dev was just seventeen years old and still discovering that he was inherently bisexual. Oz had always been so sure of his own sexuality—everything about the man with the jet black hair and dark eyes screamed sex, especially the way his long, muscular body always seemed to be in motion.

"You saved my life," Dev said softly, felt as though he could say it over and over—and he had—and it would never be enough.

Oz closed the distance between them and hugged Dev, murmuring, "I did what you needed, Devlin. That's what I've always done, that's what I'll always do."

"And what about what you need?"

"That's all part of the same package."

"Darius is gone—right, Oz?" he remembered whispering to Oz right before Oz brought him to the psychics for the mind blocks.

"You're safe, Devlin. Now it's time for you to save the world again. You're ready."

Yes, Dev was ready. With Oz by his side, he could take on anything.

Wyatt made infinitesimal corrections on what he called the cyclic, and for the millionth time in the last ten minutes, Faith thanked God that he was a trained pilot. This was so much better than holding a gun to one of Sean's pilots.

"Where are we headed?" she asked as she stripped out of the orange jumpsuit that was a size too big for her.

"Florida. A buddy of mine will take us in."

She wadded up the jumpsuit and tossed it behind her seat. "And this buddy . . . you trust him?"

"Mostly."

Mostly. Perfect. Maybe dealing with Sean's pilot and leaving Wyatt behind would have been easier. Not that she could have done that. Faith gazed out the side window at the rough ocean, the cloudy skies, reminders that Itor's weather machine might have been destroyed, but the damage had already been done. The hurricane they'd nurtured could yet strike a blow.

Wyatt glanced at his gauges. "So why was Sean surprised to hear your sister was alive?"

Faith turned to him, her first instinct to lie. But after all Wyatt had done for her, and after all he'd continue to do for her as she dealt with whoever had taken Liberty, she owed him.

"My parents sent Liberty away when she was five. They were afraid of her."

"Afraid of her why?"

God, she hated talking about this. "My biokinesis didn't develop until I was eight, but Liberty was born with it." Hazy images filled her head, of Liberty healing their cat after it had been struck by a car, of Liberty sealing the cut on Faith's skinned knee, of Liberty choking a man who had abducted Faith out of their yard and tried to drag her into his car. "She couldn't control it, and . . ."

"She hurt people."

"Yes. She didn't hurt anyone who didn't deserve it, but the fact that she *could* . . . it scared people." Her heart thundered in her chest as she remembered the day she heard the knock on the door, so clear amongst the fuzzier memories. "Some strange men came for her one day—now I know they were from a psychiatric hospital." Faith felt more than saw the tension that made Wyatt's body go taut, but he quickly relaxed, did something with the foot pedals.

"And?"

"And I never saw her again. I searched, but the trail went cold several years ago."

"Until the ransom call." He flipped a series of switches on the control panel. "What about your parents? Sean said they were dead."

"Yeah." She gripped the satchel containing the motherboard and Mr. Wiggums to her chest. Both represented family—the ratty stuffed rabbit was all she had left of her family, and the motherboard . . . well, now that it was out of Itor's hands, it couldn't be used as a weapon to kill other families.

Wyatt reached across the space between them and took her hand, prying it away from the leather case. "You don't have to talk about it."

"It's okay," she said, even though she wasn't sure it *was* okay. She'd worshipped her parents, her dad especially, who had played with her endlessly, filling a void left by Liberty's absence. "I was eight. England was hit by the Great October Storm." She remembered the roar of the wind, the crash of thunder, the sounds of metal groaning and glass breaking. "My mum, she went after an elderly neighbor who had gone outside to find her pup. My dad ran to help, and as they were coming inside . . ." She drew in a long, calming breath, surprised that the old memory still had so much power. "The side of our house collapsed. Right on top of them. I heard my dad shout at me to stay back, and my mum cried out my name . . ." She paused before saying, "It's the last time I heard their voices."

Wyatt's thumb made long, soothing passes over the skin of her hand. It amazed her that a man who had cut through enemies like butter with such cold, brutal efficiency could be so tender and caring. It also amazed her that she'd opened up to him in a way she'd never done to anyone else. Not Paula, or even Sean.

"What happened to you?" he asked softly.

She shrugged, because mercifully much of what happened next was a blur. She'd run out into the storm, calling for help, then watching as her parents' mangled bodies were dug out of the rubble. She'd screamed until she lost her voice, had tried to use her powers to bring them back to life, but her parents were far beyond help.

"I wandered around for days, healing injured people and animals where I could. That's when the men who took my sister came for me."

Faith had asked later how they'd known about her skills, and the truth was that they hadn't. When SIS learned about her parents' deaths, they'd seized the opportunity to snatch Faith in hopes that any potential powers could be developed.

"They took you to a mental hospital?" Wyatt's voice sounded a little strained, and his thumb froze mid-stroke.

"Only for a few days. It was the same one Liberty had been taken to, but I didn't know that at the time. I learned later that she'd been kidnapped a few months before."

After an assessment at the mental facility, Faith had been moved to a private school where other kids like her were being raised. She'd still been in shock, and it had taken weeks before she could function in a school setting. Her parents had been everything to her, and without them and her sister, she'd been a lost soul for months. It had taken even longer for her to recover from her fear of storms. The sound of thunder would send her scrambling beneath the nearest bed, desk or table, where she'd cower, crying and trembling, until it was over. The pain of that time still wrenched her gut when she thought about it, and dammit, if she could prevent someone else from going through that kind of pain, no matter her own personal cost, she would.

She covered Wyatt's hand with her other one, letting the satchel slide to the floor. "I really don't want to talk about this. And shouldn't you be flying this thing?"

"That's the wonder of autopilot, babe. This bird is amazing. Itor must have stolen an autopilot patent and had this beauty custom-built. I still have to keep my feet on the pedals, but so far so good. Look, Ma, no hands."

God, he was cocky, sitting there like every day he wiped the deck with bad guys, saved the world and won the girl. Of course, as an ACRO agent, he probably did do those things on a regular basis.

How many other women had he seduced over the course of a mission? The guy was definitely an American version of James Bond. Jealousy flared once again in a rush that made her heart ache. She crushed the emotion ruthlessly, because although she couldn't deny that she was starting to feel something for him, she would not allow her feelings to expand any further.

Except, how did one stop a rolling tide?

With a weather machine, maybe, she thought wryly.

"Tell me," she said, "why did ACRO want you to destroy the machine? Why not keep it, use it themselves? Your agency could protect America's coastlines, save lives, property..."

"It's too dangerous, Faith. The temptation to destroy an enemy with it would be too great."

"Not in the right hands."

"You can't know that. Collateral damage could be catastrophic. And just by having the thing, you'd invite enemies to try to steal it. You'd always be worried about someone on the inside betraying you for power or money."

Not anyone on *her* inside. She trusted her people completely. "I'd think the benefits would outweigh the risks."

"Doesn't matter. It's not my call." His gaze, sharp and intelligent, also revealed utter resolve, and it struck her that he really wouldn't consider using the machine for his own purposes, no matter how noble.

"You always follow orders?"

"ACRO has never let me down."

ACRO was lucky to have him, and she experienced a spark of resentment that TAG had missed out. "Your loyalty is admirable."

"So is yours. If misplaced."

"You're talking about Sean."

He rolled his shoulders as though Sean's very name made his muscles tense. "Christ, Faith. What did you see in that guy?"

"He wasn't always like that." She paused, waited for him to look at her. "After the mental hospital, I was taken to a very small, very secret boarding school."

"Run by who?"

She hesitated, but hell, she'd already said enough. "A well-known intelligence agency."

"So basically, you were raised to be an agent?" He looked at her for a long moment, as though taking her measure. "We've got an operative with a similar background." That didn't sound like a good thing, but he didn't dwell on the subject. "I'm assuming Sean grew up in the same school?"

"He arrived a couple of months after I did. We became great friends, were inseparable for years. But eventually, his gift became too much for him. He grew angry, power-mad. But I always believed he could overcome his bitterness and need for control."

"He really played you, didn't he?"

"It wasn't like that."

When Wyatt shook his head, like he still didn't get it, she huffed and stood, intent upon taking a seat in the rear of the helicopter so she wouldn't have to answer any more questions. "I don't need to explain anything to you. I'm going to see if I can catch a nap."

He caught her elbow, and suddenly she found herself sitting in his lap. "No running away."

"How dare you?" She shoved at his shoulders, but his grip tightened and he tugged her closer.

"Be careful," he murmured into her ear. "One little bump to the wrong control, and we end up in the ocean. But if you want to rock your hips a little, that would be okay."

"You're so ... so ..."

"Insufferable?"

"Yes!"

Grinning, he gripped her waist and helped her out with that rocking thing he'd mentioned. He was aroused. Shockingly aroused. The rhythmic pulses of the helicopter engine made their contact vibrate, made him grow even harder. "We have a few minutes to waste."

She cocked an eyebrow at him. "You want to go at it now? Right here?"

"The shocked act won't fly with me." He kept one eye on the

view in front of them and said, "You fucked me in a boiler room while security guys were hunting us, remember?"

"Perhaps danger turns me on."

"You're a secret agent. It's supposed to." His hand slid up to cup her breast through her cotton and lace top, and her nipples tightened in response. "But what about helicopters? Do they turn you on? Ever done it in one?"

"No . . . You?"

He opened his mouth over her bare shoulder, bit down lightly. "Never."

"Why don't I believe you?"

Taking her shoulder strap in his teeth, he dragged it down her arm. "Because you're trained to think everything anyone says is a lie?" His tongue made a warm, wet stroke along her collarbone.

"That could be . . . mmm, yes, right there . . . the reason." God, she was falling for his seduction skills again. No, she didn't feel light-headed and out of control, but with Wyatt, all it took was a look, a touch, a lick, and she was instantly reduced to a quivering mass of lust.

"As much as I love to remove a woman's bra, I love more that you don't wear one."

"Never have," she moaned, not wanting to think about him removing any other woman's clothing.

His hand smoothed down her belly to her thigh, and she felt herself spreading her legs in invitation. In fact, when he slipped his hand beneath her skirt, she arched against him, seeking his touch where she needed it. His other hand came up to cup the back of her head, and he pulled her down until her mouth brushed his.

"We haven't had enough time to explore each other," he murmured against her lips. "We're going to do that soon." His fingers tunneled inside her panties and found her center. "But right now, I'm going to make you scream my name."

"Cocky bast—"

He cut her off with a kiss, took her mouth like he was on a

mission. And she supposed he was, if the way he stroked her core with his fingers was any kind of clue. When he penetrated her, she cried out. He caught the sound with his mouth, inhaled it like a drowning man taking his first lifesaving breath.

"Oh, yeah." His mouth curved against hers. "I love how you respond to me."

"I hate it." Her head lolled back as he began a seductive rhythm with his finger. "I hate how you affect me."

He kissed her exposed throat, his breath a warm caress on her ultrasensitized skin. "You'll learn to love it. Crave it. Beg for it."

So arrogant. And so right. She could see herself growing addicted to him. "You're making a lot of assumptions."

His thumb made a slow circle around her clit, and she nearly gasped. "I'm stating fact."

She'd have argued, but he pinched her swollen nub between his fingers and began to roll it between them, gently, slowly, and God, she was going to come exactly the way he said, screaming his name.

You'll learn to love it. Crave it. Beg for it.

No, she wouldn't. They wouldn't be together long enough for that. She wouldn't be screaming his name or begging or any such thing, dammit.

"Stop," she moaned, and then more forcefully said, *"Stop."* She squirmed away from him, nearly falling out of his lap.

"What are you doing?"

"Nothing. I just... I need air."

I need to not fall for him.

She'd had lots of sex on assignments, most of it no more personal than the relationship between a waiter and a customer, and she regretted none of it. She'd completed her missions—if not successfully, then alive.

The key to mission sex was to stay detached. But she was having a hard time with the detachment thing when it came to Wyatt.

Frantic, she scrambled to a seat in the rear of the chopper, ignoring Wyatt's demands for her to go back.

"Faith, dammit. I can't leave the cockpit. What are you doing?" He was peeking around the partial divider between the passenger section and the cockpit. She just stared at him.

Wyatt's expression grew determined, and he shot out of his seat. The helicopter banked to the right and pitched forward. Wyatt seemed to have no trouble moving toward her despite the rolling and rocking.

"What are you doing?" she yelled. "Get back there!"

"Not without you." His arms came around her, and with effortless grace, he picked her up and carried her back to the cockpit. He planted her in the copilot seat, sat in his, and straightened out the helicopter.

"You're a fucking nutter," she breathed. "What happened to the damned autopilot?"

"It only stabilizes altitude and speed as long as you're still working the cyclic and pedals."

"Jesus effing Christ."

"Come over here and let me finish what I started."

Her adrenaline was running hot, the scare making her shake, only ramping up her sex drive. She longed for him to finish, but nothing had changed. He wanted more than what she was willing to give.

"What's wrong, Faith?"

"You. Us. This is just mission sex, yeah? Nothing but danger-induced fits of lust and madness."

"Yeah, this is danger-induced fits of lust and madness, because I am crazy, Faith—make no mistake about that. But this"—he motioned between them—"is a hell of a lot more than just lust and madness. So you can keep protesting all you want, baby... and I'll keep doing exactly what I'm doing. Now get over here."

They stared at each other like rival tomcats, neither willing to give an inch. A mischievous glint lit Wyatt's eye. One corner of his mouth twitched. She knew she was in trouble, and damn him, he released the cyclic. The bird banked sharply, throwing her backward.

"Stop it!"

"Wanna play chicken, Faith?"

God, if he'd chosen any other place and time, she'd have taken him up on it. But she couldn't fly the fucking helicopter, so her bluff wouldn't go far. She could, however, turn the tables.

"Fine," she snapped. "Grab the fucking stick!"

Smiling that cocky smile of his, he leveled them out again. She crossed the span between them, but she didn't sit in his lap. She kneeled on the floor, unzipped his jumpsuit and jeans, and released his hard cock before he could so much as blink.

"What are you up to?" he asked, suspicion and desire making his voice lower into a deep rasp.

"Did you really think I'd give in completely?" She ran her hand up his thigh, which flexed beneath her palm as he made tiny adjustments to the pedals. "I'm not as easy as that."

"I've never had a problem with easy . . . ah, yeah . . ." He trailed off when she closed her hand around his erection, the hot length flushing dusky crimson from the ring of her fingers to the tip of the head. "You've got magic hands, Faith."

"You haven't seen anything yet." Gathering her power, she let his aura come into focus. She'd seen it before, but she was still shocked by how it was so tattered, threadbare.

She cleared her thoughts, probed one of the many weak spots, and penetrated with her power. She kept stroking with her hand, and when she found his prostate with her mind, she stroked that too.

Wyatt nearly came out of his seat. "Holy fuck." He gasped, swallowed, gasped again. "Stop. That."

Leaning in, she dipped her tongue into the weeping slit at the top of his penis. "Stop what?"

"You know." He was panting now, his knuckles white around the cyclic. "Shit, I'm going to pop . . ."

She pulled back her power, using it to squeeze gently instead of stroke. A low groan from deep in his chest told her how much he liked it.

Another groan, a bit strangled, vibrated his body when she took him in her mouth. He was hot, hard, tasted of man, sweat, battle. It was such a turn-on that she slipped her hand under her skirt, her panties, and began to stroke herself as she sucked on Wyatt.

His hips began to rock upward, meeting her deep-throated swallows. Pre-cum flavored his cap as she swirled her tongue around it on each upward suck. Still, she kept up the mental stimulation of his prostate, sometimes sliding to his balls and back.

Between her legs, she was dripping with arousal, swollen to the point of pain. Her fingers worked furiously, alternately circling her clit and penetrating her slippery core.

One of Wyatt's hands came down on her head, tangled in her hair. She smiled around his shaft, let him pump into her mouth, his grip in her hair tightening as his breathing came faster.

Under her knees, the helicopter thumped, vibrated, rocked. "You're not going to crash us, are you?" she asked against the head of his cock.

He moaned. "And ruin the best blow job ever? Not. Fucking. Likely."

She closed her hand around the base of his shaft, squeezed as she drew it up to where her lips made a seal around the smooth ridge of his head. Applying strong suction, she flicked her tongue and fisted him with hard, firm strokes. At the same time, she thumbed her clit, fucked herself with her fingers.

Trembling with the desire to come, she let it happen, cried out around his cock. Her release sent him over the edge, his hips bucking, his hot seed filling her mouth. She took it all, sucking until he began to jerk and his thighs quivered.

"Land," he rasped, as she ran her tongue from his crown to his balls, catching the last of the juices they'd made.

"What?"

"I have to fly."

Smiling, she tucked him back into his jeans and climbed into her seat. "Who won, do you think?"

He wiped his brow, his breath still coming faster than he probably liked. "Won?"

"Chicken."

His dark, heavy-lidded gaze made her breath catch. "I'll give you that one. But once we're alone with a real bed? You're mine."

CHAPTER
Fourteen

It took Wyatt a few minutes before he could actually see straight again, the orgasm from the blow job making his legs tremble slightly and his entire body throb and shiver.

Yes, that was one battle he'd gladly concede to Faith, over and over again.

She wore a sexy, smug smile, as he was hit with the realization that Faith was maybe the first woman in his life who didn't bring out his love jones every single time.

"You do know this heli has GPS tracking." Her voice broke into his thoughts sharply.

"I know. No way to disable it without taking the whole bird down."

"So you're taking it down, then?"

"Yeah. Can you handle that, Faith?"

"Anything you can do, I can do."

"Oh, we're still playing chicken. That's good. I've got some ground to make up."

The helo was a full-body machine when it wasn't on autopilot, and he worked it the way he'd learned years earlier, mainly through self-teaching. Taking a chance at hovering the helo over the water while they jumped out was better than risking a crash landing.

Faith could handle this. "We're going to have to dump her at a klick in about five minutes." That would put them about one thousand meters from the shoreline—not a bad swim, but they'd use the raft. They couldn't afford any rescue attempts from the wrong people.

"Won't the crash attract a lot of attention?" she asked.

"It shouldn't. But we don't have much choice—I'm counting on the fact that the average person can see maybe six miles of detail when looking at the horizon of the ocean. With darkness and low clouds compromising visibility, much less."

Faith peered out the window into the fading evening light. "I like to swim as much as the next agent—"

"The jump will really get the blood pumping."

She cast him a doubtful look, and yeah, it wasn't going to be pretty—the seas were ten-foot swells, which would be rough as shit on her. But then again, the entire atmosphere was in an uproar. Keeping the helo level was becoming a real bitch, even with the autopilot, and it was ruining his afterglow.

Having Itor come after them now would ruin it much, much more.

"And what will we do as the heli banks and nose-dives, the way it did before?" she asked.

He tapped the side of his head. "Under control, Faith. It's all under control. Grab the bag with the raft—it's somewhere. But don't inflate it in the cabin."

"I know when, where and how to inflate, Wyatt. I thought I made that perfectly clear."

He watched her get up from the seat, the soft leather skirt molding her curves. "Lose the boots."

"I know that!" she called over her shoulder.

"And grab two life vests," he said, and smiled when she grumbled and cursed him behind his back even as the wind picked up, tossing the bird from side to side. Fucking amazing that any of these motherfucking metal hunks of shit stayed in the air to begin with.

She brought his vest to him. He continued to work the pedals as he stripped out of his coveralls and then put the vest on.

"I'm ready. Shall I open the ramp?"

"Give me a second." He grabbed the cell from his pocket and shot a quick text message as his feet continued to keep the helo steady. He got the return confirmation within seconds. "Rock on, man."

"Everything all right?"

"Never better. It's game on." He noted that she'd tucked the main part of the bag that held the motherboard under her life vest. "When I say go, put the ramp down and throw the raft."

The raft would inflate when it hit the water, and they'd have to go within seconds of its launch to prevent it from getting too far behind them. He could pull it back with his mind, but he'd still be trying to prevent the helo from crashing around their heads, and while multitasking was something he did well, that might prove too much of a stretch.

She nodded. "Are we going to clear this?"

"She's got forward motion—that's all we need."

"It's going to be close."

"Close calls are the best kind. Make you appreciate living that much more. When we unass this bitch—"

"Elbows to sides, tuck the chin, fists to face. Knees and feet together tightly," she said with a small, satisfied smile—and oh, yeah, he wasn't going to be able to wait for a bed.

"Yeah, see, I was going to say to jump into the crest of the wave so you don't fall into the trough and break your legs. Because that would suck."

She rolled her eyes and went to the back of the helo. When he heard the ramp go down, he was ready. "Throw it now, baby," he called, took his feet off the pedals and mentally kept the bird steady as he walked quickly toward her.

She waited confidently by the open door, hair blowing wildly, the leather skirt with the high slit up the back looking fucking amazing, and out of place.

She was excited about the jump.

He grabbed her hand as he stood at the ramp with her, and yelled, "Don't let go, Faith. No matter what, you hold on tight."

She nodded, and they jumped down the fifteen feet into the water—ten-foot seas, at least, and for him, not a bad swim at all. SEALs would call this a good night.

The waves pushed and pulled at them, attempted to wrench them apart—but neither one let go, held fast until they both resurfaced, the life vests pulling them up rapidly.

He had no doubt Faith could handle herself out here, but they needed speed to get away from the helo. He stared at the orange raft bouncing in the waves in front of them and willed it to close the distance between them, using his gift. As the raft responded by hurtling toward them, Wyatt turned Faith's body, her back to his chest, and did a side swim with her to meet the oncoming raft, despite her protests that *she could bloody swim, dammit*.

"Get in," he yelled over the rushing roar, pushed her into the orange raft and then dragged himself in next to her.

"Why didn't you let me swim?"

"Because I didn't want to let go of you," he said as he began to push the raft with his mind, because, fuck, the farther away from the crash site, the better. And that Chelbi was going down fast now that he'd taken his mind off it, let it bank, and bam—it hit the surface with a force that made the water surge, pushed the raft forward with a sickening intensity that nearly toppled them into the ocean.

He pushed Faith to the floor of the raft, covered her body with his and concentrated on moving the raft as rapidly as he could away from the fast-sinking helo and the parts that ripped off it on impact with the water.

The water temp wasn't bad, but with the wind, they were both chilled, and nestling into her made him so damned warm.

She peered over his shoulder to stare at the explosion that lit the night sky. Even though they were both in shape, both breathed fast from the rush of danger.

"You all right?" he yelled over the sounds of the ocean.

"Never better."

"Good." He sat back and helped her to sit up in the raft. He ran his hands through his hair, slicked the wet strands away from his face and took a deep breath. They were almost there—but they certainly weren't done, not with this mission or with each other.

"Is that shore?" she asked, squinting into the darkness.

"Yeah, we're all right—the current is on our side," he said.

She nodded, fixed the bag that had remained wrapped around her, the strap crossed at a diagonal between her breasts under the life vest.

He could easily take that bag from her—could've taken it at any point during the jump or right afterward, destroyed it and left Faith to her own devices. Could've left her the raft and swum in himself after smashing the motherboard beyond recognition, and for a second earlier, when they'd first gotten into the raft, he'd almost used his mind to rip the bag from her body and throw it into the ocean.

But he didn't. And it wasn't because sex was the only thing on his mind—far from it.

"We can walk the rest of the way in," he said, dumped himself over the side to test the depth and helped her into the water. She looked at him as if she wanted to ignore his hand, his help, but she didn't.

He pulled the KA-BAR that he'd strapped to his arm earlier out of habit—a habit that would probably never die—and slashed the sides of the raft so it would deflate and float along with the rest of the debris. Better Itor think them dead, even though they'd never stop hunting for him, or for Faith.

He followed her out of the water, watched as she stripped off the life vest and threw it next to her so that it would also float back into the ocean.

As a free agent, she was far more vulnerable than he was, but he wasn't about to let anything happen to her. Not until he could convince her that their connection was much more than just their mutual interest in the weather machine. Not until he could break through the fear that had held her back on the helo.

The beach was deserted and there was no sign of the man he'd called yet. Still, they were in the right place, coordinate-wise, so he'd give the guy a few more minutes.

"What are we waiting for?" she demanded.

"We're getting a ride—he'll be here soon."

"So we're just going to stand around on the beach, vulnerable and exposed?" She stared him down angrily and he shook his head and thought about how fucked-up it was that someone with her abilities could ever feel vulnerable and exposed.

Although he felt the same way around her—and it had nothing to do with the freakin' motherboard. "We'll be fine, Faith. My friend will give us a ride to wherever we need to go to make the exchange for your sister. We'll have room and board for the night. Just hang on—"

"Don't tell me what to do, Wyatt. You've been micro-managing me ever since we got on the Chelbi."

"Right, I forgot, you're big, bad spy girl, ready to take on the world all by yourself at a moment's notice."

"We're going to find someplace to stay tonight that I choose," she said, standing directly in front of him, arms crossed, and he could see her eyes blazing in the moonlight.

"I didn't realize we were still playing chicken," he said. "Didn't realize this was going to be an ongoing theme in our relationship."

Yeah, she was panicking, tugging on the damned choker the way she had back on the helo. Probably more so now that she'd done exactly what she'd told him she wasn't going to do. She'd flipped out when he'd told her he wanted her to crave him, and she'd done so on that helo.

Hell, they were both in the same position—he'd just been a little better about not showing it.

"You play chicken all the time—with yourself. You take chances," she shot back. "Sometimes, you take stupid chances that you don't have to take."

He nodded. "Yeah, more than sometimes."

"Why? Talk to me, Wyatt. Please." She paused. "I've seen your aura. It's full of holes, and it only looks like that when someone's not well—and I know for a fact that you're fine physically. So it's got to be... well, I tried to heal you, but..."

"Don't bother," he said shortly.

"It's not a bother." Her voice was soft, her touch to his shoulder more so.

"Let's just say that I understand your family situation. I know you might think that I'm not ruthless enough—that any other agent wouldn't give a shit what your sob story is."

She raised an eyebrow, but let him continue.

"I get it, Faith. I get the family thing. The guilt." He shook his head, hard enough to make it spin, wished the fucking memory would fall out rather than rattling like a loose spring. "But you never let the bad guys win, even if it means the biggest personal sacrifice you can think of. That's what being a good agent is all about."

"I understand that, Wyatt. But I'll do whatever it takes to get Liberty. You have no idea what it must've been like for her, in that institution—"

"I have every idea," he heard himself roar. She took a step back from him, stumbled a little in the sand, and he fought for control. When he spoke again, his voice was lower. "I was committed too—for a nice, long spell when I was in my teens."

"You spent time in a funny farm?"

"That's right, baby. I told you, every time you called me crazy, that you were right. Certifiably right."

"Shit—behind you," she said, reaching for the weapon he knew she'd tucked into her bag, but Wyatt put a hand on her arm and pushed it down.

"He's here for us," he told her, turning to see the man known to just about everyone merely as ML. ML wore his trademark, awful Hawaiian shirt, bathing trunks—a tall, tropical-looking drink in his hand. "Hey, ML, whassup?"

"I could've picked you up in the water."

"I had other plans."

"Like coming back from the dead?"

Wyatt shook his head. He pushed his wet hair away from his face. "I'm still buried."

"Hot date for a dead man." ML lifted his drink in a toast to Faith. "Come on, let's get you two back to the house and into some dry clothes, before we all get arrested."

"Nothing to arrest us for, man," Wyatt said, and ML just laughed and said, *"Bullshit"* into the wind.

CHAPTER
Fifteen

Annika couldn't remember the last time she'd been so exhausted. Dev had ordered all available ACRO personnel to participate in hurricane preparations now that Lily appeared to be heading their way.

The base was far enough inland that storm surge wasn't a concern, but a category five hurricane could pack destructive winds inland for hundreds of miles. Dev wanted the base and the nearby town to be as prepared as possible, and he wanted everyone on standby to assist in search-and-rescue and hurricane recovery.

Haley had stressed that no matter where the hurricane struck the eastern seaboard, they were going to be dealing with Katrina-like devastation—in a best-case scenario. A direct New York City strike would not only be ten times worse, but could set the entire U.S. economy back twenty years.

After hours of shoring up shelters and prepping staging areas, Annika was ready to fall into bed with Creed, and for the first time, not for sex. Unfortunately, she still had a night martial arts class to teach. Dev had insisted that the new recruits' schedules not be altered if possible.

"You hungry?" Creed looked at her from the driver's side of

her Jeep, where she sat in the passenger seat. He claimed he liked to drive, but she had a feeling that her wild antics behind the wheel made him nervous no matter how many times she explained that she'd taken hours upon hours of stunt- and evasive-driving instruction.

"Starving. You cooking?"

He pulled into the driveway of his two-story hilltop house. "If you don't mind spaghetti, with sauce out of a jar."

"I can deal with that."

Twenty minutes later, they were at the dining room table eating spaghetti and sharing a bottle of red wine. She loved coming to his place, which, though sparsely decorated, was large and homey. She lived in remodeled barracks on base, and since she was rarely there, her place had about as much charm as a prison cell.

"What did you get stuck doing today?" she asked, as she sprinkled Parmesan cheese on her pile of noodles.

He took a swig of his wine. "Since we're expecting significant casualties, my department began preparations for soul recovery."

"Which is?"

"When a lot of people die suddenly, especially in major disasters, souls are lost. They need help crossing over."

"Isn't that something that can wait until the survivors are taken care of?"

He eyed her from across the table, the intensity in his expression sending shivers of appreciation over the surface of her skin. He was so sexy when he talked shop. "Our bodies are just shells. The true essence of any human or animal is the soul, so caring for the spirit is priority. Where we're really alive is on the Other Side, not here on earth. If the lost souls aren't helped quickly to cross over, they grow even more confused."

"What else?"

Creed reached for his fork. "What do you mean what else?"

"I'm sure that saving souls is important," she answered, as she wiped sauce off her mouth with a napkin, "but I get the feeling there's more."

He nodded, his dark eyes sparking with excitement, and she realized she'd never truly understood how much he loved his job. "Prophets, psychic scholars, heck, even ancient civilizations have predicted an apocalyptic event in our near future, as well as an impending period of darkness. No one can agree if these events are one and the same, but what they can agree on is that some sort of disaster will result in an overflow of souls for evil to seduce. There will be a war of souls."

"What, like ghosts fighting against the living?" The very idea creeped her out. She could handle anyone or anything in a tangible, physical form, but facing a foe she couldn't see tapped into her feelings of frustration and helplessness, something she already experienced too much of when she was forced to deal with Kat.

"Pretty much. One of the goals of the Medium department is to prevent something like that from happening. It's why we're always dispatched to large-scale natural and man-made disasters."

The phone rang, and Creed answered in the other room, leaving Annika to ponder what he'd said. She remembered Dev saying that ACRO scientists had been trying to explain the surge of people born with special abilities, and that it might be tied to the apocalyptic event Creed had mentioned. The creepy period of darkness, though . . . that was new. But again, Dev had also said that there were more mediums in existence today than at any time in history, so obviously, something was up.

"Sorry," Creed said, and she was grateful for the interruption from her disturbing thoughts. "It was my mom."

"Your mom?" She couldn't keep the surprise out of her voice. Parents were not a hot commodity at ACRO. Many agents had none—those who had parents, they were of the soul-suckingly horrible variety. Dev had once mentioned that Creed was adopted, and she'd assumed his parents were either dead or out of the picture.

"Do you have a father too?"

He must have taken for granted that she knew his story—his whole deal. Clearly, he'd forgotten that, as of just a year earlier, if it didn't concern her, she didn't give a shit. "Yep."

Wow. "So . . . are they normal?"

He laughed. "They didn't raise me in a cage or abuse me, if that's what you mean. They were typical, all-American folks who just happen to see ghosts. We had barbecues and went to church and had big, happy family holidays."

Creed twirled some noodles on his fork and grinned. "When Mom and Dad weren't out hunting ghosts, she was Ms. Domestic. She worked in the garden, sewed, cooked her heart out. Man, she put out great spreads. Sundays were the best. She'd make a huge dessert, and Dad and I would fight over who got the first piece."

Annika couldn't help but wonder what growing up with them would have been like. The warmth she felt from Creed as he talked about his parents . . . it was something Annika couldn't quite wrap her mind around. She bet they baked cookies and colored Easter eggs and went trick-or-treating, all as a family. Annika hadn't even been allowed to go to CIA holiday functions, for fear she'd shock another kid.

She shoved the thought aside because she was a grown-up and who cared about coloring Easter eggs anyway, and sipped her wine. "You told me you were adopted."

"I was, in a way." Creed put down his fork. "They found me in a cave. Abandoned as a newborn."

"Oh, my God." She fumbled her fork, nearly dropped it. "Who would do that?"

"We never knew. But we suspected why. The tats," Creed said, drained his wine and poured more. Annika resisted the urge to reach out and stroke the symbols on his face, the way she did at night sometimes, when he slept and she just wanted to feel closer to him. She knew he'd been born with them, but he'd never explained. Then again, she'd never asked.

"My mom and dad were investigating the cave the Bell Witch was said to haunt. People had been claiming they heard wild talking, singing and moaning coming from the cave, but that particular morning they also heard a baby crying. My mom and dad went into the cave when no one else would, and found me there."

"And they just kept you?"

He shrugged. "Yeah. I guess they'd been trying to have kids for years but couldn't, so they said I was a gift."

Chewing slowly, Annika let Creed's words sink in. His parents had taken home some strange kid and raised him? How could they have loved him? He wasn't theirs. Annika's CIA parents hadn't loved her, not even a little, and she'd always assumed it was because she wasn't their natural child. Well, that and they had a job to do at all costs, and a lack of emotional ties was part of the price.

In fact, when the CIA had moved Annika, at the age of thirteen, to a dormlike facility to live under strict, military-like supervision, her "parents" had barely blinked. They'd been happy to be done with the ruse, the fake marriage and fake family. Annika had long suspected that Patricia and Joseph White weren't her parents, but all doubt had been blown away that day. It had taken nearly three more years to learn the whole truth, and when she had, the rampage had been bloody.

Patricia and Joseph had not been spared.

Martha and Dave had found a strange, tattooed kid in a cave and had loved him, so how could Patricia and Joseph not have felt even a small measure of affection for her? And why did it suddenly bother her now when it never had before?

"When did they discover your ties to Kat?"

"Right away, I guess. They're both mediums, so they knew instantly that Kat was protecting me."

Annika knew there was a difference between a normal medium, who could sense and communicate with spirits and ghosts, and what Creed did, which was to communicate with ghosts through Kat, who was, herself, a ghost.

"So . . . growing up—with the tattoos and the spirits—did you go to regular school?" she asked, suddenly needing to know everything about the man who set her world right.

Creed finished the last of his wine. "Mostly I was home-schooled."

"Mostly?"

"Sometimes I'd get a bug up my ass to go to school and be with other kids, and my parents always let me, but it didn't last long."

"The markings?"

He nodded. "Teachers, other kids...they didn't understand. No one believed I was born with them, and a teacher went so far as to report my parents for abuse, thinking they'd forced me to be tattooed."

Annika reached beneath the table and gave his knee a squeeze. When she was very young, she'd craved contact with other children, so in a way, she understood what he'd gone through. "I'm so sorry, baby."

"It's nothing compared to what you went through."

"Maybe not, but at least no one ever made fun of me." She was lucky to not have gone through that pain. And those who had messed with her in other ways—for any reason—had paid dearly.

"No, you went through worse. You were only two when the CIA took you from your mother and left you in the care of people who raised you like a prized pit bull instead of a daughter."

Everyone at ACRO knew she had been raised to be a weapon for the CIA, but only Dev—and now Creed—knew the fine details. She'd only last night shared how she'd made her first kill at twelve, and how, until she came to ACRO, the only thing she knew how to do was kill.

And here he'd been raised by gentle, loving parents to be a gentle, loving adult. Despite his hard appearance, he was a giant teddy bear, all soft and squishy. She was about as opposite as she could be. What had someone called her once? Robobitch?

"Ancient history," she said with a dismissive wave.

"Why the Q and A anyway?"

She played with a single noodle, using a finger to push it around the plate.

"Tell me," he urged.

She sighed. "I guess finding out your parents are still alive made me realize how little I know you."

"You know me better than anyone ever has, Annika."

"Maybe I know who you are now, but I don't know about your past. I've been too selfish to ask or even care until now. God, I'm such a shit." She couldn't even look at him, she was so ashamed.

"If you weren't, you wouldn't be the Annika I fell in—"

Her breath froze. Then she felt the harsh rise and fall of her chest as her lungs tried to catch up. "Fell in what?" she asked softly.

He winced, and she wondered if Kat had done something to him. "Bed. If you weren't so tough, you wouldn't be the Annika I fell into bed with at Dev's mansion."

"Right," she snapped, disappointed at the lameness of his I-fell-into-bed crap, when he should have said he loved her. "Bed. That's what it's always about, isn't it? Bed or Dev."

Panic squeezed her chest, because what the hell? Love? Was she really ready for that? Creed was looking at her like she'd grown another head, and she knew she was all over the place with her emotions.

"Annika," he said tiredly, "you're the one who always makes it about sex. As for Dev—"

"Let's not go there." She squeezed his knee again, gently. "Not tonight. I'm exhausted and I still have a martial arts class to teach."

"For the record, I know you're trying."

She smiled. "For the record, I don't have to try that hard."

THE OLD GUARD at ACRO called Oz a rogue, a gypsy, a charlatan. Oz was fine with the first two labels, resented the last one because he'd never deceived anyone who didn't want to be deceived.

They were worried about Devlin—he got that. But they never did realize that Oz would be the last person ever to hurt Dev.

A then seventeen-year-old Devlin had walked into the bar Oz had been hanging out in—living above, actually, and working in most nights, bartending to pay the rent. Oz had been waiting for him. Oz had known his own destiny, his fate, since he was fifteen years old and his spirit posse revealed it, laid out his life's path like a board game. There was nothing he could do to change or alter it.

You'll fall in love with this man. Totally and completely. You'll do anything for this man. You'll have to do anything.

And dammit, Oz had fallen, madly and completely, for the tall, handsome young man—and Devlin had fallen for him as well.

Of course, Dev hadn't known just how much hell both men would have to go through in order to just be together. Never would.

And it's not over yet, Oz reminded himself. It was only Devlin's second day back at ACRO, and as of a few hours ago, Haley confirmed that Hurricane Lily was now an imminent threat to New York City. Dev had stopped home to rest for a few hours, was exhausted, but the second he'd laid eyes on Oz, it was apparent that neither man was going to get rest anytime soon.

Their lovemaking had been fast, furious. So much was imminent now, so many things Oz needed to reveal—some he could and some he couldn't, but all of it was his destiny, always had been. And so he sat on the edge of Dev's bed, in the dark. Though they'd spent time with each other since Dev's return, this would be their first full night together in four months, since Oz had helped Devlin banish a ghost named Darius from Devlin's own body—a possession that was fourteen years in the making and had taken so much from both of them.

You're together now. That's what counts.

And still, the chills that had wracked his body all day long remained, his feet and hands numb from cold and pain—pins and needles no matter how many blankets he piled on or how much he massaged them.

The only thing that helped was Dev touching him. "Dev?" he whispered over his shoulder, and Dev was there, pressing his naked chest to Oz's back in the darkness.

"I'm here," Dev whispered.

Yes, Dev was here, and still there was so much left unfinished—so much left to do.

"This is too much on you," Dev said. "I'm back now. Things

are handled at ACRO. You've got to tell Creed everything. Soon."

Dammit, he should've known that Dev knew all about Creed. Dev knew just about everything. "How long have you known?" Oz asked, suddenly feeling too vulnerable to have this discussion.

"That Creed is your brother? Nothing I hadn't suspected for years."

"Bullshit, you suspected. You've been reading me while we've been fucking."

"It was the only way I could find out more about you," Dev said, and no, he wouldn't let himself get pulled into Oz's anger—Oz knew that, hated and loved him for it.

"You knew that I loved you—and that was everything you needed to know," Oz said.

"You'd never tell me about how you grew up. Always wanted to keep it such a deep, dark mystery," Dev murmured against his neck, his chest pressed to Oz's back as Oz tried not to think about his past.

It didn't matter anymore. Oz knew that Dev had discovered it bit by bit, had mined for the information year after year until Oz was so open to him that he couldn't keep his mind blocked. He hadn't wanted to either, had found it almost a relief that someone else knew his burdens.

"I keep thinking about you . . . all alone, no one to watch over you." Dev's hand smoothed down his chest, palm ending up over Oz's heart in a protective grasp.

Oz had grown up as a kid of the streets. He'd been too old when his mother abandoned him and his day-old brother to get into any kind of decent adoption deal, and he'd already been abused so severely for his powers by his own mother that he'd decided he'd rather just be on his own.

"You've been seeing them—your spirits—as long as you can remember," Dev continued. "It was a normal way of life for you. For your mother."

Oz shook his head. "It wasn't normal for her."

His mother was a haunted ghost-seer too—but she found it

overwhelming, took drugs to quell the voices and eventually overdosed on the streets a day after giving birth to Creed, essentially abandoning both Creed and Oz.

She'd managed to stay clean throughout her entire pregnancy. She'd been beautiful and brilliant and temperamental, much like Oz himself, and there was no way Oz could blame her.

The abuse he blamed on the priests, who told her that by locking Oz in a dark closet for days at a time, the evil spirits could be driven from him.

"Those priests were wrong," Dev said, breaking into Oz's thoughts, the way he'd broken into Oz's life years and years earlier.

Dev always thought he needed Oz more than Oz needed him, but Dev was wrong about that. So goddamned wrong.

"I know the priests were wrong." His spirit posse wasn't evil—they were more like the bad boys of the spirit world, attracting troubled souls like rock stars collected an entourage. The souls were forever changing—some of them finally got it that they were dead and went toward the light, some got tired of him and his I-have-no-fucking-sympathy-for-the-dead routine. Some of them latched on to other mediums. So change was a constant in Oz's life, as though preparing him for the biggest change of all.

"I wanted to keep Creed with me, Dev. It killed me to have to leave him like that." He remembered holding the smiling baby, remembered clearly casting the spell and calling out to the spirit who could help him, waiting for the protective tattoos to appear. They'd come up as if being drawn before Oz's eyes, the intricate scrollwork patterning the lifeline Creed would have.

Quaty had been the spirit that had answered the call first, the one whom Oz had entrusted to be the protective, possessive spirit for his brother. She'd been both a blessing and a curse, and Oz had always known there was sometimes very little distance between the two things.

"You knew the McCabes would find him," Dev said.

"I knew. I heard there were ghost hunters in the area, searching for the Bell Witch's spirit in that cave."

"They would've taken you in too," Dev said quietly, but that was something Oz didn't want to hear.

"My gift was always much darker than Creed's."

"Creed needed the protection, but he couldn't have caught your gift, Oz."

How could he tell Dev that it was his own fault that his brother was saddled with a spirit who tried to rule his love life, who tried to keep him from finding everlasting happiness?

For someone as realistic as Oz, that shouldn't have bothered him. And when Dev got quiet, Oz could sense his partner's frustration as he tried to unravel the one part of the story he couldn't see.

No, Dev would never see that part, not with his second sight or with the help of any of the ACRO psychics—he would never know just what destiny had in store for both of them, until it was too late. Oz kept that information partitioned and blocked, thanks to his spirit posse, and it was better that way. It was the only way to ensure Devlin's happiness.

"I shadowed him," Oz said, in an attempt to stop Dev from thinking too much. "I watched how Martha and Dave treated him."

To keep an eye on Creed, he'd gotten a job in the tarot shop in the town where ACRO was located, reading fortunes and doing a damned good job of it. Until he realized that most people were upset with the truth and he learned to sugarcoat the impressions he doled out to them. He'd worked there until ACRO tapped him, and for two years he avoided his fate—and Dev—until the day Dev sauntered into the bar.

He held on to Dev's hand, which was still on his heart.

"Like I said before, you're doing the right thing. For Creed and for Annika too," Dev reassured him. "True love needs to run its course."

There was a possibility that Creed could lose his powers in

exchange for true love—and as tempting as losing his own powers sounded to Oz, he knew he'd be lost without the dead.

Dev was probably the only one who understood that, even though his powers were far different from Oz's.

How Creed would deal with it was anyone's guess at this point, but his love for Annika was strong.

Dev was pulling him back into the bed, pulled him until Oz relented and lay with his head on the pillows, Dev poised above him.

"Would you give up your spirit posse for me?" Dev asked.

"You'd never ask me to."

Dev smiled before his tongue smoothed along Oz's neck, traced a slow, lazy path down his pecs and ended up circling a nipple. Oz jumped slightly, the way he always did when Dev played there—since his triumphant return to ACRO his touch was more electric than ever.

"Make it better, Dev. Even if it's just for an hour."

Dev raised an eyebrow. "An hour? Have you completely lost faith in me?"

Oz felt the smile play on his own lips—a smile for the first time in days, as he closed his eyes and let Dev move over his body.

He tensed, the way he always did when Dev decided he wanted to be on top, until Dev's mouth and hands began to work their magic and things began to fall away.

But when Dev pulled out the ropes, Oz shook his head. "No, not tonight."

"Yes, tonight." Dev grabbed Oz's wrist and yanked it upward, over his head. "Get on your stomach."

"No."

But even as he argued, Oz knew it was a losing battle. Dev knew plenty more moves than he did, could overpower him in half the time. Especially now.

Dev hauled him up and onto his knees, even as his arms remained bound tightly by the wrists to the bedposts, stretched out on either side of his head so he was pulled taut as a bow. He arched involuntarily as Dev's tongue traveled down every bump of his spine, and Oz tried desperately to move somewhere, any-where, before Dev's tongue reached its final destination. The place that would make Oz come undone, completely and totally, and Dev knew that.

And when Dev's tongue turned to steel and began to rim Oz mercilessly, Oz bowed his head to the pillows and gave up the fight, shoved his ass against Dev's face until he heard himself begging Dev to *fuck me now*.

Dev wrapped his hand around the base of Oz's cock, stopping him from coming, and he didn't listen to Oz's pleas, not until Oz was floating in that space where nothing else mattered. And when Dev finally entered him in a long, hard thrust that sucked the breath from Oz's body, Oz accepted him easily. Hungrily.

"Are you mine, Oz? All mine?" Dev asked, fucking him so hard that he was nearly incoherent, so that his head hit the head-board, and either way he was seeing stars.

"I'm all yours," he ground out as he came, and God, he wanted that to be the truth more than he'd ever wanted anything in his entire lifetime.

CHAPTER
Sixteen

ML's car was a vintage Aston Martin DB9—he put the convertible top up and the heat on in deference to the fact that Wyatt and Faith had been in the water and both were shivering in their damp clothes.

Of course, Wyatt wasn't exactly happy at having to squeeze his tall frame into the small back of the car, but ML had insisted Faith sit up front.

"What does *ML* stand for?" Faith was asking Wyatt's friend— a man he'd known since his earliest ACRO days. One of the few people who knew Wyatt wasn't dead. He was a do-anything and get-anything guy for his friends, which was a skill set Wyatt always appreciated. There were the usual rumors surrounding ML, everything from him being a direct descendant of the Rockefellers to the illegitimate son of Elvis.

"You do look a hell of a lot like Elvis," Wyatt had remarked to him once. ML had just smiled, the way he was smiling at Faith now, that surfer-dude, I-don't-have-a-care-in-the-goddamned-world smile that got him more ass than a toilet seat. "Doesn't stand for anything."

Wyatt bit his tongue—because the only thing funnier than the fact that ML was actually an escaped Amish farm boy whose name was Moses "Mose" Lapp was that his initials spelled out his profession—money launderer.

ML was the best in the game. He was thirty-two, and his empire stretched wide. Even his enemies weren't true enemies—ML had too much dirt on anyone for them to bother to mess with him. No, everyone from the Irish Mafia to the Colombian drug lords needed ML, and that was fine by him.

"I don't know how long we'll be staying with you. And we're going to need a ride out when we leave," Wyatt interrupted before ML could take it too far with Faith. Who was periodically shooting Wyatt death rays—and what the fuck, he was the one who was pissed.

"Not a problem. I suggest waiting at least twenty-four hours, though," ML said as he pulled through the front security gates. His mansion was on Marco Island—an exclusive area off the Florida coast. For the most part, ML refused to travel with bodyguards—he was wearing a Sig Sauer, the one Wyatt had given him a few years earlier.

ML also had a flair for numbers that was almost inhuman.

"How's your sister?" Wyatt asked as they entered the revamped Spanish villa–like mansion.

ML shrugged. "She's doing her own thing. I haven't seen her for a while—she's still a little wild."

"Yes, she's the wild one of the family." Wyatt rolled his eyes.

"You guys can have the west wing," ML told them. "Plenty of privacy, and I'll send extra security that way. Not that you'll need it." He stared at Faith for a second. "I assume you're, ah, *special* too, right?"

She smiled. "I'm going to need a safe."

"Not a problem. I'll find you some clothes too, for the night— tomorrow I'll have some stuff brought in new for you."

They followed him up the winding staircase and long halls. While ML took Faith into one of the bedrooms, Wyatt purposefully went into another and headed for the phone.

Dev picked up on the first ring. "Where are you?"

"I'm at ML's."

"With the motherboard?"

"Yes. It's in hand, but not destroyed."

Dev paused. "Problem?"

"There's another agent who's after it—not Itor, a free agent. Her sister's been kidnapped."

"And they want the motherboard in exchange."

"Yes."

Dev was silent. "By the time we figured out the code you sent, it was too late, Wyatt."

"I know. I blew it."

"No you didn't—you had no way of knowing their ultimate plan. None of us did. It's in Remy's hands now. You follow the lead, Wyatt," Dev said quietly. "Follow the trail to the end. We might've lost control of the hurricane, but we can't lose sight of the ultimate goal—destroying anything else out there that resembles this motherfucker. Whoever wants the machine is someone we want to get to know."

"You got it, Dev."

"I trust you, Wyatt. And I've never not known you to be able to trust yourself."

"Yeah, well, I've never met a woman like this one."

"Mission first."

"I know. It will be. I can handle this." He just hoped ML's sources came through with Wyatt's special order.

"I know you can. Keep me informed."

"Will do, Dev," Wyatt told his boss. He hung up the phone, muttering to himself, stripped and headed for the shower.

Plan, I need a motherfucking plan.

Of all the times *not* to admit anything about his past to an agent of unknown origin or status, this would have been the time.

She had him by the balls, and he'd let it happen.

He was going to need to handcuff himself to Faith for the night, there was no way around it.

The shower door jerked open and Faith walked in, completely

naked except for the black choker with the small white flowers on it. Her hands weren't playing with it the way she did whenever she got a little nervous. Instead, her body was loose, languid, as though the swim and the sex—and the fight—had gotten her back on track.

"ML gave me access to the floor safe in my room," she told him. "The bag didn't leak. I have it drying out now."

"You had to be naked to tell me that?"

"I wanted to tell you that the motherboard is in the safe—safe and sound, as they say. But I'm not going to give you the combination."

"I don't need the combination, Faith. I can take the door right off its freakin' hinges." His calming meditation had been interrupted by her entrance. Worse, his cock acted all we're-so-glad-you're-here, which was not the vibe he'd planned on giving out. "There are three other bathrooms in this wing. This is my shower."

She ignored him and sat down on the teak bench. "We need to finish our discussion. From the beach."

"Consider it finished."

"You tell me that you've been institutionalized, just like Liberty was, and you expect me not to ask about it? I've been there too, Wyatt—"

He laughed bitterly. "For what, a week? In some fucking fancy place that's more like a spa than anything? You don't understand, the place they took me to was a full-on psych hospital. I was in the lockdown ward at fourteen—the floor with the most dangerous patients."

Again with the true confessions. He sighed and stuck his head under the water in an attempt to drown out her voice. Which didn't work, since he'd been trained to listen for intel under running water, by both the SEALs and ACRO.

"Am I supposed to be afraid of you? Feel sorry for you?" she was asking.

He came out from under the shower spray and attempted to grab her, but she stopped him, fucking froze him in place like she'd done in the oil platform's torture chamber, and it was on the tip of his tongue to tell her that he didn't want her to feel anything for him.

But that would be a lie. "Let me go, Faith," he said quietly.

"If that's what you really want."

"You know what I want. I told you on the helo—I want you to love it, crave it. Beg for it . . . beg for me."

"You got it, Wyatt, got me to crave you. I'm attached to you. Something I shouldn't have let happen."

He remained motionless. Naked. Vulnerable. She took a step toward him, her bare body glistening under the soft lighting in the shower, the steam rising around them. "So you're attached. What now?"

"Any good agent knows what should happen next. It's the same thing you were probably thinking about me when I walked in here, whether or not you should take me out or trust me." She cocked her head, probably because she sensed the large wooden loofah brush that he'd picked up with his powers hovering at the back of her skull.

"Like I said before, Faith, at some point someone's got to lose the game of chicken."

"I could kill you where you stand," Faith said. "Just a thought is all it would take."

"Are you so fast that you could do it before the wood cracks your skull?"

"Are we going to find out?"

Wyatt stared at her, his expression unreadable. She hoped her face revealed as little, but the way her heart was kicking her rib cage and her adrenaline was running like lit petrol through her veins, she doubted it.

She was utterly turned on by this little game of life or death. From the looks of things, so was he.

"You're a pain in the ass," she said, and suddenly, the loofah brush whacked her on the butt. She yelped and leaped forward, nearly smashing into Wyatt. "What the hell was that for?"

"You threatened to kill me and you're outraged that I gave you a little spanking?"

She shoved him against the wall and used her gift to pin his arms to his sides. "I'm outraged because you are a complication I don't need."

"Which part are you pissed about? That I'm not letting you waltz away with the motherboard, or that you're starting to feel something for me?"

He'd hit both nails on the head, infuriating her even more. She'd lost control of her mission and her body, and with her sister's life on the line, none of this was acceptable. Making matters worse, the man at the center of all of it was an enemy ... someone she couldn't trust. But someone she *wanted* to trust.

She'd reached a critical stage, where she felt too much for him to turn back and was angry at herself for letting it happen. She had a feeling he was at the same place. They were both on a precipice, a precarious edge, where if they didn't take the other out now, it wasn't going to happen at all.

"I don't need another Sean in my life," she said, earning herself another stinging whack on the ass.

"Don't compare me to that piece of shit."

"Oh, come on. Can you honestly say you could ever trust me?" Resisting the urge to rub her bottom, she used her power to squeeze his sac, gently, smiling at his harsh intake of breath. "What makes us attractive to each other, what makes the sex so good ... it's exactly what makes us impossible to trust."

"I trust the people I work with, and they're just like you."

"So if I worked for ACRO, everything between you and me would be perfect?"

"You going to send in your application? Because I could put in a good word for you."

She snorted. "Thanks, but I'm quite happy with my current situation." She moved closer to him, noticed the brush followed her. So did a bar of soap. She ignored the items, ran a finger down Wyatt's chest while using her power to contract and expand the tissue of his cock, creating a rippling effect similar to a hand delivering soft, squeezing strokes. "I get to make my own rules. I don't have to answer to anyone or follow orders I don't agree with."

That wasn't entirely true. As the head of her own agency, she had a responsibility to those who worked for her and with her.

Something slid down her back. The soap. It slipped around her waist and up her belly, to her ribs, her breasts.

"Two can play at this game," Wyatt murmured.

"The more the merrier, I say."

She sent a stream of vibration into the sensitive area between his balls and ass. He groaned. The soap smoothed over her breasts in a figure eight, speeding up when she increased the amount of power she was funneling into his groin.

The bar lowered, slipped between her legs and began to work back and forth in her slit. Damn him, it felt good, and she allowed herself a moment of pleasure before she stepped back into the stream of water.

"This is pointless, this battle of wills."

"Then release me."

"What then? You don't let me out of your sight, even though you told ML to have his men watch me?" It was a guess, but it was what she'd do if the situation were reversed. "I don't like being a prisoner."

"So you hold me like one?"

With a shrug, she released him. "Now what?"

The man moved like lightning. She found herself pinned to the wall by his hard body and his big hands on her shoulders.

"Now we see how you like it."

"Like what?"

"Feeling vulnerable."

She laughed. "I can kill—"

"Yeah, yeah, you can kill me with your mind, blah fucking blah." He slid one hand to her throat, and for a moment, she thought he was going to threaten to strangle her. Instead, he stroked his thumb over her choker. "Tell me what you're hiding, Faith."

"Hiding?"

He leaned close, put his mouth to her ear and whispered, "Under the collar."

Gravity reached up and grabbed her, and if it hadn't been for Wyatt's weight holding her upright, she'd have gone down to the wet tile. "I don't know what you're talking about."

"How did you become a secret agent?" His thumb continued to play with the strip of fabric, and she had to concentrate to keep breathing. "Because you lie for shit."

You lie for shit. As far as insults went, that was one of the worst. Right up there with "You're a terrible shot" and "You stand out in a crowd." Her life frequently depended on her ability to lie, but with Wyatt it was as if she'd forgotten how. She rarely slipped, and even Sean, who had known her better than anyone, hadn't seen through her professional façade—not until Wyatt had cracked it wide open, leaving her weak and exposed.

Her voice quavered humiliatingly. "Fuck you."

"Been there, done that, and we'll do it again. But first you'll tell me what you're concealing."

"I'll do no such thing," she growled, jamming her hands between them to shove him away.

He didn't budge. "Guess we do this the hard way." He ripped off her choker.

Instinct had her reaching up to cover herself, her heart pounding, her breath coming in shallow gasps. Wyatt blocked her arms, grabbed her wrists.

"Let go!" Struggling wildly, she crunched her foot down on his and in the same motion lifted her knee to nail him in his dangly bits, but he pressed against her, crushing her, preventing her from causing much damage.

"Faith! Stop!"

But she couldn't. She kept her head down, hiding her throat as she pushed against him, too worked up now to even try reaching for her power. He'd stripped her of one of her shields, leaving her vulnerable, just like he'd said.

"You bastard!" she screamed, her struggles growing more

frantic, more vicious. Despite his grip on her wrists, she managed to land a blow to his chin and scratch a bloody streak down his cheek.

"Dammit," he breathed. "What is wrong with—*oof!*—you?" He took a risk then, let go of her left arm and grabbed her hair to wrench her head back, exposing her throat. His eyes went wide. "Jesus."

"Let go of me!"

He released her, stepped back, but the damage had been done. She couldn't move, her legs too rubbery, but she did bring one hand up to cover her throat.

"What happened?" he asked quietly.

For a moment, Faith did nothing but tremble, suddenly chilled despite the steam. Finally, she looked up, saw a man watching her with concern. A man she could fall in love with. A man who would kill her if ACRO ordered it.

"I let down my guard," she said. "I trusted the wrong man."

With that, she fled.

FAITH STOOD in her bedroom, staring at the bundle of clothes ML had left on the bed while she'd been in the shower with Wyatt. She was still dripping, practically hyperventilating after fleeing Wyatt's room. She'd been in such a rush that she'd left her robe on his floor, had run naked down the hall to her room. Security guys had stared from their posts at the top of the stairs, but she hadn't cared.

Well, shit.

She had not handled things well. She'd been off her game from the moment she'd seen Wyatt on the offshore platform, had lost complete control when she'd stepped inside the helicopter, and now she'd allowed him to see her mark of shame.

She fingered the thin white line that circled her throat, the scar even Sean hadn't seen.

God, how stupid was it that she was worried about a damned scar when her sister's life was on the line?

Selfish twat.

She needed to check the safe where she'd stashed the mother-board and video phone Liberty's captors had sent. She planned to make the call late tonight, let them know she had the merchandise and needed new instructions.

Hopefully, this nightmare would be over by the end of the week.

A fist pounding on her door made her jump. "Faith? Open up."

"Leave me alone, Wyatt," she sighed, even though she knew him well enough now to know he wouldn't do anything of the sort.

Quickly, she grabbed another robe from the closet—the dodgy ML guy must keep the entire wing stocked like a hotel—but instead of using the sash to close it, she wrapped it around her throat. She looked ridiculous, no doubt, but she didn't care.

"You know the lock won't keep me out," Wyatt said quietly.

She sank down on the bed, utterly exhausted. "That's why it's not locked."

"Oh." The door opened, and he strode inside, wearing a pair of sweat shorts and nothing else except the beads of water that said he hadn't bothered to dry off.

The bed sank as he sat down next to her.

"I don't want to talk about it."

"Then I will." Wyatt tipped her face toward him with a finger under her chin. "Your throat was slit, and it had something to do with Sean."

"You're mostly right."

Wyatt's gaze locked with hers, holding her as his fingers slowly peeled away the bathrobe sash. Her hands formed fists in her lap, but she let him, tired of fighting. The sash dropped to the floor, and only then did Wyatt's gaze drop to her neck. Instinctively, she flinched, hunched her shoulders to hide the mark, but his long fingers stroked her throat with such gentle care that she relaxed by slow increments.

"A wire," he murmured. "A garrote. Sean tried to kill you?"

"One of his men." She tugged the edges of the robe together, hugging the sleek material to her body. "Sean's team and I were in Paris, both after the same thing."

She remembered it so clearly, the only recurring nightmare she had that didn't involve her sister or parents.

"I'd just seen Sean at his hotel. He swore to me that he wouldn't interfere in my search. He'd never given me cause not to believe him, so I took him at his word." God, she was such a fool. Couldn't believe she was telling Wyatt this. He was going to think she was a complete idiot. Especially after their discussion about Sean on the helicopter.

"I found the artifact, a bone fragment dipped in gold and stolen from a Spanish monk's tomb, in the catacombs beneath the city. I thought I'd been careful, but . . ."

"You'd trusted Sean."

"Yes." She closed her eyes, took a deep breath before continuing. "Two of his men ambushed me. I killed one, but the other, Marco, he got the upper hand. Would have killed me if I hadn't been able to get to the stiletto in my boot. But he got away with the artifact." She rubbed her throat, the pain of the event still lingering. "The wire cut deep, nicked my jugular. I barely made it to the hospital in time."

"And Sean?"

"He sent flowers. Said right on the card that Marco hadn't been authorized to kill me and that he'd be punished. Which would explain why he followed me into the bar the day I met you. He wanted revenge."

"That fucker was the one who nearly killed you?"

"What, you thought I was really running from an ex?"

He shrugged. "At the time. I've been a little busy since finding out who you are to think about how we met."

"What did you think you'd find beneath my choker?"

"A birthmark, maybe. A small scar. You play with your chokers when you're nervous, and you never take them off, so I figured there was a story there. I didn't expect . . ."

"A horror story?"

His eyes, so green and clear, with a ring of gold near the pupils, leveled at her. So intense. So expressive, but only at times like this, when they weren't in danger and no one was trying to kill them. Which seemed to happen a lot.

"I'm sorry, Faith. I didn't mean to—"

Smiling, she placed her palm on his cheek. "Yes you did. We were both trying to strip each other down, and we were playing dirty. It's what we do."

"I don't want to do that anymore."

"Neither do I," she murmured.

She opened herself up to her power, sent a thread of it to his brain's pleasure center while at the same time smoothing a healing wave over the scratch she'd made.

"Shit," he rasped. "I can't decide if your gift is cool or really fucking scary." He covered her hand with his. "You said you learned to recognize Sean's power. Could he do the same?"

"Yes."

"How?"

She shook her head, not wanting to give away such crucial secrets, but something inside her, something strangely protective, wanted to make sure Wyatt was armed with knowledge that could save him in a fight with someone like Sean. Or her.

"In telekinetics who can affect the human body, there's always a tell. An individual signature that's different for everyone. It's usually extremely subtle, hard to pinpoint—"

"Just before you use your power on me, my teeth hurt. Like when you bite down on aluminum foil."

That was how Sean had described her signature as well. Real bloody subtle.

His wound healed, she cut off her power. Dropped her hand and her gaze, hoped Wyatt would drop the subject. "Don't you ever wish . . . no, never mind."

"Wish what?" His voice was low, soothing, and when his hand engulfed hers, that was soothing too.

"This is going to sound so silly." She felt herself blush. "Do you ever wish we didn't have to do some of the things we do?"

"You mean like hurt each other when what we want to do is be together?"

Her cheeks grew hot, and something low in her belly fluttered. "Yes," she whispered.

She longed to be able to let down her guard with someone who knew about her gifts, but she couldn't trust anyone outside her agency, and she couldn't date anyone on the inside, not when she was the boss.

"Do you plan to hurt me now?" He cupped her jaw and lifted her face to his.

"No." Swallowing dryly, as if she was an untouched virgin, she took him in, his thick, dark eyebrows, his sharp cheekbones, his firm mouth, which had pleasured her well and often.

Her body pulsed with desire at the thought, at the way his muscles tensed beneath his deeply tanned skin, as though preparing to pounce. As she watched, the rise and fall of his chest grew more rapid, as did hers.

"You're not—"

"This isn't my mojo, Faith. This is us. Together."

He lowered his mouth to hers, touched her with his lips, his hand on her face. She softened instantly, turning inside out at the tenderness of the kiss. His tongue flicked over her lower lip, but when she opened up to him, he didn't enter, keeping the heat at a low simmer instead of the white-hot inferno they usually shared.

This was exquisite. Though she wanted more, so much that she squirmed as her sex flooded and her breasts tightened, she didn't push. She let him give and take, let him build the tide of need until they melted together and she was clinging to his biceps like he might change his mind.

"Please, Wyatt," she gasped against his lips, too late realizing she was begging. Again. Just like he'd said she would.

Still kissing her, he wrapped his arm around her and lowered her onto the bed.

Cool air whispered over her skin as her robe fell open. Wyatt's hands, warm and a little work-roughened, slid over her body, leaving tingles everywhere he touched. When he cupped her breasts, used his thumbs to circle her hardened nipples, she moaned. He swallowed the sound with his own deep growl and then broke off the kiss.

His lips were red and glistening, slightly parted. Without thinking, she reached up and traced them with the pads of two fingers. They were softer than they looked, silky and moist. Perfectly shaped, like the rest of him.

She wanted to spend all night exploring his body this way, and she would.

"You're so beautiful, Faith." He caught her fingers in his mouth and drew them in, sucked on them, laved them with his tongue, and she swore she could feel it in her core.

As though he couldn't help it, his hips surged, rocking the hard ridge of his cock against her thigh. He released her fingers on a ragged breath and ducked his head to suckle her breast instead.

"Oh, yes," she breathed, shifting on the bed so he was between her legs and his shaft was rubbing in exactly the right place.

They knew they'd both reached the end of their slow fuses when suddenly his hands were all over her and her hands were shoving his shorts down over his hips. Somehow the shorts ended up on the floor alongside her robe, and then Wyatt pulled her up onto the pillows and slid down her body.

He trailed his tongue over her belly, rimmed her navel until she began to whimper and pump her pelvis against him wantonly.

"Easy," he murmured. He opened his mouth against her mound and blew hot air over her sex. "You're a greedy little thing."

"Always." She'd barely got the word out when his fingers delved between her labia and made her gasp.

"God, you're wet. So sexy..." He grasped her hand, brought it down so she could feel her own silken cream. "I like that I do this to you."

She shuddered with pleasure, let him guide her fingers through her slit and into her core, spreading her moisture up to her swollen bud. Bolts of pleasure shot through her as he worked her delicate flesh with her hand. Every skimming pass across her clit made her writhe, needing a firmer stroke, but he took his time, torturing her slowly.

Finally, he arranged her fingers so she was forced to spread herself wide for him. She watched as he lowered his head between her thighs, and she cried out when the first firm stab of his tongue pierced her pussy.

He lapped at her as if he was starving, pushing his tongue deep inside and then swiping upward in a long, hot stroke. One finger dipped into her wet hole, caressing the inner pillow of nerves with superlight, circular sweeps. She writhed and groaned in desperate urgency. Little flicks of his tongue at the very tip of her clit made her buck, but when he rolled it between his lips and drew on it like a straw, she came apart violently, punching her head back into the pillow and pumping against his mouth.

An entire ocean of ecstasy crashed over her until she was practically drowning with breathlessness. Before it was over, he reared up and entered her, stretching and filling her. He took her mouth with as much enthusiasm as he took her body, and yet none of the tenderness from before had been lost.

He kissed her like she was more than a temporary diversion. He kissed her like she was his mission, and his goal was to make her feel more special than she'd ever felt with any man.

Mission accomplished.

Something was shifting inside her, changing her, because she'd never felt this way before. He challenged her, fired her up, made her feel feminine, whole, protected.

She hugged him to her, with her arms, her legs, her sheath. Tightening everything, locking him down and inside her, she welcomed every slow thrust, relished every groan that dredged up from deep inside his chest.

Clinging to his shoulders, she reveled in the flex of his muscles, his strength, his devastating skill in bed, in battle, in everything he did from flying a helicopter to fucking. Searing pleasure speared her, and she arched against him, encouraging him to hammer into her, but he maintained his torturous pace.

The crisp hair on his chest tickled her breasts as he moved

against her. His richly textured cock slid in and out, the head catching on the tight ring of her entrance, where the nerves popped. She felt it all at ten times the normal sensitivity, and as another climax grabbed her, she screamed ten times louder too.

"Ah, fuck," Wyatt groaned, finally unleashing into her with an intensity that, for all of their wild couplings, seemed even more raw, more ferociously carnal.

She dug her nails into his back and he came with a roar, his hips hammering into her without mercy. A rush of warmth filled her as his seed did the same. He shuddered and collapsed on top of her, shifted his weight to the right just enough so she could breathe.

"Jesus," she said, when she could talk again.

"Yeah." His breath fanned over her neck, sending pleasant little shivers down her spine.

She knew what he meant. With that one softly spoken word, she knew that, like her, he hadn't made love to anyone like that before, so intensely, drawing it out.

"We have all night, yeah?"

He nodded weakly. "Wanna eat first?"

Her stomach chose that moment to growl. "I could do grub. Lots and lots of grub."

"And beer."

"Beer is good."

She felt him smile against the skin of her throat, realized with a start that not once during their lovemaking had she thought about her exposed scar, even when he'd pressed his lips to it.

Ruthlessly, she shoved away the significance of that thought. This was nice, but nothing more than a diversion, no matter how thoroughly Wyatt had kissed her and touched her and made her want more.

It had to be, because once they left the safe house, the mission started again, and though he had no way of knowing, they would soon be rivals again.

CHAPTER
Seventeen

Creed stretched out on the couch and tried to get lost in an old black-and-white horror movie until he had to be back at HQ for hurricane prep. Annika had left sometime after ten—she had an evening martial arts class to teach at ACRO. Where she'd no doubt run into Devlin.

His fists clenched involuntarily at the thought of Devlin's name, and yeah, that was still a sore spot between them.

It was one of the many reasons why they couldn't come to an agreement over whether or not Creed should give up Kat. Although Annika's admission in Greece the other night had gone a long way in Creed's decision-making process.

He'd just need to speak with Oz about it.

Oz. Just thinking the name made him double over in sudden, excruciating pain. He rolled off the couch and found himself crawling toward the door, breathing heavily as though he were dragging a thousand pounds behind him.

Kat was literally on him, nearly choking him, trying to pull him away from the door. And she was nearly succeeding too.

Oz's face flashed in front of his eyes—his friend, brother in ghost-hunting arms—and the pain got worse. He managed to pull himself to his feet, hung on to the hall table while Kat tried to pull him back down again.

"Back off, Kat," he whispered, his gut cramping as if he were breaking in two. It was like fighting a hurricane, and he was losing. "Stop fighting me."

But Kat began to wail and Creed felt the sudden sharp pain in his heart, a premonition of something he couldn't comprehend.

He needed to get to Oz, to Dev. Something was very, very wrong.

DEV LAID HIS HEAD against Oz's chest, listening to the other man's steady heartbeat, and thought about how good it was to finally be home.

There was a lot to deal with, at ACRO and beyond, especially in regard to his own lineage as the reluctant son of Itor, but at the moment he felt on top of the world, as if he could handle anything. And tonight he didn't want to think on anything ACRO-related, which was why he didn't bother to pick up the phone he heard ringing downstairs.

"You're really not going to get that?" Oz asked.

"I'm going to fly again, you know," Dev said instead of answering Oz's question. He spoke into the dark and felt Oz shift beneath him.

"I figured there'd be no way to stop you."

"You'll come up with me, right?" he asked, pictured the view of the horizon he'd had from the cockpit right before Darius had possessed him for the second time, eleven years earlier, the possession that took his sight. And he was all right with remembering that horrible day, all the terrible days when Darius tried to possess his soul in order to use him as a vehicle for revenge against Itor—the memories, for better or worse, were all back. He was healing. No more surprises, and that made him smile . . . until he felt the cold.

He sat up quickly, arms folded around his chest. "Shit, Oz, do you feel that?"

Oz was up next to him in a second, a protective hand on Dev's shoulder. "What do you feel?"

"Freezing. I'm fucking freezing." He could barely get the words out. His throat constricted with the sensation of a hand squeezing it. "It hurts, Oz."

His body was being invaded again, much more forcefully than the last time—and oh, God, this couldn't be happening again. They'd gotten rid of it...

Never getting rid of me, Darius whispered, and the choke hold on Dev's windpipe grew stronger. *Mine.*

"Not...yours," he croaked, flashed back to four months earlier when Darius had invaded his body, intent on full possession. Oz had gotten rid of the ghost then—he could do it this time too. And so Dev reached out for Oz, but his lover's hand was no longer on his shoulder. "Oz, please."

"I'm here, Dev." Oz's voice sounded sure and strong, much stronger than Dev had ever heard it before. "Darius, you get your dirty hands off him. He's not the one you really want."

What was Oz talking about? He struggled to turn to see Oz, but realized that he was surrounded by darkness. "No," he whispered, rubbed his eyes desperately. Darius had taken his sight away again.

I want Devlin, Darius whispered.

"Devlin doesn't have the means to get what you want. But I've got it—I know the way to take down Devlin's father once and for all. But in order for you to gain that information, you have to come to me."

To you, Darius repeated, releasing some of his grip on Dev's throat. Dev coughed and choked and tried to turn on his CRV to see what the hell was happening, but he couldn't—he was trapped in the dark and the cold and Oz was doing something he shouldn't be doing.

"Come to me," Oz commanded. "Move to inside me, and I'll grant your every fucking wish, Darius. Your every desire for revenge—I'll carry it out. Together, we'll take down Itor. I know what needs to be done."

You'll carry it out, Darius repeated Oz's words again, as though Oz was hypnotizing the ghost, and Dev felt some of the warmth come back into his body.

"I'm stronger than Devlin, always have been. I have more resources. You don't need Dev's bloodlines to take down Alek—you need the resources from my spirit world."

"Oz, no," Dev whispered as a deadly sense of dread climbed his spine. His lover was pushing the boundaries, playing a very dangerous game with Darius—one that Oz could potentially become trapped by.

"You come to me, only me. That's the deal," Oz continued. "Possess me, bond with me. No escape for either of us, Darius, no way out."

You'd go far to save your lover, Darius said. A bond was much stronger than a possession—once you invited a ghost inside, getting him out typically required death of the human.

Death of a human. Devlin began to hyperventilate.

"I'd go further to destroy Itor," Oz said. "I'd go further than Dev ever could."

"No." Dev wanted to scream the word, but it came out as a whisper. Within seconds, his body was his own once again, and his vision clicked into place, in time to see Oz drop to his knees, face contorted in pain.

He was taking Darius inside him, bonding with a ghost bent on revenge. Dev watched helplessly as the man he'd loved since he was seventeen allowed it to happen.

Darius is gone, right, Oz?

You're safe, Devlin.

It was only now that Dev realized Oz hadn't lied—he'd just avoided Dev's question. Darius had never been gone for good, would never be until the spirit died after bonding with a human.

Oz was about to sacrifice himself.

When Oz's eyes met his, Dev knew exactly what he needed to do to save Oz, knew he needed to get Darius back inside of him to stop Oz and his plan.

Devlin also knew that Oz would never, ever allow that to happen. As if reading Dev's mind, Oz struggled to his feet and toward the door. Dev flew off the bed to stop him, but found himself held back by strong hands—not Darius's, but others, Oz's spirit posse, as the grip wasn't unkind or painful, just necessary to keep Devlin in place.

"Don't you dare do this to me—not like this, Oz," he called, because Oz was searching the cabinet frantically as the floor began to shake.

When Oz turned to face Devlin, he held the silver pistol in his hands, the one Devlin had gotten from his father when he was eighteen and just accepted into the Air Force Academy. Oz nodded as if to reassure him, and then he pointed the gun inward, toward his chest.

Pictures came off the wall, the entire house seemed to howl with grief and Oz struggled to keep the gun steady.

"No!" Dev heard himself roar, but Oz fired, two shots, which Dev knew would echo in his mind for the rest of his life, and still Oz kept his eyes on Dev, even as he began to slide to the floor.

"He's still alive—let me go," Dev shouted as the mournful screams filled his ears, and the spirit posse had no choice but to release him.

They were dying too—again—just the way Oz was.

"God, no." Dev was on his knees, cradling Oz's head in his lap, putting his hand over the bubbling chest wound in a futile attempt to staunch the blood. He could call ACRO, get one of the healers over here... that would take care of everything.

"I'm going to save you, Oz," he whispered. "Don't you dare give up on me."

"I'm not giving up." The words came from Oz with great effort as he stared into Dev's eyes.

"Why would you do this?"

"It's the only way Darius was ever going to leave you alone, Devlin. He's trapped with me. He's dying. And he can never hurt you again."

"Let me get help."

Oz shook his head, weakly. "It won't work. This is the way it's supposed to be. The way I've always known it would be."

Dev's blood ran cold. "What do you mean?"

"From the day I met you, I knew I'd die for you." Oz sucked in a gurgling breath. "I knew one day I would have to die to save you. And I fell in love with you anyway."

The sob rose in Dev's throat, but the howling and screaming in his ears had stopped and the house had gone quiet, and for once it was just the two of them in the room together. "No, Oz. We've got to get you help. Please let me do that."

"This happened too soon...expected a few more days," Oz ground out. "You've got to tell Creed for me, tell him what I did. Why."

"Yes, of course I will."

"Kat stays," Oz said, a sudden last fierceness rearing its head. "I brought Kat in for his protection—I can't leave him in the world alone, without her."

Dev couldn't argue—not with a dying man. His heart began to crumble in his chest and he could barely breathe, let alone talk as he just held Oz for the last time.

"I'm going to send you someone," Oz murmured.

"Shut up. Shut the fuck up, Oz." Dev could barely see through the tears in his eyes.

"Listen to me—you're not spending the rest of your life grieving for me. No way." Oz took a deep, shuddering breath and his eyes closed for a second.

"Don't do this to me," Dev begged, but Oz wasn't about to be deterred. His eyes opened and he took Dev's hands off his chest and held them, the blood connecting their palms.

"After midnight. Sometime after the worst of the winter passes, I'm going to send someone to you. And you're going to resist it—hard. And so is he."

"There's not going to be anyone else for me."

"Going to send you one of the most handsome men," Oz

whispered, his voice fading and growing slurred. "He'll need you as much as you'll need him."

"Oz, please. Stay with me for a few more minutes."

"The love will always be there, but the grief shouldn't."

Dev could barely bring himself to do it, but he bent down, pressed his mouth to Oz's cool lips, a final good-bye. "I love you, Oz. Always and forever. So you go do what you were destined to do."

Oz gripped Dev's hand one last time. "Destiny's a bitch, Dev. But I'd do it all again."

"Me too," Dev whispered, and in that second, Oz was gone. And then he heard screams—horrible screams.

It took him a few minutes to realize they were coming from him.

CREED HEARD the screams from the driveway of Dev's house, had to practically crawl up the driveway because of the pain in his chest. And then, as suddenly as the pain had started, it lifted, and Kat was clinging to him.

"It's all right, Kat," he whispered. "I think it's all right now."

But they both knew he was lying. He beat on the door for a few minutes, rang the doorbell insistently but got no answer. Not caring any longer, only wanting to get rid of the heaviness in his heart, he walked around the back by the pool and attempted to shatter one of the sliding glass doors.

The glass was shatterproof, bulletproof... and still Dev wasn't coming to see what the commotion was.

Creed didn't stop pounding on the glass, trying to get through it with chairs from the deck, even the umbrella pole, and finally, finally, Dev was at the door.

He was covered in blood.

Creed rushed over to him. "Shit, Dev, we've got to get you to the hospital."

"It's not my blood."

"Whose—no, it can't be." Creed pushed past Dev and followed the blood trail up the main stairs to Dev's bedroom, where he found Oz's lifeless body on the ground. The gun was still in Oz's hand, and as Creed bent down, he automatically pressed two fingers to the man's throat to check. Just in case.

"He's gone, Creed." Dev's voice came up softly behind him.

Creed stood swiftly, turned to Dev. "What the hell happened here?"

"Darius, the spirit . . . he came back."

"No, he was gone. Oz took care of him."

Dev gave a wan smile. "Oz took care of him so I could get help. He knew Darius would come back. He'd always known."

Creed stared at the man who'd been his mentor in so many different ways, and the pain in his chest began again, spread around his heart and made it hard to breathe. Hand on his chest, he knelt by the body and felt Dev's arms pulling him to his feet.

"Breathe, Creed. Fucking breathe, all right? You're blue."

Breathe, Creed. Breathe, Kat begged him.

"There are things I need to tell you . . . about Oz. Things he wanted you to know," Dev said, and Creed drew in a deep, painful breath, over and over, until the light-headed feeling stopped and he was able to stand up by himself.

"We're not going to do this here," Dev said. "I can't look at him this way. When we're done talking, I'll call over to medical—they'll come and help."

Creed nodded, followed Dev out the door of the bedroom. Dev closed it behind him and then sat on the floor of the upstairs hallway, as though betraying his earlier words of not wanting to be near Oz's body.

"Oz did things in his life that he thought he had to, things that made the most sense. I know it might not seem that way to you," Dev said, drew in a deep breath and paused. "Fuck, there's no good way to say this. Oz was your brother, Creed. Your blood brother. You weren't put into the cave as a sacrifice. Oz was the one who put you there."

Creed thought about the man who'd always been a nontatted version of himself, an older, wiser version, a brother in arms—but that's not what Dev was saying. "As in . . . my real brother?"

"Yes."

"So he left me in the cave? All these years, that fucking curse story—he left me there?"

"Yes."

"Bullshit, Dev. That's bullshit. Because if it were true, the psychics here would've known, someone would have told me."

"It was Kat's job to block all of them out. She's the one who makes your mind unreadable."

Something rose up in Creed, something dark and violent, and he wasn't sure if it was Kat who was angry as hell or if it was him. But there was no separating the two at this moment.

"He wanted to tell you himself," Dev began. "He thought he had more time."

"Time for what?"

"The reason Oz told you that there was a certain window of time for you to get rid of Kat was because he knew, for certain... he knew that he was going to die."

Creed stared at Dev, who stared back with clear, red-rimmed eyes. "He predicted his own death?"

"Not to the day, but he knew. Knew when Darius came back after the mole was discovered what sacrifice he'd have to make. He did that for me. He's lived with that since he was nineteen years old, maybe even earlier. He said he knew about me before he even met me, knew he was going to take his own life to save mine. And he still loved me. God, he should've hated me for what he went through, the way I pushed him away. "

"Jesus." Creed felt the pain beginning again, and he rubbed his chest, realizing it was the same spot where the bullet had gone into Oz. "Wait a minute... the window of time... because Oz is dead—"

"The window is closed, Creed. I'm sorry. So fucking sorry. But Oz didn't want to take Kat away from you now, didn't want to strip you of her protection. He had to make the decision so fast—you have to understand, he did it for your own good."

"No," Creed heard himself say. "This can't be possible. I was supposed to get to choose—both Ani and I, together. We're so

close to that total commitment, we just need a little more time...
I thought we had time."

"I'm sorry, Creed. But the only person who could separate you
from Kat was Oz."

Creed heard the sob tear out of his throat, and blinded by tears
and rage in equal parts, he felt his way down the steps and out
Dev's front door. Dev didn't bother to try to stop him, and Creed
got onto his bike and took off down the road, at a speed not meant
for someone who could barely see.

But at that point, he didn't care about anything. Any hope he
had of living in peace with Annika was over anyway. Kat would
never let that happen and he would be powerless to stop her. Oz
had ensured Creed's protection...and in the same breath had
taken away the love of Creed's life.

CHAPTER
Eighteen

While ML's personal chef cooked up some food for him and Faith, Wyatt strolled along the back deck and down to the beach.

It was nearly midnight—the moon, brighter than it had been earlier, cast shadows on the water, and his muscles, loose and relaxed from the sex, buzzed as soon as he saw the water.

He stripped off his shirt and took off at a dead run toward the water, tore through the small waves, let the current take him out as he stayed underwater and held his breath for as long as he could. When he broke the surface, he shook his head, floated on his back and stared up at the sky.

He loved the water, the weightlessness, the push and pull on his skin. He was comfortable out here—could spend hours just floating, diving, letting the waves caress him like a lover. There were no problems when he was out here, nothing he couldn't solve.

"Wyatt!"

He turned, saw Faith standing at the edge of the water, the white foam rushing over her bare feet and legs, and he smiled to himself as he swam in.

"What's up?" he asked as he approached her from the surf.

"Food's ready."

"Excellent. I'm starving." His stomach growled as if in response to his words.

"You didn't have enough of the water earlier?" she asked.

"Never enough," he told her, wrapped his wet body around her dry one as she laughed. Together, they strolled up the beach and sat outside on the deck where the food had been laid out. One of the housekeepers brought Wyatt a towel and he dried off a bit before sitting down, and they ate in silence. It had been at least twenty-four hours since either of them had eaten—Wyatt had learned to turn off his response to hunger and pain early on, but now that he was able to relax for a bit, he was ravenous.

When his belly was full, he leaned back in contentment and watched Faith eating the last of her meal.

"Delicious," she said. "I think I need a personal chef of my own."

"Can't cook?"

"Not worth a damn. I never had the time or the desire. ML must do well for himself."

"ML does all right," he concurred. "He's cool, and he'll get us where we need to go."

"That's good."

He noted that she'd put her choker back on. "So, where exactly do we need to go?"

She played with the beer bottle for a second, and then decisively put it down on the table. "I checked in with the men who have Liberty. They want me to go to Belfast. Once I'm there, I'm supposed to ring them again."

He nodded, drained his own beer and tried to get rid of the growing feeling that none of this was going to end well.

"Wyatt?"

"Yeah?"

"You mentioned your family—that there were problems. Are you in contact with them at all?"

"They're all dead. I wasn't ever close with them, anyway. They put me in the institution," he said quietly, and realized he was holding the neck of the beer bottle in a fierce grip. He set it down and flexed his hand and wished the conversation was over. "They weren't special-ability types, they were oil riggers. And my telekinetic skills were supposedly just part of a teenage psychosis—one the doctors assured my father they could rid me of. And they tried everything."

"It must've been horrible," Faith said. She'd moved to the chair next to him, rather than across the table, and he glanced at her before he continued.

"Lots of crazy people in this world, but that doesn't mean they should necessarily be locked up for it. Most of them aren't violent—and if they are, they mostly do damage to themselves because they feel like freaks. I can think of a whole lot of operatives who thought they were freaks at one point too, but without them around, the world would be a really unsafe place."

She nodded. "Then again, some of them can do damage to the rest of the world. They need to be helped—controlled."

He laughed, couldn't help it, because it was something he'd heard over and over from the shrinks. *Your boy needs to be controlled. Your boy has a severe mental problem. Your boy shouldn't be allowed out in public.* "Yeah, like you can't do fucking damage, right, Faith?"

"I've upset you. Again."

"Don't worry about it. Nothing I haven't heard before. Everyone who has superpowers pays a high price for them— sometimes it almost doesn't seem worth it." He thought back to the time, months earlier, when he'd come across Remy—then simply a man ACRO was recruiting. Remy was trying to make the decision as to whether or not he should go on living, having realized that his powers made him a threat if he was ever to get into the wrong hands. Wyatt remembered telling him, *It's not your time, Remy,* and Remy had asked, *How will I know?*

Wyatt told him, *You'll know.* Every agent ran up against that decision at some point in their careers—some, more than once. Times when the choice to end their own lives for the good of the world seemed like the only option.

It was nothing new to the military world—special operators made choices like that at times too, talked about what would happen if and when they were captured.

If Remy had made the wrong choice back then, he wouldn't be able to help handle a major hurricane that was threatening New York now. So yeah, Wyatt had been right about that one.

And now he was risking himself in a way that Dev would have his ass for—in a way only Dev could probably understand. The woman sitting next to him was his nemesis, his kryptonite, and the only woman he'd ever met who could handle all his shit . . . and like it. Maybe even love it.

"How did you finally get released?" she asked.

"I pretended I was normal," he said. "Sold out myself and my powers in order to get back to the real world. Stayed on the family rig for a while and then went into the military. Chose the SEALs because I love the water."

"And you never used your powers."

He shrugged. "Rarely. Some of them saved my ass, but I didn't want to count on them. I was finally in a place where I was accepted as normal—as crazy as I could be, as crazy as I felt, there were other normal guys around me who were just as crazy, for all different reasons."

"Did you ever . . . try to hurt someone?" she asked tentatively. "I mean, without realizing that you were doing it?"

That question hit far too close to home. "I don't want to talk about this anymore, Faith." He stood and felt the earth shift under his feet. Faith was by his side in seconds.

"Wyatt, what's wrong—are you all right?"

"I'm fine," he told her through clenched teeth, even as another wave of dizziness overtook him. "Shit."

"Come on, let's get you inside."

He leaned on her as they made their way through ML's house, up the stairs slowly and into Faith's room, which was closer.

Wyatt sank down on the bed and scrubbed his face with his hands. "Something weird is happening to me."

"Can you explain more?"

"Things inside of me are shifting. Changing."

Faith sat next to him. "When did you first notice this?"

"My powers are gaining strength, faster over the past months than they had in my previous years at ACRO. But they also fail me sometimes. Something that's never happened before." He'd gone to Sam after aiding in the rescue of Remy—when he'd tried to take down a helo during that op, he couldn't do more than make the bird wobble and had to resort to throwing shit at it instead.

Fucking humiliating.

"What happened when you tried to take down the helo?" Faith asked, and he realized he must have been voicing his thoughts out loud.

"I knew it was something I should've been able to do—I knew I could do it," he said, running his hands through his hair in extreme frustration. "I tried and I couldn't do shit."

"How did you feel?"

"Fucking pissed. Agitated. Tight."

"You'd probably been underutilizing your powers for too long. They don't like that—you must've had to fight to get them back."

Yeah, he'd fought. Practiced, watched his powers return. "My powers feel uneven, like I'm constantly off balance in so many different ways, always trying to right myself. But when you touch me, when your hands are on me—even if it's just a light touch—I feel better. Whole. Like things are connecting."

"You said something when we were on the beach, about understanding what it's like to feel guilty about family. That's not the first time you mentioned your family to me in an unhappy context." Her hands covered his gently, hands that were capable of killing man or woman. Hands that roamed his body as if claiming him for her own . . . hands that connected him.

"I don't see what this has to do with my powers," he told her.

"It might not. I think I can help you, but if you don't tell me, if you don't let me in, I'm not going to be able to."

He wanted to snap that, in so many ways, she *hadn't* helped him—she'd thrown off his game, put him in a perilous position, with the fate of the world literally in her hands. But she'd let go last night, had shared her most painful memory. The least he could do was match like for like.

"I might've killed my half brother."

She blinked. "I don't understand—how could you not know?"

"I can't remember. I've blocked it all. ACRO nabbed me before the MPs got me. Saved me, renamed me and gave me a new life. And I can't remember anything about the night Mason was found murdered. So when I told you that I understand guilt, Faith, that I understood what it meant to want to help family . . . well, if the motherboard held the possibility of getting me my memory back, I'd use it any way I could, to the point right before it actually got into enemy hands."

He hung his head, felt as if that confession sucked the life out of him. But Faith was there, at his side, urging him down onto the soft mattress with firm hands on his shoulders.

"There's no shame in asking for help—in needing help, you know?"

He laughed a little. "Yeah, you're really good at that yourself."

"I'm trying, Wyatt. With you, I'm trying."

"I know that."

"No, you don't know it yet. But you will." She spoke slowly, staring at the floor instead of looking at him. "Lie back, make yourself comfortable. I'm going to be here the entire time with you, keeping you safe."

"You're afraid I'm going to hurt myself?"

"I'm afraid you're not going to let yourself heal. And you need to heal."

"Tell me about it," Wyatt muttered, let himself relax on the bed. "Look, I'm tired—maybe I can get some rest and we can get to the touchy-feely shit later . . ."

"No. Not later. We've got to get this figured out, Wyatt. Otherwise, you're going to become a loose cannon."

He felt like one already. "All I remember is standing in the office of the oil rig where I grew up. Mason's there—my half brother. And he's laughing."

"Are you?"

Wyatt closed his eyes, shook his head hard and the colors in the scene in his mind began to change to reds and oranges. "No, I'm not laughing at all."

"And then what?"

"Then next thing I remember, my hands are on either side of Mason's face." Wyatt knew it was only a matter of one sharp turn to break a man's neck cleanly. "I killed him, Faith. There's no other explanation. There's a tape of me sneaking onto the rig. Why else would I be there?"

Faith rested her hands on his chest and immediately the now familiar rush of comfort enveloped him. The room stopped spinning, his brain stopped spinning and he heard her say, "Think, Wyatt."

He screwed his eyes shut and thought about that day in September. He'd been on leave, had gone to the rig...but for what? He hadn't kept in touch with his family from the time he left for the military at nineteen. So for him to go back there, something big must've been going on.

"Who else was on the rig that day?"

"My father."

"Did you see your father, did you speak with him?"

"Not until after Mason was dead. He came in, found me over the body."

"Where was your mother?"

"She died right after I went into the military."

He hadn't been very close to his mother—had respected her the way a son should, but had always lived with the sting of her betrayal at not understanding his gifts. He'd shown them to her when he was younger, in private—and as he'd learned each new trick, he'd shared it with her.

And she'd sold him out to his father when he was a teenager, the final nail in his coffin that sent him on his way to the hospital.

"How did she die?"

"They said it was a heart attack. I wasn't on the rig when it happened." A chill began at Wyatt's feet, and within seconds he was shivering and curled up in a fetal position. All around him, he could hear things breaking, his telekinetic powers looming out of control.

"Listen to me, Wyatt, you need to calm down. What did Mason have to do with any of this?"

"I don't know." His teeth were chattering so hard, he could barely understand himself.

"Wyatt?" She put her hand on his biceps and squeezed. "You're going to feel a tingle in your head. It's just me. I'm accessing your hippocampus, your memory center."

Instantly, warmth flowed through him, easing the shakes that wracked his body, and a tingle spread over his scalp. "I feel it," he whispered.

"Good. Now, why did you go to the rig?"

"Mason called. Said he had something important to talk to me about." Weird. That little forgotten detail had popped right into his brain and out of his mouth.

"When you got there, was Mason alone in the office?"

"Yes," he rasped, because now the memories weren't a pleasant tingle. God, it hurt, made him feel like his brain was popping and ripping, and his entire body burned. But he stayed in the flashback and watched himself holding Mason's head.

Mason was lying on the desk. "My hands are on his face."

"Look closer, Wyatt. Something's not right."

Wyatt forced himself to look into Mason's eyes, to feel. The tape in his mind began to play backward, excruciatingly slowly.

Mason, dead on the desk, Wyatt holding his face. And then, Wyatt was pulled back, gently replacing Mason's head on the desk and backing up.

"I didn't do it," he heard himself say softly. "It wasn't me."

"Go farther back, Wyatt...back out of the room."

In his mind, he did—stayed with the vision in a way he never had. When he was completely out of the room, he watched what really happened—Mason was laughing, laughing at something his father said.

"I've got proof, old man. And Wyatt will too. He has every right to know what you did," Mason said.

And then suddenly Wyatt's father was breaking Mason's neck, cleanly, while Wyatt stood there, stunned. And the shock only grew worse when his dad revealed everything—that Mason had been about to turn their old man in for killing Wyatt's mother.

"He killed her."

"Who?"

"My father. He killed my mother. She was divorcing him— she had proof that he'd been embezzling money from his investors and she was going to come forward. He would've been ruined. So he killed her, and Mason knew it."

"What are you going to do about it, boy? Everyone knows you're crazy. Everyone knows you have the training to kill with your bare hands. If I tell the cops you killed him, you think anyone will believe you didn't? You, who was institutionalized in a mental hospital? Who lied about it to get into the military?" His father pointed at Mason's lifeless body. *"If you leave now, maybe the police won't catch you."*

"I didn't do anything, Faith."

"You didn't. You know that now."

"I mean, I didn't do anything about Mason, I didn't turn my father in. I . . . just left."

"You were scared and in shock. Your family put you through hell and you'd just found out about your mother." Faith paused. "Where is your father now?"

"He's dead. Died on the rig a couple of years ago."

"Then he's already getting his punishment in the afterlife. And you've got to stop punishing yourself."

It was all Wyatt could do not to cry. "Just leave me alone. Leave me the fuck alone. Please."

* * *

SENSING THAT Wyatt needed time, Faith left him, but she didn't like it. Mainly because she didn't want to think about the revelations that had come out of the session with him—the things he'd remembered were only a small part of what he'd revealed.

The larger part, the part that left her stunned, was his unintentional revelation.

He trusted her.

He might not have admitted it to himself, but on some level he trusted her. He'd opened himself up and shared his past, had even trusted her inside his head, inside his memory center—where, if she'd decided to make it so, she could have scrambled him up so badly he wouldn't remember his own name.

The level of confidence he must have felt rocked her, hard—left her on shaky ground, when she was used to walking with confidence in any situation.

He'd realized too late where his openness had left him, and she had no doubt that he was regretting sharing so much with her. He'd be rebuilding his shattered defenses even now, and she had to decide whether she should let him do it, or if she should interrupt and strengthen the bond that had started to form between them.

A wise agent would choose the latter; fostering trust would be to her advantage, mission-wise. But on a personal level, it could be disastrous. She was already dangerously close to falling for him, and it wouldn't take much to push her over the edge.

Cursing silently, she wiped thoughts of Wyatt from her mind, needing to clear it, needing to gain some perspective. Out of habit, she wandered around the big mansion, mapping out the exits, the phones, the locked rooms, the locations of cameras.

She ran into ML, almost literally, in the kitchen. He was staring into the refrigerator, wearing nothing but a pair of shorts, a cigar hanging from his lips.

"Heya, Faith," he said, without looking at her. "Want a beer?"

"Thank you, no. I'll take a Coke if you have one, though."

He tossed a can of cola at her, closed the fridge door and leaned back against it, arms crossed over his chest, legs crossed at the ankles. "You got everything you need for the night?"

"I'm very comfortable. Thank you."

He watched her as he took a drag of his cigar and then blew out the smoke. "What about Wyatt?"

"I'm sure he's quite fine."

"He's a good friend. A good man." The warning in his voice was only slightly more subtle than the blatant subtext in his words. *Don't hurt my buddy or you'll have me to deal with.*

"Yes, he is," she said, turning to leave. "Thank you for the drink."

"He saved my life once," ML said quietly, and she halted, as he no doubt guessed she would. "It was a stupid thing. I met with the wrong people on the wrong yacht. Didn't know ACRO had it under surveillance. Didn't know it was a target for pirates. Shit went down faster than a summer storm. Suddenly Wyatt was there with a couple of badass special-ability dudes and Wyatt was dragging me out of the ocean, bullets flying and the water around us burning from the lit fuel. If he'd been smart, he'd have saved his ass and let me drown. But no, he took a bullet and still fished my nearly dead ass out of the water. Got in trouble for it later. Boss said he took an unnecessary risk."

Like he'd done on the platform when he'd rescued the diver. Ultimately, the choice had led to the confrontation with Sean that landed him in the torture chamber. No, Wyatt was not a man to let an innocent person die if he could help it—nor was he someone who would let another get away with murder.

The incident with his father hadn't made sense when he'd remembered it, and the more she thought about it, the more she was convinced that something wasn't right. The Wyatt who had saved ML and the diver at great personal risk would not have run away from a man who had committed murder in front of his very eyes.

"Why are you telling me this, ML?"

"I think you know."

ML owed Wyatt his life, and ML was willing to return the favor at any cost. Again with the don't-mess-with-my-buddy message. ML was a good friend.

"I'm sure he appreciates your loyalty. Good night, ML."

She hurried back to her room, anxious to test her theory. Wyatt was still lying on the bed, arm over his eyes.

"Go away, Faith."

"That command works as well to keep me out of a room as locks work against you." She sank down beside him on the bed, set the drink on the nightstand. "Thirsty? I brought a cola."

He brought his arm down to his side and stared at her. "What do you want?"

"I want to probe your memories again. I think there's something you're missing."

A harsh bark of laughter shook his body. "I ran like a fucking chicken from the murders of my brother and mom. What I'm missing is my balls."

"Stubborn git." She probed his aura with her power, slipped easily through the damaged barrier. He stiffened the moment she entered his brain.

"Knock it off," he growled, but she did no such thing. She pierced his hippocampus, triggered some pathways to fire.

"Go back to the scene, Wyatt. Go back to when your dad told you he'd killed your mum."

He cursed at her, but closed his eyes. Beneath his closed lids, his eyes moved, as though he was seeing it all like a movie. "The son of a bitch just laughed. He'd gotten away with killing her." He frowned. "He said...shit. He said I was an accident that shouldn't have happened. That the only son who had been worth anything was the one who died when I was born. Tim."

"What did you do?"

His hands formed fists at his sides. "I was pissed." He swallowed, opened his mouth as though surprised. "Shit started flying around. My dad grabbed a pistol from his desk and—oh, *fuck*."

"What is it, Wyatt?"

His eyes shot open and he sat up so fast, she nearly fell off the bed. "He started choking. God, he turned blue. Eyes bugged out of his head. He was clawing his throat and I just stood there, watching. He collapsed. I think...I thought he was dead. That's when I left." He scrubbed a hand over his face. "I didn't remember any of that. God, did I do that to him?"

She saw the regret, confusion and pain in his eyes. She closed her hand over his. He jumped, as if the contact startled him. "It's okay."

"Okay?" he echoed incredulously. "*Okay?* How the hell could I have done that?"

"I don't know, but if you did, that would explain your memory loss. Another power manifesting like that... wow. It could have been traumatic." And Christ, if he was biokinetic in addition to his already extraordinarily powerful telekinesis... "Wyatt? I'm going to probe your cerebrum and neocortex. Those are your psychic centers. I want to take a look at what's in there."

His gaze caught hers, and for a moment she thought he'd refuse. A heartbeat later, he gave her a slow nod.

She dove in, easily located his telekinesis. That part of the brain was like a topographical map, something she could visualize in her mind. Scientists had determined that humans used about ten percent of their brains, but psychics easily used twenty, and very powerful psychics used upward of thirty. Wyatt's telekinetic center spread like a field through his brain, taking up well more than thirty percent of his brain matter.

Amazing. She probed nearby, seeking the pocket most likely to house the sexual part of his gift—a minor power like that should be connected to a parent power—but strangely, she couldn't find it. Expanding her search, she shuffled through cells and nerve clusters, traveled along neural pathways... and discovered a bundle of energy that might be the area responsible for sexual output. At first it appeared to be its own little island in the middle of untapped brain matter, but on closer inspection, she discovered a string of cells connected to an area she couldn't access. A large portion of his brain had been partitioned off by an invisible shield her power could only bump up against.

Closing her eyes, she concentrated, let her power feel for cracks. The energy signature surrounding the shield felt familiar, vibrated at a frequency identical to hers. Her pulse picked up.

Wyatt was definitely biokinetic, and the area of his power was huge. God, if he were to access that section, his overall psychic potential could be almost limitless.

She pushed against the wall surrounding the power. Harder. Harder... and Wyatt cried out, clutched his head. Immediately she retreated.

"Are you all right?" She peeled one hand away from his scalp. "I'm so sorry. Wyatt?"

"Yeah," he rasped. "What did you find?"

Relief made her sag a little. "Everything is so scattered in there—it's amazing that you can control your powers at all." She cleared her throat and spilled the rest. "But no doubt about it; you're definitely biokinetic."

WYATT LET OUT a long, slow breath as his mind attempted to process the avalanche of intel Faith had unearthed. His first instinct was to question it or deny it, but hell, he'd seen the truth in his memories. Everything she said made so much sense, and still, the relief he felt at finally knowing what happened on the rig the night Mason died was short-lived.

"I could've killed him, Faith. I could've killed my father. And even though I didn't have a relationship with him—shit, that means I lost control."

"Wyatt, it wouldn't have been your fault. You didn't know what you were doing or what you were capable of."

"I still ran, Faith."

"Your father would've put you away for trying to kill him— on some level, you knew that. It was self-preservation, not cowardice."

"It proved everything my father said about me was right—the reason he put me in the mental hospital was because he said I couldn't control myself." Frustrated, he tugged his hands through his hair.

"Remember when you were younger—it was probably difficult for you to control the telekinesis, but you learned. You can learn to control this."

"Give it to me straight, Faith, how much learning are we talking about?"

She sighed, a soft sound of sympathy. Her hand wound through his and the tilt in his brain immediately righted itself. He had a feeling that until he learned to combine his powers, that familiar, scattered sensation would remain.

"There's a pretty big learning curve," she said. "Your gifts are all strong and you've been denying the biokinesis for so long that they naturally fight against one another rather than integrate. It's going to take practice and patience."

"Until then, I'm a loose canon. Just like always."

"You have control, Wyatt, plenty of control. If anything, until you learn to work the power, the person you stand to hurt most is yourself."

Yeah, he got that. "Is the sex thing tied to it?"

"Yes. Explains a lot, actually. Such as why I remembered having sex with you. My own biokinesis must have acted as a shield."

"Why wouldn't I have known about the biokinesis earlier? As a kid?"

"I think you suppressed it. And now you've got this wall around it. Subconsciously, you've probably been building barrier after barrier to keep it hidden. I have a feeling the telekinesis and the sex thing was all you could deal with, so your mind filed away the biokinesis. Did you always have control over the telekinesis?"

"For the most part I did, except when I was younger and my temper got the best of me. Or when I was hurt. I'm lucky I was a pretty easygoing kid. I just tried to hide the telekinesis. Shit, it was bad enough hiding that one power. If my parents had known about this one?" He shook his head.

"*This one* is what got Liberty shipped off to the mental facility."

He finally took the can of cola and popped the top, and hated the way his hand shook a little. "How did your parents explain it to you?"

She shrugged, but he knew it was not a casual subject for her at all. "They tried to pretend everything was normal—told me that

Liberty was sick, in a regular hospital, with doctors who would make her better. I was too young to know any better, but when my powers started up three years later, something told me to keep it to myself. I found out the truth after my parents were killed and I ended up in the hospital where Liberty had been sent."

The sound of the ocean came in on a breeze through her open patio door as he downed the rest of the soda. He needed to get back on firm ground, back in mission mode. There was nothing he could do now about the integration of his powers—he'd just have to ride it out, the way he'd been doing for years, until the completion of this mission.

And he owed Faith. Damn, he owed her so much. She'd given him back a part of himself he thought he'd never recover. He didn't have to fear his memories anymore.

But he had a feeling Faith's memories of her sister weren't as clear. "Listen, Faith, what you said before, about me having built up barriers about things as a kid, to help me deal...well, I can't help but think about your sister."

"What about Liberty?"

"You haven't seen her in years. And now she's been kidnapped, and suddenly the kidnappers come to you to find the weather machine."

She stiffened. "What are you saying?"

"You haven't been able to track down your sister since your parents were killed."

"There were rumors that an Irish nurse from the hospital took a special interest in her. The nurse disappeared from the hospital the same time that Liberty did."

"And Liberty had an Irish brogue in that video you showed me. So did the kidnappers." He kept his tone low, gentle, even though she'd be upset with his next question no matter what. "How do you know Liberty's not in on this whole scheme?"

"How do you know she is?" she snapped. "Just because I couldn't follow her trail doesn't mean someone else, an enemy of mine, couldn't have tracked her down. She could have been living a normal life, maybe didn't even remember her past, but was kidnapped and forced to help the people who took her."

"Maybe. But what if the nurse who took her did so because of her powers? What if the nurse belonged to a terrorist organization? Liberty could have grown up in the life of a terrorist, and once you blipped on their radar, she could have found the perfect use for you."

"She wouldn't do that!"

"Why? Because you're her sister?"

"Yes! My sister wouldn't give out information about me," she insisted.

"How would she have had information about you to begin with?" he asked quietly. "If she's known about you this entire time, if she's had any information to give, why wouldn't she have contacted you sooner? Why wait until now?"

"You don't know anything, Wyatt. You have no idea what you're talking about."

"Faith—"

"Don't." She made a beeline for the sliding glass door that opened to the deck. "It's my turn to be left alone."

WYATT, OF COURSE, ignored her. She'd had about thirty seconds of peace when she turned away from the deck railing to see him looming in the doorway. Behind him, the bedroom light outlined him in a warm, golden glow, while from the front, the moonlight bathed him in cool silver.

He was good and bad, an angel and a demon . . . and heaven and hell for her.

"I'm sorry." He gazed out into the dark night. "You helped me more than I can thank you for, and I turn around and accuse your sister of being a terrorist."

A lump of emotion formed in her throat. The same thing had occurred to her, but for someone who had never met Liberty, who knew nothing about the sweet child who had used her gift to heal Faith's scrapes and bruises, for him to make the accusation . . .

it had lit her like a match. His questions had been barbs, hurting even more because his concerns were valid. But their time together was limited, and she didn't want to spend it fighting. With a sigh, she collapsed into one of the cushioned deck chairs.

"It's okay. You didn't say anything I haven't thought of. And if you hadn't thought of it, you'd be pretty worthless to ACRO."

"So who do you think is involved?"

She closed her eyes and let the salty breeze wash over her face. Too bad it didn't take away the sting of Liberty's possible involvement. God, she couldn't take someone else she loved turning bad on her.

"Could be anyone," she said finally. "Could be an organization such as Hamas or Al-Qaeda, using an outfit with a smaller profile, like the Irish National Liberation Army, to acquire the weather machine. Or it could be an Irish-born group wanting it for themselves. My money is on the Irish Liberation Force."

He nodded. "The ILF has had dealings with Itor before. So they could have caught wind of the machine through their contacts."

"That's what I was thinking. They might have tried to legitimately obtain the machine, and when that failed they decided on more drastic measures."

"I hope Liberty isn't involved," he said quietly.

"Me too." She smiled weakly. "Can we stop talking about this now?"

He moved to her, bent and locked her in place with his arms on either side of her. "What do you say we go inside and forget all of this?"

She tipped her mouth up to his. The kiss was fleeting, barely a brush of her lips against his firm ones. "Why go inside?"

"Another game of chicken?" he teased. "You think I won't take you right here on the deck?"

The very thought sent a flare of heat straight to her center. "You think I'd object?"

A slow smile lifted his mouth, taking her breath away. He was so damned handsome, a menace to everything that made her a woman. "You wouldn't, would you?" His brows knit together. "But would it be because of the game, or because you want to?"

"That would depend on you." She palmed his cheek, used her thumb to stroke his cheekbone. "I'd have sex with you anywhere. You have to know that by now." His expression became shuttered, and she felt the loss of his warmth in her gut. "Wyatt? What's wrong?"

He pushed away, stalked to the deck railing and stared out at the ocean. The breeze ruffled his long hair, brought the scent of him, earthy and male mixed with ocean, to her. She loved the way he smelled, loved the way he sometimes stood still like that, unmoving yet alert. The small muscles in his sharply cut back twitched, the only sign that he wasn't a statue.

"Are you going to feel the same way when all of this is over?" he asked after a long moment.

"Are you implying that I'm using you? That I'm only fucking you to get a ride to Ireland and help with my sister?"

"I'm not implying. I'm asking."

"Does it really matter?" She stood, moved to the rail beside him.

He shrugged, like it was no big deal, but he wouldn't have asked if he didn't care.

This time with Wyatt had been the best of her life. She didn't want it to end. Ever. But how could they possibly have a future once he learned that she had no intention of destroying the weather machine?

The thought blasted through her like a bullet. Since meeting Wyatt, she'd intentionally avoided thinking about the second phase of her assignment, which was to secure the machine for her own agency after Liberty was safely in hand. Thinking about it meant realizing how badly Wyatt was going to take the truth, and she couldn't afford to get hung up on how he'd react—not when, since learning of its existence, she'd been obsessed with the knowledge that if she could hand over the machine to TAG scientists, no other child need go through what she had the night her parents were lost.

He turned to her, braced one hip on the rail. "Once we get your sister back, let's take some time off. Go away. I know this private tropical island where the sand is white, the water is blue and the nights are made for one thing."

"Sounds lovely," she sighed. "But then what? We go back to work, an ocean apart? See each other on holidays and when we happen to run into each other on missions, with opposing goals?"

"That doesn't have to happen."

"Oh, really. I've come up against ACRO before. If it happens again . . . what if I kill one of your operatives? Are you going to stand for that? What if ACRO puts out an order for my capture or kill? Or what if one of your agents kills me? Will you shrug it off as part of the job?"

Wyatt shoved his hand through his hair. "I don't know, Faith. But it doesn't have to be that way. Aren't you tired of being alone? Of having no backup? Limited resources? Come to ACRO."

"I can't."

"Why the hell not?"

God, she wanted to tell him the truth, that she had backup and resources. Before, the omission had been for the protection of her agency, but now . . . now it just seemed like a lie. A lie he'd understand on a professional level, but would probably see as a betrayal on a personal one.

Then again, he'd opened himself up to her, had put his trust in her, so maybe it was time to put a little faith in him. It would be a big step for her, to trust him with the truth, but the more he knew, the better their chances were of surviving the meeting with Liberty's captors.

Captors, because she refused to believe Liberty was a terrorist.

"Faith? Why can't you come to ACRO?"

"Because I have my own agency." She took a deep breath. "There. I said it."

Even in the pale moonlight she could see the blood drain from his face, and she both sensed and saw the change in him, the subtle tensing of his muscles, the shutter that came down over his gaze.

"If you tell me that you really are Itor," he growled, "that Sean went rogue and you were getting the machine back or some shit—"

"No. *No.* God, I'm not Itor." She reached for her throat, caught herself and dropped her hand. "I run my own agency. The Aquarius Group. We're not private, like ACRO and Itor. We're very small, paid by a secret department in the British government, which hands down most of our orders."

His curse blistered her ears. "I'd heard rumblings of a mysterious third agency, but ACRO never uncovered any solid evidence. Why didn't you tell me this sooner?"

"Because I've put everything into my agency. It's all I've got, and I won't risk it. We don't have the resources you have. We don't have the numbers, and we certainly don't have the ability to seek out skilled operatives. We've got a ragtag staff, many of whom are severely limited in their powers. We take the people who aren't powerful enough for ACRO and Itor. I can't put them at risk."

"You should have told me."

"You know what we are, Wyatt. You know we can't run around spilling secrets to everyone we meet."

"I didn't know I was 'everyone.'"

"You're not. That's why I'm telling you now."

"Shit."

She let him stew in silence for a few minutes before saying, "I guess it's my turn to say I'm sorry."

"We do too much of that." He sighed. "I get why you didn't tell me."

"So you also understand why I can't come to ACRO."

"Yeah. But maybe you could—"

"Could what? Give up my life? Come to America and get a nice desk job while you and I play house? Or do you want more than that? You want to get married and have me barefoot and fat with your babies?"

His gaze darkened as he looked her up and down and then focused on her belly, like he was sizing her up for exactly that.

"I'm not a brood mare," she snapped.

"That whole playing house and baby thing wasn't what I was going to suggest." He touched her stomach, his fingers splayed wide. "But would it be so bad?"

His voice was husky and thick, and she swallowed hard at the sudden sexual awareness that shivered through her body. Her nipples tightened, her sex flooded, and bloody hell, she felt a pinch in her abdomen as though she'd started ovulating from merely talking about this.

His gaze bored into hers, intense and magnetic, but even as she began to lean toward him, he swore and jerked away.

"Jesus. I can't believe what you do to me."

"*Me?* You're the one with the crazy aphrodisiac superpower."

"I'm starting to think you've got a touch of that yourself," he muttered.

She sighed, turned to watch the moonlit ocean waves. Wyatt's arm came around her shoulders, a casual, comforting, familiar touch that should have made her feel weak for wanting it, but only made her stronger.

Which really scared the piss out of her.

She had to get away from him before she made a huge mistake. Like telling him she was falling for him. Bad enough that it was happening, but she needed to keep a few truths to herself, especially the ones that had the power to cut her deep.

She started to pull away, but his grip tightened, and he drew her into the shelter of his big body. "Don't go," he whispered against the top of her head.

"Wyatt—"

"Shh." He maneuvered behind her, skimmed his hands up and down her arms as he nuzzled her ear. She closed her eyes, let herself absorb his heat, let his strength and overpowering masculinity consume her.

It wasn't enough to feel him on the outside. She wanted him inside her. Buried balls deep, possessing her, pouring everything he had into her.

Apparently, he wanted the same thing, because his hands eased to her hips. Gripping them firmly, he pulled her bottom against his erection.

"Perhaps we should retire to a bedroom?" she offered, hoping he didn't notice the catch in her breath when he began to grind his hips.

"So proper." He brushed aside her hair and pressed a hot kiss to the back of her neck. "Makes it so hot when you let loose and talk dirty to me."

"You want me to talk dirty?"

The sound of him shoving his shorts down made her heart skip a beat. "No. I want you to make other noises." His hands slipped beneath her skirt. He pulled aside the crotch of her panties and entered her in one smooth, hard stroke.

She bit her lip to keep from crying out. Her fingernails scored the wooden railing, her knuckles cracking under the force of her grip.

His hands came down next to hers so their bodies touched only where his cock slid in and out of her slick core. The sound of the ocean blended with the erotic slap of skin on skin, the harsh rasp of their panting breaths.

Pounding into her with raw, brutal thrusts, Wyatt urged her toward climax with sheer force. At the first tremors, he stopped, ground his hips to stave off her release.

Still, he didn't touch her. It was torture and teasing and by far the most amazing sensation in the world. She groaned, tempted to beg.

"What do you want, Faith?"

"I want to come before one of the servants looks out of a window and sees us." Her voice was little more than a moan, surely as gravelly as his.

"Probably too late." He rapid-fired a half-dozen thrusts into her, keeping her straddling the edge of detonation. She felt like a grenade that had been unpinned but hadn't yet exploded. "That's why I'm not on my knees doing what I really want to be doing to you, licking you from the inside out, making you come against my mouth. You know how much I love doing that, right?"

Lust clogged her throat, so she couldn't answer.

"Yeah, you know. But I don't want to give the servants that big of a show. Remember when I said that no one sees my woman naked but me?"

Swallowing the lump of lust, she managed to rasp, "I remember I told you I'm not your woman."

"Yeah, you are."

She didn't have time to protest, didn't know for sure that she even would have, because he started pumping into her with a vengeance, possessing her exactly the way she wanted him to. The primitive cavewoman in her rejoiced at the me-man-you-woman routine. The modern-day, I-don't-need-a-man-to-complete-me woman bristled a little, but with every relentless thrust, the cavewoman beat Modern Day Ms. Proper down.

"Mine," he growled. "You're mine, Faith."

"*Yes.*"

Ecstasy ripped through her core and shot up her spine all the way to her skull. A wail escaped her, a cry of pleasure and pain and everything in between. The climax waned, but as Wyatt stiffened, his cock swelling inside her and hitting that spot that made her crazy, another orgasm blasted through her. Her pussy milked him, squeezed until he began to jerk reflexively from the post-climax sensitivity, his gasping curses flowing as freely as his fluids did inside her.

When he finished, then and only then did his arms come around her, holding her so tenderly, no one would have known he'd just banged her to within an inch of her sanity.

She'd shattered, blown into a million pieces, and as with any powerful explosion, she now had emotional shrapnel to deal with.

"AND THAT," Annika said calmly, as her foot crunched down on her opponent's trachea, "is why you never, ever use that type of hold, no matter what your old SWAT trainers told you."

Her opponent, a burly pyrokinetic named Chad, lay on his back, gasping for air. He wrapped his hands around her ankle to dislodge her, and she was about to make him regret that decision when the shrill ring of her mobile phone changed her mind. Chad could stay conscious for now.

"Saved by the cell." She stalked across the gym to where her duffel sat outside the ring of students she'd been teaching in her advanced fighting course. The twice-yearly late-night class was specially tailored for the Hell Month sessions that required agents to spend four weeks constantly training and running on only a few hours of sleep a day.

"What's up, Dev?" she said into the phone.

"Something has happened—"

"Are you okay?" Annika interrupted, because she knew Dev inside and out, and she'd never heard his voice sound the way it did right now, so...devastated. The long pause made a rock form in the pit of her belly.

"Never mind me. Where's Creed?"

"I assumed at his house. Why? What's going on?"

"Do you know where to find him? Where he'd go?"

"Goddammit, Dev, tell me what's going on."

"Just find him. He needs you." Dev hung up.

This was too weird. She jammed the phone into her duffel and slung the bag over her shoulder. "Class is over," she shouted to her students, who all looked relieved. For most of them, the instruction wasn't voluntary.

She took off at a dead run, hit the cold night air in nothing but shorts and the sports-bra workout top she wore for training sessions. Adrenaline made her hands shake as she started up her old Jeep. She never shook like that. Ever. But the idea that Creed might be hurting and upset...

She tore out of the parking lot and off the base. The radio, set on Creed's favorite rock station, kept droning on about Hurricane Lily and its imminent coastal strike, but she didn't listen. Lily wasn't her mission. Remy and Haley would handle it.

The Jeep rattled with speed as she shot across the backroads to Creed's house...where his Harley was missing.

Cursing, she sped to the dive biker bar where he liked to hang out, and sure enough, the bike was there, parked haphazardly near the door. Relief made her start shaking again. How irritating.

AC/DC blasted her ears as she entered the place. The first thing she saw was a wall of leather and tattoos, and none of it belonging to Creed. Just way too many bikers for her taste.

The second thing she saw was a wall of tits and too much female skin, all surrounding Creed, where he sat sprawled in a corner booth, a bottle of whiskey and a shot glass in his hands. He took a swig from the bottle and she wondered why he even bothered with the glass.

One of the skanks sitting next to him in the booth put her hand on his thigh, and Annika's jealousy warred with amusement when he spun the shot glass across the table and rather roughly removed the woman's hand. She wouldn't be deterred, though, and she leaned in, said something in his ear that made him close his eyes and shake his head.

Annika cut through the crowd like a knife through flesh. A couple of the women saw her before she got to the table and wisely cleared out. Two others were too busy sliding as close to Creed as they could, but they looked up when Annika stopped at the booth, arms folded over her chest.

"Leave. Now."

The women grumbled but scooted out of the booth, and Creed, without opening his eyes, reached out his hand for her. "Hey."

God, he looked like shit. She'd never seen him drunk, but he was well beyond that right now. "Hey, ghost boy," she said softly.

"Don't call me that," he snarled, his grip tightening on hers so hard she nearly cried out, but more from surprise than pain. His eyes, red-rimmed, bloodshot, bored into hers like red-hot drills.

"Okay." She eased next to him in the booth. "Okay, baby. I'm sorry." What the hell was wrong with him?

He cursed and took another long pull on the whiskey bottle. Before his throat stopped working on the swallow, he'd slammed the bottle on the table and pulled her into his arms, onto his lap.

"No," he slurred. "I'm sorry. Ah, fuck, I'm sorry."

"Creed, you're scaring me. What's wrong?"

"Not here."

Slowly, she extricated herself from his hold, paid the bartender and helped Creed stumble to her Jeep. Once he was loaded and buckled in, she hit the road, heading toward his place.

Creed braced his forehead against the passenger-side window and just stared out into the night.

"Creed? What is it?"

"Oz," he croaked.

"What did he do to you?" God, she'd always hated that guy. She'd been wanting to knock his teeth out for years, and if he'd hurt Creed, she wouldn't hold back anymore, not even for Dev's sake.

"He's an asshole." He slammed his fist against the door, startling her.

She wanted to ask more, but she waited until they arrived at his house, and once they were inside, she called Dev, left a message on his answering machine that Creed was with her. When she hung up, Creed was glaring at her from the couch.

"He was in on it. My parents probably too."

"In on what?" She sat next to him, rubbed his back when he leaned forward, holding his head in his hands.

"The lie. I get it now, Annika. I get why you're so pissed about the lies. Why you want revenge. CIA bastards."

A sick, sinking sensation dropped into her gut. She hated that he was hurting, even though she had no idea what had caused him the pain. And she really hated that someone had cut him so deeply that he understood *her* pain. He was too good, too decent to be that angry. He didn't deserve it, and she was going to kill whoever had done this to him.

Because she *wasn't* decent, and she had no qualms about playing judge, jury and executioner.

She reached out, pulled his hand away from his face and forced him to look at her. "What happened tonight?"

"Oz." He fisted his hands, and fury burned in his glassy eyes. "He's my brother."

Shock stole her breath. "What? Your brother brother? Like, you have the same parents?"

"Funny, huh?" He pulled away from her and lurched to his feet. He didn't get very far, though, came to a rest with one big shoulder propped against the opening between the kitchen and living room.

She was going to rip Oz apart. Dev would just have to deal with it. Then she wondered if Dev had known about Creed all along, and anger flared.

"They lied to me, Ani," Creed whispered, his head hung low, his shoulders slumped.

She crossed to him, pulled him into her arms. "You need to talk to him," she said, surprising herself. God, she was turning soft. "Tomorrow. After you've slept this off."

"I'm not drunk. And he's dead."

"You're very drunk. And don't say that about Oz. You'll talk, you'll make up, you'll get tight."

"No, Ani. He's *dead*. Fucking killed himself. Blew himself away without ever giving me a chance to know him."

Time stopped. Annika's knees nearly buckled. "But... Oh, God."

Creed collapsed on her, his weight almost too much for her to bear. His big chest heaved, his body wracked with sobs. She struggled with him to the couch, where she held him until he passed out. Then, wishing she could be two places at once, she covered him with a blanket and headed out.

She'd be back before he woke.

Annika made record time getting to Dev's place on base. She practically flew from the Jeep to his front door, was surprised to find it unlocked.

She found him in his bedroom, standing in front of the lit fireplace. Behind him, a dark stain on the carpet told her all she needed to know. Tears stung her eyes as she wrapped her arms around him and pressed her cheek to his back.

For several minutes, they stood like that, the soft snapping of the flames the only sound in the room. Eventually he turned in to her, his bloodshot gaze brimming with pain.

"How's Creed?"

"Not good. He's hurt. Angry."

Dev closed his eyes, and she knew he was keeping it together by a thread. "The thing with Kat couldn't have helped."

"Kat?"

"Oz could have gotten rid of her. Now"—he choked on a half sob—"now it's too late."

Son of a bitch. *That son of a bitch!* Good thing he was dead. She hoped he came back as a ghost, because she planned to shock the shit out of him.

"Come on, Dev. Let's get out of here."

"No. I can't leave him." His gaze fell to the spot on the floor, and he started to tremble. Then, like a dam had broken, he collapsed the way Creed had. She caught him, thankful he weighed less than Creed, and helped him to the bed, giving the bloodstain a wide berth.

Tomorrow, she'd make sure a crew came to replace the carpet.

Sinking onto the bed, she pulled him down next to her. They'd slept together more times than she could count, fully clothed, but always before she'd been the one who needed comfort. For the first time since Dev had rescued her from a hateful life on the run from the CIA six years ago, she returned the favor. She held him while he fell apart.

And he held her while she was torn apart, pulled in two different directions. She had to go back to Creed, but Dev needed her too.

Eyes watering, she stroked his hair, his back, doing what she could to comfort him, and wishing she'd killed Troy in Greece, because this caring for people crap really sucked.

CREED WOKE with the worst headache—and hangover—of his entire life. It only took a moment for the memories of the night before to rush back to him and oh, Christ, he doubled over and headed for the bathroom to get rid of the poison—in the form of the whiskey he'd poured into his body in an attempt to exorcize the pain.

It hadn't worked at all.

He crawled back to the bed and climbed in, collapsing under the weight of last night's events.

But Ani, she'd come for him—he called out for her now, but no one answered. He rose on his elbow to check the driveway from the window next to the bed; her car was gone. It was six in the morning—he didn't think she taught that early, and he needed her. Needed to tell her about Kat, the fact that, with Oz dead, there would never be a way for Creed to be separated from the spirit who protected him.

Speaking of Kat, the spirit was nowhere to be found, which was unusual. Whenever Annika wasn't around, Kat was all over him, as if to make up for time lost.

He'd expected her to be here now, in the same way he'd expected Annika to be here, holding him. Comforting him. Helping him to figure out what the hell to do now.

The pain in his chest returned and he wondered if the phantom pain, centered over his heart in the exact place Oz had shot himself, would linger forever.

He rolled off the bed and got into the shower, so the tears could mingle with the running water and he could ignore them, push them back.

Oz was my brother. And now he was gone.

He dressed quickly, and heard Annika come in through the back door. He met her in the kitchen, where she was unpacking a big take-out breakfast from their favorite diner in town.

She stopped when she saw him, walked over immediately and put her arms around him. "Hey, baby, did you get enough sleep?"

How could he tell her it felt as if he'd never again get enough sleep?

Her arms felt good around him, her body always bringing a crisp, cool air to his overheated one, and for a second he cradled her and fought the tears that threatened again. "Yeah, I got enough sleep," he heard himself mumble, not quite sure why he was lying to her. "I didn't even hear you leave this morning."

He pulled back and caught a glimpse of something in her eyes that didn't sit well with him. She smiled, rubbed his arm and then returned to unpacking the bags that held the take-out food and coffee.

"Come have something to eat," she urged.

"Am I the only one you made a delivery to this morning?" he ground out, not wanting to go there again but unable to stop himself.

"I went to see Dev, yes. I was worried about him too—even though I wasn't close to Oz, he and Dev have been together forever. And when he refused to sleep last night—"

"Last night." He heard the anger in his own voice and desperately wished he could rewind to last night, before any of this happened. But there was no going back and he was too old to believe that wishes could come true. "You were with Dev last night."

"Creed, you were asleep."

Kat's hands came down comfortingly on his shoulders, no sign of *I told you so* about Annika in her touch. He was grateful for that. "I needed you. I can't believe..." He stepped away from her. "I need to get the fuck out of here. I need some air."

"I can't believe you're going to do this now." Annika's arm shot out to grab his wrist, but he twisted away. "I want to be there for you both. Can't you understand that?"

"I understand it, Annika. And that's the biggest part of the problem." He strode out, his eyes nearly closing in response to the bright sunlight—and dammit, there shouldn't be sunlight today, not when someone you cared for, someone you loved, was never going to be there to enjoy it again.

He slid his sunglasses on, jumped on his Harley and took the winding back roads to the base and up the long hill to Dev's.

A walk around the house showed him that the sliding glass door was still open from last night, and he pictured himself walking in, seeing Dev...

Wondered what the hell it would solve. Oz's body would no doubt be gone—only a bloodstain on the carpet would still be there, as a sickening reminder. And with the anger, the grief boiling over inside of him to the point where even Kat wouldn't be able to contain nor comfort his rage, he might do or say something to his friend and boss he'd never be able to take back.

There was nothing sexual between Devlin and Annika—Creed knew that. He wasn't sure why that somehow made it worse, that Annika had such an emotional connection with Devlin, a connection she couldn't and didn't want to break.

Creed would be the one to do the breaking now.

He turned and went out the way he'd come, rode his Harley over to ACRO's headquarters and found Dylan, the head of his department, practicing meditation techniques, like Creed knew he would be.

"Creed." The man's eyes opened.

"I want to be sent on assignment. I'll take anything."

Dylan stared at him and Creed tried for any semblance of normal. "Creed, I'm so sorry about Oz."

"Yeah, me too. Thanks. Now, what about an assignment? I'm sure you've got something good on your desk that I can sink my teeth into." Creed grabbed one of the plain manila folders on Dylan's desk and flipped through it. Dylan sat back and waited patiently, until Creed closed the folder and sighed. "Please, Dylan."

"I've got orders from Devlin. He doesn't want you on assignment. He wants you here. And he's right."

"Fuck Devlin, and fuck you, Dylan. None of you knows what's right," Creed spat, and stormed out of the office, back into the sunlight.

The only problem was, Creed didn't know what was right anymore either.

ANNIKA TRIED for nearly two hours to reach Creed on his cell phone. She couldn't spare the time to physically hunt him down because she'd been too busy preparing hurricane survival kits for rescuers to hand out to victims immediately following a landfall. But dammit, she knew how to work the redial feature on her phone, and she used it every five minutes.

Her phone rang just as she was picking it up to try again for the eight hundredth time. "Creed?"

"Dev. I need to see you. My house. Now." He hung up, and she tore out of the gym, which had been turned into an emergency prep area.

She made it to his place in about sixty seconds flat, found him in his kitchen, dressed in his usual black BDUs and staring into the open refrigerator.

"Dev? You okay?"

He looked up and shut the door. "No, but I have an agency to run, and there's a hurricane about to destroy New York City. My breakdown will have to wait."

She wanted to hug him, but he was doing pretty well, considering, and she didn't want to take him back to a vulnerable place. "I can't locate Creed," she blurted. "Not since this morning."

"Dylan called. Creed tried to get an assignment about three hours ago."

"An assignment? Why?"

"I was hoping you could tell me."

"He wasn't thinking straight," she said. "He's hurt and angry. At the world, at me ... God, he must be really pissed at you and Oz if—" She cursed silently when Dev flinched.

This time she did hug him, sank into him as he wrapped his arms around her. "I have to send you on a mission," he said.

She shook her head. "I can't. I can't leave you like this."

Dev stepped back. "You have to go, Annika."

"You just lost Oz," she whispered.

"I know, and I know you want to be here for Creed too, but this is important." He blew out a long breath. "Why is he angry with you anyway?"

She waved her hand dismissively. "The usual. He flipped out when I told him I came to see you."

"His world just got turned upside down. Give him a break."

Abruptly, her emotions veered sharply to anger. "He's never understood our relationship. He's never wanted to. He's completely irrational when it comes to you."

"Is he?" Dev asked quietly.

"Is he what? Irrational? Unable to share? Yes and yes!" She huffed. "You still think I'm too immature for a relationship, don't you?" The conversation they'd had last spring brought heat to her cheeks, but Dev shook his head.

"I think Creed is exactly what you need."

That wasn't what she'd asked, but he was right. She knew it, but now wasn't the time to talk about it. Not with Dev's crazy idea to send her on a mission at the worst possible time. "I thought you wanted all available operatives here to deal with the hurricane. What's so important that I have to go out now?"

He jammed his hand through his hair, and she knew the reason was going to be a doozy. "Wyatt needs backup."

Yeah, she'd have hit the floor if not for the fact that she'd braced a hip on the counter. "Wyatt's alive?"

"And kicking like a damned mule."

Relief warred with irritation that she hadn't been let in on the big secret, but she scoured the annoyance quickly. She'd been in the life long enough to know that everything an agency did was for a reason, and Dev didn't do shit just for grins.

"What's he need?"

Dev explained the situation to her, and once he finished, she understood the need for the secrecy.

"So basically, I'm going in blind?"

"Sorry, but Wyatt doesn't yet know who wants the motherboard or where they're meeting for the exchange. All I have for you is that you'll land in Dublin. I should have more info by the time you get there. It's critical that you stay back and not get caught in the open. I'll need you to bring in the operative Wyatt's with if he can't."

"What do you mean *can't*?"

"He might have gotten too close."

She snorted. "Wyatt? No way."

"Just be ready. Backup only, until the situation requires otherwise, got it?"

"Loud and clear. How much time do I have? I need to work things out with Creed."

"How much time do you need?"

A sinking sensation made her gut feel full. For the first time, she wasn't sure things *would* work out. Before, her reluctance to commit had been an issue, but her relationship with Dev had always been a touchy subject and something that grew into a bigger problem every time his name was mentioned. The fact that Creed had tried to get the hell out of Dodge without even telling her meant that the problem had grown so large that it could no longer be ignored.

Creed had reached his breaking point.

Tears stung her eyes. "I—I don't think I need any time. Get the plane ready."

"You need to make a choice, don't you?"

Unable to speak through the lump in her throat, she just nodded.

"You realize that if you leave without talking to Creed, you've probably made it, right?" He brought his hands down on her shoulders and looked her in the eye. "You need him."

"I need you too," she whispered.

"I'm not going anywhere," he assured her. "But maybe it's time to let Creed be the one you lean on." He turned away, braced his knuckles on the counter and stared out the kitchen window. "God, I should have done this a long time ago," he muttered, almost so softly she couldn't hear it. "Remember when I changed my locks a few months ago? It wasn't because I was trying to protect you from what was going on in my life. It was because I was tired of you walking in anytime you want."

"Bullshit."

He sighed. "I'm grateful for everything you've done for me and ACRO, but I need space, Annika. No more coming to my house. No more barging into my office. From now on, you make appointments like everyone else."

Like everyone else.

She stared, unable to believe what he was saying. Her first instinct was to chew out his ass. Instead, she replayed her entire relationships with Dev and Creed. Dev had taken her forcibly out of her old life, one full of anger and vengeance, where she had been little more than a feral animal. He'd been patient, never giving up on her, and had eventually brought her around. Dev had given her a shot at a real life.

Creed had been endlessly patient with her, reeling her in slowly and carefully, situating himself so deeply in her life that she couldn't imagine it without him. He'd taught her to love, when she'd been raised to feel nothing.

Dev had given her a shot at a real life, but Creed completed it.

Heart in a knot, she realized that as much as she loved Dev, Creed was the love of her life, and she'd put him on the back burner. She'd fucked things up so badly, and this time she wasn't going to blame her inexperience with relationships. She wasn't going to blame Creed or Dev or the CIA.

She'd done this to herself, and she was going to take responsibility. But that didn't mean she wasn't pissed at Dev for being an ass.

"Yes, sir," she snapped. "I'll head out on my mission now, because heaven forbid I be in your house without an invitation."

DEV WATCHED ANNIKA GO, and once she was out of sight, he slid to the floor, his head in his hands. He hated that he'd had to force Annika and Creed together like a meddling uncle, but things between them had hit critical mass. He'd been aware of Creed's issues with him, but some selfish, dark part of him hadn't wanted to give up Annika.

Now he had a feeling that if all had gone well, she'd realize she had to make a choice between him and Creed, and if she chose Creed, Dev would lose her.

But the loss would be bittersweet. She needed Creed—he was probably the only person on earth who could handle her, and vice versa.

He pulled his phone from his BDU pants' side pocket and dialed the flight coordinator. The perky but incredibly efficient woman answered on the first ring.

"Jessie? I need a jet readied for takeoff. It'll be going to Ireland."

"Yes, sir," she said. "Time frame?"

Dev glanced at his watch. Knowing Annika, she'd need an hour to prep, an hour to hunt down Creed, and thirty seconds to strong-arm him into going with her.

"Two hours, three, tops."

"We'll have to make adjustments to the flight path. The hurricane—"

"Do what you have to do."

"You got it, sir."

Dev hung up, rubbed his eyes and leaned back against the cupboards to stare at the ceiling. He wished he could close his eyes, but there was too much in his head he didn't want to see—Oz, Annika and Ryan, the latter of whom he could no longer see at all with his CRV.

Which meant Ryan was dead.

Right now, he had to concentrate on work, because just this morning Haley had called to tell him that Remy's attempts to push the cold front forward had failed. They were leaving for the coast in an attempt to affect the hurricane itself. If they weren't successful, Dev's grief would be the least of his concerns.

ANNIKA KEPT CALLING Creed, even as she sped to his house. She'd stopped by her place to grab her always ready mission bag, which contained clothes, weapons, gadgets and disguises, and then she'd started the search for Creed. She tried his office first, his favorite biker bar second, and although it was a long shot, she had to see if he'd gone to his house.

When she saw his hog out front, she nearly let out a whoop of victory. She dashed inside and drew up short at the sight of him sitting on the couch, whiskey bottle in one hand, TV remote control in the other.

He was watching soaps.

"Um, baby? You never watch soaps."

He took a swig from the bottle. "All the backstabbing and cheating and fucking makes my life look normal. I like that."

Shit. They'd never be able to talk with him piss-drunk. But she couldn't risk leaving him either. If he sobered up and thought she'd taken off on Dev's orders without even trying to work things out, any hope of making things right would be destroyed.

"Okay, come on." She took the alcohol from him and yanked on his arm. "We're going on a mission."

"Fuck that." He threw down the remote and grabbed the bottle.

"It's Ireland," she cajoled. "They have lots of whiskey there."

"Take your precious Dev. He likes whiskey."

"Dammit, Creed, this isn't about Dev."

"It's always about Dev."

She fisted the front of his T-shirt and got right up in his face. "Not anymore. Now, get on your feet." She tugged, but he dug in like a fucking mule, and she accomplished nothing more than ripping his shirt. "I don't have time for this, Creed."

"Then you should go," he growled. "And this time, stay the fuck away."

He's drunk. He doesn't mean it. She kept telling herself that, but it did little to cut the sting. "I'll take you by force if I have to."

"You'll have to."

Fuck. She didn't want to hurt him, but he was leaving her no choice. Then again, maybe she could enlist some help. It was another long shot, but at this point, she was willing to try anything.

She left him stewing in front of the TV and stomped to the kitchen, where she paced, trying to collect herself. After a minute, she hesitantly called out, "Kat?"

There was no answer—but then, what did she expect? She couldn't communicate with the damned ghost.

"Kat?" What was the ghost's real name? Quaty? "Quaty? Look, I know you can hear me. I need your help. Creed needs your help. He has to go to Ireland with me."

A glass on the kitchen counter shattered. Clearly, Kat didn't like the idea.

"I know you aren't overly fond of me, but look at Creed. He's a mess. It's not even noon and he's pickled. There's a hurricane coming and he's too hurt by everything that's happened to care. I can help him. Talk some sense into him. At least get him sobered up so he's not a danger to himself." She paused, still feeling a little stupid for talking to the air. "Or would you rather see him miserable, drunk and watching soap operas?"

There was no indication that Kat agreed, but then, no more glasses had shattered. Annika checked her watch. She needed to get going. With or without Kat's help, Creed was boarding that plane.

She went back to the living room, where Creed hadn't moved except to lower the volume of liquid in the bottle. She swiped it out of his hand. "You've left me with no choice."

He came to his feet with roar of rage. "I'm not going!"

Annika struck. She hooked his elbow with hers and wheeled behind him, but before she could take him down, he went to his knees with a shout.

"Kat! What the fuck are you doing?"

Yes!

"Goddammit, Kat! You traitor!" His curses blistered the air, and though he struggled to get back to his feet, he seemed to be held down.

Quickly, Annika took advantage of the situation, wrapping her arm around his thick neck and putting a sleeper hold on him. He bucked for a second, and then slumped peacefully to the floor.

"Sorry about that, baby," she murmured. "But you'll thank me later. I hope."

She swallowed dryly, because she could hope all she wanted, but the truth was, she wasn't sure of anything except the fact that when he woke up, he was going to be *pissed*.

CHAPTER
Twenty

"Nice of ML to put us up and lend us his private jet," Faith remarked as she buckled herself in for the eight A.M. takeoff, her legs sheathed in the soft lambskin leather pants ML's personal shopper had bought for her. A black tank under a sheer white blouse completed the outfit, making her look part superagent, part hot mama.

Wyatt sat next to her, his long legs stretched out into the aisle, and didn't bother to hide his appreciation as his hand stroked the outside of her thigh. "ML's an old friend."

"On which side of the law?"

"Whichever side we need him to be. That's the beauty of ML."

"You know, he really does look a lot like Elvis."

Wyatt laughed. "Don't get too attached to him. He knows you're mine."

"You need to stop saying that."

"No can do," he said earnestly. He didn't remind her that she'd agreed.

Instead, he unzipped the duffel ML had handed him before they'd gotten on the jet. "We've got more clothes here for both of us. Passports." He pulled out the small green booklets and handed them to her.

"Mr. and Mrs. Lapp?"

ML's parents. The real Mrs. Lapp had given birth to eight children. Babies. Wyatt could picture himself with babies running around, one or two riding his shoulders, another couple behind him, trying to grab at his legs.

Yeah, he'd be a good father. "Problem, Mrs. Lapp?"

"No, no problem, darling. Just trying to get into mission mode."

"Plenty of time for that." He put his arms behind his head and sighed, thought about Remy and Hurricane Lily and pushed as much good karma their way as he could. Even though Wyatt had done his job, the hurricane had progressed too far by the time he'd gotten the code to Haley for ACRO to stop it without relying solely on Remy's powers. Wyatt wished there was more he could've done.

Twenty-twenty hindsight was always a bitch.

Although he hadn't destroyed the motherboard, while Faith had been taking a shower he'd made sure it wasn't going to disappear into the unknown. Thanks to his telekinesis, Wyatt had been able to feel inside the safe's combination lock until each number hit its pin in the locking mechanism. Once inside, he'd murmured his thanks to ML and his resourcefulness as he attached a micro-tracker and then replaced the motherboard in the exact position in which he'd found it. A quick call to ACRO with the tracking device's frequency, and all was set. As much as he trusted Faith to do the right thing, knew instinctively that she would, he still had a responsibility to ACRO ... to the world.

"You look very serious." Faith's voice purred in his ear, and he wondered if it would always be like this, if his body would instantly react to her touch, her voice. "Maybe you should unleash some of your sex mojo on me and I'll help rid you of the worries."

"I don't need the mojo to get you, baby. Hopefully, the pilots will stay behind closed doors for a while." He jerked his head toward the cockpit.

"Oh, right—forgot your mojo can affect everything in your path. And I'd much rather keep you to myself than share you with the men who're supposed to be flying this plane."

"Yeah, me too." He maneuvered her into his lap. "Better defuse me quickly."

"Good thing I've got just the cure for you." She wiggled on his lap, his erection already like a ramrod in the loose cargoes he'd gotten from ML's personal shopper.

He'd noted, with great interest, that Faith hadn't been happy as the woman named Leslie had offered to help dress him in the clothing. He'd barely noticed Leslie at first. He'd grown used to the extra attention from women, because no matter how good his control got, he was always going to have stronger pheromones than other men. Faith, however, had noticed plenty.

"As much as I love you in those clothes, I'm going to love you out of them more," he murmured, and waited for her knee-jerk response. He wasn't disappointed. "Get used to the word *love*, Faith."

She licked her bottom lip lightly, as if trying to decide how to handle the situation. She finally made her decision by leaning in to kiss him with a ferocity he hadn't expected, her hands twisting in his hair to pull him even closer to her—and oh, yeah, he couldn't get enough of her. While they were up here, with nothing else to worry about, he was going to make the most of this uninterrupted time.

He undid the buttons on her shirt, one by one, making sure his knuckles brushed against her nipples as he did so, then slid the soft material off her shoulders and leaned forward to kiss her breasts through the cotton of the black tank top.

She sucked in a breath as he tugged on her nipple through the fabric, soaking the material as he caressed the now hard nub with his tongue and teeth. She was busy trying to yank the tank top off while simultaneously taking off his shirt as well. Within seconds it was skin on skin, their mouths joined for long but not leisurely kisses, the kind that curled his toes and made him think about tomorrow and all the tomorrows afterward.

He'd never considered himself an easy mark—he'd always been self-reflective, even more so since spending time with the good people at ACRO, and he'd come to the realization that he might never find someone he wanted to be with for the long haul. Sam had reminded him that with his sexual pull he could never be sure if it was the pheromones or Wyatt himself that the women were drawn to.

But this, this was so different, and he had to ask himself if he'd feel the same even if their lust was controlled by his mojo, which it wasn't. He'd have to say yes, he'd feel the same, because the intensity between them, even when they were merely talking about the weather, was off the charts.

Faith was already pulling down her pants—he did the same, and once they were both naked, he had her on her back on the attached couch, which ran along the starboard wall of the aircraft.

"Are you sore, baby?" he asked before he entered her. "We had a pretty busy night. I don't want to hurt you."

"Hurt me, Wyatt—it feels too good for you not to. I can handle sore."

"I promise I'll spend time kissing it and making it better," he murmured as he slid inside her, his cock pulsing in pleasure as she contracted hard around him. Her thighs tightened around his waist, forcing him to buck into her more deeply, and he didn't bother holding back his groan as they began to rock together to the turbulent rhythm of the jet.

THE HOTEL had been closed for hurricane evacuations, but apparently someone at ACRO had pulled some strings, blackmailed someone or, heck, blown someone. Haley didn't give a shit. She and Remy had taken a room on the top floor, east side, where somehow they had to stop a hurricane.

The weather had fluctuated wildly as the outer bands of the massive hurricane spun up storm cells all along the East Coast, which naturally wreaked havoc with Remy's libido. Twice on the drive to Fire Island they'd had to pull over to the side of the road. And they'd only just unpacked her weather equipment in the suite when he'd thrown her down on the bed to take her with a ferocity she hadn't seen since that first night in the bayou a year ago.

Now they stood outside on the balcony, where at two in the afternoon it was nearly dark as night, Remy gripping the iron rail so hard his knuckles had gone white, both wearing hotel robes because it was pointless to get dressed.

"You can do this," she said, her voice barely audible over the howling wind gusts.

Remy's throat worked on a hard swallow as he looked out over the churning ocean. "I don't know, *bebe*. This is . . . Fuck, I don't know."

"You've come so far, Remy."

He turned to her, his dark eyes flashing. "She's already fucking with me, and she's over two hundred miles out." Distant thunder rolled, and his entire body convulsed.

Haley pulled him into her arms, her heart aching. Storms tore him apart, made his body react so violently that he could barely control his lust, and though he knew she could handle whatever he threw at her, he'd never fully gotten over his fear that he might hurt her at the height of his storm-lust.

"This could be bad." He petted her hair gently. "Like nothing we've dealt with before."

They'd dealt with a lot in the year since they'd met, but no matter what Hurricane Lily did, she couldn't cut the sting from the fact that for the last seven months Haley and Remy had been trying to conceive but had failed. Haley was a day late as of today, but that wasn't unusual; her periods had been screwy since she stopped taking birth control nine months ago. Still, she'd brought a pregnancy test with her . . . just in case.

"We'll handle it," she said. "Together."

A rumble started deep in his chest, joining the thunder rolling in from over the ocean. "Go set up your equipment. I'll start working." His arms tightened around her, pulling her firmly against his erection. "But don't be long. I'm going to need you. Soon."

She hurried, the tattoo that connected them tingling like a bee sting. Her equipment consisted mainly of computers, portable radars and weather recorders, all with massive battery backup. Her cell phone rang just as she was turning on her laptop.

It was Dev, wanting a status report. He sounded like hell, but she didn't think he'd appreciate her asking about it.

"Do *not* put yourselves in danger, Haley. I mean it. If things even hint that they might go south, get out of there."

"Yes, sir."

Dev cursed like he didn't believe her. Which he shouldn't. She and Remy couldn't leave now. They were here for the duration, and everyone knew it.

"I should have sent you on the Hurricane Hunter plane."

"Dev, we discussed that." Hitching a ride with the Air Force's 53rd Weather Reconnaissance Squadron would have gotten them up close and personal with the storm's eye, but there would have been some serious privacy and safety issues. She glanced at Remy, who stood on the balcony, head back, fists clenched, his chest heaving. "I have to go. I'll update you hourly."

She hung up and checked the latest satellite and radar images. Lily was strengthening, had been since Haley had left her lab back at ACRO. It would be a miracle if Remy could push the storm away from the coast, let alone weaken her. This girl was a monster, a tragedy in the making.

Itor bastards. Wyatt had prevented them from making the storm worse, but as a category five hurricane, she was going to cause mass destruction even without Itor's interference.

A noise startled her, the sound of something hitting the glass patio door. Remy's fist. Her heart leaped to her throat at the sight of him staring at her, lightning flashing in his eyes. He'd lost the robe. Rain sluiced down his hard, powerful body, the rivulets taking the paths of least resistance, the deeply scored valleys between slabs of muscle. His erection jutted upward, engorged to what she knew was the point of agony for him.

One hand, balled into a fist, braced him against the glass. The other slid down his abs, slowly, purposefully, until he was fisting his cock.

Her womb clenched and her blood rushed hotly through her veins. God, she loved it when he did that. When he stroked himself as he focused on her with such white-hot intensity that she couldn't look away.

His hand pumped, each upward stroke hitting the flared ridge she knew exactly how to lick to make him moan. Each downward stroke making his sac darken and plump with a tidal surge of blood. Her mouth watered and her sex went just as wet, until her cream slicked her inner thighs.

Unbidden, her fingers found her tight, hardened nipples through the fabric of her robe. As Remy thrust into his palm, she untied her sash, allowing the robe to fall open and expose her body to his hungry gaze. Her tattoo, a fist clutching a lightning bolt on her hip, throbbed as always when Remy's arousal rose above normal levels.

Still watching him, she slid her hand down between her legs. Pleasure sizzled through her at the first brush of her fingers over her clit. She made one slow circle around the swollen bud, and Remy jerked as though he'd been burned, his upper lip curling in a carnal snarl.

Come here, he mouthed. *Now.*

Haley had never been one to follow orders, but she couldn't resist her husband's erotic commands. Ever.

She darted to the door, had barely opened it when he yanked her outside and pushed her against the rain-soaked building. In an instant he was inside her and his teeth were latched on to her shoulder and she was coming the way she always did during storm sex.

Immediately. Loudly. Intensely.

He pounded into her, his body thrashing, slamming her spine against the wall. She must have cried out, because although he didn't slow down or let up, he lifted his head to look at her, and what she saw in his eyes broke her heart. Tears.

"I'm sorry, Haley. I'm so sorry..."

Around them, the wind howled and the rain slashed at them. She took his face in her palms and locked her gaze on his. "Don't worry about me, dammit. Stop the storm."

"I'm not going to win this one, *bebe*," he whispered, and then he peaked, roaring into the turmoil around them.

As he bucked against her, she wrapped herself tight around him. They would win this one. They had to. This was what ACRO did. They saved the world.

CHAPTER
twenty-one

"We can't be rerouted—we need to get to Ireland ASAP."

Annika's firm tone tore through Creed's skull like a knife. He was vaguely aware that the room seemed to be...bumpy. And when he rubbed the sleep from his eyes, he realized he wasn't in a room, or his house, but rather on an ACRO jet that seemed to be caught in the middle of the hurricane.

He was also damned tired of waking up hungover; he muttered as he yanked himself to his feet and into the small bathroom at the back of the jet before Annika could get to him. He splashed water on his face and gargled and tried to keep a rein on his temper as he remembered Kat and Annika double-teaming him earlier.

Kat touched his arm, as if to soothe his nerves.

"Yeah, don't even bother with that shit," he said fiercely. "Since when did you and Ani become friends?"

Kat didn't answer, merely huffed.

"Creed, are you all right?" Annika called out, and he sighed and opened the door with a heaviness in his heart he hadn't thought he'd ever have again after being with Annika.

She waited for him at the far end of the plane, and he didn't say anything at first, just sat down on one of the long seats and stretched out his legs and tried to feel human.

She sat across from him, attempting to look contrite, which never, ever worked. And he was angry at himself that he thought about how cute she looked when she tried to do so. "Are you going to tell me why you kidnapped me?"

"Wyatt's alive," she blurted out, and that shut him up. He sat there, mouth hanging open for a second, until he smiled—his first real smile in days.

"You're sure?"

"Apparently he was on a blacked-out mission the entire time—dealing with the machine that started the stupid hurricane that's rerouting us from our mission." Her voice raised as she turned her head to the closed door of the cockpit. "We're going to help him out."

He watched her carefully for a second. "And Dev thought I was the best one to help out rather than, say, Ender?"

"Dev didn't exactly want you on this mission. He wanted you home . . . to give you time to grieve. But I didn't want to leave you behind—not the way we left things." She tossed him a bottle of water and then stared out the window as the jet got tossed by turbulence.

"It's all so fucked up, Ani." He downed half of the water.

"I fucked up, didn't I? I waited too long to make my decision about us being together. If I'd said something sooner, told you how much I cared about you, then Oz would've helped you release Kat."

"I don't know," he said honestly. His head was pounding—the change in pressure wasn't helping and he rubbed his temples in an attempt at clear thought. "Oz didn't tell me much about the process, what releasing Kat would involve. Oz didn't tell me much of anything."

Oz loved you, Kat told him, but Creed shoved that thought off. "Kat won't leave us alone now."

"She's been manageable, Creed. She hasn't stopped us from being together."

"She can, though, and she will." In reality, Kat had been amazingly lax in her treatment of Annika—partially out of respect for Creed's love and partially because she knew that Ani's electric shocks could keep her at bay. "She'll never let me live in peace, Annika."

"But she loves you. How could she do that to someone she loves?"

"It's all she knows. Don't you understand, she'll do anything to protect me. If you do anything she perceives as hurting me—"

"I hurt you to get you on the plane, and she helped me. You helped me, Kat—can you please talk to him?"

He felt Kat's stony silence like a blast of freezing air. He rubbed his arms and wished he could close his eyes and sleep all of this off.

But he knew that when he woke up, the problems would all still be there. "Kat helped you because she was worried about me—she didn't want me drinking anymore. But that doesn't mean she's happy with you... with us. It's just not the way it was meant to be."

"What are you saying?"

"It's over. We need to break it off now."

"Suppose Oz had never come back to give you this option—what would've happened then? Would we be in the same place?"

"Maybe. Probably. Fuck, I don't want to do this. It's too much—I don't want to deal with this." He stared at the mini-fridge tucked into the side of the cabin and wondered if it was stocked with anything he could use to numb himself again.

Before he could check, Annika was at his side.

"Creed, before you, I didn't have any hope of getting close to anyone. I don't want to lose you. I can't lose you now."

"Look, I get it, all right—the sex thing. And I'll be there for you when you need sex, until you find another guy you can't shock to death."

"Fuck you, Creed. Fuck you if you really think that's why I'm with you." She took a ragged breath, and when she spoke again, her voice had softened. "You're much more to me than an orgasm."

Creed didn't say anything, felt like maybe, between the stress and the turbulence, he could throw up any second.

"So that's it—the end? I don't get a say?" she demanded.

"You've already had your say. That's the reason I'm ending things. It's for the best, for both of us."

She opened her mouth to say something, ended up storming off to the bathroom—the only private place on the plane. Creed thought about going after her, but his body was wracked by pain, by grief and guilt, and he was afraid he'd lose his resolve if he attempted to comfort her.

Kat rubbed his shoulders, her worry for him coming through loud and clear.

"I'm fine, Kat," he said wearily, even though both of them knew that was a complete lie.

Bite it back. Concentrate. An operative doesn't let anything get in the way of the mission.

Yet there was so much in the way.

But Creed told himself that this wouldn't be so bad, that things would be the way they were before.

You and me, Creed, Kat whispered.

"Yeah, you and me, Kat, and you're not here out of choice either," he muttered. If it hadn't been for Oz casting a spell and calling Kat to Creed, Kat could've crossed over. Been happy. And when he thought about it like that, it made him sadder than ever.

But something wasn't sitting well with Kat—Creed knew her as well as he knew himself, and yet he couldn't figure out where her discomfort was coming from.

Just then, the plane bounced and jerked, moved up and down in a sickening motion, and there was no way this rerouting was going to happen.

To concur, the pilot's voice came over the speakers. "We're going to have to land and try again for Ireland when the storm passes. For now, prepare for a rough landing."

"Shit." Annika slammed out of the small bathroom, didn't look at Creed as she buckled herself in. Creed did the same. Flying hadn't ever been his favorite thing, especially not in rough weather, and he just concentrated on the fact that Wyatt, his friend, was alive. Something to celebrate. Something to concentrate on to get him through the next hours and days.

After that, he had to hope that something else would come along that would.

ANNIKA REMAINED BUCKLED in for about ten seconds. She couldn't sit still and she didn't give a shit if the goddamned plane was bouncing around like glitter in a snow globe, and besides, they were at least several minutes from landing.

I'll be there for you when you need sex, until you find another guy you can't shock to death.

Seriously? He seriously thought that was all she wanted from him? Man, it had hurt to hear him say that. Hurt so much that she didn't know how to deal with it. Confronting emotions all by herself had been something she'd never had to do. She'd always ruthlessly beaten them back or let them out on Dev.

"Get back in your seat and buckle in," Creed shouted—but defiantly, she marched over to him.

"Not until you listen to me." She put her hands on her hips, which would have been much more impressive if she didn't have to keep shifting her weight to keep from falling. "I'm sorry I've put Dev ahead of you. You have to believe me." That sounded so lame, but she'd never been good at apologies.

He stiffened, like he wanted to be angry, but then, in the dim light, she saw the tiredness in his eyes. "That's the thing, Annika. You don't need to be sorry for being who you are. Even though I can't deal with it, how can I fault you for your loyalty to Dev?"

"You can fault me because I gave him what I should have given you." She ignored the slap of an invisible hand across the face, no doubt Kat's way of telling her she agreed. "I've felt torn in two for so long, and when I had to go one way, I almost always made the wrong choice."

"I didn't force you to choose."

"No, you didn't. But I'm making that choice now. I choose you, Creed." She threw out a hand to brace herself on a seat back when a particularly bad gust of turbulence knocked the jet around. "You've been so patient with me. So much more than I deserved. I was blind and stupid. I didn't put you first, and I should have. I'll do anything to make it up to you. Anything. Even if you say no, I won't give up."

His face fell, as if he wanted to believe her but couldn't allow himself to. "It's too late."

"It's never too late," she said fiercely. "I love you. You're all I want, and I'll do whatever it takes to make our relationship work. I'll cut back on my work schedule to spend more time with you. I'll move in with you. I'll——"

A screech nearly shattered her eardrums. What felt like fists slammed into her chest and knocked her against the forward bulkhead.

Creed swore and unbuckled himself. "Kat! Stop it!"

It took everything Annika had not to charge herself up with a million volts and turn that little spectral bitch into a smoking blob of ectoplasm. Instead, she held still, let the ghost mash her into the wall with such force, Annika could hardly breathe.

"Let her go, Kat," Creed growled. "See, Annika? That's why it's too late." The bleak look in his eyes tore into her heart like a bullet. "Oz died before he could . . ."

Get rid of Kat.

It really was too late. A raw, keening noise ripped from her throat, echoed through the tomblike cabin, which had seemed so spacious before. "I waited too long to decide, didn't I?" she whispered, partly because Kat was strangling her.

He didn't say it, but she knew. This was her fault. Utterly, completely. She'd dicked around for months, stringing Creed along because she couldn't make up her mind, and now she'd truly lost him, even though she had no doubt he wanted them to be together.

"It's over, Kat." He sounded resigned. Empty. "Release Annika."

The pressure faded, but Annika remained where she was, slumping now that Kat wasn't holding her up. Creed's strong arms hauled her against him, banded around her.

"I love you," he said hoarsely. "I'll always love you." She felt him jerk, knew Kat had done something to him, and he pulled away. Didn't look her in the eyes. "We need to get back in our seats."

"No. No, dammit. It's not going to end this way." Squaring her shoulders, she braced herself for what was sure to be the strangest, most humiliating suck-up job she'd ever done. Hell, the only suck-up job.

"Quaty," she began, and saw Creed blink in surprise. "I know you don't like me, and honestly, the feeling is pretty mutual." That probably wasn't the way to start the grovelfest, but Kat wouldn't believe anything else. "But I know you love Creed. And I know that you're a big part of why he is who he is. You also helped me get him on this plane, so obviously you want him to be happy."

Annika paused. "Is she listening?"

Creed gave her a stunned nod.

"Okay, good." She closed her eyes. Opened them and locked gazes with the man she loved. "Quaty? Creed needs you. That will never change. You protect him. Keep him safe. But think how much safer he'd be if I were around. I love him, so much it hurts. You know how that feels, don't you? When we talked about getting rid of you, it hurt you.

"We were wrong," Annika said, looking around like maybe she could catch a glimpse of the ghost. "He needs you in his life. And I need him. I want him to be safe; I also want him to be happy. That's what you want too. I can make Creed happy. I know I haven't done a great job of it so far—"

"That's not true," he said in a guttural whisper. "I've never been happier. I hate being apart from you. It's like—"

"Like part of you is missing," she finished, and he nodded. Tears welled up, making her vision blurry. "I don't like that feeling. I hate it. I can't . . . I can't live like that. I can't live without you. I don't want to." A massive, shuddering sob shook her body. "Please, Quaty. I'm begging you to share him."

God, if someone had told her a year ago that, in tears, she'd be pleading with a ghost to let her play a part in some fucked-up threesome, Annika would have forcibly committed that person to a nuthouse. She certainly wouldn't have asked anyone or anything to share anything of hers. One of the few things Annika did not do well was share.

The air stilled. Grew cold. Dead silence hung like fog around them.

"How about it, Quaty?" Desperation made Annika's voice unsteady. "Will you let me be with Creed?"

Suddenly, a warning klaxon filled the cabin with deafening shrieks, the oxygen masks dropped and the pilot's voice blared over the intercom: "Brace for a rough landing."

Creed grabbed her hand and yanked her toward the seats. She'd never seen him as pale as he was now, and he went even whiter when the jet banked hard and sent them both crashing into the port bulkhead. "Shit," he said hoarsely. "Thanks for dragging me along."

They crawled toward the nearest seats. "Sarcasm duly noted." He really must not like to fly.

His hand tightened on hers, pulling her to a halt in the middle of their mad dash to get seated. "I was serious. If something is going to happen to you, I want to be there. We're in this together."

"Oh, Creed," she whispered. "But what about Kat? What's her answer?"

The plane began to shake. A blow like a strike from a baseball bat connected with the back of Annika's skull. Pain exploded in her head and she landed in a heap of agony on the floor, blood streaming from the corner of her mouth.

It seemed that Kat had given her an answer.

"ANNIKA, SHIT." Creed rushed to her side and helped her to sit up, even as she resisted his help. Appearing weak was not something Annika did well—or at all—and she tried to shrug off his concern.

"I guess that's a no," she mumbled as with his thumb he gently wiped some of the blood from her lip.

"That wasn't Kat," he told her. "We were tossed—a box from the overhead bin caught you hard. Are you all right?"

"I'm fine." She pushed him away but remained next to him, eyes scanning the window. "We've landed—where the hell are we?" Agent Annika was on full alert.

Kat was also next to him, on his right, where she'd always been.

Flanked by the two women in his life once again, and neither one seemed very happy with him.

Suddenly, Annika stormed to the cockpit, and a minute later delivered the bad news to Creed.

They'd landed in bumfuck Nova Scotia. Annika had laid into the pilot, but he'd been as pissed as anyone. Apparently, the plane's course should have taken them well away from Hurricane Lily, but the storm had made a sudden wobble that caught them on the edge.

Remy working his weather mojo, probably.

The pilot calmly told Annika that the jet had taken minor damage, so now they were sitting on some godforsaken tarmac and waiting for repairs. "It could be hours," the pilot said.

Hours. Hours of sitting here next to the woman whose heart he'd just broken, hours of feeling like his own heart would explode out of his chest. He remained on the floor, buried his head against his knees and tried to breathe.

Oz would've laced into him for acting this way—Devlin too, no doubt.

Annika's cool hand stroked the back of his neck—soothing, comforting, everything he didn't deserve. And she was still here. Dammit, that meant something—it had to show something to Kat too.

"You've been through so much, Creed. I know you're probably

still mad at me, but can you let me help you? You can still be pissed and—"

"I'm not pissed, Ani. I'm not." He lifted his head and pulled her down to him so he could nuzzle his head against her neck, breathe in the unique scent that he would know in the dark and from thousands of miles away. "You called Kat Quaty. She liked that."

"It's time to start showing respect to the other woman in your life. I should've done that a long time ago...but I don't like to share. Now I see that I'm going to have to if I want to be with you. And I do want to be with you."

He pulled back. "I can't do the same sharing with Devlin— not the way we were, Ani. You've got to understand that. I love the man and I respect him, but..."

"But he's not a ghost."

"All I know is that when I'm with you, everything else falls away. I want it to be the same with you."

"It is, Creed. It does."

"There's still so much to integrate, to deal with," he said softly. "Still so much I want to know."

"About Oz? He did what he thought was best," Annika told him. "I didn't like Oz, that's no secret. He was intense and serious. I guess with a gift like his, he wasn't able to be any other way."

"Communicating with the worst of the worst spirits was tough on him," Creed admitted. "He didn't like to let that show, but it was beginning to take its toll."

"He and Dev always had a rocky relationship, and all I saw was Oz leave and Dev upset. But maybe that's not the way it really was." She smiled weakly. "Kills me to admit that. Oz never truly left you. He may have left you for Martha and Dave to find, but he stayed close. You were always in his sights."

"He was so little when he left me there. Still a kid himself."

"Oz was never truly a kid, Creed. He was born different."

"I know the way Oz grew up. I knew. He told me about his past, his childhood. He just left out the part about me." He turned to Annika and wiped his eyes angrily. "He could've come to Mom and Dad. They would've understood."

Annika merely nodded.

"I'm sorry, Ani. I know talking about parents can be tough on you."

"It's okay." She sighed. "Look, Dev told me some things—he wanted me to share them with you." Her voice was quiet, as if she didn't know whether or not the mention of Dev would make Creed lose it.

"I'm listening," he said instead, and she held his hand and looked into his eyes.

"Dev didn't know for very long about Oz being your brother, Creed. Not until Oz came back this last time. Dev said that it was almost like Oz knew it was time to stop keeping secrets, but at that point, Dev didn't realize that Oz knew his own fate, that Oz knew he'd have to reveal the fact that he was your brother to you before he died. And Oz was so worried about leaving you without protection that the decision he made on his deathbed wasn't easy."

"You mean Kat."

"Yes. He didn't do that to curse you," Dev said. "He just never did trust well."

"He trusted Dev."

"He did. He saved Dev's life, Creed. And he made sure you grew up safe, with parents who loved you. Don't take that away from him because you're angry. He's still your family. I mean, I don't have a family, but I know enough now to understand that there are some good ones out there."

He caught her in his arms before she could choke out the sob. "You've found a family, Ani. You've got me and my parents now."

"But Kat, what about Kat?" Annika's voice was muffled against his chest, and yes, what about Kat? He hadn't felt her since he'd taken Annika into his arms—he'd assumed she was doing her usual, giving them a few minutes of privacy before she came barreling in.

He called to her silently and she came almost immediately, hovered over him with the familiar scent of earth she always brought with her.

You've found her, Kat said.

"I know that. You know that," he answered. "I'm talking to Kat," he told Annika when she lifted her face off his chest.

"I know," she said. "I mean, I hear her."

"What do you mean you hear her?" he demanded. Because as far as he knew, the only people who ever heard Kat besides himself had been his parents and Oz.

Family. Always limited to family. His eyes welled up with tears and both Annika and Kat were brushing them away.

This was the way it was meant to be. Don't you understand, Creed? You were meant to fight for the woman you needed—and I had to be sure she'd do the same for you.

"I'll always fight for him, Kat. But I'll never fight you, not again," Annika whispered.

"You planned all this—from the beginning, you knew that you'd let Annika in?"

No plan. The universe has its own way of making things happen. But look how easily all those other women ran from you.

"I stayed away from them—you made it too hard."

I made it hard when you were with Annika too. You were just too much in love to notice. Tell her, Creed. It's time.

"Tell me, Creed. Please."

"You sure you're ready for all of this—a ready-made family consisting of ghost-hunting parents and a real live ghost? And me?"

"I'm ready. I'm finally ready . . . and it's all because of you."

"I'm finally ready, and it's all because of *you*," he told her. "I love you, Annika."

The floor of the plane began to tremble. Annika smiled, her face breaking wide open. "I love you too, baby. So much."

I love you both, will protect you both. It's the way Oz wanted it, Kat whispered, and then there was a gentle touch on his back. He heard Ani suck in a breath and realized that Kat was touching her too. Accepting her. Accepting them both.

"We love you too, Kat," he whispered, as his past and present merged with a force that shook the entire jet . . . and his soul.

His future was left in the care of two women, one watching his back and one in his arms, holding him so tight he could barely breathe.

Twenty-two

Wyatt and Faith checked into a bed-and-breakfast on the outskirts of Belfast, a small, secluded manor where she'd stayed before and where she knew the owners well enough to trust them to alert her to trouble. After settling into their room, she and Wyatt took a moonlit, hand-in-hand stroll around the area, pretending to be a married couple while mapping out potential escape routes.

ML'd had the foresight to include a wig and makeup in the purchases he'd made for them, so she'd disguised her dark hair with a curly mane of ginger, had used pale foundation and rouge to create a ruddy complexion. Though it was unlikely Liberty's captors would know where she was staying, Faith didn't want to take a chance that someone might recognize her—she especially didn't want to tip off the bastards that she had anyone with her.

After a late dinner at a local pub, they went back to their room, feeling rested despite the travel. Between bouts of furious lovemaking, they'd both managed to catch naps on the flight.

Faith had never had so much sex in her life. She was a little sore, but it was a good ache, one that reminded her that in Wyatt she'd met her match in every way. For a while, she could almost pretend they were lovers on vacation. Normal people who didn't

266 • *Sydney Croft*

hold the lives of others in their hands. In the pub they'd laughed and shared stories of places they'd been, and when the musicians played, Wyatt had dragged her out on the floor to dance.

Though she'd instinctively maintained situational awareness, and she knew Wyatt had as well, she'd allowed herself to relax and enjoy herself for the first time in years. The walk back to the B and B with Wyatt had been the most pleasant, quiet moment of her life. They hadn't spoken a word, but the incredible, magical silence had said more than any conversation could have.

Reality intruded, however, when she used the mobile phone Liberty's captors had given her to contact them.

The male voice had sent a chill up her spine. "The meeting will take place in forty-eight hours. We'll contact you immediately before with further instructions."

The timing was bullshit. They wanted her to think she had time to prepare. No doubt they'd spring an earlier meeting on her at the last minute. In any case, soon she'd have Liberty, but she'd have lost Wyatt. Unless...unless she could work something out with him. She'd have to test the waters.

"Tell me again why ACRO doesn't want the weather machine," she said, as he poured himself a glass of water from the pitcher on the nightstand.

"We don't want to risk it getting into the wrong hands."

She bit her lip, braced herself. "What if you knew it was in the right hands?"

He'd been about to take a sip from his glass, but he lowered his hand and pegged her with a dark look. "There are no right hands. Why?"

"I was just thinking that if ACRO's—or maybe TAG's—scientists studied it, we could learn how to keep others from being built, or to neutralize those that exist."

"No. If you're suggesting what I think you're suggesting..."

She shook her head, trying not to let her disappointment show. There was no way he was going to come around on this, and any further talk would make him suspicious. Her job now was to save her sister and then get the machine to TAG's scientists to study—and her feelings for Wyatt couldn't get in the way, no matter how much it hurt.

And it did. A lot.

"It was just an idea," she said with a shrug. "What is it you Yanks say? No big?"

He grinned. "Teenagers. Five years ago, maybe."

"Yeah, well, it sometimes takes a while for Americanisms to cross the pond."

He kissed her on the forehead and excused himself to go to the loo down the hall. Quickly, she took advantage of the private moment to contact her agency. She dialed, thanking God that Paula answered on the first ring.

"Faith! It's bloody well time you checked in. Where are you? Did you get the—"

"I don't have time," Faith interrupted. "I'm in Belfast. The exchange will take place within forty-eight hours. I'm guessing much sooner."

"Where?"

"Unknown. They'll call with instructions. I need you to gather a team, and stage nearby so you can be on deck when they call."

"They'll be expecting that."

"I know. And I can't risk screwing this up, so you'll hang back. Way back. And alert the Hatter Brigade as well."

"Done. Do you know who these bastards are?"

Faith rubbed her eyes, suddenly feeling the jet lag. "I suspect the ILF."

"Jesus. Haven't they had dealings with Itor?"

"Yeah. Or we could be facing Itor defectors, or free agents who want a piece of the weather-machine action."

Paula cursed. "I don't like this. I don't like you going in by yourself."

"I've been in stickier situations." Faith hesitated, and then blurted out, "I have help, in any case. An ACRO operative."

There was a heartbeat of silence, and then a screeched "*Are you mad?* Do you think this ACRO agent is just going to let you walk away with the motherboard?"

"Who are you talking to?"

Faith jumped, whirled to the doorway, where Wyatt was watching with hooded eyes, shoulder braced against the doorjamb and arms crossed over his broad chest, as though he didn't have a care in the world.

Faith knew better. And shit, how had she let him sneak up on her like that?

She spoke quickly into the phone while keeping an eye on Wyatt. "I have to go. I'll ring you later." She hung up. "I was talking to my agency," she said. "We're on my turf now. You have your resources, I have mine."

"What's the Hatter Brigade?"

"Cleanup crew." It wasn't a lie, exactly, but it wasn't the truth either. In the battle against Liberty's captors, she and Wyatt might have to deal with people with special powers, and the Hatter—as in "Mad Hatter"—Brigade specialized in handling people with special abilities.

They also contained them in facilities with which Wyatt had too much experience, and she definitely didn't want to spook him.

"Tell me what's going on, Faith. If I'm going into battle, I deserve to know everything. I'm willing to trust you, but I don't know your agency, and I'm not putting either of our lives, or the weather machine, in the hands of people I don't know."

"Like I did with ML?" she asked quietly.

"You didn't have much of a choice."

"And you do?"

"I could have the full backing of ACRO and a dozen agents on the ground in a matter of hours. So yeah, I have a choice."

"Are you threatening me?"

Wyatt snorted. "I'm exposing my throat, Faith. I'm telling you how I *should* handle this, and I'm asking you to throw me a bone and give me a reason not to feel like a fucking idiot for going against what every instinct is screaming at me to do."

He was right. Had the situation been reversed, she would be asking for the same thing. But she couldn't tell him she planned to keep the weather machine. He'd stop her, and she had a feeling he'd do whatever it took.

"My team will be standing by. They'll be close, but they won't interfere unless needed. I can't risk them being seen and compromising the mission. It's why I didn't want you to bring ACRO in on this. Coordinating my agency and yours while trying to deal with the people who have Liberty could end in disaster."

"When were you going to tell me your agency was going to assist?"

"I'm telling you now. You exposed your throat. I'm exposing mine." Her hand came up to brush her choker. "Again."

He crossed the span of floor between them in three strides, took her face in his big hands and kissed her breathless. When he finally broke the kiss, she found she'd sagged against him, needing him to brace her shaky knees.

"What was that for?" she whispered.

"Because I don't want to play secret agent right now. I want to play married couple who don't believe the world outside the room exists."

Tears sprang to her eyes. "That sounds wonderful."

He twirled a finger in one of the wig's ringlets. "When this is over, and that damned motherboard is in pieces, we're not going to play at being a couple. We're going to be one for real."

Her heart skidded to a halt so fast, she felt a burning in her chest. Scorch marks on her soul.

They couldn't be a real couple. Ever. Because the motherboard was not going to be destroyed—at least, not until TAG had studied the hell out of it. And once Wyatt realized that she'd never intended to destroy it, the only real thing between them would be hatred.

* * *

IT HAD BEEN eight hours since Remy and Haley had arrived at the hotel. Eight hours of agony for Remy. He'd stumbled in off the patio only once, to go to the bathroom and eat, and Haley had lost count of the number of times they'd had sex. Remy was exhausted, pacing the patio like a caged beast as he concentrated on the storm.

Which still raged.

He'd kept it from coming closer, but the monster hurricane hadn't weakened, and it wasn't backing off. At this rate, it would wear Remy down and burn him out long before it fizzled.

Haley had to do something, and she had to do it fast.

She opened the sliding glass door and was immediately pelted by rain. "Remy. Come inside. You need a break."

"No." His voice sounded like it had been scraped over a cheese grater. "When I came in to eat, she came closer."

He was right. With his concentration broken, the storm had lunged westward like she'd been let off a leash, bringing category one hurricane-force winds to the coastline. Haley had never seen a storm move so fast.

"You can't keep going like this."

"I have to."

Stubborn man. *That* certainly hadn't changed in the last year.

"Dammit, Remy. Get in here. Just for an hour."

Gripping the rail, he roared into the storm. Ignoring her.

Haley muttered curses under her breath and slammed the door. She knew him, knew he wasn't going to stop until either he or the storm fell apart. The phone rang, and a quick glance at her watch told her it was Dev. Right on time.

"No change, Dev," she said into the cell.

"How's Remy holding up?"

"He's not."

There was a long pause. "Haley? What are you saying?"

She couldn't help it. Tears sprang to her eyes. "This might be too big for him."

"Get him out of there," Dev snapped. "Now. The eight hours he's held the storm off has already saved lives. I won't risk yours. I won't lose any more people."

Any more? There was a story there she wasn't sure she wanted to know. "Remy won't listen."

"This is an order, Haley. Hand him the goddamned phone."

Knowing Dev was asking for something that wasn't going to happen, she opened the door and forced the phone into Remy's hand. He listened for a moment. Then heaved the phone into the darkness.

"Haley," he rasped. "I'm going to need you again. Soon." He shuddered. "She's really angry . . ."

Lily was breaking him down, slowly. Taking him apart and collapsing his walls—

"That's it," she whispered. "That's it! Remy, hold on."

Haley darted inside. Using the latest images, projections and observations, she crunched numbers. Then, using Remy's cell phone, she made a call to NOAA. By the time she was done, hope had made her giddy. After a quick trip to the bathroom, she was ready.

She opened the door. "You can stop now."

"We've been over this, Haley."

"Listen to me, you big buffoon!"

He swung around to her, fists clenched, teeth bared, and wet and naked and so fully aroused she nearly swooned despite the dozens of orgasms she'd already had. "I'm. Not. Stopping."

"I have a plan. Look, if you stop, get some rest, let Lily head this way, you can build up your strength." She held up her hand when he opened his mouth to argue. "Hurricanes have what's called an eye-wall replacement cycle. Basically, the inner wall is choked by the outer one—"

"Haley . . ." The warning in his voice told her how close to the edge he was.

"I'm getting to the point." She huffed and continued. "The hurricane weakens during this phase, but once the cycle is complete, the hurricane will strengthen, could very well be even stronger than before. But if you rest, wait until Lily hits her weakest point and then strike at her when you're at your strongest, you might be able to pound her into submission. It's already started."

Lightning flashed somewhere deep in his eyes, and she knew he was going to refuse. He was locked into his own cycle, a vortex of battle and fury he wasn't going to walk away from. Like the military man he was, he'd identified the enemy, targeted it and wouldn't retreat until one of them had won.

"I can't let her come closer."

"Remy. Listen to what I'm saying. We have a shot at weakening the storm. She'll still hit us, but she'll be a minimal hurricane. Maybe nothing more than a tropical storm."

"You don't know that. If I keep holding her off—"

"You'll burn out, dammit." Her temper flared at his stubbornness. "And where will that leave us?"

"I'll keep that bitch off the coast, Haley. I'll keep her away from you. I'll keep you safe."

She swallowed the lump in her throat, knew she had to play her ace. "I know you're willing to take chances with your life, just as I'm willing to take chances with mine. But we've got another life to consider now."

He blinked. "What?"

"I'm pregnant, Remy." She held out her hand, and for a heartbeat as he stood there, the rain and wind pummeled him. She knew the moment it sunk in, because suddenly, the air stilled around them. No rain. No wind. Even the thunder had become distant and muted.

"Are you sure?"

She smiled. "Yes."

Suddenly, she found herself in his arms and twirling around in a circle. When he put her down, the adoration in his expression made her heart turn over. She would never, ever doubt his love for her.

"Now that I have your attention," she said, "come inside." She took his hand and led him to her equipment, where the latest satellite loop showed a distinct disturbance in Lily's eye wall. "Look at that. It's starting. We'll wait until it weakens, and then you'll blast it."

"And if I can't?" he growled, and she saw that tenacious glint in his eyes start to flicker again.

"Lily's eye is still a hundred and fifty miles out. If the effort to weaken her fails, we have plenty of time to evacuate."

"*Bebe*, we're already seeing hurricane-force winds. Getting out of here won't be easy."

"We can do it."

A streak of lightning lit the room, followed immediately by a deafening clap of thunder. The power flickered. They were running on borrowed time now. Remy wrapped his arm around her waist and drew her to him, more gently than she'd have expected, given the current weather.

"We'll do it your way," he said roughly, his erection nudging her belly, "but I don't think rest is going to be a real possibility."

THE CALL FROM Liberty's captors came at six A.M., just eight hours after Faith spoke with them.

"This isn't what we agreed upon," Faith growled into the phone, because that's what they'd expect. She climbed out of bed, where she'd been doing her best to seduce Wyatt by waking him with her mouth, and stalked naked to the bedroom window.

"Plans change." The male voice, thickly tinged with an Irish accent, sounded tinny, like he might be standing in the wind. "I'm texting the coordinates to your mobile. You will arrive, alone, at 0900."

Faith swept aside the delicate lace curtains and looked out at the well-tended garden. "I want proof that Liberty is alive, or this doesn't happen."

"We'll send video."

"I want her to tell me what toy she gave me before she was taken away."

"Just be at the coordinates on time. If we catch sight of any of your *friends*, your sister dies. Don't try anything cute, Ms. Black."

Faith disconnected with the asshole by jamming her thumb so

hard into the "End" button that she heard a crunch. Wyatt's hands came down on her shoulders, kneading firmly, but the knots in her muscles felt like they'd become permanent.

"You okay?"

Shaking her head, she let the curtains fall closed. "We have to leave. Now."

He didn't bother to rail about how the bastards had moved up the timetable. He'd expected it, as well. Instead, he kicked into high gear, grabbed the duffel and packed the belongings they'd barely had time to unpack. "They're trying to rattle us."

She drew in a shaky breath. "It's working."

His head whipped up, and he nailed her with a confident, take-no-fucking-prisoners stare, which worked despite his complete nudity. "We'll get her, Faith. I won't let anything happen to either of you."

Guilt choked her more effectively than Marco's garrote had. She made a strangled sound and jerked her gaze away before she did something stupid and emotional, like cry.

Or decide to destroy the motherboard once Liberty was safe.

She couldn't go soft now. Studying the weather machine could save lives. The memory of her parents, crushed and nearly unrecognizable, strengthened her resolve. Maybe building a machine of their own wouldn't be a great idea, but TAG scientists might be able to use the knowledge gained from the motherboard to prevent future enemy machines from wreaking havoc.

The phone beeped, and the screen lit up with a choppy, grainy video of Liberty, her face swollen and bruised. "Do you still have Mr. Wiggums?" she asked. "I left him with you when Mum and Dad sent me away. I can't wait to see you, Faithie."

The screen went black. Faith closed her eyes. Breathed. Breathed some more, and wished the air didn't seem to be so depleted of oxygen. Wished her throat didn't feel raw, as if she'd been screaming.

"I'll start a shower." Wyatt's voice was the balm she needed, and she nodded.

"We'll need to make it fast. Then we'll grab some maps and you can study the layout while I drive."

Fifteen minutes later, they piled into their rented Renault for the drive to the North Antrim Coast. Traffic was light, the weather cooperative, and within two hours they'd arrived in a beautiful, untamed part of Northern Ireland Faith had twice visited while on vacation.

Liberty's captors had known what they were doing—it was early October, and nearby Dunluce Castle was closed to the public on Mondays, so witnesses and traffic would be limited. No doubt snipers would be stationed amongst the bluffs and outcrops. How many was the question.

She and Wyatt both donned black fatigues—ML's foresight coming in handy once again—and she called Paula once they'd gotten on the road. Her TAG team had been on their way to Belfast, and despite the suddenness of the call to the meeting, they anticipated an on-time arrival. They would hang back, watch from a discreet distance.

One kilometer from the meeting spot, Faith pulled over onto a dirt side road, easing the car behind a hedge. Wyatt gripped her forearm, his strong fingers gentle as he tugged her to him. "This will work, Faith. I've got your back."

Her throat felt like it had gone a round with sandpaper. "I don't deserve you."

A cocky smile and an even cockier wink made her pulse race. "I am quite the catch."

"Stop," she croaked.

"Stop what?"

"Being so damned...insufferable." She didn't mean it, and he knew it. Knew it with so much certainty that he brought his mouth down on hers and kissed her like he had to. Kissed her like they were saying hello and good-bye, like he knew things would never be the same for them after tonight.

He thinks things will be better.

Practically hyperventilating, she broke away from him and

scrambled out of the vehicle. He met her at her door, his hands coming down firmly on her upper arms, his dark hair ruffling in the salty ocean breeze. "We'll get through this."

We. *We'll* get through this.

She sucked in a bracing breath. "I know."

"Then let's do this thing." Like a switch had been thrown, he clicked into operational status, went from tender lover to lethal agent before her very eyes. Magnificent. Wicked, hot desire blasted through her, and damned if she didn't go wet right then and there.

How absurdly inappropriate.

It was with grim appreciation that she watched him melt away as they'd discussed on the drive, into the crags and cliffs that defined the coastline. Once he disappeared, becoming a fucking shadow as near as she could tell, she drove the remaining distance to the meeting spot, parked on the side of the road near the cliffs. She didn't see anyone, but then, these people wouldn't be standing around with signs hanging from their necks.

She wondered how Wyatt was doing, wondered if her team was close, wondered if she should have considered more seriously the questions Wyatt had asked her back at ML's house.

How do you know that Liberty's not in on this whole scheme?

She watched a peregrine falcon soar overhead, and once the majestic bird disappeared in the distance, she secured the satchel containing the motherboard to her side and started up the rocky trail leading to a grassy plateau. She didn't bother with stealth; the more attention she drew to herself, the less that would be focused on Wyatt or her team.

As she topped the rise, coming up on a flat expanse of emerald grass, the crash of waves against the craggy shore below drowned out the sound of her pounding heartbeat.

"That's far enough, Faith!"

She came to a halt, summoned her power so it hummed inside her, ready to go at a moment's notice. The sun was a bright ball on the horizon, casting blinding light on two men and a woman emerging from behind some stone ruins lining the stretch of land.

A glint caught in her peripheral vision and the tiny hairs on her arms stood up. She didn't need to take her eyes off the people approaching to know she was standing in crosshairs.

The men stopped, but the woman kept walking. With every step Faith's heart beat faster. Dark hair swung around the woman's narrow face, and dark eyes stared at Faith.

Liberty.

Faith's breath exploded from her lungs. She hadn't even known she'd been holding it. She took a step.

"Stop!" One of the men, wearing a white button-down and baggy trousers, gestured for her to stay put. She recognized his voice as the man who had been her contact. "What did I say about coming alone, Ms. Black?"

From a staircase near the ruins, Wyatt emerged, his hands on his head in surrender. A man with a rifle herded him onto the grass.

Exactly the way she and Wyatt had planned.

The lay of the land and the rise of the sun wouldn't have allowed for him to sneak unnoticed to the site, but this way, he'd earned a personal invite. No doubt they'd stripped him of his weapons, but that too was part of the plan.

Wyatt was more lethal without them.

Faith cocked an eyebrow at White Shirt, who she assumed to be the leader of this operation. "You know how this game is played. You tell me to come alone. I try to bring my friends. It's a tradition, of sorts."

"Enough," the man snapped. "Let's make the exchange." He pointed to the man guarding Wyatt. "Watch him. If he blinks, shoot him."

Faith almost laughed. These idiots had no idea who they were dealing with. Wyatt would bring boulders down on their heads.

On her head too, once he realized she wasn't giving up the motherboard.

Shoving aside the guilt that twisted her gut, she shouted at White Shirt, "What now?"

"Give Liberty the motherboard."

"And then?"

"She'll leave it on the ground, and you'll both walk away."

Faith did *not* like this, but she had little choice. She strode forward, watching the woman White Shirt claimed to be Liberty. Two meters away, Faith slowed. The other woman stopped.

"Faithie? It's really me."

"I know." With a cry of relief, she threw herself at Liberty, and they came together in a long-awaited hug.

Liberty didn't smell like she used to, like the licorice candy she was always getting into. Her hair was coarser. Her body harder. The embrace was stiff, awkward.

With a pang, Faith realized that Liberty was a stranger.

Of course she is, you git. Somewhere deep inside, Faith had been thinking that they'd meet and everything would be as it was before they were separated. She'd let herself believe in a mystical twin connection that would renew their bond of blood and birth.

Disappointment and grief bubbled up in her throat. Faith had to swallow repeatedly to keep from sobbing.

"This is all very fucking touching, but let's get on with it," White Shirt called out, and Liberty drew away, looking utterly unaffected by their reunion.

"If you'll hand over the motherboard, we can get out of here," Liberty said.

"Yes, of course." Internal alarms clanged, but Faith had no choice but to comply. Carefully, she removed the electronic device from the bag and handed it to her sister.

Heart pounding, she watched Liberty walk a few meters, place the motherboard on the ground, and then stroll back to Faith. "We're free to go," Liberty said. "I suggest we hurry before they change their minds."

Faith looked down at the ground as they moved toward the path she'd taken to climb the cliff. "When we get to the path, I'm going to need you to run," she murmured. "I'm not letting them get away with this."

"A fight won't be necessary, dear Faithie." Faith gasped at the tap of a gun barrel against her spine. "I'm sorry, but we can't let you go."

Slowly, Faith raised her hands and turned to her sister, who backed up, pistol leveled at Faith's chest.

How do you know Liberty's not in on this whole scheme?

Faith's skin crawled. Denial breached her lips in a soundless *no,* but it died quickly in the face of evidence she couldn't deny. Wyatt had been right all along, and thanks to him, she'd mentally prepared herself even as she held out hope.

"You're working with them."

"I grew up with them. Honestly, I don't remember much about you or our parents."

How could she not remember their parents, when every detail about them—and Liberty—had branded itself into Faith's brain? "So you really were in on this."

"From the beginning."

Faith barely contained her rage as she growled out, "You bitch."

"I knew you wouldn't understand."

"This isn't the answer, Liberty. Killing people to get what you want—"

"Is regrettable," Liberty snapped. "But we've been forced into action. With this device, we can bring the English government to its knees quickly. Efficiently." She made a sweeping gesture with the gun. "Don't you see that ultimately more lives will be spared?"

"You're no better than Itor," Faith said softly. "Do you have any idea what happened to our parents? How they died? I've spent my entire life trying to find a way to prevent that from ever happening again. And you have no problem *making* it happen? Killing entire families?"

"It's for the greater good." Liberty gestured to White Shirt. "Take her. Kill the man who came with her."

Rage seared to ash any tender feelings Faith might have for Liberty. "Fuck. You."

She lunged, ripped a series of close combat moves to disarm her sister and crack a few ribs.

Faith had trained with the Israeli Defense Forces, had learned devastating Krav Maga techniques meant to neutralize quickly, and if ever she'd needed to disable someone dangerous, it was now. Honor be damned; this was about survival.

Battle exploded around her. Guns flew out of hands, tumbled over the cliff. Screams of pain shattered the air, punctuated by the dull thud of bodies striking stone as Wyatt went on a rampage.

Liberty fell to the ground, narrowly avoiding Faith's kick. A bullet streaked past Faith's head, parting her hair. She spun, squeezed off two rounds with Liberty's pistol and brought the shooter down.

Liberty threw out her hand, the same thing she used to do in childhood when she used her powers. Faith remembered the signal too late. She gasped as her lungs crumpled into a ball inside her chest.

Liberty snarled, focusing on Faith as she clawed at her throat, shredding her lace choker.

"I don't want to hurt you," Liberty said. "But you're giving me no choice."

Around them, the sounds of battle waged on. Wyatt was holding his own, but they were outnumbered. Faith struck out with her own power, shot through Liberty's aura like it was butter. She hadn't expected that, but she wasn't about to question the ease with which she'd penetrated her twin's defenses.

The squeezing sensation in Faith's chest grew worse. Gasping for breath, she slammed down a partition on her power, a talent that had taken her years to perfect. Half her power became a vise inside Liberty, pinching her spinal cord. The other half formed a virtual fist and knocked her sister to the ground. The pressure in Faith's chest eased as Liberty lost consciousness.

Windpipe throbbing, Faith sucked in gulps of air with such force she grew light-headed.

A shot rang out. Scenting blood, Faith wheeled around. Apparently unharmed, Wyatt was throwing men around like they were toys, both with his hands and with his mind. As though he felt her eyes on him, he twisted at the waist to look at her. The blood drained from his face.

"Faith!" His shout was one of fear and fury.

She took a step toward him. The ground beneath her seemed to fall away, and she staggered, went down on one knee. Baffled, she looked down at the bloom of wetness on her shirt. As though seeing the blood triggered sensation, agony streaked through her. Clenching her teeth, she doubled over, her belly cramping. Out of the corner of her eye, she saw a rifle take aim at her. Her power was on deck, ready to go, but she couldn't penetrate the shooter's aura fast enough——

Wyatt roared in rage, his expression promising pain. The sniper's eyes bugged. He dropped the weapon, grabbed his throat. Still doubled over, Faith watched Wyatt, eyes glowing with power. The man turned blue and collapsed.

The field went silent except for the sound of Faith's labored breaths. Wyatt sprinted to her.

"Babe?" He pulled her hand away from her belly, peeled up her shirt. She couldn't look. "Hey, it's not that bad," he said, replacing her hand and holding it firmly over the bullet hole.

"Liar," she moaned, and then smiled at the sight of TAG's mission chief, coming up behind Wyatt. Nearby, another TAG agent secured an unconscious Liberty.

"Back off, mate." Gabe kneeled next to Wyatt, who looked like he might want to tear off Gabe's arms.

Faith coughed, tasting blood as she spoke to Wyatt. "He's one of mine."

Wyatt's voice throbbed with warning. "She needs to get to a hospital."

"We'll handle it."

"It's okay, Wyatt." She bit her lip to stifle a cry of pain when Gabe probed her wound. Wyatt still looked like he wanted to tear off the other man's arms—with his teeth.

Wyatt hesitated. His eyes narrowed, the message in them unmistakable. *Hurt her and die.*

"She'll be all right," Gabe promised, and finally Wyatt gave a clipped nod.

The moment he moved off, she gave in to the pain and curled into a fetal position. God, this *hurt*. Through the nausea and agony, she looked for Wyatt...where was he?

Oh, Jesus, the motherboard.

"No," she croaked, but the thing flipped up into the air and flew straight into his hands. "Wyatt."

He was going to destroy it.

"It's time, Faith."

"You can't...I won't let you." Between the pain and the memories of her parents, which Liberty had so easily batted aside, Faith didn't consider the consequences. This was what the entire mission had been about. Saving her sister and getting the motherboard for The Aquarius Group, so her parents' deaths might mean something.

She'd failed the former but would not fail the latter.

Her body trembled, every muscle spasming as though coming apart at the cellular level. She was on the verge of losing consciousness, but she summoned the last of her strength to slam her power into Wyatt. His eyes went wide, flashed at her with a combination of surprise and disappointment as she cut off the circulation to his brain.

"Faith...ah, Jesus...no..." He sank to the ground, still holding the motherboard. The amber glow signaling the power-up of his gift lit his gaze and she braced herself for a strike.

It never came. Wyatt fell over and she knew—*knew*—he could have hurt her in that single second before he passed out, but he hadn't.

Sobbing with a combination of pain, guilt and misery, Faith grabbed Gabe's hand as Paula approached, her curt hand signals sending operatives out to secure enemies—and Wyatt. "Liberty...dangerous. Take her to...Hill...Hill..."

"Hill Heritage?"

"Yes." The psychiatric hospital near TAG headquarters was the same one where both Faith and Liberty had been taken to as children, a place where they specialized in caring for and containing people with special abilities. Faith hoped Liberty could be rehabilitated, but reality had just kicked her ass, and she would never again let herself believe in happily-ever-afters when it came to her sister.

Or Wyatt.

"Wyatt. Telekinetic. Send him..." Home. To ACRO. But she couldn't get the words out. The world had gone dark, and she couldn't hear anymore.

She was bleeding out.

Body and heart.

Twenty-three

When Remy joined ACRO, he thought he'd finally understood the power behind his gift, had been relieved that there were so many ways to actually help him when the storm surged outside and hot through his blood.

But this, this was like nothing he'd ever seen before and he prayed that if he made it through this night he'd never, ever have to see it again.

His entire body had been on pins and needles for twenty-four hours—he'd been living on adrenaline, brute strength and sheer will.

And now he was living for Haley and their baby. If anything, that made their time together even more precious.

He'd forced himself to eat one of the MREs they'd brought with them, although he was beyond tasting anything but ozone and electricity, as though they'd taken up permanent residence in his body and weren't ever going to let go. And he would swear that this time Mother Nature was actually on his side, was as confused as he was by the man-made weather system that now both he and Mother Nature were forced to contend with.

Sometimes he could hear her in the wind's howl, like she was begging him for help, didn't understand the fury that swirled around them, desperate and out of control.

"Are you ready?"

He looked up from where he lay on the bed to see Haley standing over him—she'd been hunched over her equipment, muttering to herself for the last hour, like the prettiest mad scientist he'd ever seen, and he hadn't bothered her. Whatever she was cooking up had made her smile a few times, and if anyone could smile in the face of all of this shit, his Haley could. He certainly wasn't going to discourage it, no matter how shitty he felt.

He put a hand on her still-flat belly. "I'm ready. Are you two ready?"

"It's time to find out."

He stood. "Tell me what I need to do."

"The eye wall has collapsed. The storm has decreased in intensity—it's a cat three now."

"Still packs one hell of a destructive punch, though."

"She's as weak as she's going to get." Haley stroked his hair, pressed her face against his chest for a second before she spoke again. "You need to break apart the eye wall even more, keep it from building again."

"And as I break it?"

"Send wind shear into her top. An upper-level stream from the west will blow her apart."

He nodded. "Okay. Give me a few minutes out there alone. When I need you, I'll call."

"You'd better, Remy."

He jerked his head up as he saw the diagonal rain hit the window—cat two winds right now, which put the eye about fifty miles out. Reluctantly, he let Haley go, didn't bother to tell her to stay away from the windows.

The rain slammed him the second he opened the sliding-glass patio door—he was soaked through to the skin in seconds, the wind making it nearly impossibly to breathe, let alone hold steady. He put one hand on the iron bars across the patio so he could be as close as possible to the sky and still not get blown over.

Lily may have started out as a man-made hurricane, but now she was pure nature. A big part of his nature too—and suddenly he was all wrapped up in the storm's intensity, seeing into her eye with a clarity he hadn't been able to achieve before. One Haley assured him that he would, one day.

Storms are just doing their job—no one's ever happy to see them. Think of them like a little kid throwing a tantrum—concentrate on getting them to their happy place.

He spoke to the burgeoning sky: "It's okay, Lily. Everything's gonna be fine. You just need a new home to hang out in."

Decision made, he summoned all his strength, felt the all too familiar tingle tighten his entire body, toe to scalp, and as he smelled the electricity burning in the air, the acrid scent of ozone and water, lightning struck nearly right in front of his face, hit the ground below him with an intensity that seemed to shake the hotel to its foundation.

He closed his eyes and raised one fist, and in his mind he envisioned the storm, pushed her with every muscle he had, out to sea, where she belonged. "Go, Lily, go back to the water."

Still, she fought him, wanted to make landfall and do so with a twisted path of destruction.

His erection strained painfully against the soft cotton of his robe and he was going to need release soon. But he kept his eyes closed and let the sexual urge propel him harder, used the arousal to bring his mind to that floaty place he could only get to once the storm was actually over.

For the first time, he actually felt that Mother Nature was working with him instead of against, and still the pull was excruciating. And the pain of his arousal was clouding everything... The winds picked up, and shit, he was losing the battle.

"Let me help you, Remy." Haley had to be shouting, but the words in his ear sounded like a whisper, soft and sweet, and her hand slipped inside his robe and down the wet skin of his abs.

"Haley, no—I'm afraid it's going to ramp it up."

"You can't concentrate when you're in this much pain," she countered, her hand beginning a long, slow rub that nearly made him shoot off sparks of his own. He closed his eyes and concentrated on ripping apart the eye wall, let some of the pleasure give him the strength to do so.

And fuck, it was working. He thought about Haley and the baby, his friends—and now family—at ACRO, about the bayou that Katrina had screwed with, and he let all of that power loose on Lily.

He could visualize individual cloud elements as though he were standing in the eye. The ring of clouds swirled around him, holding him in a spinning vortex. In his mind, he punched through the wall of rain and clouds, shredded it like cotton candy.

Lily howled, the sound of a train barreling down on him. Haley's touch grew firmer, faster. Golf ball–sized hail shot from the sky as though it'd been fired from a grenade-launcher. Remy spun, shielded Haley with his body. The hail cracked against the building, the glass of the slider, his back.

Mother. Fuck. Lily could strike at *him*, but she wasn't going to touch Haley. As his wife's mouth closed over his cock, he emptied his lungs in a violent roar of rage and vengeance and death.

This ended *now*.

He struck out with his mind, tore through the weakened eye wall like a nuclear bomb. At the same time, he blasted her top with wind shear, blindsided the hurricane while she was trying to repair the damage he'd done to her center.

He felt the entire storm wobble. The hail stopped.

For a moment, he wasn't sure if she was done. The throbbing in his head and balls said no, and sure as shit, the winds suddenly doubled back, as if reaching for him with one last final attempt at a grasp. The air felt like a fist around him, trying to tug him over the railing. Remy refused to let it, kept pushing even as Haley pulled him closer to the brink of orgasm.

Haley licked up his length, flicked her tongue over the tip of his cock. "You're doing it! It's working, Remy!"

It was. Exhaustion had his legs trembling and his mind fading into mush, but as his balls tightened and his release tingled at the base of his spine, he found the power to send one more blast into the storm. A shriek, a long, high-pitched death wail rattled the hotel. Then, abruptly, the hurricane's winds decreased, the pressure in his head eased. While the rain continued, it fell horizontally now.

It was over. His muscles felt watery and his back stung from the hail, but nothing was keeping him from Haley. He hooked her under her arms and pulled her to her feet. He gave her a long, slow kiss, tasting rain and himself, before he picked her up and carried her inside to finish the job the storm had started on him.

"WAKE UP, SLEEPYHEAD."

Squinting into bright overhead lights, Faith blinked the fuzz out of her eyes. Where was she? She was lying down, and the room looked familiar...

The medical lab at TAG.

Her mind seemed to be as fuzzy as her vision, because she couldn't remember what had landed her here. She sat up, wincing at the stiffness in her muscles. "How long?" she croaked, her voice as unused as everything else.

Morgan, the chief medical officer with a gift for visualizing medical conditions inside a patient's body better than any X-ray, adjusted her stethoscope around her neck. "Only a day."

Twenty-four hours. The gunshot wound must have been severe. *Gunshot wound. Wyatt.* The battle on the Irish coast came crashing back in a flood of visions that made her head hurt. "What happened?"

"You were shot. It was bad, but Gabe was able to repair much of the damage on the spot. You're lucky he was there."

Gabe's skills were similar to Faith's, though not as strong or developed. Faith rubbed her belly, remembering the agonizing pain. He'd done a good job; she didn't feel a thing.

"While you were out, I gave you a post-mission workup. You're perfectly healthy. There are no poisons, parasites or foreign objects in your body. Not that I expected any, but you know Itor."

Bastards. It was because of their slimy methods that TAG had been forced to institute a mandatory post-mission medical checkup policy.

"I also performed the standard general purging to rid you of psychic tagalongs, virus-borne diseases, pregnancy—"

"What?" A curtain of red colored Faith's vision. Without thinking, she leaped out of bed and slammed Morgan to the wall, her forearm across the doctor's throat. "Did you kill it? Did you kill Wyatt's baby?"

Morgan gasped. "Y-you aren't . . . weren't . . . pregnant."

Trembling, Faith backed off, unable to believe she'd attacked like that. Not being pregnant was a good thing, right?

And yet, there was a vague sense of disappointment she couldn't explain.

"I'm sorry, Morgan. I—I have to go."

Holding her throat protectively, Morgan nodded. Dressed in a hospital gown, Faith darted out of the lab, which was on the third floor of the agency's headquarters, a converted mansion set on several acres of private property.

She ran straight into Paula, who must have been coming to see her. "Paula. Where's Liberty?" She grasped her partner's forearm. *"Where's Wyatt?"*

"They're both at Hill Heritage," Paula said slowly, as though Faith had taken a blow to the head and couldn't understand English.

Faith understood all too well, and she broke out in a cold sweat. "That's not right. Wyatt was supposed to be sent to America!" She felt her throat closing up. Her colleagues had dumped Wyatt into his worst nightmare. Nausea made her unsteady, and she had to brace herself against the iron railing that lined the third-floor balcony.

"Easy, Faith." Paula wrapped her arm around Faith's waist to keep her steady. "Let's get you back into Medical."

She shook her head. "Why did you send Wyatt to Hill Heritage, dammit?"

Paula's blond brows drew together. "You said he was teleki-netic. They're better equipped to handle hostiles. He's the ACRO agent you told me about?"

"Yes," Faith bit out. "Shit." She dragged a hand through her hair, which felt like a tangled pile of straw. Paula, with her fine features and waist-length sandy hair, always made Faith feel as if she looked like a street rat, and now more than ever.

"He's been treated well. ACRO has no reason to come down on us. We weren't sure how much he knew about us, so we figured we'd wait until you woke up before we did anything with him." A young recruit walked past, and Paula lowered her voice conspiratorially. "We also picked up an extra asylum patient."

"Don't say that," Faith said, and then barked out a bitter laugh, because politely calling Hill Heritage a hospital didn't *not* make it an asylum.

An asylum where, thanks to her, Wyatt had been imprisoned.

Paula rolled her peridot-green eyes. "Fine. Loony bin, then." She steered Faith toward the staircase. "One of the men who sur-vived the battle turned up on our SAO document."

Faith stumbled to a stop. The SAO listed special-ability opera-tives known to TAG. "Who?"

"An Itor agent named William Young. From what we've been able to piece together, he infiltrated the ILF years ago. Probably keeping tabs on them for Itor."

She remembered the warning Sean had received about a spy on board the platform. The Itor guy must have known the ILF had arranged for the theft of the weather machine and found a way to warn Sean. That e-mail Sean received hadn't been about Wyatt. It had been about Faith.

"Young also said that the ILF has been after the weather ma-chine for a long time. At one point, they offered up your sister in trade."

Faith let out a low whistle. Biokinetics as powerful as she and Liberty were rare—perhaps a half dozen in the entire world, counting Wyatt, and it must have been a tough decision to refuse the deal.

"What about the motherboard? Where is it?"

"It's in the science lab. Lab guys found a tracker on it, but we took preventive measures, constructed shields, and the bug is now on its way to Belgium to throw off anyone still tracking it. Hopefully whoever put it there—Itor or your ACRO agent—didn't get a bead on us before we got the shields up."

Itor might have tagged all important machine parts to keep track, but Wyatt could have done it as well. The idea made her even more nauseous than she already was. He hadn't trusted her—and for good reason. Her betrayal ripped through her, and if she'd had anything in her stomach, she'd have lost it.

"It's taking longer than expected to start building a machine casing for it," Paula continued. "Still, what a coup. Britain will never be vulnerable to terrorists again. If we make some preemptive strikes—"

"That's not what the device is for. We discussed this. We're going to study it, that's all."

Paula rolled her shoulder in that way she did when she was going to argue. "And we will study it. But if we build our own machine, we can stop severe weather in its tracks. We can even help out farmers during droughts and such. And if we need to, we can use it against our enemies."

"Absolutely not."

"Why not?"

"Because we aren't Itor."

"Of course we aren't." Paula's tone was condescending and careful, as though Faith were a child, and she half expected a friendly pat on the head. "But if we can use it with minimal damage to nontargets, why rule it out?"

"It's too dangerous, Faith," Wyatt had said on the helicopter. *"The temptation to destroy an enemy with it would be too great. Collateral damage could be catastrophic. And just by having the thing, you'd invite enemies to try to steal it. You'd always be worried about someone on the inside betraying you for power or money."*

On some level she'd agreed, but her drive to make her parents' deaths mean something had been as all-consuming as her drive to find Liberty. Now that it was all over, her mind felt less cluttered by emotion. She'd truly believed that TAG could do good with the machine, could at least study it and destroy it after finding out how to identify and disable any machines that might crop up in an enemy's arsenal.

But keeping it for any amount of time wasn't worth it. That Liberty had been willing to betray Faith for it was proof of that.

So was the fact that Faith had betrayed Wyatt in the same way.

And now it seemed that with power in their grasp, even TAG personnel had decided that building a machine would be a good thing in the hands of the good guys. But how long would it be before the good guys crossed a line?

Faith forced herself to not argue more with Paula, and instead flicked her hand in a dismissive wave. "You're right. I'll keep an open mind." She pulled the hospital gown tight in the back and started down the stairs to her quarters, which took up half of the north wing she shared with Paula. "Will you gather materials for a briefing this evening? I've missed a lot in the last few days."

Paula nodded. "Of course. It's good to have you back."

"Thank you. I'm going to shower and then visit Liberty." She was also going to grab the motherboard and get Wyatt the hell out of the hospital.

A stab of guilt cut through her gut, and suddenly the disappointment that she wasn't pregnant made sense.

There was no doubt whatsoever that Wyatt hated her, not only for betraying him for the motherboard but for landing him in the place of his nightmares. She'd lost him, but at least if she were carrying his child, she'd still have something of him.

Now the most she could hope for was that he wouldn't want to kill her.

HILL HERITAGE'S STAFF recognized Faith right away. They worked closely with TAG, had a private, secret wing set up to handle the special needs of people with unique abilities. Unable to face Wyatt yet, she headed to Liberty's room, the satchel containing Mr. Wiggums and the motherboard over her shoulder.

Sneaking the motherboard out of TAG's lab had been a challenge, and though she'd slipped out undetected, she wouldn't get back in the same way. She'd have hell to pay to both her colleagues and the British government.

Punishment would likely be severe.

"I've really done it this time, Mr. Wiggums," she said, and realized she'd slipped her hand inside one of the bag pockets and was stroking the stuffed animal. Hopefully Liberty would be happy to see it—assuming she wasn't too messed up from meds.

Her sister had been given psychic suppression drugs, the very ones that had probably been given to Wyatt to keep him from escaping. With any luck, he was being kept sedated as well. The idea that he might have been fully awake and trapped in his own personal hell for the last day made her stomach hurt.

Liberty was sitting on her bed, wearing blue hospital scrubs and reading one of the facility's ancient magazines when Faith entered her sterile, cell-like room.

"Faithie," she said, setting aside the magazine. "Mary, Mother of God, don't you look . . . *free*."

"It doesn't have to be like this." Faith took a seat near the door, in the only chair in the room.

"You think we can go back in time? Be a family again?"

"Maybe to start we could just try talking?" After a long silence that wasn't encouraging, Faith added, "I've looked for you all my life, Liberty."

"Am I supposed to cry now? Be grateful? Please. I have no idea who you are." Liberty laughed, like this was all a big joke to her. "And my name is Saoirse."

"Is that the Irish version of your name?"

Tugging one bare foot up on the bed, Liberty nodded. "Much prettier. Now, why are you here? And don't be giving me the you're-my-family malarkey."

Faith shook her head grimly. "I am your family. Our parents—"

"Sent me away like a dog they didn't want, like rubbish."

"That's not true."

"No? Why didn't they ever come to see me? Never once. They left me, alone and afraid in a world where I didn't know anyone. *They abandoned me.*"

"They were afraid of your power, Lib. They didn't understand it. They'd have come around."

Liberty laughed. "It doesn't matter now, does it? When Fiona took me from here, she and her husband became my parents. They understood me. They embraced my differences and abilities."

"They used them," Faith snapped. "Used them to make you a weapon for the ILF."

"You don't know anything."

"I know that your precious ILF offered to trade you to Itor for the weather machine." The flash of surprise and hurt in Liberty's eyes told Faith she hadn't known about the failed deal.

"They wouldn't do that."

"The machine brings out the worst in people," Faith said, because she knew firsthand how true that was. "There's something else I know. I know I miss my sister." Faith reached into the satchel and removed Mr. Wiggums. "I held on to him for you."

The blood drained from Liberty's face. "Sweet Jesus, you still have him."

"I took him with me. Everywhere."

For a moment it seemed as though Faith had gotten through to her sister. Swallowing repeatedly, Liberty seemed on the verge of an emotional breakdown. A heartbeat later, the cold, distant gleam came back into her eyes, and Faith felt her skin grow tight.

"You're a sentimental fool, Faithie. You should have burned it."

Faith stared at her sister, noted the fine lines at the corner of her eyes and mouth that spoke of a hard life, the scar running from right temple to cheek that confirmed it.

"You'd have killed me for the motherboard, wouldn't you?"

"Yes."

The answer didn't surprise Faith, but it did reinforce her decision to not get her hopes up about her sister's potential for rehabilitation and deprogramming. Faith carried the stuffed toy to Liberty and placed it on the bed beside her. She wanted to say something, but what?

Perhaps someday they'd find common ground and a new relationship, but not today.

Silently, Faith left the room and braced herself for one more visit.

FAITH HAD BETRAYED HIM. One hundred percent completely betrayed him, and Wyatt had done nothing about it but fall to the ground like a pussy and was now lying in a locked and padded cell in some fucking mental institution in Yorkshire.

Hurting her that same way had never been an option. He was all for a good game of chicken, but she'd made her choice, and he was finished with the game playing.

The last time he'd been put in a room like this, he'd been drugged to the gills, so much so that all he could do was lie there, unable to move a muscle, his teenage mind racing. Panicking. His powers had been immature and he'd forced himself time and time again to remain calm, plot and plan and think. No one had helped him then—they'd left him all alone in that hell that was his own mind.

Like now, except that this time his powers were far more developed, the drugs they'd pumped him full of were nearly out of his system, and he was through thinking.

When he'd woken, the anger roiled like molten lava through his body—he'd fought the urge to howl like a wounded animal and instead had remained docile, played nice so the men in white coats eased up on the drugs. He'd heard the men who brought him in here mention Liberty, knew she was in another wing of the hospital and wondered if Faith would come to visit.

He'd asked one of the nicer nurses if Faith had survived the gunshot and the woman had been kind enough to nod yes and smile. He'd wanted to smile too, with relief, but the anger had rushed in right behind the relief. She might not have died, but he had. Some part of him had gone dead on that Irish hillside.

If not for the fact that ACRO was no doubt right now tracking the motherboard and mounting an offensive to take it back, he didn't know how hard he'd fight to get the fuck out of here. But fuck that. He was going to be there when they took down Faith's agency.

Until then, he'd just revisit all those oh-so-happy teenage mental hospital memories.

This place was different, though. There were all sorts of special-ability people here, which made this a much more danger-ous place—and he wondered how many of them were institution-alized because they were thought to be simply uncontrollable.

ACRO was now full of such people. He needed to get back there, to get rid of the betrayal that hung sour in his chest. All he had to do was think about that and the heavy, double-reinforced steel door began to groan on its hinges.

He was vaguely aware that a telekinetic had been stationed outside the door to counteract Wyatt's own powers.

It wouldn't matter—Wyatt was stronger, his powers inflated with anger.

His heart was broken, his faith betrayed.

Faith.

Fuck it all—that was ironic as shit.

The door blew off its hinges with little effort on his part be-yond the internal rage of betrayal, a twisted hunk of metal that took out people in its path.

"Move aside, motherfuckers. I'm checking out," he told them calmly, heart beating double-time in his throat.

Someone shot a tranquilizer dart at him—he used his telekine-sis to stop it mid-air, and sent it back toward the man who'd thrown it, hitting him in the chest and taking him down within seconds.

He pushed aside the pain and panic he felt upon seeing all the white coats surrounding him, tried to shove down all those horri-ble days and months and years when he was helpless and scared—and shit, he had to get out and find the motherboard, had to complete the mission.

He worked the telekinesis as hard as possible, threw whatever wasn't nailed down around so he could try to make his escape, but he felt hands on him and he began to struggle.

People flew off him like objects. Fuck, something was going on.

"Don't hurt him."

Faith's voice broke through his consciousness and it took everything he had left inside of him to calm his shit down completely before she got hurt.

But the silences, the unending vortex filled every crevice of his being and his eyes focused on her.

She wore leather, like she had that very first night he'd helped her. The first night she'd lied to him.

Not that he'd been completely honest with her himself, but still, he hadn't betrayed her...had gone out of his way not to. That wouldn't happen again.

He bared his teeth. "I don't need your help. I don't need anything from you."

"I have something for you," she said quietly, the familiar accent he'd grown to crave over the past days soothing his fucked-up nerves.

"Yeah, I'll just bet you've got something for me, Faith."

He stood, flexing his fists by his sides, waiting for her next move. It came, but it didn't involve her powers.

"I'm checking Wyatt out of here," she told the crowd of doctors and security guards that now surrounded them in the mess of the hallway. "He doesn't belong here. He's never belonged here."

He nearly spat *Fuck you, love* to her, but he couldn't—wouldn't share that private pain with a roomful of strangers the way she just had.

He'd already revealed far too much here with his display of rage.

Instead, he brushed past her, grabbed his clothes from the nurse who held them out to him nervously. He stripped out of the purple scrubs they'd dressed him in, re-dressed in the dead silence all around him. When he was finished, he stalked past Faith and toward the nearest exit.

She was holding the bag they'd brought the motherboard off the platform in.

He felt her follow him the entire way out.

She wanted chicken—she'd get the game. She'd get more than she'd ever bargained for.

THEY STOPPED on the far edge of the wooded facility grounds. Birds chirped in the brisk autumn air and rabbits romped in the field and all of it felt so damned cheery that Faith wanted to scream. Instead, she reached into the satchel. Her fingers found the motherboard, and for just a moment she let herself touch it, to imagine once again how it could help save lives. But at what cost?

Slowly, she withdrew the piece of equipment. Wyatt tensed, the movement so subtle she might not have noticed had she not gotten to know him so well. She looked up at him, at the utterly expressionless look on his face, and a chill shimmered up her spine. She could deal with him being angry, but this lack of emotion left her on shaky ground.

"I'm a little late keeping this promise," she said, "but here it is."

He took the motherboard, and if she'd expected to see a softening in his expression, she'd been very wrong.

"Wyatt..." She took a deep, bracing breath. "I know there's nothing I can say to make up for what I did to you. I don't think I can even explain why, except that I honestly thought I was doing the right thing. I wanted to save lives."

He made a sound of disgust. "You wanted to play God."

"Yes," she whispered. "You were right all along. This machine brings with it too much temptation. For what it's worth, I'm sorry. And... I love you."

Nothing. There was nothing in his eyes but flat darkness and pure loathing.

She staggered backward in the face of his hatred, stung by the force of it. Her throat swelled shut, so much that she barely squeaked out a weak "Take care of yourself. Please." She spun around and fled through a break in the hedges.

The sound of the motherboard crunching beneath his boot rattled through her, the sound of her heart breaking.

Then, suddenly, Wyatt tackled her, took her to the ground in a tumble of limbs. He lay on top of her as she sprawled on her back. "I don't think so," he growled. "You aren't getting off that easy."

Tears burned her eyes. "Easy? You think this is easy? I became what I feared most. I betrayed the man I love. I'm in hell, Wyatt!"

He laughed, a bitter, harsh sound. "Hell? Baby, you have no idea what hell is. Hell is when someone you trusted takes your worst fears and makes them come true. Hell is being stuck inside your own head because no one cares enough to help you get out. Hell," he rasped next to her ear, "is being dead inside a body that still works."

He ground his hips against her, and she shivered, because yes, his body did work. His erection prodded her pelvis, an insistent, brutal presence. He wanted her. God, he still wanted her. Maybe they had a chance. And if not . . . she'd take what she could get for now.

"Wyatt," she moaned, arching up so she could feel more of his hard body. His hand slipped between her legs, beneath her skirt. The sound of fabric tearing as he ripped off her panties was heaven to her ears.

And then he was inside her. She came on the first thrust. He worked her through it, knowing exactly how her body responded to him, and when she came down, he drove harder. Powerful, driving strokes that set her on fire, burned her from the inside out.

His words about hell and being dead rang through her, but the physical connection they shared was far more powerful. This would work between them. This would heal them, or at least start the healing process.

Oh, she loved this man.

Sensation rippled through her, and the explosion took her hard, igniting every nerve ending. A scream tore from her mouth before Wyatt covered it with his lips as he pounded into her.

When it was over, he immediately withdrew. She groped for him, wanting more—not more sex, but simply to hold him. He shrugged off her touch. Confused, she reached for him again, but drew back with a gasp when he glared at her. His eyes were still cold, his breathing slow and shallow, as though he'd been doing nothing more strenuous than reading a book.

And he was still hard.

She blinked, fuzzy-headed from orgasm. "You didn't finish."

"Oh, I'm finished." He buttoned up and stood. "How's it feel, Faith? Getting fucked by someone who should care...but doesn't?"

Humiliation and hurt crawled over her skin. The way he was looking at her, like she was nothing, like any second he should be tossing a wad of cash at her, was a blow that couldn't be more painful if it were physical. "Wyatt, please. You don't mean that."

"I don't? Just watch how much I mean it." He pivoted on his heel and strode away.

"Wyatt, wait!" Without thinking, she reached out with her mind, speared straight through the bare spots in his aura, unsure what she was going to do to stop him or what she would say when she did. But God, his aura was barely there, thinner than it had been before. If she could just repair it...

He halted, went completely still. She'd forgotten that he'd learned to feel her gift. "Even after everything," he said in a low, gravelly voice, "you would still try to manipulate me?"

"I just want to heal you," she whispered.

He didn't look at her. "Heal? You mean resuscitate. And it's way too late for that. DOA, Faith."

And then he was gone. Agony overwhelmed her so that all she could do was sit in the woods and sob, until she felt as dead inside as Wyatt claimed to be.

CHAPTER
Twenty-four

The grief was so fresh, it threatened to break Devlin nearly every moment of every day, but he wouldn't let that happen. Oz would've hated him if he'd let it happen, and in deference to the man's memory, Dev held it together when he was at ACRO.

But when he was home, that was a different story. Last night, Marlena'd had to collect him from the shower floor, where he'd been curled up under a flood of freezing cold water, since that was the only place he could scream and scream and not be heard.

The loneliest part was that Dev didn't feel Oz around him at all—Oz was in that special place. Crossed over. Happy.

"Devlin, there's a call for you."

He looked up to the beautiful, dark-haired woman who'd been his personal assistant for the past eight years. "Thanks, Marlena. You can put it through."

"You got it. I also ordered lunch for you—I'll bring it in when it arrives." She shut the door before he could tell her not to bother, and he shook his head. She was probably one of the few people here at ACRO he'd allow to baby him.

He pressed the blinking button on his phone. "Devlin here."

"Hey—it's Wyatt."

"Wyatt, thank God." Dev rubbed his eyes and tried to pick up on his operative's whereabouts.

"Mission complete," Wyatt said in a thready voice that told Dev something was not right with him.

Although Dev dealt with some of the strongest men and women in the world, they were also some of the most vulnerable. "Talk to me. What do you need?"

"Just a ride home."

Dev opened his eyes. "You need more than that."

There was a long pause. "I need to come home. And you're going to need to send Annika to collect Faith Black."

"Wyatt, listen carefully—Creed and Annika are already in Ireland. It shouldn't take them long to get to you."

"Tell them to hurry," Wyatt said, and clicked the phone off... as Dev got a strange sense of foreboding. He closed his eyes before dialing Creed, tried to CRV Ryan one final time and again got nothing on the only ACRO agent who'd successfully infiltrated Itor.

One problem at a time. At least the hurricane disaster had been avoided. It was a huge relief, but his hand still shook as he dialed Creed's phone.

RYAN MALMSTROM had a migraine from hell. His head hadn't hurt this bad since the time he'd been knocked over the head with a whiskey bottle back... when? He couldn't remember.

He also couldn't see.

What. The. Fuck.

Blackness surrounded him, or at least, that was how it seemed. His eyes were closed, wouldn't open. Taped shut, maybe?

The sound of beeping—hospital equipment, he thought—penetrated his pain. Had he been in an accident?

He lifted his arm—or tried to. Something was holding it down. His other arm and both legs as well. Straps.

Again, what the fuck?

A hand squeezed his left biceps. "Ryan?"

Ryan? He opened his mouth to answer the speaker, but his

throat was dry. He swallowed. "Is...Ryan my name?" he croaked.

"Yes. Yes, good. Ryan, do you remember anything? Anything *at all*?"

He wracked his aching brain, but the only thing that came to mind was the whiskey bottle in the bar. "I remember a bar. I got hit in the head with a whiskey bottle. Is that why I'm here?"

There was a pause. "What else?"

"That's all. Everything else is blank." And he was scared shit-less.

"You're sure?"

"Of course I'm fucking sure! I think I'd know if there was any-thing else in this black hole inside my fucking skull!"

The hand released him, and two hushed voices joined the first.

"Hey." Ryan clenched his hands into fists, the only action he could take. "What's going on?"

The men, presumably doctors, ignored him.

"Dammit! Tell me what the fuck is wrong with me!" He strug-gled against his bonds, his breath coming in furious pushes of air that made his chest cut into the straps holding him down.

He had a history of about five minutes of being strapped down to some sort of hard table, but he was pretty damned sure he'd never been this helpless or pissed. Then again, there was Coco.

Coco?

Who the hell was Coco?

"Ryan, you need to calm down." The owner of the original voice drifted to him, followed by a prick in the arm. Instantly, his muscles seemed to melt. "Now, I'm going to ask one more time: Do you remember anything more than what you've told me?"

"No," he lied, because something told him to keep the Coco thing to himself.

"We still need to do one more scrub of his memory," a second voice, deeper than the first, said.

Panic strangled Ryan so he couldn't speak. Scrub. Holy shit.

The first man sighed. "Ryan, this is only going to hurt for a minute. But it's going to hurt a lot."

The agony began instantly, like his head was being run beneath a steamroller. Pain overwhelmed him so he couldn't even scream. But inside his mind he did scream, because these fucks weren't going to erase the one memory that seemed to be important. So over and over, he silently screamed, praying this one thing would stick.

Coco . . . Coco . . . Coco . . .

MARLENA HEARD DEVLIN speaking with Creed for the first time since the ghost-whispering operative had left the compound after Oz's death.

"We have to talk when you get back here, Creed—after you collect Wyatt. We have to talk about Oz." The pain in her boss's voice was evident; it coursed through her in much the same way it did Devlin. She'd been with him long enough so that the transference of feelings was unavoidable—and destined.

She'd been destined to love men who didn't love her back. Like a fractured fairy tale, she'd been cursed from birth by a jealous sister who had wanted to remain an only child, but Marlena found that linking herself to one man—Devlin O'Malley—helped to ease some of the pain.

He'd never made her feel unloved, despite the fact that his heart would always remain with another. And in return, she showered him with all the comfort and affection he would accept.

Some days, he'd allow more than others. Today, when her hands moved on his shoulders to massage, she knew he would allow anything she wanted to give to him.

"That's nice," Dev murmured, closing his eyes and leaning forward, elbows on his desk so she could have access to his muscular back. As she kneaded out the familiar tensions in his neck and shoulders, she noted the newfound strength there—he'd been training, long and hard during that time when he'd had to be sheltered from ACRO's day-to-day activities. It had been a long four months that she hadn't been allowed access to him, and she'd been as scared for herself as she had been for him.

She was a beautiful woman—there was no use denying it. So

much so that she'd been sought out by ACRO after they'd seen some of her modeling photos in a fashion magazine. The original position they'd interviewed her for was that of a Seducer—a job so powerful, so important, she'd almost taken it. She'd always been a sensual woman, had always enjoyed and understood that sex was nothing more than a power play, whether it was for love or money or something else entirely. She'd figured that the job would allow her to cut off her feelings, to stop herself from falling in love and to learn how to treat men and sex as merely jobs.

But that wouldn't have worked—she didn't have special powers, and she would've fallen in love with every single man she taught if she'd taken a position as a Seducer trainer. It would have been unbearable, and when she turned down the job, Devlin himself had come to her hotel room, right before she'd prepared to leave the Catskills.

He was the only man in her life—the only person outside of her family who knew her story.

Her sister had been killed in a car accident, effectively ending all but a tiny spark of hope there was of reversing the curse. According to ACRO, when the person who placed the curse crossed over, the curse gained strength and could almost never be broken. And so far, no one at ACRO had been able to help her. But Dev had promised her forever, and he would never go back on his word.

She was safe here. And Devlin was safe with her, would never lose his heart to her, and therefore could, in effect, ultimately give himself to her sexually, guilt free.

She also knew that, if what Oz said was true, Dev would find another love, that her time with him would be limited.

But what about her? It would have to be someone far away from ACRO, a man who didn't know she'd been sleeping with her boss for years—filling a required role for his body in return for emotional protection.

What kind of man would want her for anything more than sex, knowing all of that?

"I'm not letting you go, Marlena," Dev told her, and she shook her head, because she'd gotten so comfortable around Dev that she'd forgotten he could read minds.

"I can't stay with you forever, Dev."

"I hate it that I have to be the one who hurts you—but I won't let the rest of the world do that," he said.

"You can't take the weight of the world on your shoulders. Oz always used to tell you that, and he was right," she told him, and he smiled. She was really the only one he'd talked to about Oz.

"Maybe someday they'll be able to reverse the curse."

"Maybe." She smoothed a hand over his cheek. "Let me help you, Dev. Please. You know how happy that makes me."

She'd already begun to work the buttons on the black BDU shirt all the operatives wore, pulled it off his shoulders and suckled the sweet-tasting skin behind his ear, which made him jump with anticipation.

Yes, she knew every single part of Devlin's body—knew how to play him so he could forget everything else, even if it was for just moments at a time.

"Faith? Faith Black?"

Christ. Faith hadn't been sitting in the private park outside the mental hospital for more than ten minutes. She'd expected to have at least an hour before MI6 came for her.

As expected, she'd landed in a pot of boiling hot water when she arrived back at TAG. After being royally chewed out by Paula, she'd taken a relaxing shower and a walk, needing some time to herself before she was hauled before the MI6's Special Agent section chief for punishment.

It hadn't been enough time, and she was grumpy. She didn't even look at the speaker. "Who wants to know?"

"A friend of Wyatt Kennedy's."

Wrenching her head around so fast she tweaked a muscle, Faith looked up into the icy blue eyes of an extraordinarily beautiful blonde, who smiled the most evil smile she'd ever seen.

"Confirmation enough." The blonde planted her booted foot in Faith's face.

Faith dumped off the park bench, rolled, came to her feet and ignored the blood pouring from her nose. It was a little harder to ignore the painful throbbing. "You bitch."

"Oh, dear." Sarcasm dripped from the blonde's voice. "You hurt me." She attacked with a series of amazing moves Faith barely blocked. "And my name is Annika. But bitch always applies."

Yeah, Annika had that right. "Look at you," Faith drawled. "You have quite the pair, yeah?"

"Yeah." Annika bared her teeth. "A big, steel set."

Faith went on the offensive, landing some light blows but never doing damage. The tight leather skirt she was wearing didn't help much, and Annika moved like she'd bloody invented hand-to-hand combat. Even so, Faith held her own, blocking most of the other woman's attacks.

"You're good," Annika said. "But I'm not really trying all that hard. And I have a secret."

Faith snorted, circling the other woman. "Don't bore me with a weapon. I'll have you disarmed before you can blink."

"Please." Annika rolled her eyes. "If I'm close enough to use something as lame as a pistol or knife, I'm close enough to use this." She lunged, closed her fingers on Faith's forearm and suddenly, the world exploded into a million colors.

Well, if that wasn't a huge blow to the ego.

Mercifully, the world went black.

CREED ACTUALLY breathed a huge sigh of relief when Wyatt fell asleep on the jet. For the first hours of the flight, Wyatt paced back and forth like a wild man, muttering to himself, and with his out-of-whack emotions he'd made it hard as hell for the pilot to remain in control of the aircraft.

He wondered if Wyatt knew his powers had gotten stronger, mutated like a strange, wonderful gift he'd recently unwrapped and was still figuring out how to use.

Creed's friend and fellow operative had been sitting outside a Yorkshire inn, on a boulder, staring straight up at the sky, when Creed and Annika had gone to collect him.

From what Dev had told him in the brief call where unspoken words about Oz hung heavily across the line, Wyatt had gotten himself into some trouble with a female operative from the mysterious third agency ACRO had been attempting to get information about. And when Creed saw the condition Wyatt was in, he was more than glad that he'd sent Annika to collect Faith.

And when the call came in from Annika to let him know that she and Faith were on a second ACRO jet heading for headquarters, Wyatt woke up again and uttered a deep sigh.

"You want to talk about it?" Creed asked.

Wyatt pulled his lanky frame to a sitting position. "I...uh..." He sighed again and hung his head. "I'm just a little beat up inside right now. I've got a lot going on."

"Annika's found Faith."

"I'm sure that went well," Wyatt commented with a wry smile.

"Dev needs to meet with her—figure out where her loyalties lie." Creed spoke quietly, and Wyatt let out a snort.

"Good luck with that."

"She hurt you."

"She betrayed me. Big difference." Wyatt stared out the window for a second before his dark eyes met Creed's. "She kicked my ass."

"I know all about that."

"I guess you do."

"You love this woman?" Creed couldn't help but ask.

Wyatt nodded. "I'm hoping that feeling goes away sometime soon. I'd even take a mind scrub to help me out."

Unfortunately, they both knew that those only took away memory, not emotion.

"Can we talk about something else?" Wyatt asked. "Anything. Tell me what's going on at home."

It was Creed's turn to sigh, as he began to tell Wyatt about Oz.

* * *

ANNIKA WATCHED with detached interest as Faith stirred, jostled into consciousness when the jet began its descent through hurricane remnants on its way toward the ACRO airfield. Annika had shocked the shit out of Faith to knock her out, but the sedatives she'd injected her with later had kept her nice and quiet. The anti-psychic drugs would keep her from trying anything stupid. The biokinesis wouldn't work on Annika, but she didn't want to take any chances with other ACRO staff once she and Faith were on the ground.

Now Faith stretched, gave Annika a cool stare as she sat up straight after having been slumped in her seat and leaning against the window.

"You drool in your sleep," Annika said. "I'll bet Wyatt just loved that."

Faith shoved her dark hair back from her face. "There's no filter between your thoughts and your mouth, is there?"

Annika ignored her, snagged a cola from the fridge next to her. "Thirsty? Mouth taste like an electrical burn?"

"That's one hell of a gift you've got there," Faith said, as she reached for the offered drink.

"It's cool, huh? Gotta love evolution."

That was how some ACRO scientists explained most of the nonpsychic, physical gifts operatives had: a sort of evolutionary process that was bringing humans more in step with the animal world. Annika's own gift put her in line with electric eels and some species of fish. How the theory fit in with the apocalyptic prophecies Dev and Creed had been talking about didn't matter. Personally, she didn't give a shit about the science behind her abilities. Sure, the whole not-being-able-to-have-sex thing had been a drag, but now that she had Creed, she wouldn't give up her gift for anything.

Grinning, Annika popped the tab on her Diet Coke. "It also gives me this nifty impenetrable barrier against telekinetic attacks, so don't try anything."

"Is that why I'm not restrained?"

"You're not restrained because Dev thinks you deserve respect, being the head of a friendly agency and all that crap."

Faith rested a booted foot on the seat across from her. Goth boots with metal hoops and chains. Awful. On the other hand, they'd been packed with razor-thin, sharp blades, a micro-gun, and even tiny, drugged darts. Annika had removed all weapons while Faith slept, and not without a dash of admiration.

"I'm assuming you're taking me to ACRO."

"Can't get anything by you," Annika drawled.

"What's going to happen when we get there?"

"They'll probably torture you for a few days." Annika glanced at Faith's hands and shrugged. "You didn't need those fingernails anyway. Terrible polish. Black doesn't look good on you."

To Faith's credit, she didn't flinch, go pale or piss herself. Then again, the whole respect thing Annika mentioned probably ruined the scare factor. "No matter what they do to me, it can't be half as bad as the torture I'm going through now."

"Really? Because I'm thinking they might chain you in a cell and send Wyatt in. Something tells me he'd love to get his hands on you. And not in the fun way."

Finally, Faith reacted. It was subtle, a slight tightening of her fingers around the drink can, but yeah, there it was. Little Miss Tea and Crumpets was in love with Wyatt The Not-So-Dead Agent.

The pilot came on the intercom to announce the landing, and Annika waited until he shut up to say, "You betrayed him, didn't you? Screwed him over and broke his little heart."

The can crumpled in Faith's hand, spilling soda. "You don't know shit."

"Chill, crumpet." Annika tipped back her head and drained half her soda. When she finished, she wiped her mouth with the back of her hand. "I get it. We're operatives. We do what we have to do to complete a mission, right?"

"So if you don't care, why so outraged on his behalf when you found me?"

"Just because I've had the anything-to-get-the-job-done philosophy drilled into me for years doesn't mean I like my friends getting fucked."

Faith nodded as if she understood that. She tossed her soda can in the trash and studied Annika thoughtfully. "So you're the one," she murmured. "You grew up in the life."

"Wyatt opened his big trap?" When Faith nodded, Annika rolled her eyes. "I take back what I said about screwing him over. You gonna ask a bunch of bullshit questions now? Ask when I made my first kill? Ask what it was like to be raised as a weapon?"

"I know what it's like," Faith said softly, and Annika's stomach lurched.

She'd always believed she was unique. Not special—what she'd gone through could not be considered special—but she'd hoped no other kid had been abused like that.

"How old?"

"Since I was eight. You?"

Annika turned, looked out the window at the ground, which seemed to be coming up on them too quickly. But maybe that was because her adrenaline had started to surge as her heartbeat kicked up a few notches. She wasn't even sure why. All she knew was that she was suddenly having this weird, girly bonding chat with a woman she was pretty sure she didn't like.

Finally, she turned back to Faith. "I've been in it since I was two."

A fragile cease-fire hung in the air between them like smoke. "My parents were killed," Faith said quietly. "I was taken in for my abilities."

"Yeah. Me too." Annika studied her feet. Didn't look at Faith as she said, "Are you angry?"

"Angry?" The surprise in Faith's voice brought Annika's head up. "Why? The British government took me in when I had no place else to go. Had it not been for them, I don't know what I'd have become. I'm guessing things didn't work out quite so well for you."

"Not exactly." And Troy was still out there somewhere, completely unaware that if not for Creed, he'd be dead right now. She wondered if she'd ever feel closure about that chapter in her life.

The jet bounced and jolted as it set down, and the moment it slowed, Annika was up and pounding on the door. "Open the fuck up!"

She had to get out of there. Away from this woman who made her want to swap stories and bring up the good old days that were, in fact, as far from good as it could get.

She needed Creed.

She sucked in a sharp, stunned breath. Because for the first time ever, her instinct wasn't to go to Dev.

Creed was who she wanted.

Her choice had been made, and she couldn't be happier.

CHAPTER
twenty-five

The first instinct Wyatt had when he walked into Dev's office not long after the jet landed and the Hummer whisked him to the familiar headquarters was to give the man a hug, but he didn't. Dev wasn't one for public displays of affection of any kind, and Wyatt got that. Dev didn't have the luxury of appearing weak, even when mourning the death of the man he loved.

"I'm sorry about Oz, Devlin. He was a good man."

"He was," Dev said, his voice sincere even though he was looking at Wyatt a little strangely.

It was only then that Wyatt realized that Dev could see. For as long as Wyatt had known the man who'd saved his ass from a prison sentence, Dev had been blind, but his boss could always see better than any sighted person.

Of course, now was one of those times that Wyatt wished Dev could see a little less clearly.

He handed his boss the bag of broken weather-machine parts. "Beyond repair now—but I figured you'd enjoy the honor of doing the complete destruction."

"I also get the honor of meeting the operative who almost got you killed, Wyatt. And I don't like operatives who hurt ACRO agents."

"I don't like her much either right now."

Dev nodded slowly, ran his hands through his hair in the familiar gesture Wyatt was used to, and yeah, he was home, where he belonged. "A mission isn't the time to fall in love."

"Yeah, well, I always knew that. Never thought it would happen to me."

"You were protected by your aphrodisiac."

"It didn't work on her, Dev. Not really—she remembered, even after the first night we were together. She remembered everything." He shook his head and sunk into the leather couch. "I'm so fucked."

"You completed the mission, you did your job. And Faith will no doubt be happy to align her agency with ours."

"I don't know about that."

"She gave you the motherboard to destroy, didn't she?"

"She locked me in a fucking mental ward!" Wyatt roared, tossing Dev's desk clear of everything with his temper. "Ah, fuck, Dev, I'm sorry—I keep doing that."

But Dev wasn't looking at the desk—instead, his eyes were focused on his shoulder. "You're touching me. Again."

Wyatt shifted, hadn't realized that it was his first impulse to put his hand on Dev's shoulder to apologize, the way he would've when Dev didn't have his sight.

"You did it when you first walked into the room," Dev continued. "You hugged me with your mind. Has this happened before?"

Wyatt's first instinct was to say no, but then he realized how untrue that was. "Yeah, it has. I haven't learned to control it yet."

"Control what, Wyatt?"

Wyatt shifted. "According to Faith, I'm biokinetic. At first I thought maybe that wasn't true, that maybe there was some freaky kind of transference happening. But when she told me, when she put her hands on me, I knew what she said was right."

"You've always been tactile, but this power is one of the rarest.

The ability to manipulate the human body telekinetically...
Wyatt, if you've got that, plus the ability to manipulate inanimate
objects, you'll be working at an entirely new level."

"Yeah, but getting them to work together is another story.
Faith tried to help. Helped me in other ways too...I mean, I know
about Mason. I remember now. I didn't kill him, Devlin." Wyatt
heard his voice threaten to break but he held it together. "I love
her for helping me and I hate her for it, both at the same time."

"Getting close to someone can do that to a person, twist them
inside until they don't know which end is up." Dev's voice was
almost wistful.

"I don't want to be close to her anymore." Wyatt's jaw hurt
from clenching his teeth every time he even thought about her.

"She had an awful choice to make, didn't she?" Dev said.
"Having your loyalties split...trying to do what's best for everyone. That's not a position I'd relish being put into."

"I shouldn't have trusted her. I should've known better."

"None of us know better. That's why we're human."

Wyatt leaned his head back and stared up at the ceiling, bone
tired and confused as shit. "What do I do now?"

"You need help. Go over to the Sanctuary. They'll try to help
you with these two gifts, teach you to merge them."

"And if they can't?"

"Then you'll have no choice but to see Faith Black again."

WYATT HAD NEVER minded being commanded to do shit—he'd
always been a roll-with-the-punches kind of guy, unlike a lot of
the other operatives here at ACRO, who would've had to hold
back so they wouldn't tell their boss to go fuck himself.

Still, the *Go fuck yourself* had nearly slipped through, and
Devlin knew it. After this one, Wyatt was way too close to the
edge for even his own comfort, and he was about to face a familiar enemy, in the form of his own mind.

He had to win this time.

Now he strolled slowly across the ACRO grounds, sunglasses
on and AC/DC pounding out "Back in Black" through his iPod.

He knew that the men and women who worked at the Sanctuary were expecting him, that Dev had already called over, knew that he'd be well taken care of there, but still his gut roiled at the thought of this semi-voluntary confinement.

It's not the same as when you were growing up. Not the same as the institution in Yorkshire either.

And still, he could barely bring himself to step across the threshold of the large Victorian house and check in with the woman who worked the desk. She gave him a wide, genuine smile and directed him up three flights of stairs to his room.

He'd heard that the rooms here in the Sanctuary were large and comfortable, and his own room confirmed it—was much more reminiscent of an upscale hotel. Now Wyatt understood why so many operatives had no problem heading over to this place to recharge their energies.

His hand gripped the doorknob hard and he let go when he realized he'd bent it with his mind by accident when he'd opened the door.

"There's no shame in coming here, you know."

Wyatt turned down the hall toward the graveled voice, to see Amitola, a Native American faith healer who'd been at ACRO as long as Creed's parents had. He'd always nodded, been friendly to the tall, white-haired man, but hadn't wanted to get too close since Amitola worked in the Healing ward.

"Yeah, I know," Wyatt said, even though his words were full of crap.

Amitola stared between the doorknob and Wyatt's face. "No, you don't know that yet. But you will."

"Sorry about that. I'll fix it."

Amitola stood there silently, watched as Wyatt moved the bent metal into its correct position.

"Impressive. Now, please, make yourself comfortable."

Wyatt kicked off his shoes and sat on the bed, cross-legged, and followed the man's directions. They were possibly his only hope of not having to cross paths with Faith again.

* * *

FAITH HAD BEEN SURPRISED when Annika handed her over to three armed security guys dressed in black BDUs, but she wasn't about to argue. Her face, still throbbing from having Annika's foot hit it, was reminder enough that no matter how much Faith and Annika had in common, they weren't going to be best mates.

The security guys escorted her through what appeared to be an old but well-kept military base, to a building she guessed must be the headquarters. Inside, she was herded into a plush office complete with leather chairs, an oak desk and a handsome, dark-haired man who, while probably in his mid-thirties, was a lot younger than she'd envisioned.

He stood, offered his hand, which she shook before taking a seat across the desk from him.

"Faith Black," he murmured, as he returned to his chair. "How is it that we've never heard of you or your agency?"

"Perhaps the British are more discreet than you Yanks, Mr.... O'Malley?"

He smiled. "Call me Dev. We Yanks are a lot less formal too."

"I assume you've been in touch with the British government?"

"They don't think we're holding you for ransom, if that's what you're asking. The director in charge of MI6's TAG Division knows you're here. I don't think he's real happy we know about your operation, but he figures now that we do, we might be able to come to some sort of mutually beneficial partnership."

"I'll need to speak with him. And with my partner, Paula."

"Of course. I have a room set up for you in the guest quarters, complete with video-conferencing equipment." He stood, and she came to her feet as well. "We can discuss this more tomorrow, after you've gotten some rest."

"That's very generous. Especially considering...everything." He just stared at her with his piercing gaze, and yeah, talk about awkward. "Speaking of everything, how's Wyatt?" she asked quietly.

"He'll be okay. Which is the reason you're in my office instead of in a cell. And the reason that when we tracked the motherboard to your headquarters we didn't take your agency down from the ground up."

Surprise kept her silent for a heartbeat. How could they have countered TAG's preventive measures? She knew for a fact that her agency's technology and procedures were top-notch. "I appreciate your candor."

"Life is too short to beat around the bush," he said, his voice gravelly and low. He gestured to the door, where a tall man with a hypnotic gaze stood, staring at Faith. "Trance will show you around the base and make sure you're delivered to your quarters. I'll see you in the morning." Dev shook her hand again. "I'm looking forward to working together."

Faith was too. The trick would be avoiding Wyatt for the time she was here, because working together hadn't ended well for the two of them.

CREED HAD BEEN FUNNY when Annika found him after deplaning the jet. He'd been in his office at his department headquarters, and she'd pounced on him right there in his chair. He'd assumed she wanted sex, but when she told him she wanted to talk, he'd nearly fallen over. Well, he'd been acting overly dramatic, but still. He'd been both shocked and pleased, and it had been his suggestion that she go see Dev. It had been her idea to go together.

They arrived at Dev's office, and for a split second Annika considered having Marlena buzz her in, but hey, not everything could change. Besides, she was nervous, which had a tendency to make her pushy and demanding. She'd spoken with Dev on the phone about the Wyatt mission, but their conversation had been formal and professional. She hadn't seen him in person since the day she'd stomped off, so this was a little nerve-wracking.

Creed remained in the waiting room as Annika barged into Dev's office, where he was at his desk, working on his computer. "Hi, Dev."

His fingers froze. "Hi."

"I know what you did."

He frowned. Cleared his throat. Looked like shit. "I don't know how." He removed a file folder from his inbox and shoved it across the desk at her.

Confused, she opened it, felt her heart stop at the sight of the photos inside. "Oh, my God. Troy." The man she'd gone to Greece to kill was dead. A range of emotions rolled through her, from shock to relief, and maybe even a little anger that he'd died by a hand that wasn't hers. Then again, had she killed him, maybe she wouldn't be in the place she was now, happy to be committed to Creed and a life with him.

She'd found peace with Creed, and somehow that peace had transferred to her entire life. Just hours ago, on the jet with Faith, she'd wanted closure on her CIA past, and she only now realized that she'd found it even before she saw the pictures of the dead agent.

She was free. Free of her past, free of the anger and hatred that had been with her so long it almost felt like part of her.

"I . . . how . . . ? You did this?"

"That's not . . . Wait a second, you said you knew."

"Oh, no. Not about that. I was talking about the other day. When you said all those things to me." Before he could say anything, she moved around behind his desk so she stood in front of his chair. "I know you didn't mean anything you said."

"Annika—"

"Shh. Let me talk." She kneeled down and covered his hand with hers. "Thank you. Thank you for saving me all those years ago. Thank you for taking care of me since. And thank you for making me see that I belong with Creed."

He blew out a forceful breath, and she realized he'd been holding it while she spoke. "So you two are fine?"

"More than fine."

"Thank God." He stood and pulled her up with him, drew her into his arms. "I just want you to be happy."

"I am. I love you, Dev."

His warm lips pressed a gentle kiss into the top of her head. "I love you too."

Stepping back just a little, she lifted her hand to his cheek. "I still want you to call me. If you need anything. To talk. To hang out. Whatever."

"I will. I'll call both of you."

"Good." She studied him for a moment, admired the strength in his face, the confidence in his gaze. Yeah, he'd pick up the pieces Oz left behind and would be stronger than ever. "I have to go to Creed now."

"Yes."

With a final, affectionate smile, she pulled away. "You're coming to our house for Thanksgiving this year. Just FYI."

He laughed as she left the office. Outside, Creed was waiting for her with open arms. "Let's go home."

Home. That sounded like heaven. With ACRO, she'd always had a family, even if she hadn't realized it. But with Creed she had a home.

CHAPTER
Twenty-six

Wyatt woke to warmth invading his body, Faith's name on his lips and Amitola standing over him.

It was the first time Wyatt had felt warm in the past few hours, since he'd been lulled into sleep by Amitola's chanting.

"This is an old Native American tradition. Healing hands."

"Thanks, brother," Wyatt whispered. "I'll take all the help I can get."

"A woman hurt you."

"Yeah."

"You've been mumbling her name in your sleep. Crying out for her. That means something."

"Means I'm fucked."

Amitola actually laughed, a fluid, singsong sound. "We're all fucked when it comes to women, Wyatt. Especially once they invade our dreams." He paused. "She's already there."

Wyatt drew a deep breath, and yeah, *yeah*, something had changed. "How can I feel so peaceful and still be so angry?"

"You have to confront the anger—and the person who did that to you," Amitola said. "Your supervisor wants to see you. Can I send him in? He's been waiting."

"Yeah, that's cool." Wyatt took a long drink of water, drained the bottle as Amitola left and Josh walked into the room, shutting the door behind him. Halfway to the bed, he stuck out his hand for a shake, and before he knew it, Wyatt was shaking Josh's hand with his mind. Josh stared at his own hand and shook his head slowly.

"Do you know what this means, Wyatt? Do you know how rare this kind of telekinesis is?"

"I do now."

"We have no experience in this. You've got a lot of work ahead of you. We can't send you back out into the field until we know how fully integrated it is—until we're sure you know how to control it, to use it properly." Josh stuck his hands in his pockets. "I understand that the agent from The Aquarius Group has the same power."

Wyatt shook his head yes, and then no, because he knew what Josh wanted him to do.

"It's for your own good, Wyatt. Otherwise, it could take years before we truly know what you can do. If this woman—"

"Faith," Wyatt said. "Her name is Faith."

"If Faith can help you, it's to your benefit."

"And if I don't get help from her?"

"Then I'll work with you, Wyatt—for as long as it takes. Your place is here, at ACRO. You know that."

Wyatt nodded, stood on shaky legs and went over to the window. He pressed his forehead and palms against the cool glass for a few seconds, looked out at the rolling hills and the fall foliage and realized that he didn't feel as off-kilter as he had before. His balance still wasn't quite right, but the earth wasn't thrown off its axis either.

"Bring Faith here to me, Josh."

THE TOUR of the base was impressive. It was a sprawling, old military installation, underutilized by at least half, but it was well kept, even boasting a pub, a park and a baseball field.

As Dev had promised, the driver of the shiny black Hummer

had taken her all over, showed her exactly why her tiny agency would have been crushed if she'd ever taken on ACRO. Which, she suspected, was a large reason she was being given the tour in the first place. Dev's boastful assertion that they could have taken her agency apart from the ground up hadn't been an exaggeration. They could squash her like a bug, and they wanted her to know it.

Christ, these people ran an *animal* facility that was larger than her entire estate. And the medical clinic, which they were entering now, could have held half the TAG building inside it.

She slid a glance at Trance. He was her driver and chaperone, though she got the impression that his normal duties didn't include playing tour guide. No doubt Dev had chosen someone capable of handling her should the need arise.

Cunning bastard. She couldn't help but admire him.

TAG and ACRO might both be playing for the good guys, but that didn't mean each agency wasn't ultimately out for itself. She had to respect Dev for protecting his interests and people. She was just relieved that Annika hadn't drawn babysitting duty again.

"Is this the last stop?" she asked Trance, as they walked past the emergency room and headed down a hall lined with patient rooms. She hoped so. Every minute spent out on the base increased her risk of seeing Wyatt. She ached with the desire to see him, but she couldn't bear to see the hatred in his eyes again.

"Yeah."

For a tour guide, Trance wasn't all that talkative. But he had the most amazing eyes. When he looked at her, she felt a little of what a sheep must feel like in the crosshairs of a border collie's intense, hypnotic stare. Like Wyatt, Trance could be a menace to women if he wanted to be.

Two nurses nodded in greeting as they passed. Faith tried with Trance again. "How many people work here?"

"No clue." They exited the building through double doors in the rear and walked a few meters to an old Victorian-style building whose sign marked it as being a psychiatric unit.

I'll bet Wyatt doesn't spend time here, she thought with a pang. They traversed the halls, climbing to the third floor and slowing at a door. Trance opened it, and instantly her self-preservation instinct kicked in.

"Where we are going?" she asked, refusing to step foot inside the room.

"I have orders to bring you here." His voice was deep, commanding, and the words were as unyielding as a stone wall.

A chill ran up her spine. Maybe ACRO wasn't going to play nice, after all. On instinct, she tried to flood herself with her gift, but the power hovered frustratingly out of reach. She'd attempted to summon it on the plane, realizing when she failed that Annika had drugged her. It seemed that the drug was still working.

"And if I refuse?" She shifted her weight, readying herself for battle.

Trance looked at her, the harsh lines of his jaw tensing, his pupils dilating and then squeezing to a laserlike pinpoint. "You won't."

"You arrogant..." She trailed off, fascinated by the way he was looking at her. Her mind sort of fuzzed out, and damned if she didn't find herself walking toward him as he walked backward into the room.

"Son of a bitch," she murmured. She had enough presence of mind to know she was going to kill him the moment she was free of this haze, but not enough to actually break out of it.

It wasn't until she heard a low-pitched growl that she snapped out of the spell she'd been under. "I'll take it from here, man," Wyatt said, and Faith's legs buckled as the shock of surprise took her straight down.

WYATT CAUGHT FAITH in his arms as she fainted. Trance crossed his arms in front of his chest and kept his eyes trained on her.

"She's trouble, this one. Mind of her own," Trance said, as though that was an entirely bad thing and something that needed to be changed immediately.

"Always has been, always will be," Wyatt muttered as he carried her over to the bed.

"I could work on her. Do a little training," Trance suggested. Wyatt had heard of the excedo's predilections as a Dom, and while the rumors of Trance's tendency toward hard-core kink were barely a blip on the ACRO radar, the idea of Trance's body anywhere near Faith's made Wyatt clench his fists.

"Easy there, SEAL. It was just a suggestion. I could always lend you the St. Andrew's Cross and the flogger. You'd be surprised how effectively, and quickly, they can work when used in tandem."

The idea of Faith bound and stretched out for Wyatt himself was suddenly strangely intriguing. "Thanks for the offer, but I've got this. You can head out."

Trance laughed. "Don't knock it until you've tried it, Wyatt," he said before he shut the door behind him.

"Are you planning on tying me up and horsewhipping me, or was that talk just part of the ACRO show?" Faith's voice came from behind him.

He turned to face her and she continued. "It's not that I don't deserve it, really."

"I asked them to bring you here because I need your help. Because you owe me. That's the only reason," he said, and he wondered if she could see right through him, could tell that he was lying through his teeth—because, man, seeing her again was like coming home. All he wanted to do was lie back on the bed and let her take him, over and over, until his body was spent from passion, not heartache.

Sitting up, she bit her bottom lip and nodded.

"I'm going to need help integrating my powers. I don't know how to work the biokinesis. I can't seem to control it—it just keeps happening, even when I'm not trying," he told her, and she stared first at one of his arms and then the other. "What is it?"

"It's just that . . . I felt you—hugging me when I first came in here, but I thought it was just wishful thinking."

Fuck. "Fuck, I didn't want to do that," he told her accusingly, as if that part of it was her fault too. "I don't want to hug you. I didn't even want to see you, but it's either face you or be sidelined for the next couple of years until I can figure myself out. And I'm done with that."

She stood and moved toward him. "You're so angry with me."

"Yes. And at myself," he said, wondered why the hell he was still sharing things with her. He didn't have to prove his god-damned mental state to anyone, least of all her.

But she'd be the one who understood the most.

She touched his cheek gently and he closed his eyes, because the cool palm felt so good on his skin, smelled like sunshine, and this working together and not feeling anything for her was never going to work.

He opened his eyes and watched her watching him.

"Liberty's going to stay at the facility," she said. "There are people there who can help her. Thing is, I don't know if I can ever trust her again."

"Trusting someone who betrayed you is damned hard, Faith. I trusted you enough, after you told me about TAG, not to call for backup. I could have, easily, but I didn't. Because I didn't want to risk what was happening with your sister. If it had been anything else, that scene at the battleground wouldn't have happened."

"Are you in trouble, Wyatt?"

"No, I'm not in trouble. Is that all you care about, that my job is intact? Because right now I could give two shits about that." A vase rose and smashed against the window, shattering both, and Faith was holding her arm as though Wyatt was squeezing it. Which, *dammit*, he probably was. "How soon could you give me control over these new powers?"

"Can we talk about us first? Please, Wyatt, I need to tell you..." She stopped, waited to see if he would interrupt. But he didn't. "When I found out where my people put you, all I could think about was getting to you. I was terrified of how you would feel when you woke up there—especially after you'd shared so much with me about your past. God, Wyatt, I'm so sorry. I know what that must've been like for you—I can never ask you to understand why I did what I did."

"You can ask," he said, aware his tone had turned harsh, and he forced himself to swallow his bitterness momentarily. "I know why you did it, Faith. It was for your family. I get that, probably more than anyone. I just thought..."

"That I wouldn't betray you in the process," she finished.

He nodded, wanting to believe her.

"I knew when I woke up that I needed to destroy the machine," she continued.

He studied her for a moment, seeing the truth of her words in her eyes. "I wasn't sure what would happen when we got to Liberty, but I knew you didn't have an easy decision in front of you," he said. "That's why I'd planned to take it off your plate—if I was the one to destroy it, depending how things went with Liberty, you could always blame me, not yourself."

"Why would you do that?"

"Because I know what it's like to blame yourself for things you didn't do, things that are out of your control." He sat down heavily on the edge of the bed and stared out the broken window, the shattered glass producing a crazy kaleidoscope of images, the way he'd imagined that his mind looked most of the time.

"I can help you." She sat down next to him, her cheeks flushed, the pull between them still there despite everything. "I went through a lot before I learned, made some mistakes. I can help you to learn about it much faster. But... you'll have to trust me. If you don't, it's not going to work."

He knew that. He just didn't know if he could bring himself to do so.

FAITH'S HEART BROKE for Wyatt, knowing he wanted to trust her but was unable to do so. Somehow, she had to convince him. Not for herself, but because she wanted to help him with his new gift.

"Wyatt, I didn't put you in that hospital. Do you believe me?"

He didn't answer. Didn't even look at her.

"Dammit, Wyatt, look at me."

He did, his eyes sparking. "I don't know what to believe."

She stood. "Focus on me. Open yourself up to your power. You'll see my aura."

"How is this going to help me trust you?"

She thunked him in the forehead with her fingers. His indignant "Ow!" gave her a smidge of satisfaction.

"Do it."

Muttering something indecipherable, he concentrated on her. The muttering became curses. "I can't see anything."

"Slap me."

"What?"

"Slap me. In the face. Hard."

He narrowed his eyes at her. "Don't think that thought hasn't crossed my mind."

"Then do it." When he just sat there, she rolled her eyes. "Insufferable." She snared a shard of broken glass off the floor and slashed her cheek.

"Jesus Christ, Faith!" he shouted. His hand shot out to grasp her wrist, squeezing hard enough to make her drop the glass. "What the fuck are you doing?"

She jerked out of his grip. "Now look at me. Look at the cut. Concentrate on it."

He didn't look happy, but he did it. "Hey," he murmured. "I see your aura."

"Good. Now look for any thin spots. Should be one over the cut." She waited, and he nodded. "Okay, now envision a needle. Or a laser beam. Something small and narrow. This will only work if you find a very sheer patch in an aura. If there isn't one, you'll have to probe with your power until you find a relatively weak spot, and then you'll pick the aura's threads apart. Takes a lot of time, so your best bet is to find a thin area."

"Okay."

"Now use your needle or beam and pierce my aura."

She felt the penetration the second he did it. Felt the sudden vulnerability, as though she were a ship with a breach in the hull.

"Now what?"

"Now you can kill me."

His gaze snapped up. His head snapped back. "I can what?"

"I've exposed my throat to you, Wyatt. If you want to, you can stop my heart. Sever my spinal cord. Puncture my lung." She closed her eyes, let herself be at his mercy. "I didn't order your admission into the hospital. The moment I found out you were there, all I could think about was getting you out. I attacked TAG's doctor when I thought she ended my pregnancy. I stole the motherboard from my own agency's lab—"

Hard hands came down on her shoulders. "What did you just say?"

"I'm in a lot of trouble, Wyatt."

The hands on her shoulders began to tremble. Wyatt pulled away, scrubbed one hand over his face. "I'll be there for you. No matter what."

"Um, okay. But really, there's nothing you can do. I risked my agency and my career to get that motherboard to you. I think the British government will give me a slap on the wrist since I've smoothed things out with ACRO, but my partner, the people I work with... they won't be so forgiving."

His brows drew together. "What does that have to do with anything?"

"I'm trying to tell you why you should give me another chance." She reached up, felt his forehead. "Are you all right? You're not making any sense."

"Me? I'm not making sense?" He grabbed a tissue off his nightstand and wiped the blood from her cheek. "You're the one talking about the weather machine when you should be talking about the baby."

"What baby?"

"You said you're pregnant."

A pang of realization stunned her. He thought she was pregnant, and he wanted to be there for her. And he wasn't upset. If anything, he looked pleased.

"I'm not pregnant," she murmured.

332 • Sydney Croft

"But... you attacked a doctor..."

"Because I misunderstood her. I thought she said I was pregnant and she'd ended the pregnancy. I attacked her," she whispered, "because I wanted to be." She swallowed the lump that had formed in her throat.

"You wanted... Why?"

She turned away, unable to bear seeing the same disgust in his eyes that had been there the last time she told him she loved him. Right before he smashed the motherboard and then showed her how little her admission meant to him.

"I told you... I love you." A shuddering sob escaped her, and shit, she felt so stupid. She'd bared her body, soul and heart to him. A man who needed her only for her ability to teach him to use his new gift.

"Look," she said, still facing the door, "you don't have to believe I love you. You don't have to believe that I didn't send you to the mental hospital. But dammit, you'd better believe that I wanted to be carrying your baby. You'd better believe that I chose you over the weather machine, even if it was a little late."

She spun around, planted a finger on his sternum hard enough to make him take a step back. "And you'd better believe that losing my parents to a storm was the single most devastating event in my life—until you fucked me like a whore and told me you didn't care." The memory of the sex outside the mental hospital, when she'd been foolish enough to believe that they still had a chance, was like a bruise on her brain. "So now I'm laid out as open as I can possibly be. I have nothing to hide. I have nothing to lose. So you'd better fucking trust me to help you, because I'm all you've got."

His hand curled around hers. His big palm was warm, a little rough, and it reminded her how much pleasure his hands had brought her.

"You're all I've ever had."

"That's right, so you had better—" She blinked. "Excuse me?"

Throwing his head back, he stared at the ceiling. "I've spent my entire life living like some kind of vagabond. Even my house isn't a home." He dropped his head, searched her face, his own expression a mix of hope and hesitation. "But loving you is like being home. And when you opened yourself up to me just now, I saw more than just your aura. I saw your heart."

Which was now pounding against her breastbone like it wanted out of her chest and inside his.

"It sounds corny," he said, blushing a little, "I know. And I can't explain it."

"You don't have to. I know."

A sad smile curved his mouth. "I'm sorry for what I did to you outside the mental hospital." Before she could protest, he touched one finger to her lips. "Shh. It was cruel. Not like me at all. I think in a way I hated you not because you betrayed me, but because you were brave enough to do something I couldn't do. I couldn't face my past. But you chased yours. Hell, you slept with a stuffed animal from childhood. You didn't forget your past, and you wanted to keep anyone else from going through what you did. I didn't anticipate the lengths you'd go to in order to honor your family, because I couldn't understand it."

Tears stung her eyes. "Oh, Wyatt. Are you saying you understand now?"

He nodded. "I'd do anything for you. So yeah, I get it." He tugged her against him, pressed his forehead to hers. "I'm ready to heal. I'm ready to love you and let you love me. What do you say?"

"I say we find someplace a lot more private than this, love. Because if I show you right now how much I love you, everyone in the building is going to know about it."

A low growl rumbled up in his chest. "They're going to know about it anyway. You're mine, Faith. You have been since the beginning. My woman."

"Yes," she whispered. "Your woman."

Epilogue

"Are you ready for a drink, love?" Faith asked, as she opened Wyatt's kitchen cabinet.

"Almost," he muttered, but he wasn't talking about the drink. He was sitting at the dining room table, staring at her as he tried to break through her aura. After four months he was getting better at it, faster, but as the clock ticked down to twenty minutes, she didn't think he was going to beat his twenty-two-minute record. Not unless he weakened her with his sex mojo.

Now that he'd learned to control the biokinesis, he'd learned to control the sexual portion of his ability—which they now knew caused an aura to practically collapse. He could initiate the sex mojo and penetrate an aura with his gift in a matter of seconds. He was actually faster than she was if he cheated like that.

He penetrated with a whoop of victory. Twenty minutes, forty seconds.

"See that, honey? I'll be caught up to you in no time."

She snorted. And then gasped as a tingly sensation spread through her groin.

"Yeah," he said softly, "teach you to laugh at me." Erotic, invisible strokes lashed at her sex. "Making me come isn't—oh, God." She groaned. The glass in her hand fell into the sink with a crash. She didn't care. It was all she could do to grasp the edge of the counter and stay upright.

"This is payback for the other day. Remember?"

She'd have smiled, but she was too busy biting her lip. And yes, she remembered. Wyatt had come out of the bedroom, dressed to kill—literally—in his black ACRO BDUs, and she'd pinned him to the wall with her gift, stripped him with her hands, and then sat on the couch with popcorn to watch as she made him come without lifting a finger. For fun, she'd pinched off his urethra so he couldn't ejaculate during his orgasm.

Wyatt's chest had heaved like he'd run a marathon, his jaw clenched, his eyes went wild. And he'd still been hard, his engorged cock the color of his bite-reddened lips. A few strokes with her biokinesis had made him come again, this time so forcefully that he broke her hold as his body convulsed and his semen erupted like a geyser.

He'd only been a little mad that she'd made him late for work.

"You remember," he said, and damn him, she could hear the amusement in his voice as he filled her core with stimulation and made her cry out in release.

She slumped against the counter, cursing him. The man was a quick study. He was quick in his movements too; she didn't hear him come up behind her and pull her back against his chest.

"Want to go with me?" He was going to visit an operative who had recently given birth to triplets. He'd been looking forward to it for days.

"I can't. I need to call Paula today." Faith had remained in New York with ACRO and Wyatt, but once a month she flew back to England to handle TAG business, and as long as she spoke with Paula regularly, she was able to keep up with operations. Right now, the distance was working, especially since relations between Faith and Paula were still strained.

He turned her to him so she could look into his eyes. "You sure you don't want to go see the babies?"

"I'm sure. You go."

Framing her face in his hands with the same care he'd given her since the night they met, he kissed her. Gently, slowly, lovingly. She melted against him the way she always did, but he pulled back, his slumberous gaze full of affection.

"Marry me."

Warmth surrounded her like a summer breeze. She wasn't sure if she was imagining things or Wyatt was using one of his gifts, but it didn't matter. She was grateful for it.

Grateful for him and all he'd done for her. He'd given her a second chance, and she'd move heaven and earth to make sure he'd never have to give her a third.

"Yes," she whispered. "I'll marry you."

He kissed her again, this time in a possessive, claiming caress. One hand came up to cup her breast, while the other threaded through her hair to hold her to him. Her libido spun up again, and when his erection made itself known against her belly, she knew his had too.

"I thought you were going to see the babies," she moaned, as he kissed a hot path along her jaw and down her throat.

An erotic purr rumbled his chest. "I'm thinking maybe we could make our own."

"Oh, love." She wrapped her arms around him, pulling him as close as she could. "I can't wait."

"Neither can I." He effortlessly swung her up into his arms and headed toward the bedroom.

When it came to Wyatt, she couldn't wait for anything.

Before Wyatt came along, she'd believed her life was full. Nothing could have been further from the truth. And as he laid her down on their king-sized bed, his eyes promised a life more full than she could imagine. Full of excitement, love and children.

Yeah, she definitely couldn't wait.

About the Author

SYDNEY CROFT is a pseudonym for two authors who each write under their own names. This is their third novel together. Visit their website at www.sydneycroft.com.

**If you were seduced by Sydney's
sexy story, read on for the author's
steamy new novel**

TAMING
the
FIRE

BY SYDNEY CROFT

Coming from Bantam in summer 2009

Taming the Fire

ON SALE SUMMER 2009

CHAPTER
One

"You look like you need a daddy."

Trance merely stared down the Bear, who was dressed in all leather, and gave a small shake of his head. Wrong sex and wrong preference, but he didn't mind the attention. He had an open mind when it came to anything concerning sex, but women did it for him and always had. That wasn't changing.

So no, he didn't need a daddy, but hell, if the right woman came along, he wouldn't mind playing the daddy and everything in between.

He didn't hold out much hope for the right woman, though, which made his whole "wouldn't mind" speech easier to feed himself.

Besides, he wasn't here for a soul mate, he was on a mission from ACRO—the Agency for Covert Rare Operatives—to rescue a now free agent named Ulrika. She was on the run from Itor Corp, a powerful agency that also employed agents with special abilities. Her name means "power of the wolf," and she'd originally belonged to a small, rare European tribe of therianthropes, people who believe they are animals in human flesh. According to ACRO's cryptozoologists, therians claim to shift, spiritually and psychologically but not physically—that could be proven—into their animal.

By all reports, Ulrika had lived in harmony with her animal soul until Itor got ahold of her and mutated her powers without her consent. Now she was a powerful shape-shifter who used sex to control the angry beast living inside of her, and if she had a chance in hell of staying alive, she was going to need his agency's help.

Which was why he was here, undercover and posing as a sub rather than his Dom preference.

This wasn't one of the worst clubs, but it wasn't one of the higher-end ones either. No, Ulrika would be hiding out in a place where she could stand out without fear of being caught, and this underground London club was off the map.

He'd been watching her all night as he sat on the smooth leather stool in a stance that signaled "available." Most of the Doms avoided him, as they should. Even tamping himself down, the wild streak practically throbbed from him.

But Ulrika was drawn to that. From what he'd gathered, she liked her men hard to handle. Probably because the tamer ones were unable to handle what she had to offer during sex.

She appeared next to him, catching him off guard. He took a sip of his whiskey as if he was the one who called her over, but she wasn't buying it. She put a strong arm on his, and he let her push his hand with the glass in it to the bar, where he opened his palm and surrendered it.

Kira, another ACRO operative, an animal whisperer, had been right in pegging tonight as the night. Ulrika was definitely on the prowl.

She slid a firm finger under his chin and forced it upward, as if appraising him.

No, this wasn't going to be easy.

He forced himself to stay still under her gaze. If she was a true, born Dom, she'd have known that he wasn't a submissive, not by a long shot. But from the files he'd briefed himself on before he left the ACRO offices, he knew Ulrika's need for sex overrode most of her other senses. Especially now, when she was scared and on the run.

He was the one to bring her in, even if it meant posing as something that went against every one of his most basic survival instincts.

The wolf lady was beautiful—long reddish-blond hair, piercing gold eyes. And yes, he didn't avert his gaze purposefully, because if he was going to pull off his role as a sub, it was going to be as one who was nearly untrainable.

"Eyes down, boy," she said, her voice sure and strong, and he shot her one final glance before doing her bidding. "You won't be an easy one, will you?"

"I'm not a boy," he said.

She chuckled lightly. "You'll be whatever I tell you to be tonight."

His cock jumped at her words.

"Are you worthy of that privilege . . . boy?"

He wanted to strap her to a spanking bench and make her ass a pretty shade of red, and then they'd find out who was worthy.

He bit the inside of his cheek instead of telling her that.

"You may speak," she said, her hand caressing his ass.

"I'm worthy. *Mistress*."

"Good boy."

He brought his eyes up to meet hers again, and she merely raised her eyebrows at him. "Unless you'd rather call me *daddy*, I suggest you lower your eyes and learn to love *boy*."

He hadn't expected the sense of humor. She'd been watching him for longer than he'd thought.

He lowered his eyes, but only so he could stare at her perfectly formed breasts under the low-cut gauzy blouse she wore. Much different than most of the leather-clad mamas in this place.

She brought her cleavage close to his face. "Like what you see?"

He breathed deeply—her scent belied what she really was

underneath—part woman, part wolf . . . and he was the perfect one to tame the beast he knew was inside that body.

"Yes. I like." His voice was husky with need, and if she hadn't been able to tell from that, all she needed to do was look down at the massive bulge between his legs, straining to be set free from the black pants he wore.

"Room three. Face the wall. And keep your clothes on. I want to have some fun taking them off myself."

He nodded, pushed off the stool and walked toward the room without the requisite *yes, mistress.*

He heard her low growl follow him down the darkened hallway all the way to room three, with its heavy cuffs and chains hanging from the far wall. Which was exactly where she wanted him and the last place he wanted to be. No, he should be the one cuffing her, arms above her head, her breasts and body open to him for his pleasure.

Instead, his body would be in Rik's hands.

She was part uncontrollable predator and all danger, to herself and to the outside world, if she couldn't learn to control the change. In order to help her do that, he'd have to control her first. Slowly. Without her realizing it.

He'd have to hypnotize her into wanting him to be her sub, again and again, because word on the floor was that Mistress Rik didn't take the same sub twice. Ever. And since his skill as an excedo had, as far back as he could recall, included the ability to tame most people with one look into his eyes, he really was the perfect man for the job.

It had been two months since she'd surfaced on the scene following a botched assassination attempt on the head of ACRO's new sister agency, The Aquarius Group. Ulrika's failure to kill Faith Black had apparently led to her escape from Itor when Ulrika's handler was captured. She was now on ACRO's radar, and hopefully Trance could get her off Itor's before they tracked her down.

Now he remained facing the wall, feeling her eyes on him.

She'd picked one of the private rooms, which gave him hope that she wasn't into displaying him for the world to see.

He wasn't heavily into the BDSM scene—not anymore, but when he was in his late teens and early twenties, he was a frequent visitor to all the clubs, first in the Chicago area where he grew up, and later wherever the Army stationed him. These days, he wasn't looking so much to handle as he was a woman he could fall in love with. But here were very few women who would understand what he was and the job that utilized those special skills to the best of their ability.

It was kind of hard to explain to a date that you possessed the gifts of super-strength, better-than-average eyesight and the power to hypnotize most any human who looked you in the eye.

It was even harder for him to truly let go during sex—because Trance knew his own strength, and his worries about hurting a woman accidentally during lovemaking had stopped him from ever getting past the formal stage with any woman—sub or otherwise.

Rik's breath was warm on the back of his neck. He turned his head to let it graze his ear and she caught his lobe between her teeth, nipped just hard enough to make him turn his head back.

Her hands came around his chest—unbuttoned his shirt slowly. As she peeled it away from his shoulders, she brought her nose in to smell him, to nuzzle his neck and to nip the sensitive skin at the nape. His senses were on high alert; every touch of her fingers was like fire against his skin. His heart beat loudly, his mouth dried, and maybe this was all a mistake.

A hand caressed his heavy sac and then his shaft through the fabric of his pants. He'd wanted to wear his usual leathers, but in them he was certainly not unassuming.

"You're nervous," she said.

He didn't answer, didn't have to. It was more nervous energy than actual fear, but it all worked in his favor. Enhanced his role.

She rubbed against his bare back since he still faced the wall, eyes down, as she hadn't given him the command otherwise.

"Your safe word?" she asked.

"Daddy."

Again, the deep chuckle. "You're a funny boy. I have a feeling you won't be as funny by the time I'm through with you, though. Are there things you're not comfortable doing?"

Yes, this. All of this. "My tolerance is high," he told her instead. He didn't know if that was actually the truth or not, but he had no way of knowing, had never subbed as many of the other Doms did in order to learn how to better their role. He knew only that he preferred pleasure over pain, used restraints with his subs only to enhance pleasure. . . . He wasn't into humiliation and, from what he'd heard, neither was Rik.

It would definitely be a learning experience.

"Tell me your name."

"It's Trance," he said.

"That's your real name?"

"It's the name I use when I'm out playing."

"Fair enough. Turn toward me, boy. Arms over your head."

He did as she asked. She pulled at the chains over his head, shortening them so his arms would be held at the highest possible tension while his wrists were caught in the soft leather binding.

She fastened his wrists and his insides began to chafe almost immediately. His muscles burned slightly, and he tugged at the chains, just the way she'd expect.

"Relax," she said, and put her hands on his upper arms. But he didn't want to relax. He wanted to come, didn't realize how badly until he was firmly held down.

"Turn your head—look at me, boy. I need to make sure you're all right."

He did as told, raised his eyes and let the familiar feel of vertigo take hold of him, a side effect of getting someone else under his control. Rik stared at him, cocked her head in confusion for a second before reaching for the zipper on his pants.

Yes, she'd restrained him, but the chains would never hold. Nothing would, except his own will.

* * *

THIS ONE WAS going to be special. Ulrika could feel it. Smell it. And when she ran her tongue over the pulse point in his throat, she could taste it. Power flowed through his veins, the currents as strong as those of the river Elbe, where she used to fish as a child.

But those days were as dead as her people, and in the years since she'd been taken from her German homeland, she'd learned to tamp down both the memories and the grief, and to concentrate on nothing but survival.

And a large part of her survival depended on what she was doing now, with Trance.

Her touch as she pulled down his zipper was feather-light, and unexpected, if his quick intake of breath was an indication. Her own breathing hitched as his cock broke free from the soft denim jeans, and she resisted the urge to take it in her palm.

The man was a magnificent creature . . . broad shoulders, rugged features and muscles carved from stone. A light dusting of blond hair coated his chest, which was as deeply tanned as the rest of him. Longish blond hair, shot through with darker brown, framed eyes as blue and clear as an Austrian mountain lake. Eyes that fascinated her, drew her in when he should be keeping his gaze averted a lot more than he was.

It had been a long time since she'd encountered anything like him. Usually her customers were either handsome or fit, but rarely both, and never to such extremes.

And before this life . . . she didn't want to think about it. And yet for some reason she couldn't help it. The full moon always brought out the beast's fiercest urges, and her worst memories. Such as how Itor had destroyed her clan, had wiped her kind from the face of the earth with experimentation that only she had survived. Now they wanted her dead. After subjecting her to years of hell, they were tired of playing.

She, however, wasn't. The beast in her needed to play. If the beast wasn't kept sated, it came out, a rabid, uncontrollable thing that raged hard, killed indiscriminately, and wouldn't give back her body until it wore out. She'd wake in strange places, aching and covered in blood that wasn't her own, her memory a black hole.

Sex kept it calm. Meat kept it fed. Dominating humans kept it happy.

She'd just eaten three rare steaks. One down, two in the works.

"Mistress?"

Her gaze snapped to his. "Did I tell you to speak?"

His blue eyes gleamed, and she held her breath, unable to do or say anything until he dropped his gaze. "No, *mistress*." His voice was like a velvet whip on sensitive skin, and she felt it all the way to her sex.

This man was not a sub.

The realization found its way into her bloodstream as a rush of adrenaline. Excitement stirred the beast; nothing fired the blood like dominating an alpha, but warning bells clanged in Rik's head. Her mind raced. Itor wouldn't toy with her like this— they'd simply take her out, just as The Aquarius Group would— as payback for her attempt at killing one of their top agents. No doubt ACRO would want in on the action as well. Heck, she had to assume everyone wanted her dead.

Caution had kept her alive for weeks, and she couldn't ignore her internal alarm, even if this turned out to be a false one.

Lightning fast, she pushed his face around so he couldn't look at her, and she bared her teeth against his ear. "Tell me why you're here."

"To submit to you, mistress."

"I don't believe you. Why do something so against your nature?"

His muscles tensed, and she smelled surprise rolling off him. "I want to know what it feels like to submit," he said smoothly, "and I hear you're the best."

"I am." She pressed against him harder, letting her stiff nipples rub against his chest through the fabric of her top. "I can make you love to be dominated. I can make you learn to crave it. To beg for it."

"Then teach me."

The underlying steel in his voice sent a shiver of feminine

appreciation through her even as it raised the beast's hackles. She drew his head around and nipped his bottom lip, enough to cause pain but not draw blood. "Teach me, *please*. Say it. Now."

His moment of hesitation lasted no more than a second, but she made the mistake of looking into his mesmerizing eyes, the distraction so intense that she barely heard him say, "Teach me, please."

Nodding, she stepped back and allowed herself a leisurely scan of his body, from his bound hands to his chest, his slim waist where muscles strained, to his erection that jutted like steel from where she'd peeled back his fly.

"You will do as I say. Always."

"Yes, mistress."

His tone was better, properly subdued, and she heated all over. As a reward, she slipped her fingers between his legs and drew his heavy sac forward so it bulged over the top of his fly opening. Hunger consumed her, but she ignored her need until Trance had been properly schooled.

"You will come when and *if* I allow it," she said, as she drew one long nail up his cock, tracing the deep blue veins that circled the shaft like thick vines.

He breathed out a curse, and at her arched brow, he said, "Yes, mistress." Though he'd responded through clenched teeth, his voice had deepened, and she knew his hunger had climbed.

"Good boy," she murmured. "Very good." She scraped her nails over one nicely developed pec. "You should know that after tonight, someone else will have to instruct you. I don't do this for your pleasure but for mine, and mine alone." She tweaked his nipple, enjoying his barely controlled intake of breath. "I don't do the normal exchange of trust and power. This is about power only. My power. Do you understand?"

"That's highly unusual, mistress."

She stepped away. "It's how I work. If you object, I'll send you away now."

Several heartbeats ticked by before he finally gave her a slow nod. There was so much fight in him, and so much restraint. He was magnificent beyond belief.

Her loose clothing grew tight, confining, her skin aching for the hot, smooth contact of male muscle. She would touch him, but he would never touch her. No man would touch her with his hands ever again.

Slowly, she stripped out of her blouse, noting the way Trance's gaze darkened at the sight of her breasts. They were bigger than they looked beneath the top, the nipples hard and stiff within the gold rings that circled them but didn't pierce.

She now wore only her skirt, high heels and the radio collar, a leather-wrapped steel casing full of electronics—a homing locator and a nasty shock mechanism a handler could activate with different intensities to either control her behavior or force her to shape-shift.

The good news was that outside the ten-mile radius of a handler in possession of a controller, the collar didn't work to either give away her location or shock her. The bad news was that the collar couldn't be removed without the tiny bomb inside blowing her head off.

So yeah, she could tell herself that she could tamp down her memories, but every time she looked in the mirror, they looked right back at her.

Right now, though, her sub was looking at her, and she wasn't going to disappoint either of them.

Watching him, she cupped her breasts, pushed them together so he could imagine his cock between them, rubbing and thrusting, each upward stroke allowing her to swipe at the head with her tongue. She circled her peaked nipples with her thumbs until sensation swept from her breasts to her pussy, which flooded with her juices.

Trance's throat muscles worked on a hard swallow, his nostrils flaring, and when his tongue snaked out to moisten his lips, she knew he was ready for the next step.

Dropping to her knees, she brought her mouth close to his cock so he could feel the stirring of her breath on his skin. No touching, though, except to peel down his pants. But when he rolled his hips toward her, nearly catching her mouth with his shaft, she growled and reached for the leather-bound box behind him.

"Naughty boy," she murmured. "Time for your first lesson."

CHAPTER
Two

Trance wasn't going to like this lesson.

Kira had warned him that his hypnotic powers might not totally work on Rik—they definitely wouldn't work once the beast within her emerged. If he could keep her calm and peaceful during these sessions, he could slowly win her over.

Still, it wasn't going to stop him from having to become Rik's bitch over the next few minutes.

Fuck. Just *fuck*.

"Did you say something?" Rik asked him.

Well, hell, no one said the job of an ACRO agent was easy. Definitely not, especially after seeing the cock ring she'd taken out of her bag of tricks. She wrapped the stiff leather around the base of his cock—it would effectively keep him rock-hard and stop him from coming.

"My boy doesn't like to be told what to do," she purred. "Doesn't like not being able to do exactly what he wants to, when he wants to. But in my world, you only get to do what I want."

"Do you want to come, mistress? Because I can make you come if you put your hot, wet pussy on my cock—"

A squeeze and twist to his balls, coupled with a hard pinch to his nipple, effectively shut his mouth for a second. "You are not in charge here."

A drop of pre-cum had formed on the head of his cock—when he didn't say anything else, Rik took a long finger and spread the moisture, then pressed it lightly into the slit.

"So many possibilities—whips and chains—your skin would look so pretty marked with red, boy."

Safe. Sane. Consensual. Those words had been such a big part of his life for so long. But there was nothing safe, sane or consensual about this now. He squirmed under her words, her touch, and she slid her tongue into the slit of his cock. When he gasped, she did it again and again and then stopped as if confused at what she'd done. As he watched, she stood to her full height and tried to regain the control she appeared to have lost.

"Maybe some sounding. I think you'd like that—the cold metal sliding inside your cock until you lost all control of yourself." She slid a finger along his ass. "Or maybe—"

No. No fucking way. He'd almost let the words slip out, but he held them back, held his breath and finally said, "Anything you want, mistress."